To my dear friend Carole,

STILL HERE

Christine E. Zerillo

STILL HERE

Christine
Duffy
Zerillo

Haley's

Athol, Massachusetts

Copy edited by Ellen Woodbury.
Cover art by Dave Kobrenski.
Model for cover art: Kerri Helme

Haley's gratefully acknowledges the University of Massachusetts Press for permission to publish maps on pages 344-347 from *Historical Atlas of Massachusetts* by R. Wilkie and J. Tager, 1991

Haley's
488 South Main Street
Athol, Massachusetts 01331
haley.antique@verizon.net

Library of Congress Cataloging-in-Publication Data
Names: Zerillo, Christine Duffy, 1956- author.
Title: Still here / Christine Duffy Zerillo.
Description: Athol, Massachusetts : Haley's, [2020] | Includes
    bibliographical references. | Summary: "Historical fiction based on the
    1683 narrative journal by the actual Mary Rowlandson chronicling her
    captivity by Indians and imagining Rowlandson's relationship with her
    captor, the actual sachem Weetamoo"-- Provided by publisher.
Identifiers: LCCN 2019036415 | ISBN 9781948380140 (trade paperback)
Subjects: LCSH: Rowlandson, Mary White, approximately 1635-1711--
Fiction. |
    GSAFD: Biographical fiction. | Western fiction.
Classification: LCC PS3626.E75 S75 2020 | DDC 813/.6--dc23
LC record available at https://lccn.loc.gov/2019036415

for Grampa Duffy, who inspired my path
and
for Sam, who cleared the way

Contents

Maps and Photograph

Voices from the Seventeenth Century
a preface by Christine Duffy Zerillo

The novel *Still Here* in part considers material from the captivity narrative of Mary Rowlandson, taken from her home in Lancaster, Massachusetts, during King Philip's War in 1675-1676. She lived for eleven weeks as a captive to the second most powerful native sachem or chief, Weetamoo of the Pocasset Wampanoag tribe, who then lived near present day Little Compton, Rhode Island. Against the backdrop of one of the bloodiest wars in history, I portray the relationship between the two women and their physical, emotional, and spiritual journeys.

Still Here uses many terms from the Algonquin language, common in the seventeenth century to most of New England. English chroniclers used phonetic spelling at the time of *Still Here*, often with many spellings for the same words. No one had yet standardized orthography. I decided to use the most prevalent spellings at the time. Sometimes I quote directly from primary sources with few if any standardization to modern American English.

In colonial New England, the calendar year began on March 25 and ended on March 24. The modern calendar beginning January 1 and ending December 31 has been in use since 1752. The story begins in July 1675, and eight months later, when Indians raid Lancaster and capture Mary in February, the year is recorded as 1675 because February counted as the eleventh month of the year that had begun the previous March. Events following the raid occurring after March 25 are recorded under the new year of 1676. *Still Here* uses historical dates as recorded during the era when events occurred.

After the novel text, the reader will find maps, notes, a cast of characters, and a bibliography.

Redemption Rock

The granite ledge known as Redemption Rock in Princeton, Massachusetts, is the site of the famous release from captivity of Mary White Rowlandson. On its perpendicular face is inscribed: "Upon this rock May 2nd 1676 was made the agreement for the ransom of Mrs. Mary Rowlandson of Lancaster between the Indians and John Hoar of Concord. King Philip was with the Indians but refused his consent."

Mary White Rowlandson (1637-1711) told her own story in The Narrative of the Captivity and Restoration of Mrs. Mary Rowlandson, *which first appeared in public in 1679, three years after her capture and release. It would become a seventeenth-century bestseller on both sides of the Atlantic with fifteen editions published before 1800. According to Neal Salisbury, who re-published Mary's narrative in 1997 as* The Sovereignty and Goodness of God *in 1653, Lancaster was a frontier town in the "wild, wild west" of Massachusetts. The Rock southeast of Wachusett Lake was a point of contact between two civilizations.*

Many of New England's Native American tribes, angered by the spread of colonial settlements, the conversion of forests into farmland, and perceived injustices at the hands of colonists, joined the Wampanoag sachem Metacom (called Philip by the English) in an attempt to drive the colonists from their new homelands, in the process destroying hunting grounds, winter camps, and settlements. Mary White Rowlandson's narrative begins on February 10, 1676, when four hundred Nipmucs, Narragansetts, and Wampanoags attacked Lancaster "about sun-rising." Mary, her three children, and twenty other captives were taken into "the vast and desolate wilderness, I knew not whither." After many "removes" (shifts of locations), they ultimately rendezvoused with King Philip near the present-day New Hampshire-Vermont border north of Northfield, Massachusetts. Her bible was a source of comfort throughout, and her sewing skills, quickly discovered, placed her in good favor; for a shilling, she was asked to make a shirt for King Philip.

Mary and her captors returned by late April, 1676. John Hoar of Concord, who had instructed and protected a group of "praying Indians," went to negotiate her release at the flat-topped outcrop overlooking a meadow where the Native Americans had camped. She writes, "Philip who was in the company came up and took me by the hand and said, 'Two weeks more and you shall be Mistress again.'" Later, a ransom was raised "by some Boston gentlemen." She traveled to Boston with John Hoar to be reunited with her husband, son, and eldest daughter (the youngest had died from wounds eight days after the raid).

—The Trustees of the Reservations
Redemption Rock
Princeton, Massachusetts, 2019

Church Pays a Visit

Seconet squatted and watched from the shadows between the cattails. The breeze rustled the tall reeds above his head. When he was a small boy, he had learned to be still and disappear into his natural surroundings. Seconet stood taller than most of the cattails that hid him, but his dark skin and leather loincloth blended perfectly with the muddy water that surrounded the Pocasset camp. Seconet appeared as a shadow to anyone who might pass along this path.

The melody of swamp bird songs, the drone of lacy dragonfly wings, and the summer heat that always came with the Strawberry Moon might send a better man to sleep, but not such a keen scout as Seconet.

Seconet noticed the subtle whisper of Petananuit's English wool coat as he came along the path leaving the camp. When Petananuit brushed by within arm's length, he did not notice Seconet secretly watching.

Seconet had little use for Petananuit or, as he called himself, Peter Nanuit. Petananuit had gone with the others to the English praying town. He dressed like an Englishman, prayed like an Englishman, and ate like an Englishman. *He even smells like an Englishman,* Seconet thought with disgust, as the Praying Indian walked by. The stink of flowery fragrance did little to disguise that he no longer used a sweat lodge and river bath to cleanse his body, mind, and spirit. Seconet smiled, thinking how Sachem Weetamoo had set Petananuit's belongings outside her dwelling. She was no longer bound to that man and his stinking English ways.

A sound drew Seconet's attention further down the path. He saw a white man approaching. Petananuit stopped short, not expecting to see an English soldier on the path before him. Seconet had never seen an Englishman traveling alone so deep in the swamp and so near his summer home. Seconet drew an arrow from its quiver without making a sound and rested it across the hand that held his bow.

"What cheer, netop!" the grey-haired Englishman called out, and then again in English, "Hello, friend." He spoke in a familiar tone as if he knew the man well.

Petananuit stepped closer, recognizing the older man's voice before he could see his face clearly. He scanned the swamp behind him and then answered, "Greetings, Captain Church. Are you alone?" Although he had adopted English ways, Peter never felt sure that he could trust them.

In spite of the heat, Petananuit and Church both wore heavy English wool coats and vests. Each man wore high boots folded down above their knees to protect them from the brackish water and countless snakes that made Pocasset Swamp their home. The watery barrier protected Weetamoo's people from unwanted two-legged visitors such as Captain Church, an unwanted settler in her homeland that the foreigners called Massachusetts Bay Colony.

Seconet listened carefully so he could repeat to his sachem Weetamoo what he heard. He understood English, which he learned from his mother. She had become a Praying Indian who wanted her son to know his native ways, so he spent summers with her family in the Wampanoag village of Pocasset. There he learned more about the ways of his own people and discovered his love of being out-of-doors and learning from nature.

Each autumn, the weight of the English praying town fell upon him with its heavy clothes, drab houses, and droning schoolmasters and ministers. He wondered why anyone would choose English ways over those of his people, the many tribes or bands of Wampanoags, the coastal People of the First Light. As a young man, he rejected English ways and left his mother. Seconet's heart rested in his native home.

"Yes, I am alone I've just come from the camp of my friend Awashonks and am now seeking her cousin Weetamoo. I am unarmed," Church added quickly, close enough to see the war paint on Petananuit's dark face.

"So you had business with Awashonks, the squaw-sachem of our neighbors, the Sakonnet people? And is this to do with my wife?" Petananuit asked with eyes searching the old soldier for weapons. He hadn't yet admitted to himself that Weetamoo no longer called him sannup, the Wampanoag word for husband. In the language of the English, he was divorced.

"You are wed to Weetamoo, the squaw-sachem of the Pocasset people. Are you not?" Church scurried forward as he reached into his vest pocket.

Petananuit gripped the knife in his belt. Church withdrew a folded paper. The Praying Indian noticed it bore the governor's seal. He had seen many such letters to Wampanoag tribal leaders or sachems in recent times. Caught between alliances, Petananuit stood firmly blocking the path. He waited for Church to explain his intentions.

"I bear a message from the Plimoth Plantation. The governor received word that the Indian King Philip assembled a war council at Mount Hope this very week. The governor must know if Weetamoo and Awashonks and their people will remain neutral if hostilities commence between Philip's warriors and the colony."

It gave Peter Nanuit a strange pleasure to hear the English captain call Metacomet by his English name. Metacomet's father, Massasoit, befriended the English settlers when they arrived more than fifty summers before and remained a good friend for all his days. He had even given both his sons new English names of Philip and Alexander in honor of powerful military leaders from across the Great Water. The English had come to call the leaders of the native people kings so they could bargain with them on familiar terms in making laws, arranging treaties, and buying and selling real estate and livestock. Such concepts did not exist in this land only a half century before.

Still, with Massasoit and Alexander both dead, the English regarded Metacomet as king of all eastern native people, not only of local bands of Wampanoag people but also of other tribes along the coast and as far inland as the Connecticut River. *Like it or not, Metacomet, you are now King Philip,* Peter thought.

From his concealed place, Seconet crouched and kept his arrow pointed midway between the two men. He did not yet know if he would have to stop one or the other or both of them from undoing the will of his people to clear the English settlers from his native land.

"The governor has word of this war council?" asked Petananuit.

The old captain's awareness surprised Petananuit, although it shouldn't have. Hadn't he himself just come from Philip's war council where more than a thousand warriors gathered? Of course, the English had to have seen signs of large numbers of people streaming in from all over the northeastern Algonquin country sometimes called New England by the white men.

"Indeed, the governor has heard, and he has mustered his men to defend the colony should the need arise. He has already sent word to the governor of the United Colonies in Connecticut of Philip's refusal to turn in his guns as ordered," Church added, nodding knowingly.

Uncertain that he would find Weetamoo before his ship sailed back to Plimoth, the captain revealed information he wanted her to have. Assuming that Weetamoo trusted the man who had been her husband as a confidante, he continued with his message.

Seconet, still in hiding, cupped his ear to listen closely.

"We have the word of the Nausets, the Narragansetts, the Niantics, and now with Awashonks's consent, the Sakonnets to remain neutral if fighting breaks out. Do you think that the Pocassets will also agree to remain neutral with their neighbors?"

Seconet remained still behind the tall swamp grass and saw Petananuit take a step back. The squaw-sachem's former sannup sat down on a large stone and slowly shook his head. *How could he speak for the Pocassets? He was no longer even a member of their tribe.*

"You come too late. I warned her of this." He leaned his face into his hands and said, "Our young Pocasset braves could not be held back."

Seconet watched as Church took a step back. The captain suddenly looked very old and weary, and he sank down on another rock. He looked down at his hands. After a short time, he looked up and said, "Peter, will Philip make war on the colony?"

Petananuit thought for a moment before answering. What loyalty should he have? He had already sworn allegiance to the English. He had been driven out of Philip's war council and might have lost his life had not Philip himself stayed the hands of those who wanted to kill him.

"I have just come from Philip's council. Captain Church, I have no doubt that there will be war. The people demand it," he assured him.

"Of this you are certain?" the old captain asked. "When?"

"Philip's dance has lasted a fortnight and still the warriors come to him from all parts of our country."

With those words, Seconet thought angrily, *Petananuit ceased to be. He will only be Peter Nanuit from that moment forward. Once Weetamoo learns of his betrayal, that traitor will be marked for death.*

"This is not good, Peter." Church shook his head and looked at the muddy ground. "How long before they take the warpath?"

"Soon." Peter looked at Church. "Philip knows Plimoth will summon him to answer for the death of John Sassamon. When they found his body under the ice this winter, they suspected that Philip ordered the killing of his former scribe. And Philip must answer for his decision not to turn in all his guns. But Philip will not go to Plimoth to answer for Sassamon's death or the guns."

"But surely someone can reason with him? The governor would like to avoid war if at all possible. Perhaps a letter . . ."

Peter stopped him, saying, "Just before I left Philip's council at Mount Hope, a Mister James Brown came to Philip with a letter such as yours from Governor Winslow. The blood of the young warriors raced. They nearly killed James Brown and the other men who accompanied him and would have done so if Philip did not command them to hold. Indeed, the warriors only freed them after

Philip agreed to let the young men raid Swansea come the next Lord's meeting day. Yes, Church. I fear war cannot be avoided."

Seconet found it difficult to remain still. He burned to shoot arrows through the hearts of both the traitor and the Englishman. Trembling with anger, he stayed his hand and continued listening.

The news is very grave, Church thought. *The Sabbath is only three days hence.* "What of the Pocassets? Can Weetamoo govern them to stand aside?" Church asked.

"You must speak to her. She takes no council from me. I have tried to reason with her to join with me and the other Praying Indians. She cannot let Philip command our men to their deaths. Yet, alas, she heeds me not."

"Then I shall go to her. Can you show me the way?" Captain Church asked, standing up again.

A great blue heron rose up from the cattails and flew low across the green marshland. Seconet used the distraction to back silently away from the clearing. He had to tell Weetamoo of Petananuit's betrayal.

He fought back his anger as he made his way swiftly through secret paths to the Pocasset camp, known only to his people and their allies.

The camp was built like many others. Hidden away on high ground within the depths of the salt marsh, it was surrounded by long straight timbers sunken heel first into the muddy soil. Sufficient space between the timbers allowed an arrow to fit but not a man or even a small child. With only one entrance and one exit break in the palisades, the warriors could easily defend it.

Arriving breathless, Seconet leaned over his knees at the edge of the village.

Weetamoo knelt on a rush mat outside her home, a dome-shaped wetu made of bent branches and covered with green cattail rushes. She worked on a new wampum belt with white and purple beads drilled out of quahog shells as she heard the children shouting. They clustered near the camp entrance and jumped up and down around Seconet, her favorite scout. Weetamoo watched as the children trailed behind Seconet, who headed toward the nushweety or longhouse, the community meeting place. Similar in design but larger in scale than Weetamoo's home, it had three hearths and could hold more than a hundred people.

By going there, Seconet signaled that he had news to share.

Weetamoo stood and dusted off her buckskin skirt and watched him enter the longhouse. In the summer heat, her skirt was her only clothing. Her firm, bare, brown skin and sinewy flesh showed no signs that she had given birth only three months earlier except for her swollen breasts. Their fullness reminded her that she needed to feed her son, so she lifted him out of his papoose carrier and followed Seconet into the shade of the bark-covered lodge.

Alerted of his arrival, her people hurried to fill the wooden platforms and mats around the hearth. Weetamoo made a place for Seconet next to her and offered him a burl bowl of cool water. He drained the bowl as she settled her son on her breast and waited for Seconet's breathing to slow.

Then she spoke in her native tongue.

"Welcome, Seconet. What news do you bring to the people of Pocasset?"

"Thank you for your welcome, Sachem. An English ship is near Patuxet. It bore the English captain they call Church. He comes to talk peace with you and Awashonks. He is now close by with Petananuit."

"Petananuit returns? With an Englishman?" The information surprised her. Petananuit no longer had any ties with her people. She had ended her relationship with him and had no desire to see his face again. He was no longer Pocasset. She worried, *Has he come to spy on me and my son? What devilment is he up to now?* Following her father's advice as he taught her the ways of a good leader, she determined not to waste her time in thinking of him.

"It is good you brought this message swiftly. What of Awashonks? What does she say?" Weetamoo asked.

"Awashonks gives her word that the Sakonnets will not take part in Metacomet's war."

I don't believe that, the squaw-sachem thought. "What else?" she demanded.

"Sachem, your husband told Church that Metacomet permits the young warriors to take the warpath at Swansea on the next Sabbath day." Seconet saw her stiffen at his words. She tensed so suddenly that the baby at her breast opened his eyes and lost his grasp and struggled to regain a comfortable hold on his meal.

Seconet took a deep breath and continued, "Petananuit told Church that Metacomet agreed to spare the life of James Brown and his company when they brought Metacomet a message from Governor Winslow. Church comes here now with his own letter from the governor to ask you to remain neutral with the Narragansetts, Niantics, Sakonnets, and Nausets if Metacomet makes war. Church told Petananuit that men are mustering in Plimoth, and word has been sent to the United Colonies."

Weetamoo breathed in deeply. "Is this all?" The muscles in her neck and jaw strained. The baby flinched again and looked up at his mother for assurance.

"Yes, Sachem," he answered looking into her sharp, dark eyes.

"Take something to eat and drink and go at once to Awashonks with my message. Say to her, 'Weetamoo meets with Church.'" she ordered. He rose quickly and left the longhouse without another word.

"Make haste," she called out to Laughing Water, her daughter, who was fifteen summers in age and learning as Weetamoo had how to lead her people. "Tell the elders to come immediately to the longhouse and have the women prepare a small feast. Return to me when you have given them my word. I will prepare for this visit." She used her finger to break the infant's grasp of her nipple and stood up. Placing him on her hip, she rose and left the longhouse.

Weetamoo walked with determined strides across the open circle to her own wetu. The sun shone directly overhead in a clear blue sky. She lifted the rush flap and stepped into cool shade, briefly escaping what suddenly felt like a stifling heat. A light breeze rustled through the cattail mats overhead.

"Petananuit, that snake," she snarled. "How dare he speak to the English war captain before me!" Her thoughts raged on. "His Christian beliefs have softened his mind! He is no longer a Pocasset man! He is an English woman! That fool!" She worried, *What else has he told the English?*

The baby wrinkled up his face at the loudness of his mother's voice and the tautness in her arms. She pressed a finger to his pink mouth to ward off a cry and then slipped him into his papoose cradle board. She hung it from the roof and, with a light touch, caused it to swing gently. The baby nestled into his secure little berth and watched his mother.

Glad that she had turned her former husband out, Weetamoo knew she had to put aside her anger with him. She would decide later what to do about him. At the moment, she needed to deal with the Englishman. She had given false assurances to the governor before and was prepared to do so again. *Would it be enough to placate him another time?*

She stripped off her plain skirt and pulled on her white deerskin dress, tearing off some of its shell ornaments as she wrestled it over her head. She yanked a girdle of wampum from a basket under her sleeping platform. The long strand of wampum beads twisted and tangled as she tied it around her slender waist. She knew it would draw the Englishman's attention to her fine, feminine form. It pleased her that her skin showed no signs of stretching, unlike many other women's skin. She had carefully rubbed her belly and her breasts with nut oil during her pregnancy to keep her skin smooth. After more than thirty-five summers, she remained aware that her beauty gave her power over men, and she intended to use it.

When Laughing Water returned, Weetamoo was digging deep in the basket and drew out anklets of whelk shells and bracelets of wampum. "What do you think, Laughing Water? Will the English-man be more humbled by these or by the English beads?" She spoke in English, to practice before the arrival of the Captain. Ordinarily, she spoke only in her native Wampanoag language, but she had learned English at a young age as part of her preparation to become a sachem.

"You are more a queen in your wampum, Mistress," Laughing Water answered, in English. The young girl liked to practice speaking English, a skill she was just learning from some Praying Indians nearby. Many of the Wampanoags could converse fluently in both languages. Some chose not to try. Some, like Weetamoo, did not like to speak the foreign tongue but did so for strategic purposes. All of them pretended not to speak English when it suited them or when they did not wish others to hear their words. Few English made any effort to learn their language, which pleased Weetamoo.

"Wampum then it will be and get me my scallop shell necklace," she commanded. Laughing Water moved quickly and offered her a strand of shells. Weetamoo had been taught that a sachem must be very conscious of maintaining an appearance that commanded respect when representing her people. When she did so, she put on an air of confidence along with her clothing.

"No, not that one. I want the one with the dark colored scallop shell." As Laughing Water hurried to secure it about Weetamoo's neck, the sachem nodded approvingly at her reflection in her English looking glass.

"Yes," she said. "Now, my hair." It pleased her to own English goods. She enjoyed receiving those gifts as signs of her people's respect for her as a leader. She especially liked to see her own image in the mirror.

Laughing Water used a tortoiseshell English brush to smooth Weetamoo's long black hair. Her fingers nimbly plaited the sachem's hair into two thick, black braids. She tied off the ends with sinew and tied a small eagle feather into one braid.

"Good," Weetamoo said into the mirror. Her reflection practiced making the face of a warrior queen. She would show no fear. No submission. No guilt.

Weetamoo reached for her face paints. She darkened the lines around her eyes and reddened her already flushed cheeks. She dabbed more color on her lips as Laughing Water traced over the tattoos on the sachem's arms and legs. After another satisfied look in the mirror, Weetamoo opened the door flap and called for a runner.

A boy, too young to join the warriors at Metacomet's war dance, came to her. She placed one hand on his shoulder and pressed a string of wampum into his hand with the other. In Wampanoag, she ordered, "Take word to Metacomet that Church comes to speak of peace. Awashonks already consents, and I will talk with him. Petananuit has betrayed you and revealed the Swansea plan."

To the boy she said, "Wait for his answer. Go now." She watched the boy proudly call out to his friends and his mother before he ran from the village.

Weetamoo summoned drummers to call the women and children in from nearby cornfields and clam beds with their rhythms. Men and boys surrounded a large hollowed tree trunk topped with a tightly stretched deerskin worn smooth from use. Together they struck it with long sticks, some muffled with rabbit fur, others wrapped in leather, all uniquely ornamented with carving, beads, and colorful wrappings. The heartbeat of the people sounded with each stroke in complete unison.

"When Benjamin Church comes, we will be ready," she announced to Laughing Water. "He should not know our men have gone with Metacomet to fight the English. Let all present be seen. Hurry to spread the word."

The young squaw lowered her eyes and replied, "Nux, Sachem. It is good, my queen," blending her Wampanoag and English words together.

Laughing Water ran to the nearest wetu. She scratched the woven rush mat door to get the attention of those inside. She spoke quickly to the woman who lifted the flap, then rushed to the next wetu. The woman scrambled out and crossed the enclosed village to scratch at another wetu. At this, the hottest time of the day, many mothers cooed their young children to rest. But the drumming and sudden bustle of activity made their efforts fruitless. From each woven structure, another woman emerged who immediately alerted her neighbor.

The quiet village buzzed like a hive. Women and children danced between the wigwams. Young boys gathered wood or water. Old women tended fires or children. Young girls gathered herbs to sweeten the longhouse while others set to brushing dust from its floor. They moved within the walled palisades of their summer home as their queen readied herself to dispense with her spineless Christian lover and his friend, the cowering Captain Church.

Trouble Stirs in Massachusetts

Here's your tea, Joseph," Mary said, taking care to place his cup near at hand but not between his paper and his ink pot.

"Thank you, Mary," he replied. "I will not be much longer. But you may retire if you wish, as I know not when I will finish." He leaned back in his great carved chair and stretched his arms up over his head, interlocking his fingers. He'd been laboring at his sermon since she had cleared the board of supper. Not a man to waste precious paper, he set aside his mis-starts for reuse after they dried. It did not look to Mary as if he had much written on his finished page.

"It's no bother Joseph. I will stay with you if it will not trouble you." She settled in her chair by the hearth and turned up the wick on the oil lamp. "I have some needlework and, though it has been a tiresome day, I am not yet ready for slumber."

The minister of Lancaster reached for the crockery cup of hot tea and sipped at it noisily. "Mary Rowlandson, you make as fine a cup of tea as any noble house in England." Although childbearing had thickened her waist and the generosity of the parish had made her a more substantially sized woman, in his mind's eye, Joseph still saw the slight, blond maiden he had wed.

Mary smiled at her husband. After all their years of marriage and child-rearing, with three fine children tucked safely upstairs, Joseph never failed to thank her for her wifely efforts. She made a prayer of thanks for so fine a man, for her children, Joseph, Mary, and Sarah, and for her lovely, strong house.

Reverend Joseph Rowlandson returned his wife's loving smile as he fought back his fear for her safety and that of the children. News had come today of nine killed in Swansea, and the governors of Plimoth and of Massachusetts had issued a call to arms for militia from all the villages in both colonies. More than one hundred men had mustered out of Massachusetts Bay Colony today within three hours of the summons and already marched to Plimoth Colony. Tensions had been rising lately, and Joseph was afraid. As he sipped his tea, he searched for words from scripture that would give succor to his congregation.

Mary stitched quietly as Joseph returned to his work. There was no sound save the scratching of his nib across the paper and a quiet rustle of Mary's skirts as she fetched thread and needle from her apron pocket. She worked on an apron for Sarah, nearly five years old and wanting to be a help to her mother. The apron would be a surprise for Sarah on her birthday coming soon, so Mary could work on it only when Sarah was asleep. That child clung to her mother, following her, and mimicking her actions all the day long.

Mary embroidered a pocket with Sarah's name and her favorite fruit, the strawberry. Mary smiled and remembered Sarah's golden hair and chubby cheeks reddened with strawberries when they last picked them. Mary had scolded the child, saying, "Sarah, I declare, you have more of those berries on you than in your basket. If you want jam for your bread, you'll be paying mind to fill your basket and not your belly." Mary chuckled quietly at the thought.

Joseph's pen halted, and he noticed his wife musing in the corner. "Tell me, Good Wife, why do you laugh?"

"I did not mean to disturb you, Sir, but I just had an image of our Sarah in the strawberry patch. Your baby child is impish, but so dear. I find I cannot scold her without holding back a laugh."

"Yes, she is impish, as you say, but I, too, have no heart to scold her. We spoil her, my dear. We should be stricter with her upbringing, but I find it difficult to chide her when I look upon her endearing smile."

"As you say, Joseph," Mary nodded, noticing that he stopped writing. "I'm sorry. I did not mean to distract you from your work. I could sew upstairs if it would be a help to you."

"Nay, Mary, you do not distract but instead remind me how to choose the words for my sermon." He rubbed a hand over his tired eyes. He looked older than his forty years. *He carries the cares of his congregation*, Mary thought.

"I am burdened by the thought that many a house in Lancaster is without a father or a son tonight, and I am sure that each militia man has a child like Sarah to bring a smile to his lips. I am having trouble finding the right words to say to the families," Joseph commented. He laid down his quill pen and rubbed his glasses with the lace jabot at his breast.

"Yes, Joseph, that is troublesome indeed," Mary said. She did not stop stitching. Her own son and nephew had not been called out. Her husband was exempt as a minister, and her brother-in-law was too needed in the Lancaster home guard to be sent away. She felt sure that the uprising would concern only frontier towns, and that the governor's swift response would quickly dissipate the problem.

"What will you say?" she asked without looking up from her work.

"I want to assure the families that it will not be long 'ere their men come home again. I want to remind them of God's will for us to have these homes and to protect and defend them. I must give comfort to some who may never see their kin again. 'Tis a heavy burden." He walked over to the hearth and adjusted some logs on the fire.

"Why, Joseph, surely this will all be over soon," Mary said. She laid her sewing in her lap and continued, "My sister told me today that she heard that Governor Winslow has ordered tomorrow as a day of humiliation for all of Plimoth Colony. Would not that be a help, Joseph? Do you believe that we have brought this trouble on ourselves with wicked ways?"

"Certainly a day of humiliation could do no harm, Mary. Sure, there are some who break with the word of scripture here but not so often nor so sorely as in England. But still, in many small ways, every one of us has reason to repent."

Mary watched her husband contemplate the idea of a day of humiliation. It would involve a full day of repentance and prayer with the entire community reflecting and giving witness to others on their failures as Christians. The people would spend the day in humble prayer, begging forgiveness for errors large and small.

Joseph leaned back in his white starched shirt. Mary felt proud of the way she always kept his clothes in impeccable condition. Her family money enabled her to order the finest fabrics and trims from England. She quickly replaced any worn or discolored items with new handiwork and remade the remnants into pockets, blankets, or cleaning cloths. Mary would not have the minister going about in shoddy dress.

Joseph reflected on the spiritual well-being of his congregation. Perhaps the governor was right, he thought. Even small sleights in deed or thought or an untruth or unkindness festering in a heart left the way open for Satan's work. From such small failings, larger failings grow.

Joseph had often preached that cheats and deceptions cannot be hidden from the eye of the Almighty. Every day, he heard about court cases with neighbor against neighbor each swearing to the truth, yet surely that could not be so. Men had killed and not confessed it. The more he considered it, the more he felt that harboring such abominations would likely cause God to visit pestilence on the whole colony.

He leaned against the thick oak mantle and said, "It would do no harm to suffer a day of repentance and humiliation before the Lord here in Lancaster as in Plimoth. Men do grow to have wicked ways when we turn away from the teachings of scripture. Mary, you have given me a great help in this. I will call for a day of humiliation, and the Lord will minister to our hurts as we offer up our failings in repentance."

Mary didn't look up from her work but said, "Good, Joseph. That is good."

He crossed the room and leaned down to take her face between his soft hands. He bent down and kissed her on the forehead. "Mary, I thank the Lord for providing me with a wife as wise and good as you. You are the helpmate and handmaiden to my work. I am truly blessed."

Mary looked up and smiled, "We are both blessed, Dear." She resumed her stitching.

Joseph walked back to the table, adjusted the wick on the lamp and settled stiffly into his chair. "I shall now get on with the work of my sermon for a day of humiliation. I am much obliged to you, Dear Woman." Joseph returned to his writing and Mary continued sewing, humming a psalm quietly to herself.

When Mary looked up, Joseph was scratching his quill hurriedly across the page. She smiled and felt at peace in her world. Her fortified garrison home was safe, far from the trouble to the south. She had the love of a fine, good man. Her children were growing in good health. God protected her and all she loved.

Metacomet Steals Away

Weetamoo rose from her bed and left Metacomet sleeping. She looked down and admired his sinewy chest and arms. In sleep he was so like his brother, her late husband. Still saddened by his loss even after fourteen years, she thought, *Wamsutta should have led this war. Would war have come sooner if the English had not poisoned him? Did Metacomet trust the English courts and governors too long?* She wondered as she looked at her brave kinsman. *King Philip to all the world, but always little brother, Metacomet, to me. What is, is,* she reminded herself, and shook off her sadness. She stepped out of the wetu and into her village.

Already the women were dismantling their summer houses in the predawn darkness. *It is too early in the season to move,* she thought, *but it cannot be helped. The men must go with Metacomet, and I must take the women, elder men, and children to our cousins, the Narragansetts, where they will be safe.*

She squatted by her cook fire and had some tea and the thick corn porridge with blueberries, called samp, that her daughter Laughing Water had prepared. The purple eastern sky gradually changed to deep rose. Sitting quietly, she greeted the morning as all her people had for thousands of years in grateful thanks to Keesuckquand, Grandfather Spirit of the Heavens who showed himself daily as Nepaushet, the Sun. She felt proud to be Wampanoag, People of the First Light in this land.

When she finished her tea, she heard the mat rustle behind her and saw her kinsman Metacomet step from her wetu. "Ascowequa'ssin, Brother," she greeted him. "Good morning. Did you sleep well?"

18

"As well as you, Sachem," he answered with a grin.

She smiled and offered him some breakfast. He took the birch bark cup from her hand and nodded thanks to her.

Metacomet, the mighty King Philip, stood dressed in his full regalia. He wore a richly embroidered English shirt cinched at his waist by a wide wampum belt detailed with bird and animal designs created from white and purple quahog shell beads. Another wide strand of wampum with a metal star dangling from it, hung at his neck. Around his forehead he wore a narrower band of wampum with two beaded tails hanging down his back. The belts bore fringes of faded hair from Indian women whose husbands died fighting with or for him.

His face was dark and heavily lined for a man in his thirties. He had a long, broad chin and high forehead. He had a firm but kind mouth and memorable eyes, deep chestnut brown and full of wisdom. When he looked into Weetamoo's eyes, she felt he could see her thoughts. It had always been that way. He took the red woolen mantle off his shoulder and laid it on the ground for them to sit on.

It had been a fitful night. Earlier, the English had surrounded the swamp site of Metacomet's war council with fierce fighting and many losses on both sides. With the English barring the way at the neck of the peninsula, Metacomet and the warriors managed to slip away from Mount Hope during the night in large dugout canoes called mishoons. They had paddled across the wide Mattapoisett River to safety in Weetamoo's village, Pocasset. Metacomet and his men took advantage of the brief night to rest as the English marched the long way to Pocasset by land.

Weetamoo had been pleased to offer Metacomet room in her bed. They had always been very close as allies, kin, and lovers after her husband Wamsutta's death After four marriages, Metacom still held her heart.

As a sachem, however, she had long ago forgotten her childhood dream of marriage to him. For a sachem, marriage strengthened alliances, little more. Marriages for lust or love served no purpose. Her relationship with Metacom pleased her. Because he had married her younger sister and Weetamoo had married his older brother, both sons of the great Massasoit, they enjoyed a doubly strong kinship bond, and they remained the most powerful leaders in their country.

He sat beside her and drank the tea she offered. "We must go soon," he said, watching the crimson light growing to the east. "Are the mishoons ready?"

"Yes. The men raised them from the river bottom before first light," she answered. Nodding at the camp growing ever more skeletal as they sat, she noted, "The women will prepare to move by sunup. We can cross the Taunton River together if the English soldiers are gone. If not, we will go north through the swamp and forest to Assonet. Then you and the warriors can leave us. Awashonks and I will lead the rest to Narragansett."

"Nux. Yes. Weetamoo, you spoke wisely telling Captain Church the Pocassets would remain neutral. You gave our people time, though the scouts told me last night that Church's troops already swarmed their garrison with as many as fifty Christian Indians who they expect to lead their march here despite their lies about allying with you."

"I know which leader to follow, Metacomet," she said, looking into his eyes. She stood up and brushed the crumbs from her skirt. "I will make no more peace with the English. Now that Church knows the location of our camp, thanks to that snake, Petananuit, we must leave. Already the English have killed one of our braves in retribution for the Swansea raid. To stay here now would condemn us all to death."

"I will send warriors back to slow their way here so we can leave without their notice." For a long moment, he looked at her, his sister and wife of his true heart. "You have always been a wise leader, Weetamoo. Thank you for your help. I wish some of the other sachems thought as you do, Kinswoman." He touched her hand lightly and then resumed eating his breakfast. "It frustrates me that Ninagret and Canonchet still hold back their strength from us," he said between mouthfuls.

"True, Brother, but they offer safety to us and to Awashonks's people," Weetamoo said. "Perhaps they will have a change in heart when we stay in Canonchet's camp." She glanced sidelong at Metacomet.

The dark leader looked up at her and pulled her back down on his blanket. He lowered his eyebrows and his voice and said, "You forget how well I know you, Sachem. What are you scheming now?"

She knelt beside him and whispered excitedly, "Only that it is time for me to find a new husband, Metacomet. A strong warrior, this time, who will have no fear of the English. Not someone who carries fear from the Pequot war, but a brave, young warrior whom others will follow." Then she added, "I think a marriage between the Pocassets and Narragansetts would bring great power to our people."

He laughed. "You are a wily creature, Weetamoo. No wonder my brother chose you. He couldn't dare to have you as an enemy," he said touching her hand. "So, who will be this lucky man?"

"I have not made my choice," she answered. "But you can tell me which of Canonchet's men are the strongest, bravest, and lustiest, that I might think more on this." She rocked back on her heels.

He laughed, "You are a bold woman. Let me consider this for a while."

"Metacom, we do not have a while. I leave for Narragansett today. You must help me decide now," she urged.

"Not an hour from your bed and you must find another man?" he teased. "But you are right. Let's see. I can name several sachems, but I can think of only one who could tame a squaw as wild as you. Quannopinn. He has many warriors and will succeed his uncle Canonchet one day, and even the English call him a lusty rogue. This would be a good match for you. And for me."

"Then I shall make a union with Quannopinn. Soon."

Rising to his feet, he took her hand and said, "Let us take our paths. The warriors will go now to Nipmuc country. I will send word to you in Narragansett."

"Iotash, Metacomet. Fight well, King Philip," she said holding both his hands in hers.

"Wuniish, My Sister. Go in beauty, Sachem Weetamoo."

He turned from her and, in a moment, had gone.

Lancaster Listens

SOVEREIGN LORD,
Help me to humble myself before Thee
by seeing the vanity of honour
as a conceit of men's minds,
as standing between me and Thee;
by seeing that Thy will must alone be done,
as much in denying as in giving spiritual enjoyments;
by seeing that my heart is nothing but evil,
mind, mouth, life void of Thee.

-excerpt of a prayer of humiliation
from a collection of Puritan poems
entitled Valley of Vision

A mighty fortress is our God," sang the saints of Lancaster.

Mary sat in the first pew holding her hymn book so Sarah could look on. Her older children, young Joseph and young Mary, stood sharing a hymn book next to their mother with no trace of their rivalry earlier in the day. None could tell how Joseph's taunts had caused his sister to raise her voice and her hairbrush against him. Mary stole a glance at her family, at the moment a portrait of the perfect minister's brood. Joseph was tall and dark like his father, and both the girls had Mary's own fairer looks. Proper and proud, hers was one of the most respected families in town.

Fidgeting at the end of the hymn, Sarah looked up at her mother and tugged on her hand. "Is it time to go, now?" she whispered.

"Hush, Sarah. Not yet." Her mother spoke without looking down. She fixed her eyes on her husband, Joseph, stepping to the pulpit.

"Brethren," he began, "I urge you all to go forth in the grace of God. Keep Him in the forefront of your minds. Trust in Him to guide your words, thoughts and deeds. Pay mind to stray not toward Satan's temptations. Heed me; God is judging us by our acts. Bring not His wrath upon our house by failing in your duty to give glory to His name. Look not to find the trials of Swansea and Brookfield at our doors by your selfish acts. Humble yourself before God this day and every day. Trust in the Sovereign Lord and go in peace. Amen."

"Amen," the congregation responded. Mary's Sarah echoed loudly, openly voicing her relief that the formal day of humiliation had ended.

"Now, may I go play with my cousin Joseph?" she begged, tugging at her mother's skirts.

"Sarah, you may walk home with your cousin, but it is nigh time for bed. There will be only a little time to play tonight."

Before Mary could finish, she saw Sarah clamber over her brother and sister, swing the door of the pew open, and press her way through the somber adults to her cousin's pew in the rear of the meetinghouse.

Bless her heart, Mary thought. Sarah had withstood this long day of prayer and humiliation with surprising tolerance. *Who could expect a child of only five years to spend nine hours in worship?* The usual three hours of Sabbath worship often taxed her ability to behave properly, and this special all-day service had been excruciatingly difficult.

"Mother, may I walk Rebecca home?" Joseph asked anxiously, fidgeting even more than Sarah had and craning to find his new friend in the crowd. The formerly serene house of worship buzzed with conversation. Young people fled first.

"Yes, you may walk with Rebecca. But return home straight thereafter . . ."

"I will, Mother," he said over his shoulder as he turned and pushed past his sister into the crowded aisle.

Before young Mary even asked, her mother said, "Look, Dear, your friend Constance is waiting for you. Go on."

"Thank you, Mother," replied Mary as she left the pew with practiced poise and all the airs and graces of a young woman of status.

Mary chuckled at the differences among her children. Mary and Joseph were becoming adults. Joseph showed uncertain new interest in the opposite gender, and young Mary grew increasingly aware of her position and marriageability. Sarah, her little imp, could think of nothing else but play.

Mary bowed her head and whispered, "Thank you, good Lord, for blessing us with these three angels. Watch over them and guide us in raising them in the knowledge of your power and protection."

"Mary, my heavens. Will you stay to pray all the night?" Elizabeth tapped Mary's shoulder and held out her hand. "Come walk with me, Sister, before you grow stiff from this long day of humiliation. We'll need to make haste to keep watch over little Joseph and Sarah."

Laughing, Mary agreed. She waved to her husband surrounded by the town fathers and, after catching his gaze, set off with her sister. As Mary passed through the congregation, some worshipers stopped her to offer acknowledgments of Joseph's inspirational words.

Mary's neighbor leaned out of her pew and called to her. "Good evening, Mistress. Be sure to thank Mister Rowlandson for calling for this day of humiliation. Our son is with Captain Moseley, and we are reassured that, with God's mercy and forgiveness, we will see him safely home again. May God bless your family."

"And yours as well, Goodwife. We will keep your boy in our prayers," Mary replied.

The old woman who lived up the road had a pinched nose. She tapped Mary on the arm and said, "Mistress, thanks be to God that your husband has led us in this prayerful worship. It is our only salvation now with the heathens rising up all over the colony. May God have mercy on us and protect us. Give Mister Rowlandson our thanks, Mistress." She nodded at Mary with conviction, then pulled her son's arm saying, "Come now, Samuel, we must go before the night air gives us a chill." The young man obediently led her to the door.

"I will, Goody. Thank you for your kind words, and may God bless us all."

A short balding man came to her side. He rolled his hat brim in his hands. "Beg pardon, Mistress Rowlandson," he said. "My son is with Captain Appleton. Will you ask your husband to pray for him? He is only sixteen."

"I will, Good Sir, and our family will keep him in our prayers until this time of trial ends. We will pray for his safe return and our deliverance. God be with you, Freeman."

"Thank you, thank you kindly," he said, then faded into the stream of people edging toward the door. Slowly pressing through the crowd, Mary and her sister at last stepped out into the evening air. The early August heat had dispersed, and as if an answer to their prayers, the cool night washed over them. Mary felt purged of her dread from the awful news from all over the colony.

"Mary, do you think this war will spread?" her sister asked, slipping her shawl up over her shoulders.

"Who can say, Sister? I pray not, and I am much assured by this day of humiliation that God will see the devotion of his people," Mary answered. "Joseph tells me there are hopeful signs. The Mohegans have sent warriors to fight for us. And last week, the Mohegans killed many Wampanoag Indians in a battle near Rehoboth. God must be turning the hearts of Indians against Indians. Surely this is in answer to our prayers." Mary squeezed her sister's hand as she spoke.

"Aye. But my husband heard in town that only days ago Captain Hutchinson and Captain Wheeler were not only ambushed on their mission to treat with the Indians near Brookfield but that many settlers were killed and wounded in a siege there that lasted four days. These devils seem to grow more and more bold—and in so many places. Only today I heard the men saying that Mendon has been abandoned after savages butchered women and children there."

Mary looked at her sister with surprise. *Why had Joseph not shared the news with me? Surely he knew of this if my brother-in-law did.*

"Who brought this news, Sister?" Mary asked.

"I know not his name, but it was a rider who came through town today," Elizabeth answered. She hid her mouth with her hand and confessed, "I was listening at the window while they held council this morning. They spoke about seeking protection for Lancaster from the governor. More men will be called up to fight."

Mary's brow wrinkled. "This is harsh news, Sister. But surely we are safe here, being so close to Boston. Don't you think? Surely the governor will send men to help or leave our men here to protect us. I can scarce think how we could defend this place if more of our men leave. Could they expect women to bear arms now, too?"

Mary looked about for her children. *Was her son Joseph old enough to be considered a conscript? Would she and her daughter Mary have to learn to wield weapons? And what of little Sarah?*

"Ah, there you are, little master Joseph Kerley. Say goodnight to your cousin, Sarah," Elizabeth called out as she approached the door of her own home. "Tomorrow you will have more time to play. Goodnight, Mary. Perhaps in the morrow we should take these two to gather berries?"

"Yes, yes!" the two young children answered. "We're going berry-picking. We're going berry-picking," they chanted as they joined hands and swung each other in merry circles.

"Honestly, I know not where they find the strength!" Mary laughed. "Good night, Sister. Good night, Dear Nephew. Save your heartiness for berry-picking in the morrow. Come, Sarah."

As Mary stood outside her house, one of several garrisons for the town of Lancaster, she wondered for the first time if it could survive a four-day siege.

A Wedding of the Tribes

In the traditional society of the Wampanoags in the seventeenth century, both men and women each took part in the building of a house and in the making of a home. The men were responsible for the actual construction of the homes and were the ones to harvest the bark for the covering and the sapling poles for the frame. The women gathered both cattail and bulrush reeds to make mats for covering the houses (used alternately with bark) and lining and insulating the homes.

—Linda Coombs, 2005

Close brushes with the English punctuated tedious travel to Narragansett. Wampanoag scouts kept Weetamoo aware of enemy movements. The travelers skirted English troops in wide arcs, often going over arduous hilly or swampy terrain that avoided main footpaths. To give Metacomet and his people more time to escape, some scouts laid false trails to confuse the English and their hired Mohegan trackers. Along the way, knowing the trackers would collect anything of value, they abandoned valuable items to lighten their burden and encumber their pursuers.

A trip that would have taken a half day of brisk walking stretched into three days of furtive skulking, but at last they reached the swamp bordering Canonchet's camp. Using secret trail markings known only to the local tribes, they found their way along a nearly dry path. Two small birch saplings bent to form an arch near the entrance of the trail. Deliberately placed stones marked the right branch of a fork in the path. Carefully folded grasses pointed out another pathway. Through alert observation, Weetamoo's scouts discovered the subtle clues that led them to Canonchet's camp.

The further they walked into the swamp, the more signs of habitation they saw. Recently cut trees had familiar stone-axe markings made to look like beaver signs. Sharp saw grass they walked through grew taller than Weetamoo. Her people stepped with care in one another's footsteps to avoid leaving many footprints.

Weetamoo estimated that, together, she and Awashonks came with three hundred or more elder men, women, and children. Metacomet had taken a full force of more than a thousand warriors and their sagamore and sachem leaders with him. Metacomet chose his sister Amie's husband, Tispaquin, to stay and protect Weetamoo's band. His most trusted ally, Tispaquin, was long married to Amie, Metacomet's older sister. Tispaquin's Assawomset people had joined with Weetamoo's band to avoid trouble with the English. Because the Narragansetts had sworn allegiance to both the English and nearby Wampanoag tribes and because of Canonchet's promise of neutrality, Weetamoo and Metacomet expected safety for the warriors' families here.

Weetamoo wondered about it, however, as she approached the camp. Its secrecy did not strike her as unusual because of frequent skirmishes among all Algonquin tribes and their neighbors, but something seemed missing in the landscape. Weetamoo counted as conspicuously absent stout oak and pine trees used to make mishoons, the dugout canoes. She also saw no young, straight trees often taken to build fort-like barricades around camps in times of trouble. She saw many elder trees with narrow limbs removed and knew that wood to be best for arrow-making. By such signs, she decided that the Narragansett, too, had undertaken preparations for war. The fact relieved her. She might not find it difficult to convince them to join with Metacomet.

Joyous celebration met their arrival. Despite Canonchet's absence, his people welcomed them with a summer feast. They steamed eels, quahogs, clams, and lobsters between layers of seaweed in stone-lined pits. They built a great fire, and celebratory dancing carried on into the night. Happy reunions among relatives kept laughter and conversation going long after drumming ceased and the main fire died down.

Fatigued from her journey and the obligatory dances she had to perform as leader of the Pocasset people, Weetamoo retired early to the nushweety, a longhouse set aside for her and many of her people. She sat at the edge of a wide sleeping platform and removed her moccasins. She rubbed her feet. She noticed that her cousin, Awashonks, sat across the long room doing the same.

Awashonks had her hair pulled back into a long tail wrapped in rawhide in a style typical for a married woman. As symbols of her status, she wore eagle feathers and silver fur trimmed with valuable black or purple wampum made from seashells. Her thick middle made it hard for her to reach her feet, and she got winded leaning over. Yet, she had traveled the whole way at Weetamoo's side with no complaints or demands for rest.

A hardy woman, thought Weetamoo. *She is a great sunk squaw, known to their enemies as a grand old queen, and my favorite living relative.*

Weetamoo did not remember her mother. She and Weetamoo's grandmothers had long ago left this world. Weetamoo did not feel very close to her old aunts, who thought her too forward for a squaw. The fact didn't trouble her because she was raised to be a sachem, not a squaw. She had to know the ways of men and women to be a good leader. Awashonks, a sachem herself, understood.

Weetamoo decided at that moment that Awashonks would sponsor her marriage.

"This was a long journey, cousin. How are you feeling?" Weetamoo asked, crossing the room.

Awashonks smiled at her young cousin and said, "It was not so bad, but my feet are tired. Some parts wear out quicker than others," she laughed.

"Your feet tire more from your dancing than our walk," Weetamoo joked. She knelt down to rub her cousin's feet. "Let me do this for you," she said.

Awashonks nodded in appreciation. She had a big face with high round cheeks. She always looked as though she were smiling and about to break into a laugh. Often, that was the case. Others sought her company, and she genuinely enjoyed spending time with people. She loved dancing and usually stopped only when the drummers tired out and went to bed.

"Where is Tolony?" Weetamoo asked, wondering if they would have enough privacy to discuss her marriage proposal.

"Sitting with the other old men. You know, smoking and playing hubbub. Throwing stones. They'll be at it most of the night. I've given up wondering why. Besides, he never was much of a dancer. My husband would rather be off in a corner somewhere," Awashonks responded.

"Ahh, that feels good, Weetamoo." Ashawonks appreciated the foot rub.

"It feels like your feet have danced enough for both of you," Weetamoo said as she pressed the tight muscles with her thumbs to stretch them. She flexed Awashonks' foot.

"So you come to rub my feet, do you?" she asked. She patted Weetamoo on the head. "Tell me what is really on your mind, Weetamoo," she laughed.

"I do want to give you comfort, but yes. There is something I wish to discuss with you."

"So, tell me." She rested a hand on Weetamoo's shoulder.

Weetamoo looked up. "Awashonks, you know the importance of a sachem having strong alliances," she began.

"Yes, I do," Awashonks affirmed.

"And you also know that we build alliances from strong marital relationships."

"Aha," interrupted Awashonks. "So that is it. A man. Tell me, which one? Was he at the dance?"

Weetamoo stopped rubbing the old woman's foot and put her hand on her knees.

"Yes, it is a man, and yes, he was at the dance." Weetamoo blushed as she thought of Quannopinn dancing. His controlled movements and rhythmic grace made her think he had earned his reputation as an accomplished lover.

"Tell me, Little Cousin. Who is it?" Awashonks asked excitedly. She loved matchmaking and believed people were meant to be joined.

"I will. But before I do, I have to ask an important favor of you."

"Yes. You know I will answer you yes. What is it and who is he?" Awashonks leaned forward.

"First, I need you to agree to be my marriage sponsor. Then I will tell you."

"So, you want me to accept this great honor, but you will not tell me his name? I am not sure I can do it," Awashonks said with mock sincerity.

Of course, once asked, she had to serve as sponsor. The identity of the man didn't really matter to her. As sponsor, she had the power to prevent the marriage if she thought it unsuitable. Her role as sponsor would involve carrying on negotiations with the prospective husband's sponsor to see that the marriage was reasonable and fairly conducted.

"I will tell you, but first, give me your word," Weetamoo insisted. She sat beside Awashonks on her bed.

Sitting up very straight, Awashonks said in a formal voice, "I accept the honor of serving as your marriage sponsor." Then she huddled close and whispered, "Quick, now. Tell me who is he."

Weetamoo laughed, hugged her, and said, "He is Quannopinn. He is Narragansett."

Awashonks's smile left her face and she loosened her embrace. She waited a moment to respond.

Weetamoo drew back and demanded, "What? What is it? Do you know something? You must tell me."

Awashonks recovered her composure, then said, "It's nothing. I had only heard that he is twice married already. I expected you to seek a man who marries for the first time," she answered. "This is all." She did not want to shame Weetamoo by suggesting he was a poor choice.

"You are honor-bound to tell me the truth. What is it that troubles you with my choice?" Weetamoo grabbed her cousin's hand and held it tight.

As her sponsor, Awashonks could not keep anything secret from Weetamoo. "I will tell you."

She leaned closer as others came in to settle down for the night. "I heard that he can be hot-headed and that he has a strong appetite for the company of squaws," Ashawonks whispered.

Weetamoo burst into laughter. "Oh, only that," she said, relieved. "That does not worry me. I am hot-headed as well. I seek a man who will not wilt like my last husband. I want a strong man.

"And that he likes female company is no concern of mine. He has two other wives if I am not enough for him, although I doubt he will find much need for them once we are wed," she added confidently.

Awashonks laughed. "No, Weetamoo, I think he will find you more than enough company." She patted her cousin on the back. They hugged one another. Awashonks hoped her cousin would not be hurt in the pairing.

Weetamoo looked around the room then said quietly and quickly, "I asked you to sponsor me, Cousin, because you understand the importance of a sachem's marriage. I hear he is a strong warrior and an eager lover, but that is not what matters most to me. I want an alliance between the Narragansett and the Wampanoag people. He is second only to Canonchet, you know. Metacomet thinks Quannopinn can persuade Canonchet to join in our fight."

"Oh, ho," Awashonks said. "Now I understand. Metacomet is behind this sudden marriage decision."

"No, no. This was my idea. I only asked his help in choosing the right man."

"So it was his idea that Quannopinn be the man," Awashonks said. She thought about it for a moment. Then she said, "I am honored to be your sponsor, but understand this. If I discover him to be in any way wrong for you, I will tell you so. It is you that I care about, not Metacomet and his war.

She held Weetamoo's hand and looked into her eyes. "Yes, my little Namumpum. I will be your sponsor."

They embraced again, and Awashonks whispered in her ear, "So tell me. Did you dance with him tonight? Was he interested? Does he even know what you are planning?"

"So many questions. No, I did not dance with him. But I did see him dance, and he moves very well and is very handsome. I watched him with his young wife, and he was gentle and sweet to her. No, he does not know."

She stood up and added, "But he will soon."

Over the next month, the courtship evolved. At first, unsuspecting Quannopinn had no idea of the negotiations that went on between Awashonks and his grandmother, Quaiapen, the sunk squaw or old queen of his people. The two women dickered over the dowry, wedding date, marriage home to be built and the property to be given, but eventually, they agreed upon the match. Only then did his grandmother tell Quannopinn of Weetamoo's intentions. When his favorable response came back through the sponsors, Weetamoo made the formal proposal by leaving a basket of corn biscuits by his door. A prospective husband only had to eat one of the biscuits to signify his interest. Quannopinn ate the whole basketful.

Under pretense of berry picking, clam digging, and seeking materials for their future home, the couple went on private excursions and explored their compatibility. On one of those occasions, Quannopinn helped Weetamoo cut and strip the branches for the framework of their wetu. They walked about a mile from the encampment to a place near the edge of the swamp where they gathered the supple young saplings they needed. They worked together easily and made stacks of poles to drag back to their home site. While Quannopinn bundled the branches together, Weetamoo gathered cattail reeds to weave mats to cover the frame. Her fingers bore calluses and scratches from all the mats she had made since she arrived in Narragansett.

"Quannopinn," she said, "I think we should wed at the Green Corn Feast." She didn't look up from her work.

"That is only seven days from today," Quannopinn said, surprised by the suddenness of the suggestion. "We will scarcely finish our wetu by then," he added as he tied the loads of sticks together with strips of walnut bark. "And I have not finished making you a bride gift, since you have kept me so busy since you first proposed." He looked at her with a grin.

"I need no gift. You will be enough of a gift to me," she smiled back. "The way you work, we can have this wetu built in two days. You have all the framing, and I will have enough mats by the time you have lashed it all together." She laid down her cattail reeds and stretched in the hot August sun. "In this weather, we do not even need a wetu."

His industriousness pleased Weetamoo very much. Immediately after her proposal, he had set to work with her clearing the place for their wetu. He did not even want to stop to eat because he preferred to work, often from dawn to dusk, until the task was complete. Weetamoo liked that he approached everything he did as fully as he approached building the wetu, whether hunting, dancing, gaming, and, she had heard, even lovemaking. He put his full attention into his task at hand. Admiring his strength and coordination, she watched him bending the long branches and securing them deftly. She leaned back on her elbows, content that right now his attention focused on her and their upcoming marriage.

"You speak the truth, Weetamoo. It has not been so hot for many summers." He used both hands to push sweat from his forehead and ran his fingers through his long black hair. Weetamoo liked it when he wore it loose, and he indulged her when they spent time in one another's company. "But I can think of one reason that we will need a wetu," he said walking toward her.

"What is that?" she asked, stretching out her legs and playing with the grass between her toes.

"We will need a private place where I can bed you without all the others growing jealous." He sat down beside her and tried to pull her close.

"No, Quannopinn," she smiled. "We shall wait until our marriage for that, with or without a wetu." She did not resist him tugging her closer on the soft green grass. She leaned her forehead lightly against his and looked into his dark brown eyes. "My sponsor warned me about you," she said, "but you will wait to sleep with a sachem." She kissed him lightly on the lips.

Quannopinn fought his desire but understood her point. A marriage between sachems constituted a sacred honor. "Then we will wed within the week, for if you continue teasing me, I will have to go away to avoid dishonor or spend all my time with my other wives. Who will help you build your wetu then?" he asked. He leaned on his elbow and looked at her. "You are so beautiful. I would have wed you anyway, sachem or not." He ran his finger lightly over her forehead, nose, and lips. "I see the perfection of the Creator Manitou when I look at you."

Quannopinn's flattery and flirtation were hard to resist, but Weetamoo insisted on waiting until after the ceremony to consummate her marriage. No custom demanded it. Wampanoag women could sleep with whomever they chose, regardless of marital status, but Weetamoo believed the long wait would heighten their mutual pleasure and reinforce her position of status. Her father and grandfather had taught her well always to keep her leadership in the forefront of her mind.

She leaned up on her elbow and looked at her future sannup. In Quannopinn, she found her best match yet. Stronger than Petananuit and much more handsome than her second husband, whom she never mentioned and seldom thought about. She suspected him perhaps a better warrior and leader than Wamsutta, her first husband. Although she dearly loved Wamsutta, she had always doubted his war strategies. He was too trusting—so trusting that he walked right into the English trap and died for it. She took a deep breath.

She looked at Quannopinn. Having heard many stories of his bravery, she had no doubt about his courage and wit in war, and he shared her deep distrust of the English. "Yes, Quannopinn, I have long awaited a match with such a man as you," she said. They leaned together, and she fell back under his warm embrace.

A week later, during the Great Feast of the Green Corn, Weetamoo prepared to marry again. Awashonks and Laughing Water helped her to dress.

She put on a softened doeskin dress she had dyed bright red with bloodroot. Laughing Water painted her face red, too. Awashonks tied her hair into two long braids and tucked an eagle feather in one of them. Weetamoo tied her broadest wampum belt around her waist and hips and pulled on a long pair of red woolen stockings. She wore moccasins embroidered with bright colors. Across her breast she wore a necklace made of soft, colorful bird feathers. Iridescent greens and blues shimmered at her throat.

When she finished dressing, Awashonks gave her a pair of earrings made from feathers and porcupine quills and said, "These represent your name, which means little bird, and your character that reminds me of the porcupine, sometimes unassuming yet always sharp. Wear these to remind Quannopinn of your true nature."

Weetamoo took the gift and laughed with her cousin. "They are perfect," she said and let Awashonks help her put them on.

The women joined the feast, celebrated to honor the gift of the first fruit of green corn, the best fruit from their gardens. The thanksgiving festival had already begun. At the feast, celebrants placed baskets of first-picked corn from each garden into a ceremonial fire while the Powwow of the Narragansett tribe danced around the fragrant pyre in a sacred circle.

The Powwow wore a coat woven from corn leaves and reenacted tilling, planting, weeding, pollinating, ripening, and harvesting of the long-awaited, sacred crop. He shook green corn stalks and dried gourds as he danced around the burning basket until it had turned to ash. Only then did celebrants shuck other fresh picked ears and drop them into boiling water.

Weetamoo took special delight in celebrating her union with Quannopinn on her favorite feast day of the year. The gathering of all the tribes to taste the first corn harvest evoked her most joyful memories of childhood. The echoes of music and laughter of all the ancestors always sounded in her heart on the sun-baked days of sacred harvest.

Before long the people lined up in front of steaming pots to taste the year's first ear of sugary goodness. Everyone enjoyed eating that favorite food with shellfish steamed in stone-lined pits between layers of coal and seaweed. When everyone finished eating, Weetamoo and Quannopinn entered the sacred dance circle. They acted out the story of how the Wampanoags received the first gift of corn from the Great Spirit.

Quannopinn hid his fine wedding garments under a great cape of moose hide. He played the part of the old man Mondomin, weakened from starvation. He lay down on the ground as if dying. Then, Mondomin awakened by the sound of a partridge stuck in the branches of his wetu roof. Clasping his cape close and feigning great difficulty, Quannopinn pretended to go out of his wetu into the stormy winter night to free the bird from his roof. Since the imaginary bird was dead, he brought it back into his wetu to prepare and cook it for his supper. Just as he prepared to eat the fresh meat, he heard the sound of a crying woman.

Concealing her wedding dress under a worn out deerskin coat Weetamoo appeared. She cried and begged to be let in and have something to eat. Mondomin took pity on her and invited her inside. Then, knowing he had too little meat for both of them, he gave her the whole partridge and lay down and died.

Weetamoo pretended to bury the old man. She then danced through the passing of seven cycles of the moon while Quannopinn slowly pushed corn stalks up into the sky from under his cape. To the children's great delight, the stalks grew taller and taller until they reached full height. Then, in her native tongue, Weetamoo repeated the words of the Creator, "Listen, my children. What you see now, will be called Mondomin after the unselfish man who once fed a starving woman before himself. Tell this story to your children and their children. Always remember this story whenever you see the green corn growing. This food will grow and ripen for you for all time."

All the people gave cheers of happiness when Quannopinn grew up out of the corn stalks, shed his moose-hide cape, and appeared in his wedding attire. He wore a white shirt brightly embroidered with designs of animals, birds, and fish he had hunted or caught. He wore his hair in a topknot with a fan of turkey feathers spreading from it. His wide wampum girdle about his waist had more animal designs that matched a narrower band around his forehead. He walked to Weetamoo and removed her coat to reveal her finery to the crowd, who voiced their approval with long "Oohhhs" and "Aahhhs."

Awashonks and Quaiapen stepped into the sacred circle with them, and the Powwow waved cleansing sage smoke over them all with a large eagle feather. He stopped and asked. "Who speaks for these two people who wish to marry?"

Awashonks stepped forward and said, "I, Awashonks, the squaw sachem of the Sakonnets and cousin of Massasoit Metacomet speak for Weetamoo, the daughter of Caunbitant and squaw sachem of the Wampanoag Pocasset. She is a good woman who knows the duties of a wife and mother. She has learned the ways of the hearth, and she has learned the ways of the hunt. She has led her people for fifteen summers and has made her people happy. She has always kept the sacred ways of her people. She comes with her friends and family to join with our Narragansett brothers and sisters. We love her." A cheer of support erupted from her followers.

Awashonks took Weetamoo's hands and said, "Weetamoo, my dear little bird, take once again the duties of a wife. Make a home with Quannopinn and share with him all your talents. Share with him your dreams and your fears. Never be harsh with him. When anger, sickness, or tiredness come between you, be patient. Be strong.

"I have spoken," Ashawonks concluded. She kissed Weetamoo's cheek and backed away. Weetamoo smiled at her cousin. She bit her lip to keep tears from welling in her eyes.

Quaiapen stepped forward and said, "This is Quannopinn, my grandson. He is a good man. He has proven that he understands his duty as a husband. He is a brave warrior and skilled hunter. He is a strong sagamore to the Narragansett. He has always walked in the ways of the Great Spirit and honors the sacred gifts. We love him." Another cheer came from the crowd.

Quaiapen reached for Quannopinn's hands and said, "My son, you take on the duty of a husband to Weetamoo and a father to her son. Be faithful and kind. Use your skills to care for and protect her. Let her know your heart. Sometimes there will be difficulties; do not let them separate you. Know when to speak and when to listen. Have patience. Do not let anger or illness or want come between you.

"I have spoken," Quaiapen concluded. She kissed Quannopinn's cheek and hugged him tightly.

Then the two sponsors led the couple closer to the fire and the Powwow. He used his eagle feather to paint the air surrounding them with smoke from a braid of sweetgrass. He joined their hands together and said, "These two are one."

Quannopinn lifted Weetamoo off her feet and kissed her hungrily on the mouth. She wrapped her arms around his neck and kissed him back, eventually easing herself to the ground. They smiled and turned to face their family and friends. Loud and happy affirmations broke out from the crowd.

The drummers began a steady new rhythm and sang out in joy. The circle filled with people eager to dance with the newly married couple. Quannopinn's other two wives, one young, one old, came forward, accompanied by their families from their own hearths. They presented Weetamoo with wampum necklaces they had made and welcomed her with light embraces. Weetamoo thanked them warmly and turned away to greet other guests. The bride and groom accepted many items for use in their newly finished home.

After a long evening of eating, drinking, and dancing, Quannopinn broke away from his warrior friends to find Weetamoo surrounded by women offering advice. "Come, Bride," he called out. She saw that he would not wait to share his wife's bed until the end of the feast, which would go on for days. He scooped her into his arms and said, "Come now, Wife. I can wait no longer to make our new wetu a home."

"Nor can I, My Sannup," and leaned into his shoulder and kissed his neck with a tender smile.

Dining with a Captain
November 17, 1675
Lancaster, Massachusetts Bay Colony

Humming, young Mary danced in a circle, holding her mother's prized Delft charger in her arms.

"Mary, take care with that," her mother cautioned. "Your grandmother brought that all the way from England, and we are not like to find another of its kind on this side of the Atlantic."

"Yes, Mother," the daughter replied and gently placed the large porcelain platter in the center of the table. Its intricate blue-on-white pattern reminded any visitor of the wealth that Mary brought into her marriage. "What other help can I be to you, Mother?"

"Fetch the table linens from the press and mind not to drop the lid too heavily," her mother called, as she stirred the stew pot over the hearth.

"Yes, Mother," Mary sang as she skipped off to the front parlor.

Mary wondered if her daughter's lightness had to do with young Master Richardson's attendance at tonight's supper. She watched her daughter select table linens with care and noticed that she chose napkins that she had embroidered herself. She thought her daughter a wise girl, it being never too soon to show her handiwork to a potential suitor. The match, however, would never win her father's approval. He would not let her wed the son of a common tradesman. Even though Master Richardson's father had become a commissioned officer, Mary knew an honor such as that was only bestowed since the colony's recent misfortunes. Mary felt sure that the commissioners would soon deal resolutely and smartly with the trouble with the Indians, and soon both Lieutenant Richardson and his son would return to their usual work as carpenters.

No, Joseph would never see her wed to a carpenter. Still, Mary saw no harm in letting the girl dream for a time.

"Halloo, the master of the house is at home," called Reverend Rowlandson from the front door. He poked his head through the doorway and said, "Aha, here is Mistress Rowlandson busily attending to her evening festivities." Then, bowing deeply, he handed his wife a bouquet of winter berries and greens.

"Oh, Joseph, these are quite lovely." Mary accepted his offering with a curtsy. She turned to her daughter. "Mary, could you arrange these for our table?"

"Yes, Ma'am. Father, you are a dear to think of them." Young Mary floated over and whisked the bouquet from her mother's hand and glanced her father with a quick buss on his cheek.

"How was your day?" Mary asked her husband, turning back to her table setting.

"Quite good, my dear wife, but I must trouble you to set another place at the table, for we will have esteemed company joining us for our evening meal tonight."

"Pray Joseph, who might that be?" Mary asked.

"Captain Daniel Gookin, the Indian superintendent will be here," Joseph said. He hung his coat on a peg by the door. "He is just come from visiting the Christian Indian village at Marlborough, and I have asked him to join us for dinner before he returns to Cambridge in the morrow."

"Oh?" By not turning to face Joseph, Mary tried to conceal her dismay. "Very well, Joseph." She raised her eyes to meet young Mary's and spoke quietly, "Dear, fetch another plate and cup, if you please." She turned and smiled to her husband, "That is well, Sir."

As she counted off the places at her table, she wondered how she would stretch the meal in her stew pot to feed one more guest. There was little to be done at such a late hour to make the meal more filling. The lovely scent from her oven reminded her that she had no

43

time to fold, rise, and bake another loaf of bread. Neither did time allow for her to cook more meat, potatoes, or carrots. She could, however, thin the broth and make some dumplings for her stew and increase her bread pudding. She set about fetching more flour, raisins, cinnamon, and sugar from her larder and sent her daughter to her buttery for butter, stock and milk. As she worked, she thought the men would be more engrossed in their conversations than in their stomachs. As long as she kept them in good ale and bread, she hoped the meal would satisfy them all.

As Joseph settled into his great chair, pulled off his boots, and slipped on his house shoes, Mary set her daughter to work on the pudding while she mixed ingredients for the dumplings and dropped them into her stew. Turning from the hearth, she said, "Mary, use the sugar cutter on that cone, not a knife. It makes less mess. Hurry, Dear. They should be about any time now."

"Aye, the Lord favors me with such a fine wife and daughter," Joseph spoke. "The scents from your pot are most savory, indeed, and your bread pudding, Dear Daughter, 'tis the best, by far." He put on his glasses and looked over some papers from his waistcoat pocket.

A thumping at the back door announced the arrival of young Joseph, arms laden with firewood. "Sorry to be late, Mother," he called out. "I was talking with the young men in town and forgot the time." He dropped his load near the hearth and brushed the bark and dirt from his coat with both hands.

"Joseph, get away from my pudding. Can't you see, you're scraping your dirt everywhere!" his sister scowled.

"A fine welcome, Sister, and I am glad to see you, too," he teased. "Good evening, Mother. Good evening, Father. I shall go dress for dinner. Where is the little poppet?" he asked, hanging his coat on another peg by the door.

"Sarah is staying with her cousin tonight. With all you men about, it is sure to be a late evening, and she will not sleep if there is something she might miss going on downstairs."

"Why, who is coming to dinner?" Joseph asked. He dipped his finger into his sister's mixing bowl as he passed on his way to the stairs.

"Joseph, you are a plague! Get away from my pudding, I said!" His sister tried to slap his hand, but he was too quick for her.

"Mary, mind your tongue. The Lord does not approve of name-calling," her father said, not looking up from his reading.

Joseph gave his sister a confirming nod. She screwed up her face and nodded back, both hands on her hips.

"I saw that," her father said from his chair. "Enough, both of you. I'll have none of this before our guests, Lieutenant Richardson and Captain Gookin."

"Daniel Gookin? The Indian overseer?" Joseph asked, wheeling toward his father.

"Yes, the very same," his father nodded.

"Joseph, get dressed for dinner, please," his mother said. Nodding to her daughter, she said, "Mary, that pudding looks fine. Take the bread from the oven if it is done and put the pudding in its place."

Joseph bounded up the stairs as a knock sounded at the front door. Mary quickly wiped her hands on her apron and crossed through the hall to open the door. "Good evening, Lieutenant Richardson," she spoke. "How fare you, this fine evening? And young Master Richardson, it is pleasant to see you looking so well. Do come in."

Joseph rose from his chair and joined Mary in greeting their dinner guests. "Good evening, William, well met, Good Sir," he said, warmly shaking the lieutenant's hand. "And welcome to you, too, Nathaniel. Come in, come in."

"Now, where has our daughter gone off to?" the reverend asked, looking around. "Miss Mary, please come take the gentlemen's coats."

Tucking her hair under her coif, young Mary stepped in from the buttery. "Evening, Lieutenant. Evening, Nathaniel," she said with an awkward curtsy. "May I take your coats?"

"Thank you, Miss Rowlandson," said the Lieutenant, casually handing off his coat as he stepped forward to accept a silver tankard of ale from the minister. Reverend Rowlandson sat in his great chair and offered the lieutenant a seat to his right.

Mary brought the cooling loaf of bread to the table together with a bowl of butter. As she looked into her stew pot and saw the dumplings had turned nicely golden, she hoped Captain Gookin wasn't long in arriving. She swung the pot away from the fire to slow the cooking. Glancing back at the door, she saw her daughter Mary still holding Master Richardson's coat as she listened while he spoke. "Mary, dear, please hang the young gentleman's coat and show him a seat here at the table," she called without looking in their direction. The poor dear," Mary thought. Her daughter's cheeks were already quite flushed. "Nathaniel, may I offer you some cider or ale?" she asked.

"An ale would be fine, Mistress Rowlandson," Nathaniel said, as if he'd been of an age for a great time. Mary noticed that he threw a quick look in his father's direction after he said it, but the lieutenant and the reverend were engrossed in their conversation.

"I'll fetch it," young Mary volunteered readily and went to the cupboard to pull down another tankard.

"There's a good daughter," her father said. "Will you take the pitcher down to the cellar and draw more ale, as the captain will be soon here, and I'm assured he will have a thirst as well."

"Yes, Father." She poured slowly, smiling at Nathaniel. Young Mary filled his tankard and, not wanting to miss a moment in her dashing guest's company, hurried to the cellar .

A knock sounded at the door. Young Joseph called from upstairs, "Let me answer the door." He stomped noisily down the stairs, landing before the front door with a thump. He pulled the door open with a flourishing bow, "Welcome, Captain Gookin. Do come in, if you please."

"Good evening, Sir. Is Reverend Rowlandson about?" Captain Gookin asked quietly.

"Right here, Captain," Joseph said, crossing the great room to shake his hand. "Welcome to our humble home. You know Lieutenant Richardson and his son, Nathaniel, I trust."

"Indeed, I do. They have been of great service to me in my work here. Good evening, William, Nathaniel," he nodded to each.

"May I present my family? This fine woman is my dear wife, Mary, mistress of the house, and these are our children, Joseph and Mary."

"Good evening, all. It is good of you to take in a weary traveler on such brief notice. It is surely my good fortune to meet you all."

Mary was surprised at his appearance. She had pictured him as tall and heavy, but he was neither. He was much older than she expected and, although she knew he had been made superintendent of the Indians due to his long support of the work of Mr. Eliot, she had not pictured him a man in his sixties. His face had a kindly look, not a bit like the vile, Indian-loving savage she had imagined.

"Do come in, Kind Sir," she said. "Mary, please take the captain's hat and coat. Come, come, have a seat here by Mr. Rowlandson." She led him across the great room to a warm place at the table near the hearth. She brought the steaming kettle of stew and took her seat on her husband's left. Young Mary poured a tankard for the captain and sat beside her mother. Joseph sat next to her, then reached for the pitcher before he felt his sister's heel upon his toes. Pulling back his hand, he winced silently.

"'Tis a fine evening indeed to have such distinguished company for dinner. Now that we are all here, I shall offer a prayer of thanksgiving before we sup," said the minister. "Let us bow our heads and pray.

"Almighty Lord, Thou art truly infinite in wisdom in bringing us, your humble servants, together with these worthy soldiers for this meal. We thank Thee for the goodness of Thy gifts of the harvest and for the joy of having all these noble Christians under our roof.

Though we are not worthy of this great honor, let us make them welcome as Thou will one day welcome us all into Thy heavenly kingdom. Through Christ our Lord, Amen."

"Amen," murmured those gathered around the table.

"Mary, bring our guests' trenchers to me for filling, if you please," Mary told her daughter.

"Yes, Ma'am," she replied, eager to show her skills as a hostess to the handsome young Nathaniel. Her mother was grateful that she remembered to serve the captain first, then the lieutenant, and then Master Richardson, before serving father, brother, mother, and herself in that order. Mary noted how her daughter lingered, taking great care to spill not a drop near the young soldier's trencher. Mary smiled in approval when young Mary slid back into her seat.

"So, Captain, to what do we owe the great honor of your visit to Lancaster?" asked Reverend Rowlandson, filling his mouth with a forkful of dumpling.

"Mr. Rowlandson, 'tis an unsettling mission I am on this day. I have been sent by the council to look into the affairs of the Christian Indians at Marlborough as there has been some trouble of late in some of the Christian villages."

"What kind of trouble, Sir?" asked young Joseph. He put down his cup of cider and leaned forward.

"Joseph, don't pry," cautioned his mother. "You must allow our guest to enjoy his meal."

"Begging your pardon, Madam, but 'tis not prying," said Captain Gookin. 'Tis only a natural curiosity for a young man in these trying days, and if you permit me to answer, I shall endeavor to satisfy that curiosity.

"And enjoy this fine meal," he added with a wink to Joseph as he took a mouthful of stew.

"As you please, Sir," Mary agreed.

"I'm sure you have heard of the accusations against the Wamesit Indians near Chelmsford. Our Lieutenant Richardson here has lost of late not only a fine stack of hay some weeks hence, but now his barn filled with hay and corn has been also destroyed by fire," the captain began, pausing to spoon another mouthful of stew between words.

"'Tis so, and though I have not lodged a complaint against the Wamesits," Lieutenant Richardson continued, "there are some who impute the Wamesit Indians for these devilish acts."

"Though I know it were none of those fine praying Christians who were at the cause of this burning. But out of clamors raised by numerous colonists, the council has sent me under the protection of Lieutenant Richardson here to observe and report on the doings of Christian Indians at Marlborough."

"I am glad to report that there is no cause for alarm among these fine praying folk," Captain Gookin continued. "The council has appointed Mr. John Hoar to watch over and secure the Marlborough Indians, and he has agreed to build a workhouse to insure the protection of the Indians from harm and the villagers from fear and worry."

"'Tis a sorry state of affairs that peaceable neighbors who for nigh on thirty years have kept the Sabbath holy and lived as good Christians should now be locked up of an evening and suspected of the doings of their heathen kin," said Mr. Rowlandson.

"But so it is in Marlborough. 'Tis this sad business that brings us near to Lancaster, young Master Rowlandson," Captain Gookin said, looking at Joseph. He mopped up some stew with a fresh-torn piece of bread, still steaming inside.

"Mistress Rowlandson, I must give you my compliments for this fine stew," the captain said. "'Tis the best I've had though I'll thank you for not telling Mrs. Gookin I said so. She's a fine woman with fair skills, but her stew is not so savory as this."

"Why, thank you, Sir," Mary smiled. "Perhaps I can give you some of the herbs I use for seasoning to bring to your wife as a gift. 'Tis the Lord's own sweet seasoning that makes the meal, not the cook."

"Aye, you are modest and gracious," the captain continued. "My wife would be ever so pleased if I return to her with more than stories of my travels."

"But Captain, why would you be traveling here to Lancaster if Marlborough were your destination?" Joseph asked. He sopped up the last of his stew and nudged his sister to give him more.

"Not before the guests," his sister nudged back discretely.

"Smart lad, you know your geography," the Captain replied. "We must also see the Nashoba Indians near here to insure that there are none among them that would cause harm. We will be traveling back by way of Concord instead of through Natick. There are still many there who have no love for the superintendent of the Indians, even though all Natick's Praying Indians have been removed to Deer Island. There are some who will not be pleased until all the Praying Indians have been confined to that desolate place."

"Have you been there, Sir? To Deer Island, I mean?" asked Nathaniel.

"Aye, Sir, I have. 'twill be with great hardship that these poor folk suffer the winter on that rocky place."

"Are there not trees and animals to hunt?" asked Joseph.

"Yes, there are trees and plentiful sheep, but Samuel Shrimpton, the landowner, would only allow them there with the promise that they harm not his sheep nor his growing wood. They must make what meals they can from the sea and use only dead fallen wood for fires. Mainly, those two hundred souls survive on clams they dig and corn sent from Boston. 'Tis a very woeful place indeed. Yet they bear it with the Grace of God. They are a timid people, and I have assured them that only by tribulations such as these do we come to everlasting life."

"Amen to that good advice," said Reverend Rowlandson. "Now you curious young people will have to let the good captain finish his supper. Please, Sir, eat before it gets cold." After a quick glance in her stew pot, he added, "Mary, another serving for the captain and the lieutenant."

"Oh, thank you, but no more for me. I smell a fine pudding and want to enjoy a taste of that before I am satisfied," said the lieutenant.

"Oh!" the hostess said, jumping from her chair to the brick oven near the hearth. Using her apron, she pulled the bread pudding from the oven and set it hurriedly on the table. She was pleased to see that it had not burned and had set nicely. *Thank Thee, God, for not letting this burn,* she prayed. "Would anyone like more stew before their pudding?" she asked, grateful to see enough left in the kettle to offer second helpings.

"Not for me, Mistress Rowlandson," said Captain Gookin. "I, too, am bewitched by the aroma of the pudding."

"Mary, please serve the young men more stew while I serve the pudding," Mary said to her daughter.

"Yes, Ma'am," young Mary happily filled Nathaniel's trencher and spooned the remnants of stew into her brother's with a wrinkled look.

After dolloping out great servings of pudding, Mary noticed plenty remaining for second helpings of that. *Well done,* Mary, she thought. "More ale or tea, gentlemen?" she asked.

To full assent, Mary poured the last of the pitcher and went down cellar for more. She smiled to see her dinner party proved successful. She breathed happier knowing that Captain Gookin supervised and controlled the Christian Indians. She looked with pride upon her children who had managed to behave as they should for the most part of the meal. When she returned to the main floor, the men had retired to the parlor for a smoke. Joseph and Nathaniel continued eating, while Mary cleared away the rest of the dishes.

Judging by the sounds of their hushed voices, Mary gathered that the men began discussing other unsuitable news that they didn't want her or the children to hear. The two young men finished the pudding and began arm wrestling. She joined her daughter in clearing away the mess, then repaired to her chair for some needlework.

As she stitched, Mary Rowlandson prayed to God that her son would never serve in war. She prayed for him to attend school and preach like his father. She prayed that young Mary would one day marry a minister or a lawyer, not a soldier or a carpenter. She prayed that her home remain in the same good order as on this fine winter eve. She prayed to God to be always safe and warm with all the necessities for her family and any they might need to shelter, and she prayed that New England would one day become as fine a place as her birthplace across the sea.

Mary couldn't hear the men say that up and down the colony of Massachusetts and at the fringes of their neighboring colonies of Plimoth, Rhode Island, and Connecticut, Indian ambushes of colonial troops occurred due to the militia's inexperience with native ways of fighting. Despite their employ of Christian Indians as scouts and guides, the settlers lost valuable men of experience and countless volunteers. King Philip's men surprised and cut down soldiers at key locations, setting villages afire, and then disappeared as quickly as they had come. Colonists abandoned their homes and fled. The war moved closer and closer to her home with each passing day.

Mistress Rowlandson didn't know that the enemies made primary targets of places where land had been swindled away from native people and that they regarded Lancaster as such a place.

Thunder in the Night

Thunder awakened Weetamoo. Not spirit thunder from the west, but man's thunder. English guns. She reached for Quannopinn in the furs beside her. She felt only an empty bed. Had she slept through an English attack? She sat up and listened as she pulled on her skirt and leggings. Then she thought with a start, *Where is my papoose? Where is Laughing Water?*

More guns sounded. Closer this time. *Are we under attack?*

She heard a woman scream on the far side of the camp. Men shouted. Someone ran just outside her wetu. She threw on her mantle and pushed open the door flap. Low, grey clouds spewed heavy snow, and she saw smoke and fire on the other side of camp.

She grabbed her bow and quiver of arrows and stepped out into the frozen night. A half-dressed warrior ran past her toward the unfinished barricade that separated her people from the source of the noise that awoke her. The tall straight timbers hewn from the stumps Weetamoo passed on her way to Narragansett nearly surrounded the camp. Lines of British soldiers advanced toward the small opening in the camp's wall. As she watched, the running warrior and several others like him fell like reeds before an English scythe. He toppled onto a mound of writhing bodies piling up at the entrance to the camp. His face rolled toward her. In shock, she recognized the grimace as that of Mantowapuet, her nephew. His bleeding body blurred into the mounting wall of human flesh, the only hindrance to the advancing English.

She drew her bow and looked steadily into the eyes of the first Englishman she saw. She sent her arrow straight into his heart. He joined her killed and dying brothers in the writhing heap of death. Her heart felt no sorrow for him.

Weetamoo spun amid the smoke and chaos to seek out Laughing Water and her baby son. She saw Awashonks crawling out of the nushweety.

"Weetamoo, get down," Awashonks called. "Come quickly. We must go to the mishoons. Help me gather the women and children."

"No." Weetamoo stood tall like a brave. "I will not go without the blood of these cowards first. You gather the women and children. I will fight." Weetamoo reached out to her and said, "Find Laughing Water and my son for me. Make sure they get into the mishoons." Then she turned away.

Weetamoo took her mark on another Englishman just as he raised his weapon toward an old woman stumbling away from her burning wetu. The sachem let her second arrow fly. The soldier fell just in front of the old woman he had targeted. Weetamoo set another arrow on her bow.

Awashonks called back to her, "Weetamoo, come now! You are a leader of your people. We cannot win this battle; we must go now and fight another day. Come, gather your people, and take them to safety. We must save those we can." Awashonks' grey hair hung loosely. She looked like an old woman begging for scraps and not the vibrant leader Weetamoo so admired. Ashawonks ushered people out a narrow opening in the rear of the stockade.

The mishoons, their hollowed wooden canoes, waited hidden nearby. The women pushed their children along and muffled their sobs. Like all warrior people, they had practiced swift escapes many times, especially recently in their travels here to Narragansett, a place of supposed safety. As each mishoon filled with thirty or more passengers, one of them pushed it off, and they paddled it away.

Weetamoo turned to see flaming torches flung into the lodges and wetus of the camp. Her and Awashonks's people had come here for refuge from English retribution. *Have the English now turned against the Narragansetts? Was the attack reprisal for having offered shelter to Pocasset and Sakonnet women and children?* She shot another arrow and sent a third Englishman to meet his white god.

A child with hair on fire ran from his wetu toward Weetamoo. Time stretched out as he ran and the flames waved like yellow feathers behind his head, his soft scream like the wind whistling through it. A pop sounded across the way leaving a puff of smoke behind. The soldier's bullet caught up with the boy. He dropped to the cold ground. His fire feathers flickered, then grew still. As the firelight in his hair faded, so did the spirit light in his eyes. Weetamoo whispered a prayer for the boy and pulled her eyes away.

Her face and chest felt hot, and her blood pounded in her head. *What kind of cowards are these,* she thought, *to attack women and children in the camp of an ally? What honor do they gain?* She had distrusted them all along, but now she felt disgust and hatred burning through her very bones.

She stood still and mute in the midst of a horrible nightmare. All around, her people cried out in pain. They died in their beds or faced guns as they fled their shelters. She saw bloodied blades flashing in the firelight. She heard the heavy crunch of war clubs crushing skulls. Indian and English voices cried out as guns broke bones and tomahawks tore flesh away from bodies. English commanders shouted orders to retreat and to advance. People ran in all directions. Smoke and fire surrounded her. The smell of powder hung thick, mixed in the air with the smell of blood and burning flesh.

She saw her husband, Quannopinn, with a small band of warriors. He fired at the English climbing over the bodies of her brothers to enter the camp. She looked for familiar faces in the bloody pile and felt sickened by the sight of blood matting the white hair of her uncle. She wanted to go pull him from the pile, but his eyes stared at the sky. She knew he had already embarked on the path to the spirit world. She could not summon him back or delay his journey.

"Caunbitant, your brother comes to join you now," she whispered to her father.

She had killed before and seen others killed, but never had she experienced such slaughter. The English soldiers greatly outnumbered them, appeared all around them, and shot or burned everyone and everything in sight. Her people's leaders shouted, but no one seemed to listen to them. From Quannopinn's direction, she picked Captain Church's voice out of the crowd.

The English breached the fort. They crossed the narrow log bridge and swarmed through the passage in the outer wall of the fort. They searched wetus looking for survivors to kill. The screaming tormented Weetamoo. Her people usually did not utter anything so loud except for the warrior's cry. The sounds she heard wailed of death.

Weetamoo watched grey-haired elders walk calmly to their deaths to draw attention away from their fleeing families. Too old to run in the cold winter weather, they sacrificed themselves for the younger generations. Amid the flames and noise, Weetamoo turned and saw a mother standing and holding a blood-soaked papoose. Thoughts of her own son jolted her.

She ran to Quannopinn's side. "Weetamoo, go now!" he ordered. We can save no more."

Weetamoo sent an arrow into the neck of a man firing into a nearby wetu. She reached for another arrow but found her quiver empty. Baring her knife, she ran toward an approaching Englishman, but Quannopinn caught her by the wrist.

"It is over," Quannopinn said, overpowering her with a firm hand. "We cannot change this. We go, now."

She tugged back and threw her knife into the face of a man raising his gun at Quannopinn's back. Then she ran, her eyes squinting tightly to hold back hot tears.

She slipped through the stockade and ran down the path to the water. Flakes of snow touched her like small gifts from the spirits. They did not cool her anger. She did not look back but could not escape the death screams of her people. Cries to the living and calls to ancestors in the spirit world drowned out low moans. Desperate voices wailed like those of wounded wolves in the darkness. The English thunder did not stop.

Bitter smoke swirled down the embankment and pushed away the scent of white pines and salt water. The smell of burning hair and flesh hung in an orange mist over the snowy woods.

Weetamoo slid down the icy path to the water. Very few mishoons remained along the shore. She saw many gliding away up the river to the north. The young warriors had removed the stones from the sunken canoes and raised them from the river bottom before she arrived. From under the brush at the river's edge, they pulled paddles and handed one to each passenger stepping aboard. In the darkness, Weetamoo could not see who was or was not there. She stepped into a mishoon behind other survivors and settled into place. Once it had filled to capacity, Quannopinn pushed the heavy canoe into the river.

Weetamoo took up a paddle and plunged it into the icy black water. She had no words. She did not take stock of who had come and who was lost. She tasted the bile of hatred for the English in her mouth and used her bitter anger to drive further and further from their reach into the land of the Nipmuc. The sound of thundering guns and wailing cries behind her lessened with each stroke and were replaced by soft sobs and mournful howls wafting from the mishoons ahead of her on the dark river.

As the mishoons struck out into open water, she felt the rhythm of movement rising from the strength of her people against the river's steady current. The unity of their exertions drove them ever deeper into the land of their fathers. Her land.

She raised her paddle to the sky and shouted, "Hear me, oh great ancestors! I vow to avenge this cruel night. I, Weetamoo, and my people—the Pocassets and Narragansetts—will join Metacomet's warriors to fight these foul English until I breathe no more. Aaaiiii-yahhhhhh."

A Call to Arms

Mary talked with her sister Elizabeth as they prepared their beans for baking. The next day, the Sabbath, they would not do any cooking. They would spend most of their day in meeting and prayer. But before they slept tonight, they would take their beans to a common fire for baking. Then, after their church service, they would bring their beans and bread home for their dinner.

As Mary slid her finger down a dried pod, the beans fell one by one into her earthenware crock. She could do the task by touch, so she looked at her sister's face as she worked. "What do you think of this?" she asked. "Chaplain for the militia is quite an honorable post."

"Sure, Mary, it is. But it gives me great fear to consider the Reverend Joseph away and you and the children here alone," Elizabeth said, shelling her own beans as quickly as Mary.

"But I will not be alone, Elizabeth. You know that. Living in the garrison, I sometimes feel as if I will never be alone again. Especially now, with so many coming and going with all the talk and preparation for war."

"Aye. That's true enough. Today, I heard that the governor has called up another three hundred men from the Bay Colony, and these will join the muster of the Plimoth and Connecticut colonies to bring the number of fighting men to over a thousand by the end of this month. Surely a thousand English soldiers can put down the rebellion led by Philip's wild men," Elizabeth said.

"Over a thousand men? Where will the three hundred come from? Our towns have so few to defend them now. I have to say, Sister, this worries me. Young Joseph and his friends spend all their time in the company of the men now. I don't like the look in his eye when he speaks of the honor of war," Mary said as she wiped her hands on a linen cloth at her waist, nearly upsetting the heavy crock.

"Nay, I think you may be wise in this, Sister," Mary added. "It might be best that the Reverend turn down this chaplain post and mind the needs of his own family and his parish here in Lancaster." She walked to the buttery door, raised the latch, and pushed it open.

"I have no doubt that it would be best, Mary. How could you even imagine your husband wandering the countryside, following after the trouble loose in the frontier towns? It seems now, no matter where the governor sends his troops, the trouble arises somewhere else. There is no telling where King Philip and his men are, and they skulk in and out before any can stop them. At least here in your fine house, you can sleep well and know you are defended. It seems unlikely that they would come this close to Boston, doesn't it?"

Mary gathered up the bean shells into her apron and took them outdoors to shake them into snow over her dormant kitchen garden. She looked around in the darkness and noticed the snow-covered fortifications started at the corners of her house. These flankers should have been completed before the winter snow fell upon them. Now, they stood unfinished. Once the ground froze, no more work could happen on the earthen barriers. *Come spring, the men will finish up their work here and on the other houses,* Mary thought. She went back inside and shuddered as she pushed hard against the back door.

"I hope that is so, Elizabeth." Mary leaned close to her sister and said, "I heard the men talking last night, and they said they heard a rumor that the governor supplied Philip's men with powder."

Elizabeth's head snapped up with a gasp. "That is an abomination! For Christians to sell powder to be used for the devastation of Christians?"

"I don't know if we can consider Albany Dutchmen as Christians. I believe those traders would sell anything to anyone for a profit. Yet, if this could be stopped, I think Philip would find himself in the stocks."

"It will be more than the stocks for that one, Sister."

"Aye, Sister. 'Tis so," Mary answered. She unstopped a jug of molasses and poured it liberally over her beans and then her sister's. Her sister took a braid of onions from the wall, pulled two free, and chopped them into small pieces. Mary added a few pinches of dried mustard from her summer garden and stirred the ingredients with a wooden spoon.

"We should make a cake for tomorrow. Will you come to eat it with us if we do?" Mary asked.

"A cake?" Elizabeth laughed. "For what wedding? Are you not aware there is a war going on, Mary?"

"A Banbury cake. We have enough dried currents and have not had any sweets in such a long time. The holiday is approaching. And you know that the last slave ship brought an ample supply of sugar and spices. What do you think?" Mary said.

"I think our husbands will think us mad. But they will love to eat it all the same. Yes, let us make a cake. We will hope that it is to honor the occasion of our fine Reverend Joseph Rowlandson refusing the post as chaplain to the militia. This seems a fitting feast for a Sabbath afternoon."

A thumping at the door announced the arrival of the very man they discussed. "Ah, Joseph, were your ears burning or were you following your nose in search of baked beans? If so, you are a bit too early."

"Aha, Goodwife, it must have been the burning ears." He laughed as he shook the snow from his coat, hung the garment by the door, and said, "How is it that nary a time passes when two women are hovering over some excuse for food, but that their real ambition is to meddle in the affairs of men? What gossip is it today, then, fair ladies?"

"No gossip, Sir. Only good-natured thoughts for your well-being and that of your family," his wife replied.

"Ah, then in this we are agreed. Mary, I've just come from a meeting with Sam Appleton. He's being dispatched to the northern frontier. He departs tonight to muster in Dedham. I have told him that I will not accept the position as their chaplain. I will stay here."

"Praise the Lord in Heaven!" Mary exclaimed and held out her arms to her husband. "What happy news! Here is an occasion to celebrate."

"I'm pleased that it makes you happy," he said in a tone that told Mary he had something else on his mind.

"Elizabeth," Mary said with a nod to her sister, "be a dear and look out of doors for our young men, Joseph and William. These beans should be taken for baking now if we hope to have them for our dinner tomorrow."

Elizabeth, sensing her dismissal, got up, and pulled her cloak down from its peg, saying, "Of course, I will find our two fine sons and put them to work. Then I must hasten home, for surely my own good man will come home soon." Fastening her cloak, she said, "Thank you for the molasses, Mary. Good day to you and you as well, Joseph. I'll see you both in the morrow."

"Good day, Sister. Sleep well."

"And you, Elizabeth. Mind your step. There is ice underfoot," Joseph said holding the great heavy door open for her. As one of the garrisons for Lancaster, the Rowlandson home was heavily fortified. The door was made of thick oak planks, and it took effort to push it tight in wet weather such as they had at present. Joseph leaned against the door after the latch fell into place.

"What is it, Joseph? What worries you?" she asked.

"This rebellion grows, Mary. Five hundred have been called to muster under Sam Appleton."

"Five hundred?" Mary was surprised. "I didn't know the colonies had so many fighting men."

"That is the trouble. They do not. Sam tells me he has been given command over Jim Oliver, Nathaniel Davenport, Sam Moseley, and Joe Gardner. This concerns me, Mary, because these are not trained militiamen but a mixed lot. Some of these fellows are just farmers, apprentices, and artisans. Not combat men. Some are simply attracted by the offer of land and pay. But there are others, Mary, drawn to fight with pure hatred in their hearts. It can lead to no good."

"Wasn't it Sam Moseley who very nearly lynched those Christian Indians at Marlborough, Joseph?"

"Indeed it was. If it were not for Captain Oliver, Moseley would have been done with the lot of them."

"Were they the same Indians that Captain Gookin visited when he dined with us last?"

"Yes. The very same, marched to Cambridge and boarded on ships bound for Deer Island when John Hoar could no longer hold back the clamoring of the mob against them. That same mob got whipped into a fury by none other than Sam Moseley."

"I'm thinking, Joseph, that it's Sam Moseley who concerns you. Am I right?"

"I should bear no grudges, but that man does not seem a proper Christian, Mary."

"Well, 'tis best for them, then, to be out of harm's way. Surely no one will go out to that barren island with winter bearing down on us to wreak vengeance upon them now." Mary did not want to see innocent people harmed but nevertheless felt more secure with the Christian Indians removed from her vicinity.

"Mary, what worries me most is the vigor with which some of the unholy English rabble in our midst plays at war. These sinners are too eager to provoke the Christian Indians. For each provocation of the friendly Indians, there comes another raid on settlers when before we shared peace. Look to Brookfield where former friendly Indians ambushed Captain Hutchinson and Captain Wheeler on their way to make a peace treaty. They would have finished everyone in the garrison if rain had not put out their fires and ended their siege.

"Anger on both sides grows and grows," he continued, "and cannot be quenched without more bloodshed. Five hundred men marching in the cold can only worsen the situation for both sides.

"No, Goodwife, I cannot accompany a band such as this on a fool's errand. Mark my words. No good will come of this. I must stay here, and I have begged leave to keep our son here as well, for we have few enough men left to defend us here in the event of a reprisal."

Before that conversation, Mary had felt little alarm about the distant trouble, but when Joseph mentioned her son, a knot formed in her throat. She hadn't liked Joseph's growing interest in the war, but until now, she hadn't thought about how close war might come to her own hearth. She didn't allow herself to think that her son had grown to an age to fight in a war. Joseph's words clamped a cold fear on her chest. *What if the supply of angry farmers and seamen ran out? Would the governor then turn to sons of farmers and seamen and ministers, too, to launch and stave off new attacks?* She shivered.

"Joseph," she said, "I am much pleased that you will not march off with those men. Thank you for protecting our son from such a fate. Can you say to me that we should not worry, then? Surely the large army can put down the insurrection at last, can it not? Can we sleep soundly in our beds?"

"For a time, Wife, for a time. It is thankful I am to the Lord for the protection of this fine home and the strong men of Lancaster who will defend it, should war come. Fear not, Wife, for the fighting does not take place here but far to the south, in Narragansett country, and on the western frontier. Our family shall rest well enough this winter."

"For that, I thank the good Lord." Mary looked out the window for her son. "Now just where are those boys?" she wondered. She fussed with her bean pots. She called outside for Joseph and William. "Where did they wander off to? I need to get these to the beanery or we shall starve," Mary said as she headed for the door.

Then she remembered she had forgotten all about the cake.

A Tribe Scatters

W alking in the frigid night, Weetamoo closed her mind to
her aching limbs. Wind whipped sleet across her back and hair. She
no longer felt her toes, and the burning in her feet had stopped and
moved up into her calves. But she would think only of her people.
She determined to bring them to Metacomet.

Stepping swiftly through deepening snow, she forced her mind to
focus on the strength of her people. *How courageous they were. How
strong.* They left their refuge in the Great Swamp with little warning,
with only what they wore and what little they could carry in haste.
Now they marched north and west in winter's whiteness to join
Metacomet, the mighty King Philip, and his men.

To her left trudged Sunk Squaw Quaiapen, the old queen of the
Narragansetts, mother of her second husband who died ten years ago
of lingering disease. Though grey-headed and very heavy, Quaiapen
kept up the steady pace with no complaint and never asked to rest.
Behind her, Weetamoo saw more old women walking with their
heads high. One old woman held her arm close to a blood stain on
her mantle. Watery drops of red fell from her elbow. Her grandchild
held her other arm, letting the old mother lean on her as they
stepped along the uneven ice-crusted path. Behind them stumbled
a sea of women and children. Weetamoo could not tell how many
followed or how many remained behind.

On her right strode her new husband, Quannopinn, silent and
strong. He walked briskly, breaking way through the hard crust for
others to step in. She never saw him stumble or stop. His footsteps
fell without faltering on the dark path through the woods. A small
band of warriors followed him. Only a handful had survived the

bitter fight. Few had stayed at the fort to protect these elders, women, and children. Many others had given their lives so that these few could escape.

Ahead of her, Laughing Water walked, carrying her baby brother on her back. Weetamoo thanked the ancestors who watched over her children when the English attacked, since they both escaped in warm clothing. Laughing Water dressed warmly in thick winter hides, and he nestled snugly in his papoose carrier lined with soft rabbit fur. The woven flap that covered his head kept him warm but allowed air and light to flow through. Weetamoo checked him often and found his face and hands warm, unlike her own and many others'.

Weetamoo's thoughts snapped back to the horror in the swamp. *How many crying children stayed beside their dying mothers as the English set the village afire?* Weetamoo wondered if the English would take the survivors prisoner or if their hateful smoke had smothered the life out of everyone left breathing? Weetamoo remembered her young nephew falling face first onto the writhing mass of dead and dying men and her uncle's staring eyes as his blood darkened the snow around him. *Who would bury them and burn offerings to the ancestors for them? What would happen to the elders, the wounded and ill trailing behind them now?*

"They can never survive this journey," Weetamoo said under her breath.

"Did you speak?" Quannopinn asked, reaching down to touch her shoulder.

"Nux," she said, looking straight ahead. "I am concerned for the wounded and the unwell. I think they need to rest a while."

"I was thinking of them, too, but there is no time to rest. We will have to leave them here with some able kinsmen to tend to their needs. I saw Mohegans fighting with the English. They will know how to track us. It would be better for a few to stay behind than for all to be captured. When they have recovered, they can make their way to the Praying Indian towns." He stopped and called out to the Narragansett lead warrior, Tispaquin. The black sachem strode to his side.

Tispaquin had dark skin like many black Indians. His mother, a Seminole Indian born to a Creek sachem, had mixed heritage from an escaped Negro slave. The lineage of leadership had passed to him from his Creek mother as well as from his Assawomset father. Although the British had attempted to disinherit him from his land because of his mixed heritage, they had not succeeded. While some patriarchal English called Tispaquin a slave, he remained the free leader of his people in Assawomset. Married to Metacomet's sister Amie, he had proven himself as one of the bravest warriors in their company.

"Tispaquin, go back through the people and tell them we will part ways," Quannopinn said. "Those strong enough can carry on and follow me to Nipmuc country. Those who cannot follow will set off in different ways to confuse the English scouts. Ask for elders to lead the different bands."

Without a word, Tispaquin turned and soon moved among the people with Quannopinn's orders. He would ensure the swift following of the order.

Listening at Weetamoo's side, Old Queen Quaiapen stepped in front of Quannopinn. "I will stay with my people," she said. "We are near the old stone fort. We can seek shelter there. Stonelayer John can come with me and instruct the others on how to strengthen this shelter."

She firmly set her jaw, and Weetamoo could see no use in arguing with her.

"Old Mother, you are very wise," Quannopinn said, leaning closer to her and placing his scarred hand upon her shoulder. "Make your people follow different paths to the fort, and use the rocks to conceal your tracks as you near it. Bind the bleeding so no signs give away your path. Take branches . . ."

Quaiapen laughed and interrupted him. "Young nephew, you explain to me, the old sunk squaw who taught you and half your warriors, the ways of woods? Have no fear that I can lead this band away from the English dogs."

Quannopinn smiled at her. "Who am I to tell the wisest sachem of the Narragansetts how to find her way? Go, Mother. May the Spirits lead you to safety." He raised his hand in a farewell greeting.

Weetamoo reached for Quaiapen's gnarled hand and said, "Grandmother, I thank you for your courage. I will ask the spirits to keep you safe. Aquene. Peace."

"You are strong, Weetamoo. You must take all you can with you so the Pocassets and the Sakonnets and the Narragansetts will not become lost tribes. We will not let the English erase our names as they have the Pequot. Trust that the grandfathers are watching over you. Wuniish. Go in beauty."

"I'll never let the English take away our names, Quaiapen." Weetamoo held her hand tightly and touched Quaiapen's creased forehead with her own. The night wind had taken all the warmth from the old woman's flesh. Weetamoo opened her eyes and found courage glaring back from the old woman's brown eyes. She would not cry.

Weetamoo squeezed Quaiapen's hand tightly, then let her go back to her people. They turned from one another to take their separate paths.

Lancaster Ruined

Before dawn broke on the frigid morning of February 10, 1675, an unnatural stillness filled the air in Lancaster. Not just the muffled stillness from fresh fallen snow or the usual quiet solitude before the villagers stirred. Another silence settled on the town, one that caused animals in the barns to prick up their ears and birds in nearby branches to hold silent vigil as they waited for the sun's warmth to cast itself on their fluffed feathers.

A narrow road threaded through a flat expanse of white pasture-land carved out of the forested, hilly countryside. Dotted along the road nestled the twenty-three homes that comprised the village of Lancaster. Each homestead had a small kitchen garden with paths beaten to communal barns, wells, and pastures. In the center of town stood a modest house of worship where Reverend Rowlandson ministered to his flock. The stark, wooden church appeared tiny standing beside the cedar-clad garrison built for the Reverend's family next door.

One of several garrisons in the town, its design included fortifications to shelter members of the frontier community in the event of dangerous weather or enemy attack. Built in a rectangle, its upper story jutted out over the first floor to allow men positioned above to see and shoot down upon any who might approach. Its diamond-paned windows had wooden shutters inside and out that could be closed against the winter chill, stormy nights, or invading marauders.

Like most garrisons, the house had stone and earth packed inside its walls to prevent penetrating bullets, a feature that had proved invaluable during the recent siege and burning of the Brookfield village. Since hearing how Indians had set fire to structures at

Brookfield by pushing flaming wagons of hay against the buildings, men in Lancaster began digging stone flankers around the outside of the village's houses. On one corner, an eight-foot stone and earthen wall stretched for ten feet in two directions but did not meet its neighbors' wall.

Inside in the upper chambers, the Rowlandson family slept unaware that many visitors had slipped into their town overnight and quietly concealed themselves in the settlers' sheds and barns and on the hills behind their houses. The visitors waited to awaken the town by surprise.

Mary woke while it was still dark. She felt weary of long winter nights and short days. She found it tedious to rise before the sun, but she had work to do. She lay considering leaving the comfort of her warm bed for the cold kitchen. Yet, she knew that if she did not stoke the fire soon, it would only get colder.

Joseph had left the day before, the morning after he told Mary he would not accept the chaplaincy. He had gone with several other men to the Bay Colony to ask once again for more military support for Lancaster, the westernmost outpost of colonial civilization. With him away, she needed to tend the fire.

She reached for her lantern and struck a flint to light it. As she passed the window, she looked out into the dark night and saw a soft glow from a neighbor's window. Yesterday's snowfall had dressed everything in a fine, white fur. Stars shone clearly between high clouds. It would be another brutally cold day.

Chickens squawked in the barn. Mary thought it too early for them to be cackling over their fresh laid eggs. She hoped a fox or raccoon hadn't gotten into the barn overnight. She would wake her son and ask him to check on them after she lit the fire. She dressed quickly and pulled her garments tightly against the chill. Mary made her way down the stairs. She gave thanks upon seeing a little orange light still in the hearth. As she pulled kindling from the wood box, she thought she heard a dull thud outside and assumed it was her riley mare, Agnes, kicking to be let out of her stall. Joseph could tend to her as well.

She used a bellows to blow on the fire and watched smoke curl upward in the glow from the coals. Flames flared up with each pulse of air until they at last crept along the edge of the kindling. Once small sticks fully burned on their own, she put down her bellows and gathered up a few heavier pieces of wood. She heard another sound outside. She dropped her wood carelessly into the fire and went to the window.

Mary looked upon black silhouettes of trees against grades of blue, grey, and pink dappled light. With the stillness of a secret, an amber light appeared at the horizon. High above, deep salmon clouds layered under a brightening azure sky. As the morning awakened, trees changed from black cutouts to cylindrical grey-and-white shapes bearing spots of lichen and bands of black. Leafless maples stretched up past the green hemlocks and white birches leaned lazily in their midst. Light in the east intensified, and the bright pink diffused, dimming the sharp contrast between the high heaven and scattered clouds whose edges blurred into a murky, pale lavender dawn.

As if all the color had pulled from the sky to the eastern edge of the earth, a bright blaze rose in the distance. The vibrant show of color above faded into its brilliance. The band of luminous golden light widened at the place where heaven and earth met, and tufts of grey-blue cotton batting swaddled clear blue sky. In only minutes, the brilliant sky show withdrew, and a dim, grey coverlet of cold blanketed all. Mary uttered a prayer of thanks for the new day.

In the distance, Mary saw smoke rising from the far end of town: too much smoke to emanate from a chimney. She feared a fire. Then she heard another thud, closer. She recognized it as musket fire. She turned to the gun rack by the door. All the weapons stood in their places.

"Joseph! Joseph!" she called out, momentarily forgetting her husband was away.

The church bell rang wildly. Mary turned back to the window. Her pulse quickened. She recognized serious trouble afoot. The bell tolled furiously and then slowly tapered off. Outside, men ran into the road, pulling on their coats as they went. Far off, she heard more gunshots and a treacherous whooping that could only come from enemy Indians.

"Oh, dear God!" she gasped. "Awake! Awake! We are being attacked!"

She ran to her front door and raised the bolt for the villagers running her way. If the Lord willed it, forty or more people from her town would enter the garrison for refuge. Just then, her son Joseph came bounding down the stairs still in his nightshirt.

"Mother, what is happening?" Joseph called out. He ran to the window in time to see several neighbors racing toward his home. He saw smoke and flames clearly visible in the early morning light.

"Quickly, Son! Bring the kegs of powder and shot up from the cellar," Mary called as she let in the breathless family from across the way. Half-clothed and carrying their children, they burst in, yelling, "The Indians are coming! They have crossed the bridge and have set fires to the barns at the end of the road."

"Come in, come in. Hurry," Mary said urgently as she let the bolt fall back in place. "Did you see any others about?" she asked. "Were my sisters Hannah and Elizabeth on their way?"

"Yes, they are coming, but I think they were opening their barn first," said her neighbor, Goodwife Johnson.

"This is no time worry about the animals," Mary fretted. She went back to the window to see if she could see her sisters. More gunshots and screams came from outside, and young Mary came down, holding Sarah on her hip.

"Mother, what is happening? Are we being attacked?" she cried. Her face showed no color as she looked to her mother.

"Aye, Mary. But not to worry. The men will take care of it. You must take Sarah and the other children upstairs and keep them there. We will tell you when it is safe to come down."

Young Mary released her sister and put her hands to her mouth as her fear erupted into jagged sobs. Sarah ran to her mother, clinging to her skirts and asking breathlessly, "Mama! Mama! Are we going to die?" Her wide eyes shone up at her mother, pleading to be told all would be fine.

Mary pushed her own rising panic out of her voice as she bent down and kissed her. "No, Baby, we are in a strong fortress. You go upstairs with your sister so you won't be trampled by all the men coming here to protect us. Everything will be fine. Go along, now," she said encouragingly, masking her sense of dread. Her older daughter's lack of composure flustered her. "Mary, stop crying and take your sister upstairs. Now!" she snapped. Young Mary grabbed her little sister's hand but kept crying all the way up the stairs.

Mary pushed the inside shutters closed. Frantic pounding sounded at the door. "Let us in! Let us in!" she heard Elizabeth yell. She ran to raise the bolt again and let in her older sister, Elizabeth and her eight children. As the two women embraced, little Joseph exclaimed, "Aunt Mary, I saw Indians! And they have guns!" He made it sound like a festive occasion, not a dangerous one.

Another family crowded behind them, and Mary ushered them all in, directing all children upstairs with the others. Gunshots and whooping sounded closer. Mary didn't know what to do. They had talked about the possibility of an Indian raid, but she never dreamed it would really happen here. Especially not with Joseph away. More villagers pushed in through the narrow doorway.

When Mary's sister Hannah arrived, Mary thanked her brother-in-law Ensign John Divoll for taking charge in Joseph's absence even before he came through the door. "Get buckets of water ready," he called out. "You women can help load muskets. Men, take a station by one of the loopholes and alert us to any Indians you see. Don't wait to fire. Kill them as they enter your sights."

Young men lugged buckets of water to the back door where waiting women placed the buckets strategically around the garrison. Mary took two buckets upstairs and checked on the children. They looked out the windows and pointed excitedly.

Mary went to the window in time to see her neighbors, the Ball family, pulled out of their house by four half-naked Indians. In the next moment, she watched in horror as three of them clubbed John, Elizabeth, and their baby. The fourth Indian picked up the two other children and carried them off, their arms and legs flailing as they went. Mary gasped and buried her face in her sleeve. She slammed the shutters closed.

She leaned her back against the shuttered window and closed her eyes as if the action alone would prevent the goings on from becoming real. When she opened her eyes again, she saw the boys jostling each other for a better view at the other window. She pushed down the bile rising in her throat and rushed over to them.

"Everyone, away from the windows," she ordered. She pushed them all toward the center of the house. "Here. Come sit near the stairwell and play a game. Come, come. There, good children." The youngest girls huddled together crying as though it were contagious. The oldest boys resisted moving away from the windows. Her daughter Mary and her friend Rebecca, unable to quiet the crying children, also wept hysterically. The smallest called for their parents and tried to push their way back downstairs.

Mary had to restore some order.

"Come, dears," Mary said quietly to the older girls. She put her head close to theirs and whispered, "This will all be over soon. You children need to play quietly here until we tell you to come down. Mary and Rebecca, you need to show the others that everything will be all right. Can you do that for me?" she asked, gripping them each by the shoulder. They dumbly nodded. "There are my good girls," Mary said. "Now, go read or sing with the children or teach them a new game."

The girls wiped their eyes and nodded again. Sniffling and biting her lower lip to fight back her tears, young Mary looked at her mother. Mary encouraged her, saying, "I'm very proud of you two and thank the good Lord you are here to help the little ones.

"Help me close all these shutters now," Mary said, again pulling the little boys away from the windows. They challenged one another for the best gun loopholes where they could still keep an eye on the activity outside.

Mary was surprised that, despite the noise outside and the pandemonium below, the girls accepted her calm assurances. Her voice had not betrayed her own desire to wail in despair. The little girls followed Mary and the older girls around the big open room, and Sarah tried to wrap herself in her mother's skirts. Mary reached down and patted her gently. "You be a brave, big girl now, Sarah, and I need you to stay here with Mary. Can you do that for me?"

Sarah looked up with her bright blue eyes so full of both trust and fear that Mary thought she could see right through to her true heart. She wanted more than anything to scoop her into her arms and rock her safely to a better place. Instead, she cupped Sarah's tiny chin in her hand and said, "I'll be back to check on you soon. Mary, I'll send some of the women up to help you with the children," she called over her shoulder as she went back down the stairs.

More villagers had arrived, and the great room filled with commotion. Men shouted at one another, and women consoled their children and coaxed them upstairs. Some women cried more than the children. The young men seemed as if on a holiday. Anxious to have the chance to shoot at an Indian, Joseph and the others dashed about carrying guns, shot, and powder. Their enthusiasm dampened when Indians spotted two boys who went out to fetch water. Only one made it safely back to the garrison with no water and the woesome tale that his friend had been knocked dead.

They bolted the doors tightly once again.

Richard Wheeler shouted from one of the loopholes that the Indians shot another neighbor, Ephraim Sawyer, as he ran to the other nearby garrison. Richard raved furiously, shouting out as Ephraim begged for his life. He cried in horror as they bludgeoned, stripped, and disemboweled his good friend. Richard grew distracted when he saw Indians set his own barn afire. Before anyone could stop him, he ran out the door to protect his property.

Through the open door, Mary saw him shot dead before he could cross the road. She slammed the door shut, banged the bolt lock home, and dropped to her knees.

Through the narrow gun loopholes, the men helplessly watched the nearby garrison under attack. They saw Indians, out of range of their guns, climb atop the roof of the Wheeler barn and fire down over the newly constructed stonewall flankers upon any who tried to reach the garrison. Then they set fire to the garrison with flaming arrows and shot those who ventured out to put out the fires. Mary then understood the need for so many buckets of water inside the garrison.

She looked around at what only a short time before had been her comfortable home. She saw her furniture overturned and scattered about. Men with guns stood at every loophole, peering out with fingers ready to fire. Women sat on the floor behind them, twisting shot and gunpowder into wads that might fire or might explode in their laps if done wrong. Tempers flared and some spat out curses and bitter words, yet some prayed calmly over all the noise. The din from outside increased as the Indians beset her house. Above the shouts, whoops, and gunfire, Mary noticed the sound of children singing coming from upstairs.

Ring around the rosy.

A pocket full of posy.

Ashes. Ashes. We all fall down.

She heard them tumble and giggle and felt amazed but thankful that they ignored the chaos outside. Her moment of thanks ended when gunshot pelted her home. It seemed to come from all sides at once. They must have climbed atop her own barn and the hill behind her house. The fortifications within the walls rose up to waist height, but not above that. Bullets blasted right through the wooden walls, and anyone who stood up took the chance of being wounded. They learned the risk when three men fell as they ran for more ammunition.

Shooting went on for what seemed like an eternity, yet at only two hours past sunrise, the Indians set Mary's house on fire. A brave neighbor who ran out with a bucket to quench the fire foiled the first effort, but the Indians shot their fiery arrows into so many places in the building that soon the walls blazed all around.

The smell of burning timber overpowered the stench of gun powder. The children came running downstairs for fear of smoke rising to the upper story. In the midst of all the noise and smells, Mary realized they could not survive by staying in the garrison. Mothers and children all cried, "What shall we do?" while the men tried vainly to shoot at the Indians, who stayed safely out of range.

Mary panicked. She called to Hannah and Elizabeth, "Sisters, we will have to run outside."

"Out there? Are you crazed?" Elizabeth at first refused, but smoke thickened and flames threw off unbearable heat. At last she agreed, and the three women quickly cloaked themselves and their children against the frigid winter and headed for the door with their children tucked tight against them. When they first opened the door, guns fired so rapidly that it seemed as if the devil himself threw handfuls of stones their way. From inside, they closed the door and caught their breath, choking from the smoke.

Mary noticed that even the dogs that had come in with the crowd cowered and covered their ears and faces. She had seen the same big dogs bark and chase away any stranger or creature, but when faced with the present attack, they slunk into the corner and whined.

As smoke grew thicker, her children coughed and cried around her. Mary knew there was no choice but to leave. Fire had spread to the beams above, and if they stayed, they would burn or be crushed when the roof fell in. Never had she imagined being faced with such a choice: to stay and burn or run and risk gunshot, clubbing, or capture.

"Lord protect us," she whispered.

She opened the door and ran out first, carrying Sarah on her hip. She saw Indians all around with guns aimed and hatchets raised. She managed to dart among them. She looked back for Mary and Joseph. She saw her brother-in-law John stop still. His hands gripped his throat. A spray of blood shot forth between his fingers. He fell face first across her doorway. The Indians gathered around him and pulled off his clothes. She instinctively reached up to cover her own throat. It felt as if it was closing up.

Mary felt a sudden pressure in her side and looked down to see blood staining her dress and apron. Sarah screamed. Mary saw blood on Sarah's belly and hand. Elizabeth's older son, William, ran out and got shot in the leg. He fell down. An Indian ran by and struck him dead with a wooden club. Mary marveled at how everything seemed to be happening so slowly. *Am I really standing in the midst of this nightmare watching so calmly? Is this really happening? Why do I feel no horror or pain?*

Elizabeth stepped through the door and saw John and William lying bloody at her feet. She screamed out, "Lord, let me die with them." Before she could utter another sound, a bullet struck her in the head, and she fell down dead over the threshold.

Mary felt shock to see her sister's prayer answered so horrifically. In the midst of the terror, Mary reached out for her children, wanting them beside her as she tried to reach the cover of the trees. But her two older children had run off in different directions, she hoped to safer places.

She heard the Indians laughing and bellowing out strange cries as Henry Farrar fled the flames and fell from their relentless gunfire. She stood, dazed. A big Indian with a terribly scarred face and one good eye pulled her and Sarah out of the gunfire to a sheltered place behind an overturned wagon. He tried to take Sarah from her, but Mary would not release her. Another Indian rounded up children and ran them off into the woods.

Mary looked at her kitchen garden and her door yard and counted twelve lying dead there. A mob of Indians surrounded each body like a pack of wolves, tore their clothes from them, and pranced and howled over their spoils.

"Come, go along with us," the one-eyed man directed.

Mary was shocked. *How could he speak so clearly yet be so vicious?*

She leaned away, watching his hand that held his hatchet. She found her voice and asked, "If I go with you, what will happen to me? Will you kill us?"

He took her wrist and answered her, "If you come willingly, you will not be harmed." He turned the hatchet in his hand. "Come now." He was tall and menacing with a bare chest and painted face.

She looked back at her house. Flames consumed the roof, leaving charred timbers exposed. Part of the roof collapsed into what had been her bedchamber. She could not go back. Mary composed herself and stepped forward with the one-eyed man and asked, "Where do you take us?"

He did not answer. He pulled her by the arm down the road out of her town. They passed several burned-out houses. She closed her eyes and covered Sarah's as they walked by many bloody, naked bodies. Everywhere, savages pawed through the wreckage and crowed in delight as they held up pots or baskets of food. Two men on horseback drove all the livestock into a tight circle, as they wheeled and whooped around the animals. While crossing the bridge out of Lancaster, Mary thought with a start, *What will Joseph think when he returns home?*

Gathering Up the Christian Indians

Weetamoo smelled smoke coming from Hassanamesit before she saw the campfires. The scent reminded her of all her people lost at the Narragansett camp. She pushed that vision from her mind. She must get her people to shelter. They had walked for days without food or rest. Her legs felt wooden, and she could barely bend her knees. The flesh in her thighs trembled. Her calves felt as taut as untanned hide.

Thankfully, Quannopinn and some of her runners had gone ahead to set up camp. Through the trees, she saw specks of glowing light from the bark-covered wetus. It surprised her not to hear the people of Hassanamesit readying for their arrival. The village had never been so quiet. *Have the people gone with Metacomet? Or with the English?* she wondered.

Hassanamesit had been established as a Praying Indian town. The Indians here had adopted English ways and lived in their own separate community apart from both English and Indian towns. The English had set up Praying Indian towns along their frontier as a buffer between themselves and any hostile tribes. For over forty years these people had lived within the limits of English law, attended Christian schools, and practiced Christian faith. Weetamoo wondered who they would side with in the present war.

She wished her people had gone with Metacomet from the start. If they had, her people would be safe with him in Menameset preparing for spring raids, and she would not feel the shame for her tribe's suffering and loss. But she reminded herself that Metacomet needed her and Awashonks to stay behind so he could escape. It was good that her people helped the Narragansetts to harvest the corn that would feed them all. *Humph,* she thought. *We would have fed them all, had the English not burned their village. All lost. All gone.*

More aware of the cold when she could see the village, she walked deliberately, consciously willing each step to follow the last. Her shoulders shuddered. Quannopinn approached her.

"Come, Weetamoo." Quannopinn gently took her by the elbow. He led her through the snow toward a large wetu and pushed aside the door flap. "Come here," he said, helping her bend her rigid body through the doorway. He took off her stiff fur, frozen from sleet and cold, and wrapped her in a soft, dry, wolf fur. He touched her skin lightly as he helped her sit and pulled off her moccasins and leggings. Her skin shone nearly as white as an Englishman's and felt as cold as the sea. He hurriedly slid her feet into new dry leggings and moccasins and covered her with another fur. He turned back to the fire and added a wooden log that crackled and sizzled with moisture.

"There was little dry wood, but we will have enough for the night. I will go get water and food. You rest and get warm."

"Thank you, Sannup," she said, grateful for his tenderness. For such a strong warrior, he was also a most tender lover. Metacomet had been wise to suggest him as a mate for her. Powerful and protective, he gentled her like no other man had since Wamsutta's death. She shivered at the memory of Wamsutta when she saw him last, cold and grey from English poison. She made a prayer to his spirit in the sky and watched it rise with the smoke up and out through the hole in the bark roof.

The warmth of the fire and the wolf fur wrapped around her did not stop her from shaking. Long past feeling cold, her limbs only felt brittle. She lifted her heavy arm to wipe her eyes and nose on the soft fur.

"Here you are, Weetamoo," said her old cousin Awashonks as she ducked into the warm shelter. "Here take this," she said, putting a cup of hot sumac tea between Weetamoo's trembling hands. The red, cracked skin on Weetamoo's hands shriveled like an old woman's. She shook too violently to hold the cup, so Awashonks helped Weetamoo raise the cup to her cracked lips.

"It is good that we have come to Hassanamesit, Weetamoo. How we have come this far with so little, I do not know. I found some squash, and it is cooking now. We will have that and some nokechick to eat soon." She held the cup to Weetamoo's lips again, saying "Here. Sip some more, cousin."

"Th-th-thank you, c-c-cousin. I am grateful for your k-k-kindness," Weetamoo stammered, trying not to chatter. "W-w-we are all in d-d-debt to our c-c-cousins, the Hassanamesit."

"Our cousins are gone, Weetamoo. Gone to join Metacomet."

"They have?" Weetamoo felt palpable relief. As her shoulders relaxed a little, her red ears became visible above the soft fur draped around her shoulders.

"Yes, James Printer is here from Cambridge, and he told me that Muttaump came here two moons ago and bade them to go willingly or find themselves going as captives. He is headed to Albany to negotiate for arms and supplies. Only those too ill or too aged stayed behind. He said Muttaump took most of their food and supplies, but we have enough to comfort us this night. Tomorrow we must move on, for we have not found enough for us to stay."

Weetamoo considered the news. Fortunately, they had dry shelter tonight, but they could not ask for supplies. They would carry on with what they brought and what they could find as they traveled. If Metacomet headed for Albany, then he would follow the Mohawk Trail. They would meet him at the Baquoag River or at the crossing in Pocumtuc or possibly further north at Coasset.

Weetamoo sat up defiantly, saying "We will go to Metacomet. By now he will have t-t-traded with the F-F-French for all we need. And be on his way back . . ."

"Hush, now, just sip and get warm. We'll talk after you eat and rest. I must go now and see to that squash. Here, take one more sip before I go." She helped Weetamoo with the cup again, then left the wetu with an armful of blankets and furs for the others.

Weetamoo felt searing pain in the tips of her fingers and toes as she began to warm up. Her legs tingled, and her back, neck, and arms ached. Her cheeks felt hot. She put her fingers to her face to absorb their warmth.

I must think.

The Hassanamesit went with Muttaump but not all willingly. *Can we trust the Praying Indians?* After all, Petananuit, her former husband, had joined them, and he had led the English to the Narragansett camp. And the others recruited by the soldiers had dogged them constantly since they left Narragansett. The departure of the Christian Indians troubled her. But she appreciated their deserted wetus today so her people could rest.

Weetamoo reached for more tea as Quannopinn came in. He wore an English wool coat and held another in his hands. "This is for you Weetamoo," he said thrusting it toward her.

"No. Never will I wear a dirty English coat again! Take it away!" she cried.

"Weetamoo, listen to me," he said kneeling beside her. "You must take this, or you will not survive. Our kin in this village will share what they have. It is a gift, and you must accept it."

"I want no Christian gifts. Give it to another. I will wear clothing made only by my people, not English." She tossed her head away from him. He knew it would do no good to argue. He laid the coat on the sleeping platform and sat beside her to eat the nokechick he pulled from his pocket. He offered her a piece, but she refused it.

Awashonks pushed open the flap and entered with a steaming half squash and three wooden spoons. "This will warm us inside, too," she said lightly.

Quannopinn laughed. "I knew you would find a meal before you made a bed tonight, Sunk Squaw. You can be content only when your stomach is full, no?"

"I will eat your share, too, Quannopinn, if you tease me too heartily."

"Oh, no you won't, Old Woman," he said and took one of the spoons she offered. He plunged it hungrily into the hot, orange flesh. "This smells like a feast," he said.

Weetamoo reached for a spoon, but her fingers felt too stiff and clumsy from the cold, and she could not grasp the spoon except as a child would with her whole fist. She saw that Quannopinn struggled, too, to grasp his spoon. She realized that he had been as cold as she but had tended to her needs before his own.

She tasted the squash. It melted on her tongue. The squash was her first food in days. "You are right, Quannopinn. Awashonks, you have conjured a feast. Thank you," she said.

The fire in her legs had moved to her thighs, and she felt prickles like nettles all over her thawing flesh. She wiped her nose with her fur and looked at Quannopinn.

"What say the elders? Have the Hassanamesit joined our fight?" she asked.

"The elders say they do not believe many will fight with Metacomet. They have become too used to their Christian ways and too fearful of English reprisal. Already the English sentence Christian Indians to hanging for crimes they did not commit and take whole towns away in ships."

"In ships?" Weetamoo put down her spoon. "To where?"

"James Printer says he watched them take many women and children away," Awashonks answered. "They marched the men through the streets and locked them up in their jails. They took some to Deer Island, and some say they plan to sell them as slaves in the islands to the south. In Barbados."

"So say the elders," said Quannopinn. "The English told the Christian Indians they took the measures for their own protection against angry white men. But it really means just another push, push, push to remove us from our land."

"Quannopinn, this is harsh news. Have I not said from the beginning that we cannot trust the English? Their treaties with us mean nothing. They came like wolves in the night to hunt us down, and now they turn on their own Christian Indians after treating with them for nearly forty summers." As her blood warmed, her fingers throbbed. Her hands and feet felt as if a jellyfish had stung her. Sweat beaded under her eyes and on her upper lip.

"We must move with swiftness now," Quannopinn said. "All our people have to fight to stop the English. If we do not, there will be an end to all the Wampanoags, Christian or not. What they have done to the Pequots and the Narragansetts, they will do again and again until we exist no more."

"Nux," Weetamoo agreed. "Let us eat well and sleep well tonight. Tomorrow we join with Metacomet and add our strength to his. We cannot fail in this. This land is ours. We will stop them."

She looked at Quannopinn and tried to see conviction in his eyes. His words said one thing, but his eyes said another. *What is happening to you, my fierce warrior?* she wondered. *What is nagging at the edge of your mind? Is it creeping into mine?*

Hasty Flight
First Remove
February 10, 1675

$\mathbb{M}$ary walked without thinking, obediently following the one-eyed man's directions. Roots and rocks scarred the well-beaten trail they traveled. At times she slipped on patches of snow or ice, so she kept her eyes on the path to avoid falling. Mary had never walked as far as she had today. She wondered if the brown devils would ever let her stop to rest, but she dared not ask.

Mary carried Sarah close to her bosom. The only time the poor babe ceased her cries was when she fell into a fitful sleep or fainted from her pain. It didn't matter. Mary took her silence as a hopeful sign. Sarah's wound stopped bleeding and instead slowly seeped a brown, viscous ooze. Mary wrapped her apron around Sarah and bunched it over her injured belly. Sarah belched as Mary pulled the cloth tighter, trying to keep her child intact.

They walked the whole day, climbing steadily in the shadow of Mount Wachusett. At first Mary's fear propelled her forward. But as time passed, her feet ached where leather rubbed against her heel. Her damp skirts dragged with unusual heaviness around her ankles. Her legs trembled, and she breathed in short, dry gasps. With the day fading into twilight, cold descended quickly on the shaded side of the mountain.

Mary's eyes adjusted to darkness as the light waned. At home in Lancaster, she seldom ventured out after sunset. She usually remained inside after dark to avoid any Indians skulking about, and now here she was, tromping through the night with them.

Where can they be taking us? she wondered. The forest rose thick about her, but the path wore smooth here. *This must be a main footpath. Perhaps when they sleep, I might run back along this same trail,* she thought. She looked back and saw only trees, shadows, and the big Indian who had taken her from her home.

Black smudges and lines of paint covered his face, and he wore his hair shaved off on one side and long on the other. *He looked to be about thirty, but who could really judge with natives?* He had a strong jaw, one bright brown eye, and an ugly scar in place of the other one. He wore leather skins on his legs and a woolen mantle over one shoulder, yet his chest was bare. Around his neck hung a string of bones and claws. She shivered as she wondered where he might have gotten the bones. She closed her eyes and remembered seeing him club her nephew, William, on the head. She felt sick and coughed to hide her gagging.

She turned away and forced herself to place one foot in front of the other in a slow and steady climb. When they reached the top of a hill perhaps a mile or more from her home, they stopped. The women made temporary shelters of pine boughs, and Mary collapsed with Sarah under one of them. Through leafless trees, Mary saw a glow in the eastward direction of Lancaster. Several smoldering fires sent smoke into the night sky where houses once stood.

She prayed for her family and townspeople. She clutched her little girl and put some snow into Sarah's mouth to quench her thirst. Only then did she grow conscious of cold seeping up from the rocky ground.

Close by, Mary saw an abandoned house and prayed she might sleep there instead. But when she approached her captor with the question, he replied, "What, do you love the English still?" With a laugh, he dismissed her request.

Exhausted, Mary sank heavily to the ground under a pine tree with only its shed needles as her cushion. She hoped that she and Sarah might find comfort in sleep. Yet, the creatures who had taken them had no interest in sleep. They spent the evening roaring, singing, and dancing around a fire, celebrating their victory and feasting on the spoils of Mary's village. Her heart ached at the thought of all her family and neighbors whose lives had been shattered during the miserable day, and she could not dream of taking even a morsel of food. Indeed, she felt nauseous with grief, pain, and fear and wished only to be away from the monstrous heathens.

After hours of her captors' devilish hooting and howling, the fires slowly burned down, and the villains finally settled down to take some rest in the cold darkness. Mary looked back toward her home and saw only a faint glow of the embers of her former life.

What would be in store for her now?

"Oh, Lord in Heaven," she prayed, "Look down upon your poor children and grant us comfort. If it pleases you, send the men from our village to take us back to our warm houses. If that is not your will, dear God, bless us with your good grace and heal us with your infinite goodness."

Snowy Retreat
Second Remove
February 11, 1675

Dawn arrived too soon, and when Mary opened her eyes, the heathens around her were already tearing down their makeshift shelters and packing to go. She knew she had no choice but to follow and mutely fell into step behind them. *Where are they taking us?* she wondered again.

They walked for hours, and Mary tried hard to keep up, worried if she didn't that they might kill her. Her body ached from her own wound and from the weight of her little girl. As she shifted Sarah to her other shoulder, she lost her balance. She stumbled and fell, causing cries of pain from her daughter. She pressed her hand over Sarah's mouth and muffled her own cry.

The one-eyed man lifted Mary up by the elbow. He took Sarah from her, and Mary screamed, but he covered her mouth with his big, bloodstained hand. With his other hand, he lifted Sarah by the arm to another man riding on a stolen horse. Mary recognized the markings. It was Freeman Stokes's grey mare. *Had he lived,* she wondered? Only days before, he had asked her to pray for his son. If he lived, she hoped he would pray for her and her children now. She prayed.

Mary stopped her devotions when she heard her baby child crying again. She hurried to the side of the horse and reached up for Sarah but was jostled as the horse stepped over a downed tree limb. She fell again and winced as her bloody side scraped against mud-caked snow.

A tall warrior said something she couldn't understand to the rider, and the horse stopped. They bickered over something, and then the rider got down and pushed Sarah back at her. Mary knelt in the snow and held Sarah tightly. She tenderly stroked her hair and, rocking gently back and forth, promised her everything would be fine. The big dark stain told Mary otherwise, but she refused to think about that. Sarah's moans grew softer.

When Sarah at last quieted, the one-eyed man motioned to Mary to get on the horse. Without disturbing her sleep, he gently took Sarah and gave Mary his hand. He pulled her near to the horse and helped her to climb upon it, letting her use his knee as a step. Once she was astride the mare, he passed Sarah up to her. Mary cradled her, leaning her daughter's head against her breast.

Unaccustomed to riding without a saddle or reins, Mary found it difficult to ride the horse while holding onto Sarah. She clutched the horse's mane between her fingers and Sarah's back and used her other hand to hold onto the horse's neck. She struggled to stay on the mare. After a while, she settled into the bumpy gait and used her legs to keep her balance.

Each time Mary shifted to relieve her tired limbs, she roused Sarah who resumed her crying, "Mama, I want to die. Please let me die." Despite Mary's efforts to calm her, the child's moaning worsened and once caused the one-eyed man to warn Mary if Sarah didn't stop, he would knock the child on the head.

Mary leaned far forward on the horse to cover Sarah's body with her own to give her warmth and muffle her sounds. "Be still," she urged. "God will protect us." Eventually the steady, swaying motion lulled both her and Sarah into an uneasy sleep. Forgetting their pain, they both dozed until a sudden lurching woke them. As the weary animal stepped downhill over rough and slippery terrain, Mary lost her balance and fell head first and landed in the snow with Sarah right beside her. All the Indians around them began laughing, and Sarah resumed her anguished groaning.

Mary was furious.

She stood up and shouted at them. She picked up a stick and struck out at one of them, yelling, "How dare you!" He easily stopped her weak blow and threw the stick aside. The Indians all laughed again.

She screamed out loud, "What is wrong with you? Can't you see she is hurt? How can you laugh to see a child dying in pain?"

At those words, Sarah cried out, "Mama, let me die."

When Mary heard that, she fell to her knees. She crawled to the one-eyed man and, with her hands clasped together, begged him, "Please, please, let us rest."

Snow began to fall and the light in the west faded.

She didn't know if he understood her words and took pity or if he would have stopped there anyway, but in either case, he stopped for the night. He signaled to the others. Immediately, they began to build lean-to shelters with pine boughs and lit small fires as the snow fell around them.

Arrival at Menameset
Third Remove

February 12, 1675

The next morning, they rose early for another day of difficult walking. Mary tried to keep up and felt sure they offered her the mare again because she caused them to fall too far behind the others. She gratefully accepted the mount as she relished the warmth of the horse's body and relief for her aching feet. She had not removed her shoes overnight in the cold but felt certain that she had several blisters.

Sarah complained less about her pain and at times acted restless and talkative, although she seemed confused, sometimes speaking to her absent cousin, Joseph, or her father. She occasionally shivered, and Mary took pains to keep her own cloak wrapped tightly around the child. Mary didn't notice greenish fluid seeping from Sarah's bowels. Again and again, she found herself slumping into sleep as she rode along.

The day wore on and the band eventually came to Menameset, an established native village near a salmon fishing weir.

When she dismounted, Mary felt tired, hungry, and sore. Sarah once again spoke crazily. She had slept restlessly throughout the day, but only for a few minutes at a time. She complained of nausea and gave off a foul-smelling, fecal odor.

Mary looked around for any others from Lancaster but saw only native people wherever she looked. It seemed as though she saw many more Indians here than had been at Lancaster. The women worked at covering stick frames with rolled up ash bark and woven mats. The men greeted one another with hearty shouts and loud boasts. Frozen by the sea of alien faces, sights and sounds, Mary stood in the midst of it all. Although surrounded by people, never had she felt more alone.

Mary passed several days at that place trying to nurse her child who could only take a bit of water now and then as she lapsed between fever, sleep, and restless crying. Each cry brought on more threats from the Indians of silencing her babe with a heavy club, so Mary took great pains to keep Sarah as comfortable as she could in the rough conditions of the little hovel she had for shelter.

On the eighth day, two women whom she had not previously seen arrived and took her to a wigwam made of sticks and bark. They whispered to her, "Go in wetu." She did and found a warm fire burning inside. The women gave her an animal fur to wrap around herself and her daughter. And at last she collapsed into a leaden slumber with Sarah gasping small feverish sighs in her arms.

Sometime in the night, her child ceased moaning. No more blood oozed from her wound. No more breath stirred from her dry lips. Mary woke to find her limp and cool in her arms. Mary's cries howled into the night. Her keening woke two women, who urged her to hush before the men came to finish her off. Mary did not let on that the child was already dead. She cradled Sarah's head in her hand and, whispering soft lullabies, lay down with her.

In the morning, Mary opened her eyes, at first not realizing where she was. Then remembering the nightmare of the previous day with a shock, she peered quickly around her without moving. She looked down at Sarah's soft curls and kissed her cold forehead.

"Oh, Lord, my God, into Thy bosom I commit the soul of this brave little angel," she prayed. Her throat ached, and she wished this were all a bad dream, but the cold, heavy bundle in her arms was all too real. Mary wept as silently as she could. When she ran out of tears, she thought, *At least your mortal suffering is over.*

Daylight filtered through the cracks in the wetu, and Mary looked around the hastily thrown up structure. She lay absently stroking Sarah, unable to find the desire or strength to get up. *God, my God, forgive me, your poor sinner and redeem me from this ordeal. Take pity on me and on my children and bring us to safety.*

A New Hearth

A scratching noise at the opening of the wigwam announced the arrival of the two women from the night before. They ducked inside. Mary noticed that the younger one was with child, though she appeared a child herself. The other woman appeared to be older, maybe thirty or so, and wore clothing ornamented with shells and beads.

Mary pretended she was still asleep.

The young one shook her. "Awake. Mary Rowlandson, awake." She jostled Mary harder with no response. The girl pulled off Mary's fur cover, saw the limp child curled in her arms, and knew that it was dead.

"Come," said the older one to Mary. "You must leave this place and go to Quannopinn."

Mary resisted, squeezing Sarah tightly. The older one pulled her arm and said, "You must go. Leave the child."

Not ready to accept Sarah as beyond help or harm, Mary struggled. Then, accepting the women's unrelenting command, she sat up, pulled herself free, and gently laid Sarah between the warm furs. Moving stiffly and wincing from her aching side, she rose to her feet.

"Where is Quannopinn," she asked. "Is it far from here?"

The young one giggled. The older one said, "Quannopinn is not a place. He is a sagamore, a great leader, and he will be your new master. He has paid Monaco to make you a member of his household. Come now," she insisted.

Mary blinked. "Paid Monaco? The one-eyed man who took me from my home? Am I now chattel to be bought and sold at will?"

"Come. Now." The women lifted the door flap open.

Emerging into bright sunlight, Mary looked back to see the place where her child had died. She saw a rounded bark hovel surrounded by dark evergreens on the snowy mountaintop overlooking her burned-out town. She saw other similar shelters, but not many and none near her own. She had been set apart.

Dear Lord, she thought, *my baby has come as close to you in heaven as she could on this cold earth. Take her soul into your hand and let her sing with all your hosts of cherubim. Bless her and keep her, dear God. Amen.* She told herself that Sarah was in a better place. She tried very hard to believe it and take comfort.

Mary followed the women without protest. She asked where they were taking her, but they did not answer. She couldn't tell if they didn't understand or if they didn't want to answer. *What does it matter now?* Mary thought. *Sarah is gone.*

They led her to a much larger wigwam than the one where Sarah's body rested. It looked weathered and old. Mary stepped inside and saw a squaw kneeling by a small open fire in the center of the room. She appeared to be making tea or broth. A man stood by the doorway. Mary recognized him as the tall man who had talked the Indian off his horse for her the day before. *Was it only one day ago that Sarah cried in her arms?*

The older woman accompanying her said something in her Indian tongue, and Mary looked at the squaw by the fire.

Small and thin, she wore a sleeveless dress that covered only one shoulder. Her hair was pulled back and tied with a piece of leather wound down the length of it almost to her waist. She had a pretty face, but she looked tired. The weariness of hard travel showed in her deeply lined face. Mary wondered if the two were her new master and mistress but was afraid to ask. *Perhaps the woman will take pity on me and let me go home.*

The man stepped toward her and said, "Mistress, I am Quannopinn, sagamore of the Narragansett, and this is my wife, Weetamoo, sachem of the Pocasset."

It shocked Mary to hear such refined English coming from the mouth of a savage. *What trickery is this?* she thought. His had an odd dialect and he appeared foreign, but, indeed, he spoke to her in English. Though surprised, she made an automatic, polite response.

"I am Mary Rowlandson, wife of Reverend Joseph Rowlandson of Lancaster." She noticed that the man wore half English and half native attire. She wondered if he was half-bred. The thought repulsed her. He wore a white man's hunting blouse with the fringed leggings and moccasins of an Indian. His war paint had washed away, and she thought he had handsome features for a red man. She immediately chastised herself for the thought.

Weetamoo got up and came closer to inspect her. She looked at Mary's soft white hands and pinched her upper arm. "Too fat and lazy," Weetamoo said in English.

Surprised by such an insult from a heathen, Mary thought it best to mind her tongue. She thought, *This woman is as thin as a stick. Of course she thinks a well-fed person is fat.* Then she had a fleeting fear that they were planning to eat her. She had heard all kinds of strange tales about Indians.

Quannopinn laughed and said, "That is good. She won't need so much to eat. So, you are pleased?" He stood by the doorway with his arms crossed and watched the two women examining one another.

Weetamoo answered him in their own language. Mary didn't understand the words, but she heard disagreement. While they did not raise their voices, they exchanged words back and forth until Weetamoo seemed to agree with Quannopinn.

He turned to Mary and said, "You shall live with us now. You will travel with us, eat with us, and sleep with us." He gestured toward a knobby rack made of spindly sticks of wood. It had wild animal skins piled on it. Surely they did not expect her to sleep on *that*. For how long? she wanted to ask but dared not.

She looked around and saw large baskets under the strange beds. Over her head hung a bower of wild branches thickly layered with bark. Daylight shone in from the hole in the roof over the fire that warmed the wetu. The whole place had a strange smell of smoke mixed with pine and herbs.

Mary didn't know what to do. She worried about leaving Sarah's body alone in the small wigwam. "Sir, may I be permitted to return to my other shelter? I have left my child behind."

The request surprised Weetamoo, already aware that squaws were burying the dead child. She wondered whether English kept their dead with them and, if so, for how long, but she did not want to ask. It would not be proper.

She looked at the strange woman. Weetamoo had traveled to Boston and Cambridge and had seen many English before but rarely so close at hand. Mary's pale skin color appeared almost translucent like the shells on the beach near her home. The blond hair had an odd bending nature. It looked so disorganized, and Weetamoo wondered why the woman did not keep it better managed.

Weetamoo noticed the many layers of clothing Mary wore and thought them very impractical. Mary wore an ankle-length gathered skirt and apron with a long-sleeved blouse and a vest over it. She had a cape over that. The skirt stuck out with a fullness and length that seemed wasteful to Weetamoo, and the leather shoes appeared more pretty than useful. *The thin leather will not last many miles,* Weetamoo thought. She wondered what Mary wore under the skirt that made it stick out so. She squatted, lifted the hem, and found another skirt and another beneath that one.

Weetamoo pulled the cloth away and looked under the skirts. Mary shrieked and stepped back. Startled, Weetamoo fell back. Quannopinn reached out to catch her but not before she landed on the ground.

Weetamoo stood up and shouted, "Get out. Out of my house," and pushed Mary backward. Mary fell out the door. She rolled over, snatched up her skirts, and ran away, looking back to see if she was followed. It did not appear so.

Weetamoo's impertinence shocked Mary, but then she remembered that the same people rode around her house burning and killing her kin and neighbors. She pushed from her mind the unbidden image of her sister and her nephew lying on her doorstep and sucked in a great gulp of air.

She would have to mind her step if she hoped to live.

She set to finding the wigwam where she had left Sarah but noticed suddenly that all the hovels looked similar. Hoping to find the right one, she began peeking in doorways. At last she found the place where she had left Sarah and ducked inside. She threw aside the fur she had slept in, still stained with her baby's blood. Tossing the covers on the floor, she realized someone had taken Sarah's body away. She wailed inconsolably and stumbled outside calling, "Sarah—where is my Sarah?"

The nearby Indians ignored her or looked at her curiously, but no one answered or helped her. The two women who came to her in the night eventually heard her cries. They came down a path from the woods.

"Mary," one of them said to her, "your child died. She is buried."

"You buried her? Mary screamed. "In a heathen grave? With no prayers or consecration? Where? Take me there!" Mary pummeled them. The two women accepted her grief-stricken blows, eventually holding her wrists to subdue her. When they told her they would take her to the grave, she stopped struggling.

They walked through the wood up a path that led to an open place on the mountaintop. Between outcroppings of ledge, they came to a small patch of newly turned soil that covered Mary's youngest child in lasting sleep. Mary knelt beside the grave and wept. She clasped her hands and prayed, begging God to have mercy on the unbaptized little girl.

She looked around for flowers, but seeing none in February, instead pulled up sprigs of princess pine and winter berries and laid them over her child's resting place. *Winter berries*, she thought, *not strawberries, but red and sweet even in the snow. Rest now, my little daughter, rest well.*

Then she laid her head on the dirt and wept.

The squaws pulled her away as the day grew colder and snow began falling again. She struggled with them, but at last let them pry her away.

Quannopinn's Gift

Embarrassed at the undignified ending to their meeting, Weetamoo felt more convinced than before that she did not want the white woman in her home. It angered her that Quannopinn tried to pass the woman off as a gift. He put her in an uncomfortable position. To say no would refuse a gift. It would bring bad spirit energy between them. To say yes put her at a disadvantage. She had no notion of what she would do with the woman, and she had no gift of equal value to give Quannopinn in exchange.

She had tried to explain her feelings to Quannopinn, but he did not understand. He thought she needed help. He would not hear of trading the woman back. Weetamoo saw the woman as the first wedge between her new husband and herself. Though she felt obliged to accept the gift, she did not have to like it.

When the three women returned from the grave, Weetamoo asked the younger woman, her daughter Laughing Water, to take Mary to the cook fire outside and show her how to prepare their meal. Weetamoo stayed inside and consoled herself by playing with her son. She sat with him on her bed furs and wondered what he would be like as he grew up. She wondered, too, about the new life inside her. Which of her sons would grow up to be the sachem of her tribe? Her second son could be the leader of both her own and Quannopinn's tribes but her first son, Pocasset only. Would there be jealousy? Or would they be close friends as Metacomet and Wamsutta once were? She looked in her infant's eyes and wondered if he would one day betray his brother. Chilled at the thought, she looked away.

Quannopinn returned to the wetu. He strutted over to Weetamoo and said, "How is my bride? You must be pleased to have more help. And for only the price of a gun."

Weetamoo looked at him. She still could not believe he had encumbered her with a white woman, especially an injured one who had just lost a child.

"What were you thinking?" she asked him impatiently. "We barely have enough to feed ourselves, Quannopinn."

"That is no longer so, wife. We now have horses, cattle, sheep, and pigs to eat." He frowned a little, annoyed that she was not more appreciative.

"Think about that, Quannopinn. All those animals need food, too. Where will we find grass for them on the way to Pocumtuc or Coasset? Look around. There is snow and ice everywhere." She paced, wondering how she could turn down his gift, the first he had given her since their marriage.

"Then we will butcher them here and take their meat with us," he answered. "Or we will eat our fill now and dry the rest for later. It matters not."

"It matters greatly," she snapped. "Bringing the white woman into my home displeases me. It is hard enough to care for ourselves, my son, and my daughter. And what if the woman brings disease? Think, Quannopinn. How useful will this mourning mother be to us?"

Quannopinn crossed his arms and responded sharply, "I thought you would be pleased with another woman to help ease your burden."

"How Quannopinn? How will she ease the burden? What does she know of our ways? Did you see what she wears? She will only slow us down. And trading a gun? How can you give that away when we are at war?"

"It was a fair bargain," he insisted. "We have no shot or powder for it anyway."

"I am displeased." She turned away. She lifted a basket from under her bed and spread the contents over her sleeping furs.

Quannopinn, still angry but chastened, knew he must smooth things with his new wife.

"Weetamoo, forgive me for not speaking with you on this first. I am a guest at your hearth, and if you decide she must go, I will trade her to another. I only thought she could help you. I made a fair trade, and I think she will hold value with Metacomet. Monaco told me she comes from a wealthy family. They should pay handsomely for her. We can barter for what we need with her." He stepped closer to her and breathed into her ear, "Tell me what you want me to do."

His scent and the huskiness in his voice suggested he didn't want to continue the argument over the white woman. He tugged on a strand of her hair and turned her face to his, only inches away. "Tell me what you want, little Namumpum," he insisted, using her childhood name. He leaned toward her lips, and she stepped back.

"No, Quannopinn. This is not the way we can resolve every dispute. I am too angry with you to discuss it now." She turned away from him and rearranged her jewelry. Though frustrated with him, she wanted time to consider what value the white woman might hold for her and her people. If the woman was strong, she might be useful.

Weetamoo could not put Quannopinn off so easily. Weetamoo had asked for a lusty mate, and Quannopinn proved all she hoped for in that regard. With two other wives, he still craved the company of his new bride almost every night. No wonder she had conceived so soon. She thought that perhaps she should tell him the news and stall for time concerning the woman. She did not want their first argument to come to them over a gift given with good intentions.

Quannopinn slipped his arm around her waist and pressed her body against his. He spoke into her ear again, "Tell me what you want, Sachem."

Weetamoo knew her new sannup well enough to see that she could not stall him any longer. She leaned back against him and said, "I want the father of my next son to honor his wife." She turned and kissed him on the throat.

He lowered his mouth to hers, then stopped and said, "Next son? What do you mean?"

"I will have your son," she answered. "In six moons."

He looked at her lovely face and said, "A son? You are sure?" His eyes reflected brightly.

"I am sure," she smiled. He lifted her off her feet and spun with her in a wide circle.

He burst into a great smile, picked her up again, and carried her to their bed. He gently placed her on the soft fur and kissed her. He slid his hand under her skirt and ran his hand back and forth over her smooth belly. "In six moons? I cannot feel him yet."

"No, but I can feel him well already, and I have seen him in my dreams grown to be a strong man like his father. He will look like you, Quannopinn," she whispered and tenderly bit his ear.

"What a great gift, Weetamoo. We will raise our boy to lead his people," Quannopinn said. He slipped off his loincloth and carefully straddled his wife.

Weetamoo's first son began to cry.

Where Are the Children?

Mary followed Laughing Water to the cooking fire. Because the young girl demurred to Weetamoo's instruction, Mary assumed the girl to be another slave like herself. She didn't see the resemblance between Laughing Water and Weetamoo, her mother. Nor did she realize that the young woman behaved submissively due to the numbness of grief after losing her husband in the massacre at Narragansett.

The slender girl's rounded belly revealed a late-stage pregnancy. Mary presumed that Quannopinn may have had his way with her and worried that it could be her lot, too. She would have to guard herself from such a fate. The thought of coupling with a savage made her shudder.

Laughing Water showed Mary which basket held herbs and dried beans, corn, and peas and which held their primitive cookware. She used gestures, so Mary assumed she could not speak much English. Mary saw some English iron pots, but they used more handmade pottery urns, leather vessels, or woven baskets. With no soap, Mary wondered how they kept their dishes clean. It was no wonder, she thought, that so many had died of disease.

Mary watched the native woman prepare a small kettle of samp, a porridge made of ground corn with a small number of peas stirred in. It would be for dinner and hardly enough to feed one, let alone three women, a big hungry man, and an infant.

They carried the kettle into the lodge, and Laughing Water portioned out three spoonfuls to each. Mary had no appetite, but she tasted a mouthful. It was bland and gritty and, despite her hunger, she pushed her wooden bowl away. Her action did not go unnoticed by Weetamoo, who snatched the bowl away and scraped the remainder into the dishes of the others, one spoon apiece.

No one spoke.

After dinner, Laughing Water showed Mary how to wash dishes using leaves and sand from the nearby brook bottom, a painfully cold process that left her fingers red and stiff. She gratefully went back inside to warm her hands by the fire.

At home she might have taken up needlework or read from her Bible, but here she had nothing to do but dwell on the death of her poor babe, Sarah. She went to the bed they had assigned her to share with Laughing Water, turned her face into the furs, and wept until she fell asleep.

Mary dreamt of home, of sleeping in her own bed. The comfort of lying beside Joseph under a warm quilt and a solid roof soothed her. Her dreaming eyes scanned her bedroom with its fine paneled hearth and sweet-scented maple wood burning there. Her rocking chair where she nursed her babies nestled low by the window.

A movement at the window caught her attention in the dream, and it startled her to see a face behind the glass. She gasped as she saw the grinning face of the one-eyed man who took her from Lancaster! He held a war club in one hand and Sarah's head in the other.

Mary drew back and woke with a scream. She sat upright, choking for breath. She pushed away the evil image of Sarah's face dangling from her golden curls wrapped around dirty brown fingers. She stifled a wave of nausea and held both her hands against her violently beating heart as if to keep it from escaping her chest.

Displaced and forgetting where she was at first, Mary looked around. Seeing the stick frame and woven mats above her, she looked at the door afraid that Monaco, or One-Eyed John as the settlers called him, might come through the opening.

Dark stillness surrounded her. Her blood pounded through her veins. She tried to convince herself that no more harm could come to her. But, alone and captive among strangers, she felt her fear quicken. Her children were taken, and her baby girl was dead. The awareness started a fresh spasm of tears that lasted into the early hours of morning.

She had barely fallen asleep again when Laughing Water shook her to get up. "Come, Mary," Laughing Water said. "Come now." Her English was not as good as Quannopinn's, but her message came across clearly as she gestured toward the door and pulled on Mary's sleeve.

Mary reluctantly got out of bed. Her body hurt all over from lying on the stick frame. She felt as if she had slept on a row of bumpy, hard rolling pins. She felt worse after sleeping on the spindly sleeping platform than she had felt after sleeping outside on the ground. She longed for her plump feather bed at home.

If she still had a home.

Laughing Water coaxed her outside, relentlessly tugging on her arm. Mary lifted the door flap and, to her astonishment, she saw her son Joseph standing in front of her. With unkempt clothes and wild hair, he stood there, whole and alive. Her joy burst forth in a screech.

"Joseph! My God, thank God you are alive!" She embraced him and breathed into his ear. "Oh, my dear, dear boy. Are you hurt?" She held him away to inspect for damage. He appeared unharmed, but she could see fear in his eyes. She cupped her hands around his face and pressed her forehead to his.

"No, Mother, I am well. How are you faring?" She could see he strove to be a strong young man when he really wanted to cry in his mother's lap. Only thirteen years old and made to stand up to a heathen mob's brutal ways on his own. How she longed to make things right for him.

His courageous effort improved Mary's own will to remain strong, and unconsciously, she straightened up. "I am quite fine, Son. Where did you come from? How did you get here?" she asked, turning more questions over in her mind. "Come, come. Let's sit here and talk." She led him to a log near the outdoor cook fire.

"A different band took me from Lancaster. They camp with their company about six miles or so from here. Some of the Indians there came here to join in the fight at Medfield. After they left, my Indian dame came for me and told me you were here. She let me come to you with another band of warriors. Mother, they told me that Sarah had . . ." he couldn't finish. His strong veneer shattered, and he burst into tears. "Oh Mother, tell me they are lying. Please? Please! Please . . ."

Mary cradled her boy's head and wept with him. "I'm so sorry, Son. I'm sorry. How I wish it were a lie and this was all a terrible dream." Her words caught in her throat as she saw his pained reaction.

They hugged and consoled one another, and Mary suggested that they pray. Together, they recited the Lord's Prayer and Psalm 23. When he was quiet again, Mary offered to take him to his sister's grave.

He refused to go. "No, Mother. I dare not see something I do not wish to remember." He stood up and said, "Instead, Mother, let me take you to see Mary."

Doubly shocked to learn that both of her older children survived the wretched attack and stayed nearby, she covered her cheeks with her hands. "Oh, praise God almighty! Is she here and well?" she asked, rising up and pressing his hands between her own.

"She has no injury, Mother, though she suffers in poor spirit. Your company, however, will surely refresh her. Will you come with me now?"

"Of course, of course. Do we travel far?" Mary asked as she gathered up her skirt and wrapped her cloak around her shoulders against the cold morning.

"No, just down there," he pointed to a row of wigwams across the way. It astonished Mary to think her daughter had been so close by, probably for days, and she had never known it. "Dear God in Heaven, protect and deliver us," she whispered. For the first time in days her heart lightened and she allowed herself to imagine that she might actually find freedom once again.

They walked as freely through the heathen village as if they were on their own streets in Lancaster. No one interfered in any way. As they approached the wigwam where young Mary resided, they saw her seated on a stump with her elbows on her knees and her hands covering her face.

"Mary," Joseph called out. "I've brought Mother to see you."

The girl turned, saw her brother and her mother, and fainted. Mary rushed to her daughter's side and patted her checks and hands to revive her, but the girl stayed limp. An old squaw handed Mary a strong-smelling herb. She mimed holding it under young Mary's nose. Mary sniffed it and thought it smelled vaguely like camphor.

She cradled her daughter's head and held the herb under her nose. The girl opened her eyes, saw her mother's face, and fell straight away into convulsive crying. Her mother found it impossible to console her, and soon the Indians tried to separate them in an effort to quiet the poor child.

Mary didn't tell her daughter that Sarah had died. *Better she not hear it in her state,* Mary reasoned. She hugged her daughter desperately as the Indians pulled her away. "Be strong, my child. Pray to God and be strong. Your father will see us redeemed," she called out as the poor girl, wailing and reaching out for her mother, fell to the ground again.

Mary's heart heaved a hard stone up into her throat after the encounter with her daughter. She leaned on Joseph as he led her back to her lodge. He sat down with her and held her hand until she stopped trembling.

"Mother," he said after a while, "I have to go back before I am too sorely missed, but I promise to visit again soon. Please don't worry, Mother. I'll keep a watch over my sister," he told her.

Mary took some reassurance by that. They both pretended to be strong and clasped one another tightly before he left with his party of heathens.

Mary turned back to her temporary new home and saw Weetamoo squatting by the cook fire as she stirred something in an iron pot. As Mary approached, Weetamoo gestured for her to keep away. Mary was unsure what Weetamoo wanted and drew nearer.

Weetamoo waved her arms at her and said in English, "Go. Find food. There is not enough here for you."

She shook a long wooden spoon at Mary.

Go find food? Where? Mary wondered. She was in the wilderness, and it was February. Amidst all these heathens, they surely knew little wild food remained ungathered. She looked at Weetamoo, who again held up the long spoon and shook her head, "No."

Mary stumbled along the path that led to Sarah's grave and sought the winter berries she had seen earlier. Gone. Another had picked them. She tried poking under the snow at the base of the bush to see if any berries lay still hidden there. She found a dozen wrinkled fruit for her effort, not even enough for a mouthful. She wandered in the woods until she came to the mountaintop where her child lay at rest. She looked at the little mound and saw that they had even taken the berries from her baby's grave.

"Oh, Lord," she cried. "What more can they take from us?"

She bent over the grave and wept again until her tears flowed dry as the winter dirt.

Weetamoo's Lament

As days passed, Weetamoo grew less and less tolerant of Mary. Weetamoo and Laughing Water took her to gather dried berries and nuts as they walked and showed her how to use pointed sticks to pry roots from the frozen ground. Yet, the white woman's efforts yielded little.

"Look at her, Laughing Water," Weetamoo said in her own tongue. She nodded toward Mary who made tentative stabs at the ground with her stick. "She pokes about with no knowledge of what she does. She knows not what we can eat and leaves food untouched or trampled as she goes. Yet, she stands with her hand out at mealtime and expects her share as if she were an honored guest. I can forgive her ignorance but not her arrogance."

"It is so, Mother." Laughing Water said, not looking up from her work. She deftly loosened a ground nut from the earth and put it in her basket.

"When first Mary came, I pitied her after the loss of her child and shared our modest meals with her, but even then, she refused or spat out our gifts in disgust. I tire of her rudeness after a fortnight."

"I saw that when you turned the woman away at mealtime yesterday," Laughing Water replied.

"Yes. Perhaps a hunger in her belly might open her mind and improve her foraging skills."

"Perhaps," Laughing Water responded with a frown. She moved behind Mary and gathered up the bits Mary had overlooked. Laughing Water added a dry mushroom, some nettles, and three acorns to her basket.

Laughing Water knew that Mary had begged from other people. But she would not share that news with her hot-headed mother. She quietly continued her work until the time came to go prepare the next meal. As usual, Mary had disappeared, probably off begging again.

When word of Mary's begging reached Weetamoo, her cheeks flushed and she stomped back to the camp looking for her. She felt the eyes of her people on her as she went. Not only did Mary's actions reflect poorly on Mary, showing a lack of resourcefulness and pride, but worse, it reflected badly on Weetamoo as a sachem unable to provide for her own household. Mary had not adjusted to their ways, and Weetamoo felt ashamed for her and by her.

In the custom of Weetamoo's people, children learn life skills from birth by watching their elders. No one has to instruct or reprimand children, as they mimic their parents and learn by example how to find and prepare food, craft fine baskets or pottery, or develop toolmaking and hunting ability. One adult would never tell another adult how to do something, for fear of insulting the other person. Weetamoo could tolerate someone doing a task poorly but could not abide someone who wouldn't even try. She resented Mary expecting others to do tasks for her without attempting them herself.

Weetamoo threw open the door to the lodge. Both relieved and angry that she did not find the white woman there, she tossed her cape on the sleeping platform and leaned against it to release the tumpline holding her papoose's cradle board on her back. He still slept, so she gently lifted the board to suspend him from the roof support of her wetu. She touched it lightly to keep it in motion so he would not awaken.

Weetamoo knelt by the cook fire and rolled a stone over dried corn to crush it into meal. The more she thought about Mary, the faster her hands moved. Though Mary observed her and Laughing Water in their daily tasks, the woman showed no interest in making herself useful. Weetamoo thought, *I'm tired of trying to help her adapt. After all, she is an unwanted gift, a gift that is more trouble than she was worth. Why didn't Quannopinn discuss this with me before bringing her home? And now, to hear that she's been begging or stealing food from others! This has to stop and quickly!* Weetamoo looked down and saw that, in her pique, she had ground the corn to an ultra-fine powder.

As Weetamoo brushed the corn dust into a leather sack, Mary came into the wetu. As usual, she lifted the flap more widely than she needed to, sucking warmth out into the winter day. She noisily stomped snow off her shoes and flung her cape onto her sleeping platform as she knocked against the papoose carrier suspended overhead.

The baby stirred.

Mary pulled a dried ground nut out from under her apron and sat on the side of her bed picking mildew off it with dirty fingernails. By its withered appearance, Weetamoo knew that the nut was not newly dug but had come from someone else's food cache.

Weetamoo threw down her grinding stone.

"Did you steal that? Give it to me at once!" she demanded.

"I most certainly did not steal it. It was a gift," Mary answered. "Since you offered me no food, I requested a share from one of your neighbors. I found some Christian Indians of good heart who did offer me this, and though it is nearly spoiled, 'tis better than to starve."

The infant whimpered slightly. His mother stood up and patted his cheek to calm him. She steadied the rocking papoose.

Weetamoo thrust her palm toward Mary. "Give it to me," she ordered again. When traveling, they followed the custom of sharing food within households for variety and nutrition. But Weetamoo's demand did not imply sharing.

"No, this is mine. It is all I have had to eat this whole day." Mary clutched the ground nut to her breast.

"You will give it to me," Weetamoo commanded, surprised by Mary's open defiance. Her people would never consider such disobedience. As a sachem, she always received great respect. She inhaled deeply, stuck out her chin, and reached for the ground nut once more. Then, meaning to take the root forcibly, she stepped forward.

Mary stood up and jostled the papoose again. The baby cried, and Mary backed away. She shouted, "No!" and raised the root up to her lips.

Weetamoo closed on her and yanked her by the hair. She spun her around just as Mary crammed the tuber into her mouth and grinned at the angry woman.

Weetamoo's eyes narrowed, and she wheeled a kick against Mary's backside. Mary landed on her face in the grey dirt. On impact, her teeth let their prize escape. Mary raked the rotted root back into her mouth. Heedless of the scraping grit, she bit down furiously and swallowed it in two gulps.

"You dog!" Weetamoo cursed her. "You shame me with your begging. This you will not do."

Mary knelt on all fours and turned to face her mistress. "I was hungry," she snarled. She tried to stand. Weetamoo pushed her back into the dirt.

"Silence!" Weetamoo growled at her. She saw the white woman's dress tear as she fell. "Look at yourself! She shouted. "Your English clothes are soiled and worn thin. Your skin and hair are dirty. Have you no pride? No honor?" The sachem smirked at the useless clothes the men of the village coveted. Her son cried out.

Shell beads clicked as Weetamoo rocked the papoose to calm him. She looked down at her own soft deerskin dress embellished with intricate bead work designs. She had made it long before and always kept it clean and in good repair.

She stared at the small, weak white woman lying in the dirt. Weetamoo felt protected and safe, warmly surrounded by the skin of birch bark. But Mary Rowlandson looked as uneasy as a salmon caught in a bear's grip.

Never taking her eyes off the angry sachem, Mary crept as far from Weetamoo as possible in the small space.

Mary's hands were cracked and bleeding, and her skin hung on her arms. She waited for the tirade to end and to be sent on some other task, away from the unyielding woman. But Weetamoo had not finished.

"Hear me, Woman. I am Weetamoo, daughter of Caunbitant, sachem of Pocasset, a people with rich hunting and fishing grounds. And now, because of you and your people, we have only old roots, berries, and nuts to fill our empty mouths.

"For many months, my warriors of my sannup Quannopinn and Metacom fight. For many days, the people cannot hunt and fish and harvest crops. Like the animals, we wander, eating what we can find. The people are sick and hungry. What makes you feel that the people should give more to you? You shame me with your begging."

Mary gave no answer.

The sachem adjusted her beaded bracelets and anklets and continued, "You are a burden to my people. It is only for Quannopinn's interest in ransoming you and the others for food and guns that you live. I say, you are of no use. We should kill you for all for the trouble you have caused us."

Mary did not speak. She moved her hand under her apron and felt a worn scrap of paper in her pocket, a scripture passage from one of her husband's sermons. She clenched it tightly. Weetamoo noticed her movement and yanked at her arm, pulling the tattered page from her hand.

"You reach for this for protection!" Weetamoo shrieked as she grabbed it and held it above her head.

"Ha. Your god will not help you here," she continued. "I know of your bible. Many of the people have learned to read that book. Like my second husband, Petananuit, they leave their homes and families and land to hear the white man's lies. They think if they wear white men's clothes and live in white men's houses they will have white men's respect and will not have to fight. But they are wrong."

She rumpled and threw the page on the dirt floor, narrowly missing the fire. Mary dared not reach for it.

Weetamoo peered into her English looking glass fastened to the wall and smoothed her hair.

"Too long my people trusted the white man's lies," the sachem said. "They use the Praying Indians to learn more ways to harm our people and take the land of our fathers. Your white men hunger for more than they need." She lifted up her skin cape dyed with symbols of corn, beans, and squash and shook it at Mary's face.

"For many years, we helped the English. Our fathers showed them how to plant the three sisters: beans, squash, and corn. Our mothers gave them food from our baskets when they had none. We shared the gifts of the sea and forest.

"But it was never enough," she railed. "White men pushed our people off our land and built their walls and fences. They asked our sachems and Powwows to put their mark on their English papers, and they said our leaders' marks mean the land no longer belongs to us.

"White men lied and cheated and made our people drunk to get what they wanted," Weetamoo said.

Mary didn't stir as Weetamoo lifted a small drum from a peg woven into the frame of the wetu. The Indian woman stared at its stretched leather and felt her connection to the animals of the earth. The drum's white feather called to the spirits of the air. She held it near her ear and heard the soft echo of water that gives life.

Weetamoo spoke quietly. "White men do not hear the voices of the fathers who breathe still in these woods. They do not hear the voices of the spirits who guide us and make signs for us to know where to hunt, when to plant, and how to harvest." She tenderly hung the drum back in its place. "They only want more land, and we are in their way. But we will stop them. Metacom has joined the people together, and we will drive the white man away."

Scratching on the wetu's leather flap announced a visitor. Weetamoo smoothed her dress and hair and lifted the skin aside. Wanahee, the older woman who buried Sarah, stood holding a dead partridge. "Sachem, please accept this be-nah-nah. My sannup offers this for your and Quannopinn's evening meal."

114

Weetamoo took the bird from her grasp and told her, "It is a good gift, fitting for my man's meal. Go to your sannup and thank him. He is welcome at our hearth this night."

Momentarily relieved by the intrusion, Mary flinched when Weetamoo threw the bird into her skirt. "Prepare this well, or you will be beaten," she snarled.

"Yes, Mistress." Mary scooped the bird into her apron and, hoping to leave the wigwam without further abuse from Weetamoo, skirted the fire. Weetamoo became distracted with wiping the bird's blood from her hands as Mary half crawled and half tripped out into the cold air, retrieving the remnant of Joseph's sermon as she went.

Mary whispered thanks to her God for His mercy.

Sagamores' Council

As the afternoon sun faded, Mary thanked God for the warmth of the fire. A partridge stewed in the steaming skin pot. She added hot stones to raise the temperature and put in scrubbed ground nuts and some dried corn from Weetamoo's basket. She added herbs she had gathered and wished for salt to flavor the soup. Mary knew it must taste good or she would suffer Weetamoo's wrath.

Never mind the wicked dame, she thought as she put her shoulders into grinding corn for a blood pudding. This will certainly taste better than the meal they gave me. She looked at her own bowl, empty except for small bare bones and claws. *Lord, never did I dream I would savor entrails or relish scant meat sucked from the bones of a bird's foot.* Mary's hunger abated slightly from the morsels, and she slaked her thirst with a small taste of the broth.

Mary expected a brief respite from her mistress's scorn because Weetamoo would spend hours primping and preening for the important evening to come. All the sagamores, the lesser chiefs, would attend the meal and conduct important talk of war and peace. Weetamoo kept busy inside her wetu, readying it for her visitors by freshening it with sage and sweetgrass smoke. She had announced that she would also prepare the tea and tobacco for the sagamores' council. Mary felt grateful that Weetamoo would at least handle those tasks herself.

Mary rose to gather more sticks for the fire. As she picked up dry deadfall protected from the weather under snow laden pine boughs, her thoughts wandered to what Weetamoo had let slip about the possibility of ransom. Mary thought about how she might listen in on the council. She decided to make a place to hunker down near the wetu where she might glean information about her ransom and release.

Mary wanted to believe that she might soon go home. "Lord, let it be so, that I am ransomed and soon home again with my fam . . . " she stopped. Guilt rose in her throat, choking her selfish words. How could she pray for herself when her poor dear children were still lost to her in the vast wilderness. Her home was gone. Her family was slaughtered and scattered. The Lord only knew what had become of her husband.

She amended her prayer. "Lord, if it be your will, please make my children's plight less harsh than my own, and when you deem us worthy, please let us come together in safety. Amen."

✳ ✳ ✳

Choosing just the right wood to keep the scent and heat pleasing for Quannopinn and the sagamores, Weetamoo laid sticks carefully near the fire. She would attend the council as a sachem in her own right, and as hostess, she insured that nothing would disrupt the discussion.

She laid out the woven reed mat next to the place reserved for Quannopinn. In Metacomet's absence, he was leader, due in part to her own kinship with the Great Sachem and his with the leader of the Narragansetts. She took a ceremonial clay pipe and sacred tobacco from their mink pouch and carefully tamped some tobacco into the pipe bowl. She gently laid the pipe down, cautiously keeping it and the fur and feathers that adorned it on the reed mat. She laid the tobacco pouch beside it. *This at least is plentiful here by the Baquoag River*, she thought.

She dipped her sweetgrass and sage brush into the fire until the ends caught, then blew the flames out, leaving hot, orange tendrils curling with smoke. She rose and waved the smoking bundle over the areas where the sachems and sagamores would sit, over the sleeping areas, and all around the bark walls of the wetu. She murmured incantations to Ke-che No-din, the Spirit of the Wind, seeking his blessing on the place. Smoke tinged the air with its sweet incense and drove away unpleasant odors left behind by the filthy white woman. When she felt satisfied with the cleansing of her home, she pushed the brush end into the dirt, snuffing out any small embers. She dipped it in a gourd filled with water and put it back in its ash bucket. She placed a small stick on the fire and backed out of the wigwam, allowing the flap to fall into place to seal in the smoke-scented air.

She saw Mary hunched over the fire, rolling dough of cornmeal and bear oil onto moistened corn leaves as Weetamoo had shown her. The white woman clumsily folded the leaves around the dough and dropped them into the bubbling stew. Weetamoo resisted the urge to reprimand her. She told herself that the bits that fell out of the loose wrappings would thicken the stew.

Weetamoo walked down the worn path to the river. She stopped beside a white birch tree and knelt to leave a small offering of tobacco at its roots before peeling fresh bark to make a vessel to boil her guests' tea. She placed another offering at the base of a spruce tree before pulling free one of its long, stringy root fibers. Bending near the river's edge, she dropped more tobacco into the water before using a hollow gourd tethered at her waist to crack the skin of ice and scoop fresh water. She hastened back to the cooking fire to select stones for boiling the tea.

Because Mary was a gift from Quannopinn, Weetamoo had tried hard to tolerate her but felt continual frustration over her lack of basic skills. The English woman had put too many stones in the stew pot. The steaming liquid sloshed over, quenching the fire below. Weetamoo pushed Mary aside and deftly fished out a number of stones with a forked stick. She dropped them from the lip of the skin pot onto the hissing, angry coals. She sat by the firelight and fashioned another boiling pot from the supple birch bark and stitched it with a bone needle and the length of spruce fiber. Satisfied that Mary had arranged sufficient wooden dishes and gourds for the meal service, Weetamoo stepped into the wigwam to set the water boiling for their tea.

Weetamoo's wetu appeared ready for the arrival of the sachems and sagamores. She hoped they would agree during the council to forge ahead with the war and hoped she might persuade them to lessen her burden of Mary Rowlandson by trading her to the Mohicans for weapons and ammunition. For the moment, she busied herself dressing and preparing for the important evening ahead.

✳ ✳ ✳

Council members sat in a ring around the fire in the wetu. Quannopinn represented the Narragansetts of the south and held the seat of honor. Wonalancet of the Abenakis from the north sat directly opposite, flanked by Matoonas of the Nipmucs from the west and Monaco of the Nashaways from the east. Awashonks and Weetamoo sat on Quannopinn's right, representing the Sakonnet, Pocasset, and Wampanoag people of the south and east.

Weetamoo kept her place near the entrance to the wigwam so that she would be ready to fill any needs. The men had eaten well. After thanking and honoring Monaco for his gift, Quannopinn lifted the pipe to the Great Spirit, Sha-wain-ne-me-shin, signifying that the council would begin. He offered the calumet to the four corners of the spirit world and bid Monaco to accept the first smoke.

Quannopinn began, "Welcome, my brothers and sisters. It is good we are all here together. In four days' time, we will meet Metacomet and Canonchet at Squakeag to speak more on this war with the English." He paused while the other guests shared the pipe. They all understood that sharing of sacred smoke signified that all who spoke would speak the truth. Each would have the others' full attention to share what lay on each mind and in heart.

"At the council in Montaup," Quannopinn continued, "the Wampanoags, Pokanokets, Nipmucs, Pocumtucs, and many Narragansetts chose the warpath to stop these white men before they become too strong. This war is a great burden. We must decide what is best for our people. War is not the way of the Narragansetts, but it has been pressed on us, and we are unafraid.

"War with the white man was not always so. In the time of my grandfather, white man did not come and stay. Before the time of the English, the people lived in peace, aquené, on the land. Our councils came together to decide what the people needed. We warred over hunting or planting ground, but our wars were just, and the stronger tribe claimed only enough warriors and squaws to replace their loss and enough ground to provide for their people. The sachems chose the best way for the people. But now our sachems have been made powerless by white man's law.

"Ours was not the way of the white devils, who seek to leave no red man, woman, or child in their path. When I was just a child, I saw their evil against our enemies, the Pequot nation, where they burned villages and killed with their guns any who tried to escape a death of fire and smoke. I heard the screams of the children and the cries of their mothers again in Narragansett. We will speak today of what is in our hearts. Wonalancet, what have you to say to this council?"

Weetamoo looked proudly upon her husband for his opening remarks.

Wonalancet stood to speak. He came from the northern forest country with high mountains and a cold climate. He wore a bearskin coat and thick moosehide boots. He was younger than Quannopinn, perhaps in his late twenties, early thirties. Weetamoo thought he was very attractive. She wondered if he might be a good marriage choice for Laughing Water, although she had not yet ended her mourning for her sannup killed at Narragansett. It had only been three moons since his passing. Still, Weetamoo thought a pairing between the north and south would strengthen their alliance.

"Quannopinn speaks the truth. Aquené, peace, was on our land for many years. Some white men came and traded goods with us and went away. In my home, we have lived long in peace. But now trouble has come to the heart of my people. They hear of the unjust ways of the English and the deaths of our brothers, and many of our warriors will not listen to the words of my father, Passaconaway. He has told us of his vision of pale faces coming as many as there are leaves in the forest, red man's hunting ground bare of trees and furrowed under white man's plow, and our rivers and fishing places choked with dams and whirring mills.

"This the Great Spirit whispered to him. He will not fight with us. He will not waste his young men before the white man's fire and thunder. He will only use his spirit power against them. He has gone away from us.

"But many of our young warriors fight alongside me, and we have taken back much of the land. We have driven the white people away, killing them and burning their houses so they cannot return. We show our warrior pride, and each one of us strikes their corpses to count coup on their bodies so they will not enter the spirit world in strength. And we take some of their people so that we can come to know more of their strange ways. I have spoken."

Weetamoo stood and spoke. "Their ways are strange to us, as you say. I have lived with this woman, this Mary Rowlandson who Quannopinn has bought, and see that she has few skills. She can make English clothing. The people want the white man shirts, so they come to her for them. Now, in the season of popping trees, many ask her for the warm leggings and stockings of the white man. But she spits in disgust and tries to bargain with each one for more food. She does not give freely of her skill. She expects to be paid much for her effort.

"I do not understand a woman who has no pride, who will not make a gift and accept the proper honor for her work. Are all the white people so unkind and selfish? If each one makes only for himself, how will they survive? They do not honor the gifts they have from the spirits; they do not share their own gifts freely so all have more. I cannot understand these people. And after they have driven us from Pocasset and done violence to our people in Narragansett, we are committed to war. My people will fight to rid the land of them. I have spoken."

"Weetamoo speaks the truth," said Monaco. His face looked more grave than usual. He lacked so much sleep that his good eye sagged. "So hungry are the English for white man's money that they kill one another, and they kill us, too. If they did not hang our three brothers, Mattashunnano, Wampapaquan, and Tobias, for greed, war would not have come so soon. We all know they hung our brothers for the killing of John Sassamon, the Praying Indian who once sat as a sagamore with Metacom, yet all the people know it was the Englishman Pattuckson who killed Sassamon, all for Christian money. The English let our people witness their trial but did not hear our voices for our Wampanoag brothers. That great dishonor brought the tribes together in anger. So now the Nashaway, Quabaug, Natick, and the Pennacook at Marlborough all fight with me against the white man's ways. I have spoken." He took his seat.

Awashonks stood and spoke quietly, "My people, the Sakonnets, cannot be held from war any longer. The English made treaties with our people and bade us give up our guns and agree to live by their laws. We have tried to abide by their treaties, but they still came to us and poisoned my sons against me and took more land. They struck against our people with many fighting men and torched my home. They have broken our treaty again with blood and fire in Narragansett. We will fight alongside Metacom. I have spoken."

"Matoonas, what is your mind on this?" asked Quannopinn.

Matoonas rose. He was as tall as Quannopinn but older by ten or more years. He dressed in the light clothing of the Nipmuc, the lake people. Even in winter, he went about bare-chested. "My people will fight until the English are gone from Nipmuc country. We have already raided their village they call Mendon near the Muddy Brook, but the English have not gone. They have sent more to fight. We will war on them until they are no more. I have spoken."

Quannopinn stood and agreed with the sachems around the fire, "I, too, am on the warpath against this English army that chases us down in our own country. Their paper means nothing to me—or them. There is no honor in it. What they say today they will change tomorrow. My people have tired of their lies. I will fight alongside my brother Metacom. It is good that we are of one mind. Tomorrow we leave this place and cross the river, and we will soon meet with Metacom and Canonchet of the Narragansetts. I have spoken."

"What of these white people we have among us?" Weetamoo asked. "Some of them only add to our burdens. We should trade them for corn or guns before we fight again." By bartering her for the supplies they desperately needed, Weetamoo hoped to be rid of Mary without offending Quannopinn.

"Weetamoo is wise. We will need more food and powder before we fight again. We should sell them to the French and Mohicans. They camp nearby and pay well," agreed Matoonas.

"This is wise, I agree," said Quannopinn. "When we meet with Metacomet, let us speak of this again. Let this council end in one voice with all in favor of war."

The men rose to leave. Her brows lowered, Weetamoo eyed Quannopinn for ending the council so abruptly before she could have full agreement on her desire to trade their captives. But the time had passed to change the outcome. She would speak with him later about his dishonor to her in not providing time for all to speak on the matter so they could go to Metacomet's council with a united voice to dispose of the captives. She had to hide her dissatisfaction and accept the greater outcome of support and commitment from all the tribes to finish the war.

She would have to wait to rid herself of Mary.

Outside, Mary huddled close to the wigwam. She had found a small opening between the layers of bark where she could hear if she lay on the cold, wet ground. Although she understood only a few of their words, she grasped the gist of the conversation.

The mention of ransoming the captives to the French excited her. She thought they would surely sell her back to her husband. She clearly understood that tomorrow they would travel to meet with King Philip or Metacom as they called him and was relieved that her salvation might be only across the river and a few days. She gathered up her damp skirt and apron and walked back toward the fire. Her wounded side felt stiff and ached from the cold.

As she neared the fire, she saw an English gentleman walking in her direction. Mary was astonished. *An English man amid all these heathens? What sort of witchery was it?*

"Are you Mary Rowlandson?" he asked.

Meeting Mr. Pepper

"Mistress Mary Rowlandson?" The Englishman's voice spoke from the darkness just outside the camp.

Dumbstruck, Mary strained her eyes to see beyond the campfire in front of Weetamoo's lodge. Her lip quivered at the sight of an obviously Christian man wearing English clothes.

Wigwams surrounded her. Sounds of pagan chanting and smells of wood smoke filled the dark, starry night.

"Mistress Rowlandson?" he repeated.

Mary barely knew what to say. In a fortnight, she hadn't been addressed with proper formality. She staggered to her feet and shook dirt and ice from her skirts. She smoothed her hair.

"Sir, by what means do you know my name? Who are you and how do you come to me here in this great wilderness?"

Mary overcame her astonishment to ask the questions.

"Mistress, my name is Robert Pepper of Roxbury. When I learned that you were among this band, I obtained leave from my captors to seek you out. How do you fare?" He stepped toward her from the edge of the woods. "Are you well?"

Her reaction to Mr. Pepper's arrival surprised her. His presence disturbed the ease she had felt moments before in her growing expectation that her ransom could occur soon. Something was not right that the Englishman should cause her fear even as savages held her captive. How had she become so unperturbed in that hostile world? What made her start so at the sight of her own fellow?

A cry caught in her throat. She could not speak.

"Please. Take my arm, Mistress Rowlandson. You appear unsteady." He reached out and caught her by the elbow.

Mary willed her tongue to form words. "Thank you, Sir," she said. She brushed dirt from her apron and rose to her full stature. "What a great providence it is to meet you, Mr. Pepper. Please come warm yourself by the cooking fire." She gestured toward the fire outside the wetu. "Have you journeyed far to come here?" Though she said words she might have used in her home, her voice betrayed a quiet desperation.

"Only a mile or so tonight. A short distance in comparison to the many miles I have walked in the midst of the heathen since my captivity."

"You must be weary, Sir. Let me offer you some tea." She played the hostess, relying on her rearing as a lady of prominent status, despite the rude setting and primitive resources. From an iron kettle, She poured a liquid steeped with chamomile and nettles she had foraged into a drinking gourd and gave it to him. They settled themselves on wooden stumps near the fire. She bore herself as a proper English woman and resisted her desire to cling to the man and cry. She had a hard time forming the right words.

"Tell me, Mr. Pepper, are there many other captives with you?" She asked it casually, but her voice shifted in octaves, giving way to the gulf between her words and thoughts. *Could I grab him and beg him, please take me from here? Tell me there are others and we can leave together. Will you lead me home?*

He looked briefly away, then said, "No. Not many."

He accepted the tea she offered and said, "Thank you, Mistress. You look well. Are you fairly treated?" His eyes showed a quiet despair and a longing to be comforted by a fellow Christian. His words also rang false.

She hesitated. She could not reach out to hold the man and let him hold her. Instead, she replied, "I am not unfairly treated. Their words affect me more than their actions. Oh, I have been hungry because their food is not plentiful or savory, and I have an injury to my side that causes me stiffness and pain. But it is mending, thank you."

She paused as if distracted, then said numbly, "My direst sorrow is caused by the loss of my dear babe, Sarah, who was buried only weeks ago on that hilltop." She gestured. "Only six years of her life spent, to end in bitter anguish at their hands."

"My deepest sympathy for your loss," he said and patted her hand to comfort her.

"Thank you, Mr. Pepper," she said quietly as she looked down. After a moment, Mary asked, "Have you any news of Lancaster?"

"Nay, Mistress, I have been in the company of these Indians since September. I was taken at Northfield. We were ambushed in a ravine while crossing a small brook. We retreated to a hill to make our stand but most unfortunately ran out of powder and shot and were overcome."

"I heard of your fight. Many were lost that day. Were you injured?" Mary asked.

"I was shot in my leg. Save three of us, all fell, including our Captain Beers. I have been with the Indians since and gone nearly as far as Albany to see King Philip."

"Walking all the while on your wounded leg?"

"It has been difficult, but I learned it would be to my greater misfortune to show weakness. Two taken with me were tortured and put to death. Although they carried me at first, I did not want them to tire of it, and so I learned to heal my wound with a poultice of oak leaves. Perhaps, brave Madam, you should use it, too, for your own injury."

"I would be much obliged, Kind Sir, with your instruction in the method." A usually modest woman, Mary barely lifted her apron to show the place where her dress was torn through by the gunshot. She had tried to keep the wound and dressing clean by using only icy water and torn bits of her dress. The wound smelled fetid.

Mr. Pepper collected handfuls of large dry oak leaves from under a stand of hemlock where the snow had not yet moistened and rotted them. He loosened the torn strip of cloth binding her dark sore.

Amazed that she winced only slightly, he pulled away the inner cloth dressing. He gently laid several leaves in place of the soiled dressing and carefully refastened the strip of binding cloth. "'Tis healing well," he offered encouragingly and brought Mary a fresh cup of tea. "Do this daily and you will be healed more quickly."

"Mr. Pepper, I cannot thank you enough for your presence and your help. You must call on me when we are both restored so that my husband and I can show you our proper gratitude." She leaned closer and whispered, "I overheard the leaders tonight speaking of selling me to the French for guns and food. I am much comforted by the prospect, though 'tis bitter to think that my redemption may lead to more havoc on our good people.

"'Tis a bad time, this, but you mustn't dishearten yourself. Think only of your return to your home, and trust that God will support you. It is from Lancaster that you hail?"

"Lancaster as it was. It is no more, Mr. Pepper," she said, looking into the burning campfire. "After they fired our houses and shot us down as we fled, they took many of the women and children as their captives. We have all been sold to different masters and have little chance to gather in prayer and sorrow. It takes all our strength to keep up with the wanderings of these heathens. My own two children are in captivity nearby with different masters, but I have seen them only once. It is for them that I continue to hold myself strong." Never in her past life would she have revealed so many details to a stranger. "Forgive me prattling on, Kind Sir. I need not trouble you with my woes."

"Do not fret, Mistress Rowlandson. I am honored to have met such a courageous woman as could endure these trials. You must bear up under these burdens, but you will be redeemed, I have no doubt." He stood and straightened his breeches and buttoned his coat. Mary caught her breath and her eyes darted about at the thought of his departure. She rose, took his hands in hers, and looked into his white face as she burned the details of his countenance into her mind. *How long might it be until I see a friendly face again?*

She clasped his hands tightly.

"Mr. Pepper, I should like to tell you that it has been hard to be among these heathens these many days with naught to eat or drink but their musty corn swill and icy water chipped free from the river." Her words tumbled out like a fast-moving mountain stream. "And me with a gaping wound here at my side being forced to march along through the snow and mud, with them pushing me all the while, never caring if I should stumble or tear my skirt. Why, they even laughed at me and my poor dying babe when we fell from their naked horse, unable to remain secure, for you see, they use no furniture or bridle when they ride.

"This awful wilderness they drive me through grows deeper every day, and every step brings me farther from what is left of my family, if any." Refusing to let go of Mr. Pepper's hands, she paused and then rambled on, "I saw my sister shot dead in our doorway. For running to her son, the devilish beasts knocked her on the head. I know not what will become of my eldest children, Joseph and Mary, taken captive with me from our burning house all the while with our own blood running down to our heels . . . And then to be forced to leave my poor tender babe, Sarah, back there, buried in one of their pagan graves, with no Christian comfort for her tiny soul . . ." Mary's jaw trembled, and tears welled and ran down her cheeks.

Mr. Pepper patted her hand and nodded, unsure what to say.

Mary sniffed, wiped her eyes, and shook her head as if tossing away her horrid thoughts. She released Mr. Pepper's hands and said, "But Sir, what pains me more than all of this hardship, which I must know that God the Almighty has been pleased to provide for the redemption of my soul, what is worse than all this is to be deprived of the fellowship of Christians such as you. Why, when you stepped out of the darkness into the campfire light, I was certain I'd seen a ghost. It has been so long since I have had good Christian company that I thought I might never see a white man again. It would be a righteous gift to me, Sir, for us to bow our heads together here to pray. Would you do that with me now, Mr. Pepper? Would you kneel with me in prayer?" She nudged toward him as she spoke.

"Dear Madam, it would be an honor. Yes, let us pray together," he helped her to her knees.

She reached under her apron into her worn pocket and drew out her tattered verses. "I have these scraps from my husband's last sermon but loathe for them to see me with it, as my mistress has no love of Christian ways. But this evening she is detained at a council of the sagamores, so let us use this time to pray."

Together they read a passage from the book of Psalms and prayed for Sarah's small soul, for Mary's other children, for her husband, her family, and the good people of Lancaster. Then they prayed for Mr. Pepper's safe return to his family. They prayed for humility and acceptance of God's will for them and thanked Him for His comfort and healing for their penitent souls. Just the act of touching the pages and speaking the words of scripture aloud with another made Mary feel the restoration of a piece of her heart.

When they finished, Mr. Pepper helped Mary sit on the log stump. He warmed her drinking gourd with the last of the tea from the kettle over the glowing coals.

They heard stirring from the direction of Weetamoo's wigwam, and Mary whispered, "Their council must be ending." Mr. Pepper saw a cloud of fear in her eyes and thought it sensible to take his leave before they noticed him.

Mary gripped his hand tightly, unable to let him go, yet knowing he couldn't stay. The heavy dread of being alone again among those strangers pressed a weight upon her shoulders. For just a moment, she considered going with him, then realized there was nowhere to go. If he, a strong man, hadn't escaped, how could she imagine that she could?

Mr. Pepper gently freed his hands from her tight grip and rose. "Fare well, brave Mistress. I pray that we will meet again in better times."

"Go with God, Mr. Pepper, till we meet again. I shall be forever in your debt for your kind words and tender ministrations. May the mercy of God be with you."

Weetamoo lifted the flap and emerged from the wigwam just as Mr. Pepper faded into the blackness outside the encampment. Freshened by his company and assistance, Mary thought that tonight she might sleep restfully for the first time since that most doleful day.

Grains of Discontent

"Why did you not wake me sooner?"

"I thought you would have need to rest after your late council, Mistress."

"Where is Quannopinn?" Weetamoo demanded.

"I saw him smoking outside One-Eyed John's wigwam, Mistress. He and the other men who were here last night . . ."

"Do not call him by your English name!" Weetamoo snapped. "You will call him Sachem Monaco. He is a great warrior chief."

"I am sorry, Mistress. I meant no disrespect. It is how he was called by my people."

"Sachem Monaco, do you hear me?" Weetamoo insisted.

"Yes, Mistress," Mary said as if she were tired of being berated.

Weetamoo ignored the tone of Mary's voice and took her drinking gourd from its hook on a cut branch that supported the wetu. She took Quannopinn's too, put some crushed cornmeal into the gourds, and poured hot water over the meal. She stirred it with her knife and set it aside. In a larger gourd, she added crushed herbs to make her morning tea. She took the tea and Quannopinn's corn mash to him near the wetu of Monaco. The sachems were in the middle of a heated discussion.

"We must send someone to our summer home for food. We do not have enough for the people," Matoonas was saying.

"Nux. It is so. The English have left their villages bare and have little more than we do. We cannot fight on nokechick and ground nuts," Quannopinn agreed.

"No, we cannot spare our men or risk going back with the English so close. I say we take more English villages," Monaco argued.

"There are no villages—we have burned them all behind us. Now we can only go to the north or east," Wonalancet said. "In my country to the north, the people have been untroubled. The settlers have had time to fortify their garrisons. It will be a hard fight. To the east, the English are many in number and gain new men and supplies by sea. And Metacomet waits for us across the river."

"We must meet with Metacomet and his sagamores," said Monaco. "But we must also provide food for the people. Near my home, there is a village the English call Medfield. Their people are foolish and do not cut the trees near their houses. We can fall on them by surprise in great numbers and take what we need and be away before they can call out for help."

"Nux, I know that place. We can take Medfield with ease," Matoonas said. "It is far from their army in Boston and wooded right to their very doors. I will go there with Monaco to get food for the people." As Medfield was the heart of the Nipmuc territory, Matoonas would not be left out of a fight in his own country.

"My men, too, would be honored to help in the raid," Wonalancet offered. "They long to wet their knives with English blood. My father holds them back too long."

With that, Quannopinn decreed, "Taubut, it is a good plan. Take your two bands and go now. When you return, we will strike camp and meet again at Baquoag. Wuniish, Netop."

"Wuniish, Netop." Before Quannopinn could put out his pipe, they had gone. Their warriors, anxious to be on their way after nine idle days, mounted their horses and departed the encampment within moments. So many followed Monaco, Matoonas, and Wonalancet that Menameset looked suddenly barren.

Weetamoo was glad that the other three sagamores were taking swift action to replenish their supplies, although she was annoyed that they had not brought her and Awashonks into the conversation. She understood that some warriors had to stay behind to protect the people, yet Quannopinn assumed independent leadership without her advice. She held back from complaining in front of the others but vowed to have it out with Quannopinn once they were alone.

"So you rise at last, sleepyhead," he said and reached out to pat her head.

Her annoyance changed to anger, and she felt fire rising in her cheeks. "Don't touch me, Quannopinn. I am not a child to be teased. I am your wife. And much more than that, I am a sachem."

"I didn't mean any harm, I only . . ." His proud face wrinkled with confusion.

"Am I not the only one of you who did not let the English swindle me out of my land? Am I not the only one who brings three hundred warriors to fight for us? Am I not the sister to Metacomet and one of the first to fight beside him in this conflict?" She struggled to keep her tone calm, though a tempest raged inside her chest.

"Of course you are all those things, wife, but none of that gives you a right to be discourteous to me, your sannup." His placating tone edged toward defiance.

It was too much. Weetamoo shouted back, "And what, pray tell, gives you the right to be discourteous to me? How dare you meet with the sagamores without me, making important decisions outside of our official council? And how dare you dismiss a discussion I raise in council? And while we are on the subject, how dare you bring someone into my household without my consent?"

"Oh, no, not that again. Weetamoo, we have discussed and settled the matter already."

"Have we? Perhaps you and I have an agreement, but why did you not bring the matter before the council last night? We need more than just us two in agreement to sell Mary and any other captives, yet you ended our discussion and closed the council before the others had time to speak." She closed in on him, making each point with a finger directed at his heart.

"Hold on there, Wife. You are right that we need more than just us two to agree, and that is exactly why I ended the discussion. We need Metacomet's consent before we make any agreements with the Mohicans, the French, or any other party."

"Oh, no we don't. This is where you are mistaken. Metacomet will consent to any wise decision I put before him because we are well-trained leaders and always put the people ahead of our pride. You seem to think that because you have fallen into a position of power and married a sachem, you suddenly rise above all of us. You make unwise moves without the benefit of good advice from seasoned leaders. This does not follow the ways of our people." She turned away from him.

"Fallen into power?" He spun her around to face him. "I've inherited my right as a sagamore, just as you did. And I, too, am well-trained to lead!" He shouted. Since they still stood outside Monaco's wetu, it was clear that others in the camp heard their raised voices, but no one stopped what they did nor did they look in their direction.

"Oh, and is that why you have spent time in English jails? And had to escape and pay fines? And brought disgrace upon your family?" She spat. "Taking single-minded action unwisely leads to trouble. All important matters must be brought to the attention of our whole community. You must stop and take measure of their thoughts and words. We cannot afford rash decisions at a time like this." She wrestled her arm away from his grip.

"So you think raiding Medfield counts as a rash decision? Am I squandering resources for my personal benefit? No, I support doing what we must to feed our people." He loomed over her at his full height, as if that made his argument stronger.

"Had you asked my opinion, I would have agreed with you, Quannopinn, but you cannot treat me as you might your other wives who have no authority of their own. We are equals, and you must be wise enough to see that if you expect our marriage and our alliance to continue and if we are to win this war together. And more than that, you must consider my counsel before you take action, not after."

Weetamoo noticed Ashawonks approaching from her wetu and lowered her voice.

"You married a man who has never had to ask permission from a woman for any action. At least not since childhood. I won't start now," he shouted back.

"You are no longer a boy, and you must behave as a man and as a sagamore who has responsibility not just to himself or his own people but to his wife and to his fellow leaders and their people as well." She bit back further words. "This is my counsel on this. I will say no more until we both take time to think on this."

"I am through talking, too." He stomped away, nearly knocking Awashonks off her feet as she drew near.

"Well, good morning to you, too, Quannopinn," Awashonks shot over her shoulder, then turned to speak with her cousin. "So it looks like it will be a cool morning."

"Are you not furious with him? Did you see what he did last night and this morning?"

"What?"

"Truly? Did you not notice how he dismissed my conversation about ransoming the captives last night? And this morning, he went off and met with the other sagamores without either of us and sent them off to raid Medfield, never even discussing it with us."

"Well, that's not quite true. He and I spoke of it earlier, and I suggested he see if he could get the others to form a war party to gather some resources nearby. He wanted to wait until you awoke to discuss it, but I urged him to send them quickly as the English follow us closely. It was I who suggested he let you sleep. Do you think I do not see that you are with child? You cannot keep pushing yourself so hard. It is bad for the baby."

"Bad for the baby! Awashonks, this is not my first child. I have never let being with child get in the way of my duty. Do not ever, ever do something like this again. Do you understand me? And now look at the rift you have caused between us. How am I to mend this? Harsh words cannot be unspoken."

"Well, if you ask me, he had it coming anyway. Oh, yes, I heard every word, and you were right to tell him how you feel. He is a hot-head, but I know him. He'll have a good think on it, and he will realize you are right, although I will let him know that I took the blame for this morning."

"As you should. I hope you are right. I am worried that I may have made a mistake with a bad marriage choice."

"Oh, believe me, no one worries more about that than I do. But as your sponsor, I will try to help you both work things out together. Let us both see how your words this morning sit with him, and in time we will know if a change comes from it. Now, let us go and have something to eat. Whatever you have there has gone cold by now, and you must keep up your strength."

"Awashonks, you and your appetite will be the death of us all." Weetamoo laughed and swung her arm around her cousin's thick waist as they walked back to the cooking fire for their tea.

A Brief Moment

Mary saw the riders leaving and bowed her head in prayer for Medfield. If only she had a way to warn them, that they might not befall the same fate as her kinspeople in Lancaster. The fear of what awaited those good folk weighed on her all the day long and made her think again of her own family.

She finished up her chores as early as she could and thought to look for her son and daughter, hoping she might see them once more. She had no way of knowing if they were all in the same place or if they had been split up again, but it seemed that the latter was the way the Indians traveled. She noticed that she always traveled with small groups with no way to know which way any of the others went, especially in the thick forest.

She walked toward the place where she had first seen her daughter Mary, all the while looking about for Joseph, but she saw neither of them along the way to their encampment. As she neared Mary's wetu, she saw her daughter sitting under a nearby tree. To avoid upsetting her, Mary went around behind her and then sat quickly beside her and covered her daughter's mouth before she could cry out. At first, she jumped, but then with tears filling her eyes, she clung to her mother with all her might. Mary hushed her and held her and waited for her tears to subside. She stroked her hair and rocked her in her lap, as a babe, even though she was nearly eleven years of age. She barely felt the weight of her child, and Mary clasped her as tightly as her daughter did her.

"My darling girl, please do not fret. These strangers will not hurt you, though they keep us apart. Show me which of these are your master and dame, and I will make sure I always know where you are."

Young Mary pointed out the two Indians who lived in her wigwam. Mother and daughter leaned behind a tree so they might not be seen by them.

"Oh, Mama, I am so frightened. And hungry."

Mary reached into her apron pocket and gave her the bit of nokechick she had saved from her breakfast. Sarah gobbled it in a single bite.

"I will bring you more next time, dear daughter. Until then you must be a big strong girl and do as you are told. Never give them any reason to complain about you, and before long we will both be freed."

"Will we, Mama?"

"Yes, dear. I heard it myself from their council. I think we are drawing very near the place where we will be restored to freedom. So you just be good and say your prayers and I will see you as often as I can get away."

"I love you, Mama, and I will never be bad again. Was it my fault that this happened? Like Father said in Church, are we being punished because we did something bad?"

"No child, not you. Not you. There are some grownups who have brought these troubles our way, but God tells us He loves us and the more He gives us as a challenge, the more we can show that we love Him. You will keep saying your prayers, now, won't you?"

"Oh, I will. I mean, I do. Every day and night like you and Father taught me. It's just that I sometimes forget the words."

Mary laughed. "Don't you worry about that. When you forget, you can say what is in your heart, and God will hear you and know what you mean."

Young Mary hugged her hard. "Thank you, Mama. I so miss you and Father and Sarah and even Joseph. I just want to go home."

"And you will and soon. Now here, let us pray a little together before I have to go." Mary pulled her tattered paper from her pocket, and they said the words together until young Mary heard her dame calling for her. Mary gave her a hug and sent her off with a promise to visit again. The short moment made her feel at once normal and at the same time so very estranged from the world where she was now living.

Mary returned to her own hearth and finished out the day, completing her usual tasks without complaint. That evening, she whispered a special prayer of thanks to God for allowing her to see her daughter once again and to hold her in her arms. She prayed for her strength and comfort and made an urgent plea that her hopes of release might be soon at hand. For the first time in a fortnight, she fell into a deep sleep.

Warriors Return from Medfield

Distant whooping and shouting abruptly shattered Mary's heavy slumber. Her heart pounding, she leapt to her feet and fled toward the woods. She hid in the thicket before the first rider reached the camp. *Is this another attack? Are these rival Indians? Was she possibly being rescued?* Her palms sweated. Her throat tightened. Her mouth dried out. She crouched behind a large tree and watched.

Riders charged into the camp with thunderous gunshots and great whoops. The villagers rising from their furs answered with more whoops. As they got to their feet, Mary saw them all smiling and laughing. Confused, she took time to realize that the excited riders had returned from Medfield. From their excited shouts, she gathered with dread that they had succeeded in sacking the town.

Some held the belongings of settlers like herself. Some held bloody English scalps and other morbid trophies. Though she could not understand their crazed words, she recognized their boasting and teasing gestures. Mary cowered at the sound of their screeching. She saw riders jumping from unfettered horses and falling upon the waking Indians. Even as the people embraced one another in excitement, she panicked.

Drumbeats sounded, and soon the whole village was afoot chanting and singing. A rekindled fire grotesquely lit their frenzied dancing and shouting. She watched them throwing something into the fire. As it sizzled, the people raised their voices to the sky amid the smoke. Women fetched cauldrons and set them to boil with booty from the returning warriors. In the red firelight, Mary imagined herself in hell. The demonic screeching increased and overpowered her muffled sobs.

Too afraid to retrieve her fur from the wetu, Mary hunkered down in the woods. Her only warmth that February night came from her own shuddering and shivering. The noises kept her awake until nearly dawn when the celebration subsided and she dozed off into a restless sleep.

Ceremony of Triumph

The uproar in the night had awakened Weetamoo, who knew at once that Matoonas and the others had returned from Medfield. She counted the number of gunshots and understood that they had killed twenty-three white settlers. She was on her feet as the first of the warriors arrived at the encampment. Whooping triumphantly, Wonalancet leapt from his horse holding several scalps in his raised fist. He crushed Quannopinn with a great bear hug and announced loudly, "My brother, this raid was an easy victory! You should have come!"

Yelping wildly, Monaco flew off his horse and raised a jug of English rum over his head and shouted, "Nux, the English fools barely put up a struggle!"

Matoonas rode up carrying a young, squirming pig that he tossed to Weetamoo. "Here is an offering from the English for the Great Spirit," he said. Weetamoo deftly caught it by the hind legs, pulled her knife from her belt, and slit its throat. Its struggle ended quickly.

She whispered thanks to its spirit, and then lifted the piglet towards the fire already being built up in preparation for a great celebration.

Excited warriors filled the camp, and the people crowded around to hear of their exploits. The young men boasted of their bravery and conquests, and the older men goodheartedly praised and teased them. Although they had fought hard and ridden long, they felt full of spirit and eager to tell war tales. Squaws received gifts of iron pots and woolen garments, and sons got knives and hatchets taken from the homes of the enemy. But the most prized spoils were the English cattle and sheep driven in by the last arrivals. Weetamoo's mouth watered at the sight of meat the people had long been without.

As tradition commanded, the first gifts were offered to the Great Spirit. Although hungry, no one would eat until the gifts of corn, peas, beans, and meat had been burned to ash with tobacco and sage and the smoke risen to the Great Spirit Sha-wain-ne-me-shin.

Drummers and dancers gathered around the great fire. The Powwows or medicine men from the different bands lit bundles of sage and sweetgrass to purify the sacred dance circle. Holding their smoking bundles, they danced in thanksgiving for the safe return of the warriors and for their abundant rewards. Using sacred eagle feathers, they smudged each of the dancers as they entered the sacred circle. They fanned the sweet scent of sage and sweetgrass into their mouths and noses and bathed their bodies with swirling clouds of smoke. Circling the fire and acting out their feats of battle, warriors preceded the others. Then came the elders followed by the women, and finally, the young people. All danced and chanted as they made their way around and around the fire, always circling to the right.

The warriors still wore greasepaint and bloodstains from the battle. Many had war clubs, tomahawks, and knives in their hands. The followers put on their best clothing before joining in the dance. Swirling capes, leggings, skirts, and other garments adorned with shells, beads, feathers, or quills flashed colorfully in the firelight. The revelers made honors to the fallen. Songs of bravery rang out. Chants to the Spirits sounded in loud unison. People danced till they grew weary and others replaced them in the joyful circle.

As the first gifts turned to ash, people melted away to prepare a feast. Some men slaughtered the beasts, and women butchered and dressed them. Children fetched water and built cook fires. Elder women worked to grind the corn for bread. The eldest men gathered in clutches with the warriors, anxious to relive their days as braves. Everywhere, people smiled and sang.

For a time, tonight felt as it had been before the English, thought Weetamoo. Yet even in such a joyous moment, thoughts of how they had hurt her people soiled her happiness. She wanted to weep at the thought of how little they had after fleeing their burning homes under gunfire. She mourned for those left behind in Narragansett country who did not have the chance to escape. Every family had suffered loss. Those who escaped Canonchet's village came with what they wore. They had not taken food or clothing or other necessities. All they currently owned they had gathered on the trail or taken from the raids on the English.

She felt at once grateful for and resentful of the prizes taken. She wanted her way of life returned. She hoped that the victory at Medfield revived people's spirits and made them eager to pursue the English again and again until the ravagers left her country. As she saw dawn's first light through the trees, she struck her knife deeply into the belly of a fresh lamb.

Nearby, Awashonks laughed, "Weetamoo, this is not an Englishman, only a lamb. Use care or you will split it through."

"I only wish . . .it were . . .an Englishman. . . .I yearn to . . .redden my knife . . .with their blood," Weetamoo spat between thrusts.

Awashonks steadily beat corn in its wooden pestle with her pounding stone. "Our warriors have done that for us, and we will all feast today, thanks to them."

"Today, yes, Awashonks. But what of tomorrow? And the next day? How long can we run like wolves? The old ones weary of this journey, and now I'm told we have a coughing sickness among us. We should be in our winter homes, warm in our wetus, making wampum and baskets and enjoying our season's harvest. It is not good for so many to be in one place. We never have food enough to satisfy all." She continued hacking furiously at the lamb, severing its limbs with single blows.

"Weetamoo, you must learn to accept today for today. Only the Great Spirit knows what is in our path for tomorrow. We must be grateful for what we are given here and now," her older cousin said without looking up.

Standing, Weetamoo gathered the pieces of meat into their skin and brushed her hair from her face with the back of her bloodied hand. It left a mark like a warrior's on her cheek. Her eyes were full of fire as she looked at Awashonks. "Never will I be grateful to have what already belongs to me. The English have stolen from us and fail to appreciate that we have allowed them to live here so long. The time has come for them to go."

Weetamoo turned her back on the old woman and walked off. Sadness filled Awashonks's eyes as she watched her cousin go.

Medfield Spoils
A Precious Gift

Their food is generally boiled maize or Indian corn, mixed with
kidney-beans, or sometimes without. Also they frequently boil in this
pottage fish and flesh of all sorts, either taken fresh or newly dried.
These they cut in pieces, bones and all, and boil them in the aforesaid
pottage . . . Also they mix with the said pottage several sorts of
roots; as Jerusalem artichokes, and ground nuts, and other roots, and
pompions, and squashes, and also several sorts of nuts or masts, as oak
acorns, chestnuts, walnuts; these husked and dried, and powdered, they
thicken their pottage therewith.

—Gookin, 1674

Mary slept fitfully until she felt someone tugging on her arm. She
opened her eyes to see a little girl in braids bending over her.

"Ascowequa'ssin," the girl said as she pointed up toward the sun.
"Yo wuttut'tan."

Startled, Mary struggled to her feet before understanding that
her greeting meant, "Good morning. The sun is high." The cold
ground had numbed her usually sore side and stiffened her limbs. She
awkwardly rose and felt the warmth of the sun. She saw clouds of
mist rising off the river. "Praise be to God that today will be a better
day," she murmured.

The din of the night had gone. She could hear happy chatter and
singing, clay pots rustling and mortars thumping corn into meal. The
smell of meat cooking filled in the air. The men had returned with
food! She took the little girl's hand and hurried back to camp.

Mary saw the remnants of Medfield all around the camp. Squaws
wore English coats, and men flashed metal hatchets and knives.

Cook fires warmed English kettles, and great joints of English meat simmered in English pots. The sight and smell of it brought a smile to her face, and her stomach rumbled at the thought of such a feast. Yet almost at once, a shadow of shame crept into her heart for sensing pleasure as a result of Medfield's peril.

"Dear Lord, forgive my selfish hunger and want. I beg for your mercy on the souls of the good Christians who were the hosts of our feasting. Let me not forget my thankfulness to them and to You, who are all powerful. Amen."

Mary walked to the communal cook fire and found a woman there singing and smiling as she filled her children's wooden bowls with juicy lumps of lamb in broth. She beckoned Mary to join them.

Mary needed no second invitation. Using her bare hands, she tore into the meat. Hot juices trickled down her face and chin as she gnawed on a rib. Even with no seasonings or vegetables, never had a meal tasted so good to her. Mary nodded in thanks to her hostess as the squaw and her ravenous children devoured their meal. All shared in the meat and broth until they drained the pot dry. Mary thanked the squaw and helped wipe out the pot and bowls, then took her leave to find her mistress.

All around her, people celebrated. Mary passed between campfires, feeling invisible to her captors as they reveled—laughing, joking, singing, and dancing—in their good fortune. Their merry ways sharply contrasted with their haggard, spent hunger just twelve hours before.

A warrior saw Mary approaching, stood up in her path, and bade her stop. She was about to turn and run when he said, "Mary, hold out your hand."

She took a step back, noticing he held a war club in one hand and a basket in the other. She didn't dare refuse. She raised her hand to him.

"Will you have this?" He bent down and lifted a black, leather-bound Bible out of a basket and held it out to her.

148

Mary looked at the man who stood offering her the Lord's word. He wore English clothes like her own, but his face and hair belonged to the red race. She wondered if he had stolen the clothes or if, somehow, they belonged to him. She assumed the book came from some settler's house in Medfield, reduced to smoldering ruin.

What was she to do with his offered gift? She yearned to pull it from his grasp and hide beneath a tree to savor the words. She wanted to mouth the familiar verses and again touch the thin leaves of paper. For the first time in her captivity, Mary gazed upon something she considered sacred from another world. *From my world. Not this nightmarish struggle among the savages.*

Mary eyed the book and the man with caution. *What would her mistress think? What would she do to her if she found Mary with it? What if the man conjured some evil trick? Would the man snatch it away as she reached for it and toss it on the fire? Could she, would she trust him?*

"Sir, why do you offer such to me?" she asked.

"Mistress Rowlandson, because I am a Christian like you, I know this good book will give you comfort in your captivity." He gave her a slight bow.

Mary's mouth dropped open. He spoke as well as she did. Her eyes told her one thing but her ears, another. She didn't know how to reconcile her reactions to a second Christian Indian in the midst of wild savages. She wanted to despise the man she saw, but his actions and words conflicted with her expectation.

"My name is James Printer. I am from Hassanamesit, Madam. You may know of my work in the Harvard Press. In Cambridge."

"James Printer, you say? Yes. Yes, I have heard of your fine printing, but I had no idea that you were . . ." She stopped.

"Yes, I am an Indian. What you call a Praying Indian and have been for all my life. I know no other ways."

Mary looked down at his hands still holding out the book to her. She reached out and touched the worn leather binding. "Thank you, James Printer. I am thankful for your gift."

As he released it, she vowed not to think about how he came by it. She refused to think about the last hand to hold it or the gathered faces who may have listened to the final reading, perhaps only days earlier or even in the midst of a hellish siege the night before like what her own family had suffered.

She knew that, if God put this book into her hands, He surely wanted her to have such sustenance during her time of trial.

"Thank you," she murmured as she stuffed it under her apron. She smoothed her skirts and looked around briefly.

"Tell me, James Printer, will I be killed for reading this?" Mary asked.

"I daresay not. There are many here who pray."

"Yes, but do they live with Weetamoo?" Mary asked and lowered her gaze to her worn out shoes.

"Ah, yes, then you may do well to keep it in your pocket, Madam," he replied with a glance toward the ceremonial fire.

"That I will. I thank you again, Sir. I will remember your kindness when I am restored. You shall be rewarded." Just speaking English with a man who believed in her God, even a red man, made her feel more whole. She spoke with an assurance she had not felt in days, an assurance such as she might have in her home.

Home, she thought and closed her eyes. Again in her mind she saw her last view of her hearth with smoke curling down the stairs behind her children. She heard the frantic yells of men in her drawing room calling for water or shot and of women and children praying for their lives. She heard again the rattle of bullets pummeling her garrison walls and war whoops screeching outside as the stink of gunpowder and wood smoke burned her nostrils. She sucked in a breath and opened her eyes to see her savage captors stomping around the fire reenacting their hateful acts in victorious celebration. Her tears blurred that vision, and she turned away, stroking the precious gift under her apron.

She forgot about finding her mistress and sat down under a small bower of hemlock trees that left a dry bed of leaves beneath and opened the Bible. It fell open to Deuteronomy 28:1, which reads,

Now if thou wilt hear the voice of the Lord thy God, to do and keep
all His commandments, which I command thee this day, the Lord thy
God will make thee higher than all the nations that are on the earth.

That thought nourished Mary, but when she read on, the passage
warns,

But if thou wilt not hear the voice of the Lord thy God, to keep and
do all his commandments and ceremonies, which I command thee this
day, all these curses shall come upon thee, and overtake thee.

A litany of curses and blights follows, and Mary felt the full
weight of the condemnation and dreadful curse that had befallen her.
She and her people had been lax. She became frightened that her
redemption was at risk. But as she read on to 30:1-4, she was once
more reassured that,

when all these things shall come upon thee, the blessing or the curse,
which I have set forth before thee, and thou shalt be touched with
repentance of thy heart among all the nations, into which the Lord thy
God shall have scattered thee, and shalt return to him, and obey his
commandments, as I command thee this day, thou and thy children,
with all thy heart, and with all thy soul; The Lord thy God will bring
back again thy captivity and will have mercy on thee, and gather thee
again out of all the nations, into which he scattered thee before. If
thou be driven as far as the poles of heaven, the Lord thy God will
fetch thee back from thence.

The passage lifted her so that she thought that, if she repented,
God, in His mercy, would gather His people, scattered upon the
earth, together once again and turn all those curses against their
enemies. The reading restored in her a reason to be hopeful. In spite
of all her trials, she had assurance that God would bring her and
her children together in safety if they only kept their faith in Him.
Closing the book on her knee and closing her eyes, she prayed, *Lord
let me not forget these words and keep them all my days. I will repent and
put my trust in You who will always lead me home.*

Raising her eyes, she became aware of the passage of time, and
worried that Weetamoo must surely have missed her. She tucked her

Bible away carefully and stepped into the chaotic scene around her. Gluttony in food and drink had made the men, already heady from their victory, even louder and more boastful than before. Women worked at tidying and storing their new treasures, and the little boys ran all about playacting war scenes and whooping like their fathers.

Mary made her way through the mayhem to the sagamores' fire, where all the leaders gathered. She guessed by the severity of their looks and ritual passing of the pipe that an important council had begun.

As she tidied up around the cook fire, she caught bits of their conversation but did not understand many of their words. She wiped out their wooden burl bowls with leaves and water and stacked them neatly in a basket, taking great care not to let them clatter together and disturb the leaders.

Matoonas, Monaco, Awashonks, Weetamoo, Wonalancet, and Quannopinn formed an inner circle. Outside that circle sat old men and women, some Mary recognized as Powwows. Others—many warriors, but also some squaws and even children—encircled them. Each sagamore took his or her turn to speak. No one interrupted. Each finished matter-of-factly, and the next one began. Sometimes murmurs rose from the crowd. Sometimes they turned to their neighbors with expressions of doubt or agreement. At length, Quannopinn raised his hand signifying that all had spoken.

From the finality in his voice, Mary judged that the council had made a decision, but Quannopinn announced something she did not understand. Then he gestured toward Matoonas and waved his hand toward the trail leading west. Toward Monaco, he indicated a path to the east. For himself, Weetamoo, and Awashonks, he pointed toward the central path. Wonalancet, it seemed, would leave the band and head to his home to the north.

Weetamoo stood abruptly and stomped away without waiting for Quannopinn. Mary took a deep breath, dreading her mistress's wrath. When Weetamoo's temper flared, Mary thought it dangerous to be near her, for she struck out at others with harsh words and harsher deeds.

As the others rose from the circle, Mary understood clearly that they would once again remove from their camp. With the departure of the other tribal leaders, she feared they would take the few Christian whites among them away and she would again lose her children.

Mary slipped away with the departing people to seek out other settlers she had seen before. She had been told that this band of people held at least nine other captives. Although heathens crowded the camp, she hoped she could find her son or daughter again among them or at least learn which way they might travel. She felt reassured by the promise of her Bible that they would all be gathered again in a better time, but she wanted to see them in the flesh before parting once more. Seeking other pale faces like her own, she stepped through the mass of native people.

Mary had difficulty finding any white people. Smoke of the cook fires and dirt from traveling veiled everyone in the same grey pallor. To no avail, she scanned the tops of heads gathered near fires as she sought the lightness of blond or brown hair or even a dusty coif.

But then she heard a woman's shrill voice, sobbing and crying behind a wigwam. Mary followed the sound and found a white woman sitting with her face in her hands. A small child stood at her side, crying, too, and patting the woman repeatedly on the shoulder. Ringed around her were another seven white children, all crying and holding onto one another. Mary stepped toward the woman and asked them, "What is this, then? Are you not earnest with God for deliverance?"

At the sound of her English voice, the children turned to her and the woman looked up.

"Mercy!" the woman cried. "Mistress Rowlandson, Providence has sent a sign of deliverance in you. I had thought until now that I was the only Christian woman among these heathen." She sniffled and leaned back with her eyes wide.

As she looked up, Mary recognized her as Goodwife Ann Joslin, one of her neighbors from Lancaster. Her face was streaked with dirt and tears, and she appeared disheveled and worn. "Take heart, dear friend. You are not alone. There are others of us in captivity, but I do hear that we will be leaving this place, so I was hoping to find among this crowd my own two children before they are lost to me again."

"I have not seen other children. These eight children are those of my own and my sisters," the woman answered. She straightened up to her feet and reached for Mary's hand saying, "But please, Mistress, do stay a while and talk with me, for I am of weak spirit." She sniffed again.

Goodwife Joslin struggled to rise, as she was heavy with child. Mary took her by the arm. "I will stay but a moment, Sister, to pray with you, but nay, do not trouble yourself to rise. Your child's birth must be near at hand. Sit. Sit you down and let us give comfort to these poor children."

Mary turned to look at the crying children and said, "Hush. Now, hush, children. Has not our Sovereign Lord watched over us all these days? Do not fret yourselves now. Our God will abide in us His promise to return us safe to our homes. This will be but a brief time to remind us all to give praise to His goodness."

Stroking their hair and placing her hands on their shoulders to reassure them of their safety, she walked among the children. She wiped the tears from one child's face with the hem of her apron. The little girl looked up at her with eyes full of fear and hope. Mary smiled and looked away before the child could see her own doubt. She tilted the chin up of one of the oldest and whispered, "You must be quite strong now and help the others to be brave. It will not do to have them falling into despair. Can you do that?" she asked. The little fellow put his shoulders back, stood up tall, and gave her a nod as he wiped his nose on his shirtsleeve.

"Come, now, children. Let us all pray together. Come. Come. Hold one another's hands," she said, shepherding them into a little circle. She led them in the Lord's Prayer and then asked for God's help to remain strong while they waited for their redemption. All but one had stopped crying. The babe near her mother continued to suck in great gasps of air and furrowed her brow as tears etched wet channels down to her dusty chin.

Mary picked up the little girl and sat her on her knee. She sat beside the mother and placed her arm about her shoulder. "Tell me, Dear. When is your time?" she asked.

"I've lost track. In all this mad wandering, I no longer count the days. Though there have been pains, I yearn not to give birth and have thus far held it off. I would that my child be born dead than be dragged through this sufferance."

"Listen, Dear. This is very important. I know that this is a very hard time for you, but it will do you no good to show them your despair."

"A very hard time?" Goodwife Joslin looked at her, shouting and nearly laughing in incredulity. "My husband was killed before mine own eyes. I have been made to walk countless miles while I am starved of food. My child within is tormented in its efforts to be born, and I am desperate not to let that happen. Nay, Sister, this is not a very hard time. There is no relief here save to run away from this place."

A few Indians at nearby households looked up at Ann's outburst. Mary, alarmed by Ann's raised voice, put her finger to her lips saying, "Goodwife, it will do you no good to harbor thoughts of escape. As you have said, this child will soon be born. There is no food out there for you or your children. You will find no way to cross the rivers or find your way home from here."

"I am strong. I will find the way. My child will not be born into this heathen world. I must find the way," Ann answered through gritted teeth.

"Goodwife, I implore you to speak no more of this," Mary said urgently. "It will do you no good. And it will frighten the children. Look at them. They need you, poor motherless whelps that they are." They both scanned the little mob. "No, Sister. You must stay and be strong for them, for you and for your own children. Can you make that promise?"

"I fear not, Mistress," said Ann quietly.

"Then let us look to the Lord for encouragement," Mary said. She pulled her Bible from her pocket and asked, "Will you read with me now?"

Ann looked at the English Bible with such surprise, it seemed as though she had never seen one before. Mary allowed it to fall open in her lap, and together they read from Psalm 27. They were both especially heartened as they read aloud, "Wait on the Lord, be of good courage, and He shall strengthen thine heart, wait, I say, on the Lord."

Waiting for strength and courage was all they could do. Before she left, Mary reassured them that, in His own time, He would raise them up out of bondage and restore them to their kith and kin.

More than anything, she wanted to believe that.

Leaving Menameset
Fourth Remove
February 22, 1675

In the morning, Weetamoo awoke to the sounds of the people dismantling their wetus. Today, they would leave and venture through the snow on the way to meet Metacomet. She lifted her warm fur and slipped on her leggings and moccasins. Thankfully, the white woman had left the wetu. Weetamoo hoped she had already made tea. She would eat lightly. Taking time to pull back her hair and paint her face before she stepped outside, she threw her beaded cape over her head and stood before her mirror. As she did, she could see remnants of many broken-down wetus.

Ordinarily, people left their frames for the next time they might pass this way, but not at the moment when they knew that enemy scouts skulked nearby. To make it difficult for the English and their Indian traitor scouts to use the camp or take advantage of what they might leave behind, they packed all they could and burned the rest. Smouldering shelters littered the campsite. And some warriors had gone back to block the English from following.

"Wuniish, Sachem Weetamoo," Awashonks called. She pulled the reed mats off her wetu frame, rolled them quickly into tight bundles, and placed them in her pack basket.

"Wuniish, Cousin," Weetamoo replied and then asked, "Have you seen the white woman and Laughing Water?"

"Mary has gone to fetch water, Cousin. And Laughing Water has already left with some of the others. With your son on her back and another in her belly, she decided to leave early so she won't lag behind." Awashonks looked up at the low-hanging, grey clouds. "The sky foretells a snowy, wet day. Most are setting out early. It will be a tiresome journey."

Weetamoo grunted and turned to remove the bearskin that covered her wigwam opening. With the knife she always wore in her belt, she quickly cut the sinew fastening the skin. She rolled it loosely and stepped inside where she wrestled it into an ash-wood pack basket taken from under her sleeping platform. She removed the wolf skin from her bed and rolled that into her basket as well. She tucked in her black mink tobacco pouch and pipe, her mirror, and her beaded pouch with her face paints. From under her sleeping platform, she pulled another basket filled with garments and folded them into her pack.

Amid bustling sounds outside, she heard the familiar swishing of Mary's skirt and her clumsy footsteps returning from the river. *The English move about so noisily*, thought Weetamoo. She called out to Mary, "Put the tea water on. Quick. Use the bark pot and bring the leather and clay ones in here to pack. Hurry. Can't you see the people are ready to leave?"

Mary did as she was told. She gathered up a small collection of clay pots, drinking gourds, wooden cooking tools, and Weetamoo's one prized iron stew pot and brought them into the wetu. Weetamoo put them into her own basket. To Mary's, Weetamoo added a meager supply of maize, beans, squash seeds, and dried meat.

"Do not take any of this for yourself, for I will know. This is Quannopinn's, and he must remain strong to fight the English. Take the furs from the sleeping platform and the mat coverings in your basket. We leave soon."

Weetamoo finished filling her own basket with her wampum and jewelry and rolled the inner woven mats into her pack. She rested it on her bed and backed up to it, squatting slightly. She pulled the tumpline over her shoulders and onto her forehead. Standing with grace and ease, she tested the weight of her burden, found it bearable, and set it down again to have her tea.

On the other side of the camp, Quannopinn talked to the last of the warriors gearing up to leave. He had slept somewhere else overnight. Weetamoo wondered if he had thought about what she said. She found it hopeful that he held a full council the day before and included all in the decision to move on immediately. After taking a town like Medfield, they would be sure to have disloyal native trackers looking for them, and the snow today would provide good cover if they moved swiftly.

Weetamoo watched her sannup saying goodbye to his men and loading his own horse to go. He did not look her way before mounting and leaving the camp. So it is, she thought. Weetamoo tossed her empty birch cup into the fire and lifted her pack basket onto her back. She took a stick and set fire to the remains of the wetu and ushered Mary into line with the others.

The camp disappeared bit by bit. Naked, charred bones of wetus stood amid smoke from doused fires and dust from hooves of departing warriors' horses. Nearly all left behind were women, children, and old ones. As if of one mind, the remaining people picked up their loads and walked toward the west just as snow began falling.

The Path to Nichewaug
Ann Joslin's Demise

Mary stooped to hoist her basket and felt the tumpline pull taut against her forehead. The ache in her shoulders and neck surged back with the weight of her load. She would not complain. Her own load was lighter than most, since she was still injured. She had no idea how the Indian women bore so much. She shifted the basket slightly and set off after the others.

The sight and smell of burning wigwams reminded her again of the day she was taken from her home. Fire over her head and behind her, she had faced Indian gunfire to escape with her Sarah. A dry ache wrung a tearless, soundless cry from the back of her throat. *Poor Sarah . . . If only the bullet had run through our two hearts, my babe wouldn't have died in miserable anguish, and I wouldn't be wandering this howling wilderness with a band of heathens.*

Ashamed of her selfish thought, she uttered a prayer for humility in accepting the lot God chose for her. "My dear God, who knows best what is needed for my redemption, grant me the patience and endurance to suffer what you deem best for me. Give me strength to survive and courage to persevere as I declare your righteousness and submit to your will. Blessed be the name of the Lord."

As far as she could see in every direction, only heathens met her eye. She was the lone white women in a tapestry of Indians undulating across the landscape. Each step she took drew her further from her home and her husband and brought her deeper into uncertainty.

Fallen branches from winter's ravages littered the coarse land. Brambles and brush reached up through uneven snow. Stepping into footfalls ahead of her, she frequently crunched through the crumbling crust. She felt pebbles of ice gathering in her shoe about her ankle. She wanted to stop and push the ice crystals away but dared not for fear of being trampled.

Mary noticed the easy stride of a woman beside her and realized it was the woman who shared her meal the previous evening. Mary asked if the leggings she wore prevented ice in her moccasins.

"Nux," replied the woman. "Have you no leggings, Mary?"

"No. Only stockings. They are warm, but they do not keep ice and snow out of my shoes."

The woman nodded. "It is difficult without leggings. You should make some. Ask your master for deerskin."

"Hmm." Mary nodded, unable to imagine Weetamoo allowing her such an extravagance. She would not share a morsel of food with her. Why would she part with a skin? "Perhaps if I made you stockings, you could help me to make leggings," Mary offered. She had benefited from the Medfield spoils, not only in increased food, but also in acquiring wool, cloth, and needles for knitting and sewing.

"Nux," agreed the woman, giggling at the idea. She hummed a rhythmic tune that Mary recognized as a hymn from *The Bay Psalter* that she used often in her worship.

Mary started. "You are Christian?"

"Yes, Mary. I am Rachel, and I am learning Christian ways from my husband, John Printer. We lived in Hassanamesit but came away when Sam Moseley began taking our people to Deer Island. My husband worried for our safety. So my children and I returned to our families in Nipmuc at what you call Mendon. James has long lived among the English, but I have only been among them for the past four years. James did not want to see me or the children harmed."

"How come you to be with this warring band?"

"When Mendon was attacked, James thought it best for us to come away with our families. With troops being called against us and the English fearing us in their midst, we knew we could no longer stay among the Christians." She did not mention that James had already been captured three times and lost his faith in Christian promises or that he had been recently released under the pretense of spying for the English.

"And you sing a Christian hymn here? Amidst the heathens?" Mary asked.

"Nux. I do. Today is the Sabbath."

Mary had nearly forgotten. Only weeks from her world, and she had forgotten the Lord's Day. "Lord, forgive my selfishness," she murmured. "Let us sing." She began a familiar tune, and her companion joined in.

I to the hills lift up mine eyes,
from whence shall come mine aid.
Mine help doth from Jehovah come,
which heav'n and earth hath made.
He will not let thy foot be moved,
nor slumber, that thee keeps.
Lo, he that keepeth Israel,
he slumbreth not, nor sleeps.
The Lord thy keeper is, the Lord
on thy right hand the shade.
The sun by day, nor moon by night,
shall thee by stroke invade.
The Lord will keep thee from all ill:
thy soul he keeps alway,
Thy going out, and thy in come
the Lord keeps now and aye.

The hymn lightened Mary's step and lifted her heart as she moved along among the mass of people. Tears fell down her face to mark her joy in praising the Lord on His day but at the same time exposed her sorrow over her loss and her fear for the future. She glanced over once and saw tears welling in Rachel's eyes as well. Mary couldn't know that Rachel, too, had lost family to this war. After a few psalms, the two women continued on quietly, immersed in their own thoughts.

As they walked, snow fell in thick, wet flakes. Mary's cloak and skirts grew heavier with each step. By mid day, she was soaked through from head to foot. Though warm enough in her wool, she found the weight of her clothes and pack difficult to bear. Wet leather straps rasped against her skin. She lost step with her friend and worried that she could not carry on, yet she willed herself just to keep placing one foot ahead of the other.

When they came to the bank of a river, everyone dropped their loads, and Mary feared they would have to cross it. She thanked God that instead they stopped for the night, even though it meant another night in the wilderness.

Never had she seen a more inhospitable, desolate place. Thick, wet snow covered the ground. This site offered no frames for houses and no established campfires. Nothing but trees and thicket surrounded them and no road led in or out of the wilderness. She dropped her sodden pack and, eager to get inside away from worsening weather, helped others gather sticks to make a shelter.

Though she had looked for her children and other captives during the morning's trek, she had not seen any of her kind. Only heathens wherever she looked. She hoped they might remain in the new encampment long enough to find them again.

✳ ✳ ✳

They remained in the place, which they called Nichewaug, for four days. Men hunted, women foraged, and they all rested and ate what they could find, supplemented in small part with remnants from Medfield. Though great in number, they dispersed widely along the edge of the river and in the woods beyond.

Each day after finishing her chores, Mary tried to find her children and the other captives. She asked any who would speak to her if they had seen them. For three days she had no success finding any of those she sought. On the fourth day, she at last encountered captured settler women who knew of Goodwife Joslin and the children, so Mary inquired about their well-being.

The disheveled women crowded round her, all speaking at once, some of them crying, and all clutching at her as if she would save them from drowning.

"Good sisters," Mary said. "Pray tell me what has happened. Where is Goodwife Joslin?"

One of them wiped her eyes and pushed her hair back under her coif. She took Mary's hand saying, "Oh, Mistress Rowlandson, 'tis dreadful news. Goodwife Joslin has been killed in a most gruesome manner." She erupted into another wave of tears and fell heavily into Mary's arms.

Mary tried to comfort her and led her to a place to sit. Still the woman could not control her sobs. Seeking even one person who might tell her what had occurred, Mary looked from her to the others, but not one of them could stop crying. Though they uttered phrases between their shrieks and wails, Mary could not understand a word.

Mary put on her best minister's wife's face and stood before them saying, "My Sisters, I have no doubt that you have seen great horror, as have we all these last few weeks. I want to comfort you and remind you all that our God is still watching over us, and though He may have placed a great evil in our path, He has only done this to help us in our own path to righteousness. Yea, we must bear this burden with strength and sureness, knowing that it is only through our suffering that we are brought to His side. Now I urge you, dear Sisters, please share your burden with me, that we may pray to God for understanding together."

The seated woman rubbed her face with her apron and rose to her feet. Her eyes still brimming, she said. "You are right, Mistress," and turned to the others saying, "Let us lighten our hearts by sharing this pain and finding comfort in the Lord. I will tell you what we know."

"Goody Joslin, as you know, was in terrible distress when last she saw you, and I am sad to say that she only worsened after you parted. She was unable to refrain from begging them to let her go home. She remained in such a state of grief, wailing all the day and night to be freed.

"After a time, the devils who hold us grew weary of her ceaseless crying, and before we left our last camp, all at once, they fell upon her and stripped her naked. Singing and dancing in a hellish manner, a great many of them gathered about her. And when at last they stopped," the woman drew in copious breath, "they knocked her and her child on their heads and placed them in a fire to be burned." The narrator's head sank down and she twisted her fingers together. She sobbed again, more quietly than before.

Mary tried to keep her face steady, though she had scenes of their evil dance and deeds swirling in her head. That her neighbor and innocent child were dealt with so cruelly raised emotions that she couldn't quell in her breast, and her throat ached to cry out. Fear and anger fought inside her trying to will her into action. She wanted to run from her captors and hide, yet at the same time, she wanted to run at them with her voice raging.

While Mary struggled to contain herself, the woman sniffed and continued, "Dear Mistress, what is most distressing of this all is that the children were made to watch. And after that horrible sight, they were warned by the savages that it would be their own fate as well if they attempted to go home." She stopped again with her mouth drawn tight, biting back more tears. "Oh, that we could unsee these woeful sights and erase our anguish. But yea, though they tormented her and her child, Ann cried not. She only prayed and prayed to God through it all."

Mary's heart burst with pain for Ann and her child. She found little comfort in hearing that Ann had found solace in prayer until the end of her miserable life. *Where is God in all of this?* Mary worried that her own children been made to watch the executions. *Were Joseph and Mary somewhere nearby, cowering with the idea that it might be their fate as well?*

She suppressed the rising thought that she herself may have come close to the same end with her own babe Sarah. A fresh stab of terror struck her breast as she remembered how inconsolable young Mary had been when she last saw her. She felt an urgent need to rejoin her daughter and son and pushed down wave after wave of anxiety about their safety.

Mary vowed to herself in that moment that she would not show weakness before her captors or the goodly women. She pushed aside her desire to rush out and find her children and pretended courage, saying, "Sisters, though our tormentors have visited such atrocities upon us, we must remain strong and find our way back to our families. We cannot let ourselves fall into the same hell that took our sister, Ann, from us." Some murmured in agreement.

"Fall down on your knees with me now and pray for strength and for protection for ourselves and our children. Dear God in Heaven, send Your strength upon my son, Joseph, and my daughter, Mary and the children of all of Your good people who are with us in captivity. Make them to be strong in the sight of their enemies. Let the goodness of Your grace fall upon their hearts and keep them steady. If it is Your will to restore them, let that be at some day near at hand. If it please You to show mercy on our penitent souls in this request, we will give You glory all the days of our lives, as well we know we should. Accept into Your kingdom of heaven Goodwife Joslin and her child. May You forgive them and us for any failures to praise You and trust in Your goodness always. In Christ's name. Amen."

"Amen," they all uttered, some echoing Mary's resolve, others mutely mouthing the familiar word.

Mary rose from the cold, wet ground and looked at the women clustered before her in the wide camp of heathens all around them. Amidst all of them, she felt very alone. She told herself that only with the help of God would she survive. Yet something inside her said that repentance and begging for God's help might not be enough.

Flight Again
Fifth Remove
February 26, 1675

As she walked away from an early morning council fire, Awashonks called out to Weetamoo. "Wait up, Little Bird. I'm an old tired woman."

Weetamoo did not wait. She walked to her cook fire and knelt on a woven mat and set to grinding corn for the next day's travel.

Weetamoo banged her grinding stone against the hard kernels in the hollowed-out rock. The muscles in her arms tightened as she worked to crush the dried corn with repeated blows.

As Awashonks neared Weetamoo, she said, "The men are wise in this, Weetamoo. The warriors are tired and few and hungry. We need to join Philip's forces before we strike again." The grey-haired woman grunted with effort as she folded her knees and lowered her heavy body to the ground to join Weetamoo in grinding corn.

"So you, too, think we should run and hide like scared rabbits?" Weetamoo snapped, looking bitterly into her eyes.

She didn't wait for her answer. She focused back on her work and said, "No, Awashonks, I cannot agree. We should stay and send the scouts to Philip to bring his men and food. All this travel has been a heavy burden. Every day we bury another child or elder. The wisdom of my grandfather tells me that the English, too, have not had enough to eat. We can stop the men who supply them. They are such fools, always walking known paths by daylight and gathered together like a flock of turkeys. It would be easy for us to ambush such fools."

Awashonks used both hands to roll her grinding stone over the corn on the worn flat stone in front of her. She kept her neck, shoulders, and arms relaxed as she worked. She allowed the weight of her body and the stones work for her.

"Easy for a few, yes," Ashawonks replied, "but they always send more men, Weetamoo. As old Passaconaway said, 'They number as many as the leaves in the forest.'

"It is wise to listen to the warriors' plan to strike the English hard and in many places at one time," Ashawonks continued. "We need time to find food and seed corn for the people. If you and I take our people to a camp that we can hold against the English, we can raise corn before winter comes again." As she spoke, her hands swept the ground corn into a leather traveling pouch.

"For Quannopinn's honor, I have agreed, Awashonks," replied Weetamoo, "but I think we will wish we had not done this. The snowfall makes our way even harder. The English can sit warm in their garrisons eating our food and waiting for more help to come. They grow stronger as we grow weaker. They make their own each country that we leave behind."

She looked up from her work and said, "Hear me, Awashonks. We will regret this decision. I have spoken."

By those words, Weetamoo let Awashonks know that the conversation had ended. She could not admit to herself that the men might be right. She didn't know what lay in the path ahead, so she had agreed that Philip's camp with their neighbors to the north would be safer for the women and children. She, too, had grown weary of travel, and she feared for the health of her people. And she had grown tired of trying to convince others to make a stand and attack in great force.

She could only hope that all of them had chosen the right path.

Weetamoo scooped cornmeal into her leather pouch and rose to start packing for the next days' travel. She looked for help from Mary Rowlandson, but as usual, the white woman had disappeared. The stupid settler woman constantly wandered off or sought excuses to avoid her work: reading her bible or looking for her children or begging others to give her a meal. She was more trouble than she was worth. "She had better fetch a good price," Weetamoo snapped.

The sachem stuffed the few supplies they had used the evening before and during the morning into pack baskets made heavier with food and stores taken from Medfield. With her gleaming knife, she cut a lambskin down from the frame where she had stretched it the day before. She had not had time to finish softening it. The skin would be less supple without soaking it in water mixed with brains, but Weetamoo could not help it. She would work it further at the next camp. She rolled it into her pack.

Looking up, she saw Quannopinn heading her way. His progress slowed as each family stopped him to ask questions or thank him for recent provisions from Medfield.

Weetamoo had to admit that she admired her new husband. Not only was he handsome and strong, but like her, he had no fear of the English. He had already shown his defiance to the colonists, and when jailed for his actions, he had escaped. She knew he would not betray her or the people as her husband Petananuit had done. Quannopinn honored the ways of his people and had not been poisoned like the Praying Indians by white man's lies. Despite their recent quarrel, she felt a wave of pride at the sight of her sannup. They had reached a tacit agreement about their current strategy.

"Come, Weetamoo," Quannopinn called. Let us ride with Monaco for a hunt. He will tell us of the raid on Medfield. Leave that chore to Mary."

Weetamoo lifted her basket onto her back and positioned the tumpline comfortably on her forehead. She would not let him see her disappointment in the decision made at council. Showing her anger to her dear cousin Awashonks could be accepted, but she must not let it again come between her and Quannopinn. Although he, like her, favored making a stand immediately, he had acquiesced to the wishes of the weary people.

She took her husband's hand and walked quietly with him to where the leaders conversed with their chief men. Laughing and clapping his back as he passed, Quannopinn spoke briefly to one of them, asking him to lead some of the bands to the next encampment. As usual after any raid, everyone would spread out to avoid being followed by the English They would keep to smaller trails in swampier places to make it difficult for enemy scouts to find them.

At least their travel the next day would be easier with the horses they gained from the Medfield fight. Weetamoo swung her bare leg over the back of her new horse, a bay mare. The sleek, dark animal whinnied and shied and backed up a few steps, but Weetamoo firmly and quickly calmed her.

"Quiet, Sister," Weetamoo told the mare. "It is your work to carry me for this day. I thank you for you help."

The horse tossed her head and nickered and then allowed Weetamoo to direct her with subtle leg movements. From a young age, Weetamoo learned to watch an animal closely to understand it better and allow it to understand her. Her quiet assurance around animals made them listen and follow her lead. In moments, she and Quannopinn rode out with Monaco between them.

"I will tell you how it was at Medfield," said Monaco. The big, one-eyed man loved to brag about his victories. Weetamoo settled into a comfortable position and let the horse's motion drain away her tension.

"As we thought," Monaco began, "it was no trouble to creep close to the houses with woodland leading right up to their doors. We reached the town before dawn and spread ourselves throughout the village. We took hiding places in their barns and sheds. Just before sunrise while most of the lazy English were still in their beds, one farmer came out to milk his cow. I had burrowed under a pile of hay in his barn. How was I to know that he would choose that pile to feed his cow that day?"

He laughed, and so did Weetamoo and Quannopinn.

"I pulled in my foot quickly when he turned around but felt sure he saw me, because he kicked over a pail and ran back to his house. I whistled a signal, and we began setting fire to their barns and houses before he could wake the others. We easily surrounded them and burned most of their houses."

"Didn't they have any guards posted?" Weetamoo asked.

"No, Weetamoo, I saw none! And if any others did," Monaco answered, making a chopping motion across his throat, "we silenced them."

"So they did not all hide in their garrisons?" she asked.

"Many fled from their houses to the garrisons," he replied, "but we killed all we saw. We counted coup on twenty-three men altogether. And the rest you know. We came away with the livestock and provisions." Weetamoo was well acquainted with counting coup as part of the warrior tradition. Enemy dead must be struck by each warrior to insure they cannot enter the spirit world whole, thus insuring that the warriors would not have to fight the same enemies again.

"You were fortunate that they did not follow after you," Quannopinn said.

"Fortune had nothing to do with it," Monaco snorted, "We burned both their bridges, so they couldn't follow."

"Nux, that was wise," Quannopinn said. "I heard you left a message there. What was that?"

"Nux, yes. James Printer left a note on the bridge. He wrote, 'Know by this paper that the Indian that thou has provoked to wrath and anger will war this twenty-one years, if you will. There are many Indians yet. We come three hundred this time. You must consider that the Indians lose nothing but their life. You must lose your fair houses and cattle.' It was a good fight."

"Yes, Monaco, you fought well, and so did your kinsmen. I only wish the council had agreed to keep up the fight," Quannopinn complained.

"And I," said Weetamoo. "We have strength and food now. I know we could destroy more towns while we wait for Metacomet."

"Nux, you are right, Weetamoo. We should keep up our efforts, and I am angered that some among us would run. I say we must continue to surprise the settlers as we have done in Medfield. Attack them before they can take shelter in their garrisons. Once inside those fortified houses, they can defend themselves too easily from many sides. Only fire will get them out."

"Agreed, and by slipping into their villages at night and burning their houses and barns all at once, just as you did, we have a strong chance of killing their warriors before they can arm themselves or call in help," Quannopinn said.

"And we make their villages uninhabitable," Weetamoo said. "As at Mendon and Lancaster, they have no choice but to abandon the burned-out towns."

"Taubut, this was a good plan. To let them gather in their garrisons is no good for us. You are right that once they are in position there, we have little we can do but stay out of range of their guns and contrive ways to burn or starve them out," Quannopinn commented.

"Nux, Quannopinn. Haven't we learned at Brookfield that a siege is of no use to us? In only four days, other militia came to their aid, and rainfall thwarted our efforts to set fires. No, we should undertake no more sieges of garrisons. Ambush and surprise are the only way," Monaco stated firmly.

Weetamoo thought about it. "It is frustrating that some of the others choose to wait. Are we now outnumbered by the Christian Indians? And can we trust their loyalty to us? Perhaps it is they who have swayed the people to withdraw from fighting.

"As Awashonks said," Weetamoo continued, "we should strike the settlers in many places at the same time. There is wisdom in it. If together we all strike at once, they cannot send men from other towns to fight—not when they are too busy defending their own homes. I do not like to wait, but it is the decision of the council."

Amused by her unusual less than fiery facade, Quannopinn smiled at his wife. "That is so. Once we join with Metacomet, we may number enough to do just that. And Metacomet, I have no doubt, can convince the others that this is a good plan."

Monaco grunted in agreement. "Yes, Metacomet will be ready for this fight. And they will listen to him. We won't have so many cowards and praying fools to outnumber us in his camp. And by now, he should have raised arms from Albany and maybe even convinced the Mohawks to join us. He'll have no trouble convincing the rest to finish this. Once we join forces with Metacomet, we are sure to succeed in driving the English out."

Relishing the idea of driving the English into the sea, Weetamoo rode on in silence.

Across the Baquoag
Sixth Remove
February 27, 1675

Mary thought they might stay longer at the new camp to rest after their long trek, but in the early hours of the morning, scouts rode into camp shouting something unintelligible, and it was as if the world had come undone. She watched Quannopinn and her captors, many who looked like armed savages as they mounted horses, some two to a beast, and rode out in several directions, while the others tore apart the camp and set fire to it.

"Go, Mary," Weetamoo shoved her toward their wetu. "Take your pack basket. Leave everything else. We leave now."

Mary rushed inside, grabbed her pack while taking time to put her Bible in. She added a fur to cover it before leaving. She had never unpacked her few personal belongings, so she had only to light the shelter afire. She made sure Weetamoo had her pack first and took note that Laughing Water had collected her pack and Weetamoo's papoose. Using a stick from the cook fire, Mary set it against the woven mats she had been made to carry for so many days and watched the dried rushes burst into sizzling flames. Though covered in wet snow, the very dry hollow reeds produced a raging blaze that hissed and whistled as it consumed what had been her shelter in Nichewaug.

It gave her pleasure to burn down the hovel, and she hoped the reason they could do without all meant that her redemption would happen very soon, perhaps just across the river. Or perhaps they rushed to leave because her redeemers pursued them from behind. The possibility gave her a moment's pause. Should she dawdle to see if she might be rescued or should she keep pace with the others stretching themselves into long lines moving quickly downriver? She had no time to consider options as Weetamoo grabbed her and pushed her into the long queue of departing heathens.

She noticed that many carried papooses or aging mothers or helped those who could not walk unaided. Four were carrying one wounded man on a litter, and yet they moved swiftly, as if they were being chased by the devil himself. They marched on without rest through thicket and wood, sometimes lifting the injured man on their backs until they came to a clearing by the riverbank.

As they all poured into the glade, no one said a word. As if by instinct, the native women and men worked at taking down trees and lashing them together for the river crossing. Mary watched in wonder as the forest around her transformed into transportation, though she doubted that it would be possible to move so many across the swift flowing current on such crude devices. With great haste, the workers built makeshift rafts and dragged them to the river bank. Even as that happened around her, Mary turned and saw the first of the rafts loaded and pushed out into the frigid water. The industrious way they all seemed to know what to do stunned Mary.

"Now! Get on the raft!" Weetamoo barked at her, shoving her towards the next raft waiting at the shore. Dreading that she would soak her footwear already in tatters from all her travel, Mary stepped aboard. Her once lovely boots had carrieid her to church services and tea dances. After her travails, scuffs and tears marred them and her stockings showed where they had worn right through. Would she never see the likes of them again?

Others pushed Mary to the front of the craft. She sat on her baggage and marveled that her feet stayed dry the whole way across the river in spite of the furious current. Everyone alighted on the opposite side, and others shoved and pulled her up the embankment just moments before the raft took off again for more passengers.

Just then, shots sounded in the distance, and Mary had to wonder at the meaning. *Will today be my last day with the heathen band? Will*

Captain Moseley or Captain Church come riding in to rescue me while leading my captors away in chains? Oh, please God, let this be so.

More shots rang out but further in the distance.

Could the rescuers be retreating? she wondered. *Surely, they can find us with the smoke billowing from the ruined camp on the other side of the river. How could all the heathen women and children, old and wounded alike. make such a hasty crossing, and how could so few warriors frighten off seasoned soldiers? What trickery is in a God who makes hearty men fear to go where weak and starving, half-clothed women could? Are not our Massachusetts men strong enough and wise enough to manage to cross a river such as this? Do they not care so much for us that they would turn back when we are so near at hand? Where is my God in this? Why have even You forsaken me in this wilderness?*

She looked up and down the river and saw no sign of colonial men, only many more rafts bearing across hundreds of Indians and their goods. First, mainly women and children, several with papooses. Then the elderly and wounded. Last of all, the warriors.

The crossing took the rest of the afternoon and continued on into the night. Mary was astonished by the number in their company and tried to count them but couldn't as they were always in motion.

In the evening, many warriors returned, some taking rafts and others just riding into the water on their horses. By the next evening, all had crossed. They had left a good deal behind, and Mary felt troubled that once again they had no food. She knew she had some stores in her bag and took them to Weetamoo.

"Mistress Weetamoo, would you like for me to make us a dinner with these?" she asked, still hoping that they camped very close to civilization at the other side of this forest.

"No, Mary. These are our reserves."

"But, surely, we could have but a mouthful, after all our long journey?"

"No! Do not ask again." Weetamoo stared at her as if she were a headmaster ready with a cane.

Fuming over Weetamoo's stinginess with her food, Mary turned away and put the provisions back in her pack. She walked toward the river in hopes of finding some dried berries or ground nuts before others did. Mary found the area already depleted by other foragers. She went to bed with a gnawing hunger and only water from the river to soothe it.

Baquoag

Weetamoo and Quannopinn had no success in their recent hunt, no doubt due to the sheer number of others seeking quarry. They had gleaned all they could from their surroundings and needed to feed their people. They lay in their bed speaking low while Mary, Laughing Water, and the baby slept in the rough shelter they'd made earlier that day.

"We're agreed then. We will eat the horses," she said.

"Nux, it must be so," he answered. She could see his disappointment as he leaned back and looked at the roof. Starlight and moonlight winked between the layers of evergreen above. The crystal clear night brought dry cold in the season known to her people as the time of popping trees. Listening quietly, she heard the creaking and snapping of birch and pine boughs so frozen they could not bend with the wind. Tomorrow would be frigid, a good day for stewing the horse meat.

"Good. We will not need them anyway, as we do not have far to go and must cross the Ashuelot and the Kwinitekw. The horses would only slow us down. Besides, Metacom will have supplies from his talks with the Mohawks at Hoosic. They will have more than just our corn and peas when they arrive."

"It is so. Tell me, Wife, are you well enough to travel with our little son inside you?" He reached over and rubbed her stomach. The mound of their future son grew riper, though not as quickly as Petananuit's son had grown. Perhaps another girl this time. It had been sixteen summers since Laughing Water's birth. And she would soon have a child of her own. Weetamoo hoped to find her a husband when they reached Coasset.

"I am well," she patted his cheek. "Do not worry. You will have a strong son."

She rolled over and regarded her papoose in his basket. His face had reddened. She touched his forehead and found it warm. She loosened his covers slightly. She closed her eyes and asked the ancestors to keep watch over both her sons and her daughter. *Help me guide them in the ways of our people and keep them strong.* She lay awake for a long time thinking about her children and what the future might hold for all of them.

✳ ✳ ✳

The next day, the warriors slaughtered all the horses taken on their raids and divided them among the people. With over three hundred to feed, each hearth received sustenance enough for a meal or two. Weetamoo boiled a leg for her family, and all shared in the broth. Mary used a forked stick to tear a bit of meat free, but Weetamoo pulled her hand away and told her to wait until they boiled it again. The sachem knew she must drain every bit of possible nutrient from it before sharing out the meat. Mary, who had never wanted for food in her prior life, did not understand the concept of limited provisions nor the fact that filling herself on broth equal to a small portion of meat would effectively curb hunger. Ordinarily the Wampanoags would dry any meat left over, but with so many hungry travelers, not a morsel remained.

Weetamoo settled down after their meal and worked on her wampum beads. She and her household had collected and carried along many shells. She polished beads by rolling them on a stone, then bore a hole though the many white and less bountiful purple beads. The work took time and patience as she manipulated a boring tool rolled between her hands or sometimes a small bow and string. She had no time to make tools and so worked by hand.

Mary entered the makeshift shelter and settled on her sleeping mat. She searched in her pack for her Bible, drew it out, and thumbed the pages. The sight of it disgusted Weetamoo. "Mary, put that aside, for you have work to do. I need a pair of stockings, and you have not worked on them in days. Others also need your work, so you should not waste your time in reading."

"Today is the Sabbath," Mary responded. "We cannot work on the Sabbath as I said to you before. I will work all the more on your stockings tomorrow." She lowered her eyes to her book but did not rest comfortably on her bed. She looked ready to spring out the door.

"There is no Sabbath here," Weetamoo answered. "You have no special privileges. Work is work and must be done everyday. By all. Put that away."

"Nay. If it troubles you, I will go outside and not be in your way. But I must keep holy the Sabbath."

"Enough of that talk. You will work or I will strike you and erase that look of pride from your face. Put it down. Now."

Mary was about to object, but Quannopinn stepped over, reached down, closed her Bible, and put it back in her basket. Glaring at her as if he might do her harm, he sat back down without a word. Mary did not dare take the Bible back. Instead, she took up her knitting and faced away from the two of them.

By the bobbing of her head, Weetamoo knew Mary made prayers to her God, Jehovah. *Let her pray,* thought Weetamoo. *It will do no harm, nor will it do any good. At least she is working.*

Mary's Descent into Exile
Seventh Remove
February 28, 1675

The next day, a scout roused the campers when he shouted that the English troops approached. Although still on the other side of the river, the Indians knew it would do no good to let the enemy gain any ground. With no breakfast nor even tea, they tore down, fired their camp, and set off.

They passed through a swampy place, and it became harder to stay in one another's tracks. Mary tried to find high spots to set her foot on but sometimes slipped and fell through into icy water. She thanked God that her wool stockings did not soak through. She secretly felt glad she had not yet finished Weetamoo's stockings.

The Indians took a turn and picked their way through a frozen swamp over a beaver dam. Clawing roots and branches threatened to catch her foot and send her sprawling, but she felt pride in her improving ability to traverse such difficult terrain. Her wound had healed well thanks to the oak leaf remedy Mr. Pepper had recommended. She had grown stronger despite her hunger. She found herself adapting to the native ways. As Mary emerged from the swamp, the sight of a rising mountain ahead deflated her momentary pride. She saw the mass of moving savages creeping up its side like locusts over a field. Chastened, she realized that so closely did God attend to her needs that He saw her pridefulness and took it from her in that very moment.

Reaching the hillside at mid day, the party that included Mary stopped for a meal before climbing over the mountain. Another meal of peas and ground nuts, it barely whetted her appetite. Although they had all feasted on horse meat the previous night, they had had not enough livestock nor time to have saved anything, so they would find themselves foraging once again.

Before she ate, Mary offered a prayer. "Thank you, God, for this sustenance and for your wisdom to choose that which will sustain my body as well as my spirit. Forgive me for such little thought as I have given before to the food you provided. Never have I worried about running out of food or eaten any food that did not agree with my taste. In God's great wisdom, You chose to make me aware of my wastefulness and self-indulgence, caring not for who might have little or none." After her prayer of thanksgiving, she shared her food with Rachel, the Christian Indian who had walked beside her. In return the woman offered Mary some of her nokechick and a bit of deer meat. Mary felt refreshed by variety and kindness.

"You are a true Christian," Mary said. "I am grateful for your kindness and your friendship."

"You are a good woman, Mary," the Indian woman replied. "I can see your strength, and it is good to be your friend. Netop."

"Netop," Mary replied, smiling.

Crying excitedly and pointing at her brother, a little Indian girl scrambled into Rachel's lap. Her plaintive voice sounded like Sarah's when Joseph teased her. Mary turned away to hide her tears that suddenly welled up.

Mary listened as Rachel explained to her son how Weetucks taught the people to give to each other, not to take. She reminded her son of Matahou, the jealous brother and doubts he had about the goodness of the Creator. The story reminded Mary of Cain and Abel. Unlike Cain, however, the Indian boy repented and then shared with his sister, even giving her an affectionate pat on the cheek.

Her thankfulness to God faded after watching the family that lived in two worlds, half-heathen, half-Christian. Mary picked up her burden and started off toward the hillside. Her tears fell freely as she made her way up the incline. Heedless of branches scratching her legs and ice filling her shoes, she tramped on.

Why were my children and I being punished? Sarah killed. Joseph and Mary lost to me. Why did God provoke the settlers with the heathen rage? What have I done to evoke God's wrath?

Her stride lengthened as anger replaced her sadness. She knew herself as a dutiful mother, an honest Christian, a model minister's wife. She had filled all her roles with no complaints. She had entertained even the most difficult of guests with charity and kindness. Even in her captivity, she tried to set a good example with other captives despite her own fear and doubt. Yet, God had forsaken her.

She examined herself for fault and thought about her husband's sermons. He said that God's anger with their ways caused the war. He preached the need to praise and glorify His name and the need to humble oneself and submit to His infinite wisdom. She heard Reverend Rowlandson's voice ringing from the pulpit, "When challenges face good men, they have been chosen to learn a special lesson." The sound of his voice and his words comforted her. She had to remember that God chose her burden for her. She had been chosen to hear God, and in His great mercy, He would deliver her when her lesson completed.

She trudged on.

Breathless from her efforts, Mary eventually neared the crest of the hill. Resting her bundle on a rock, she climbed the last rise to see what lay ahead. At the summit, Mary's heart fell at the vista spread below. She saw nothing but trees covering the hills that spread far into the distance. *What is this vast wilderness? With so much land, why were the Indians so murderously attacking the small English settlements?* She sunk to the ground, sitting on a windblown granite slab.

As she rested, she murmured a new prayer to the Lord. "Make steady my feet on the path to righteousness."

She looked at the tangled mass of trees below and wondered who would ever find her. *How could the commissioners send someone to this place?*

No. My only hope of restoration rests with Philip and his desire for guns. She vowed to petition him to trade her for guns at Albany, for surely, she supposed, they were destined to make their way on foot to Albany. *The Indians could trade me for guns to the vile papist French. And they will ransom me to the English for money.* She had heard that the French had resorted to human traffic for wealth after draining inland streams of animal pelts. *I have no use for French religious practices if traded in Albany, but at least I would be among civilized people.*

A ribbon of river threaded far below. Mary thought that, after they crossed it, they would meet Philip. Relieved to think they were nearing their destination, she unknowingly began her deepening descent into exile.

Weetamoo Walks with the Grandfathers

Weetamoo walked with Awashonks, the sunk squaw sachem, or old queen, of the Sakonnet people. In spite of her age, Awashonks walked quickly. Weetamoo took longer steps to keep pace with her.

"Weetamoo, you are wrong to suspect all white men. There are some good men among them. There are some who are not good. Think of Captain Benjamin Church. Has he not kept his good word with our people?"

"Awashonks, how can you say that? Did you not see him at the village of Canonchet? He was there that day. I saw him. When they fired our wetus with us still inside them, he cared not for the women and children and elders there. Those who fled the flames, he greeted with his gun. How can you think him a friend?" She looked up at her older cousin.

"Weetamoo, as with our people, sometimes leaders heed not the voice of good men among them. I saw him there, too, and I heard him arguing with the captains as he urged them not to fire our village. He argued for our lives and, failing that, he begged them to preserve our lodges and our food. They would not listen to him."

Awashonks stepped lightly over a fallen birch.

"No. I cannot find honor in those ways. They do not fight like men. They offer peace in one hand and death in the other. I made treaties and still they threatened my people and used my cousin's help to us as a reason to break their word with us both. No, Awashonks. They are no good. You can never trust a white man's word."

"You are young, Weetamoo. In time you will grow to see many men and many promises. Men's hearts will change, but good men will befriend you, and you will see what I see in Captain Church."

"I have seen all of Captain Church that I need to until I see his head on a pole. It would please me to take it myself." Weetamoo spat in disgust.

"I see I cannot change your heart. We will see if time will change it. I am tired. I will rest here. You can go on. I will rejoin you when I am refreshed," Awashonks said.

"As you wish, Cousin." Weetamoo did not change the sunk squaw's heart.

Awashonks felt more weary from Weetamoo's contentious company than she did from walking. She welcomed time away from the young sachem's angry words.

So young and so hot-headed, Awashonks thought, *like so many of the tribe today.* As she set her basket down and settled on an outcropping of stone, she wondered at how things might have differed if the young people listened more to the elders.

Unwilling to admit she also wanted to rest, Weetamoo walked away. She climbed up the rise to rest at the top. She could not bear to hear Awashonks defend the treacherous white men. Her anger started to give way to her pain. She had lost two good husbands to the English, one to poison and one to disease. She had been betrayed by another husband, Petananuit, who had led the white men to Canonchet's village, so long hidden in the Great Swamp. And now she feared that her voice did not command the power it once did at tribal council and that Quannopinn sometimes believed he could speak for her. She felt her own power draining from her with each new marriage.

Quannopinn was now her husband, but only because she and Metacomet thought it a wise alliance. Rightfully, she should be Metacomet's wife, but as the older sister, she wed Wamsutta, the elder son of Massasoit, not Philip, who attracted her more. She liked Philip's courage, humor, and most of all, his defiance of the

English. Their fathers, Caunbitant and Massasoit, chose her younger sister Wootonekanuske as Metacomet's wife. The two marriages doubly strengthened the bond between the Pocassets and the Pokanokets, and fixed the position of both families as leaders of all the Wampanoag people. A wise choice, but after Wamsutta's death she felt her power slipping away. Quannopinn's inexperience led to hasty decisions, without deep consideration of a true leader. And she had lost so many in the great fight, her complement of warriors had greatly diminished. She wanted her power back.

Still, she knew that when she reunited with the other tribes, Metacomet would listen. With him, she would stand strong and always say the words held in her heart. She and Metacomet agreed that they must push white men back into the sea from whence they came.

He agreed with her belief that the old Spirit of Matahou had found white people and turned their minds away from Creation. The colonists pulsed with a desire to possess all and left no way for others to live in peace.

She looked out over the valley before her. The caravan neared Kwinitekw River, and she hoped to join forces there with Pocumtucs and Wampanoags. She could see trails below that followed the river and clearings in the distance that marked camps along the way. *This country is so beautiful,* she thought. She thanked the Great Spirit for refuge from white men's guns and fires. The valley below, she felt sure, still looked as it must have during the time of the grandfathers.

She remembered summers as a little girl in her home country. At the Feast of the Green Corn, the people gathered from all the Algonquin nation. Dancing and feasting lasted for days. She ate shellfish and corn until she could eat no more. Her grandfather told her stories of her people, and she begged to hear more. He made her laugh when he told stories of him and his brother as young braves just learning the ways of men. He taught her to be a warrior, for she had no brother, and he told her she would grow to be a great sachem one day. She heard his voice in the place where she stood on the mountain.

"Listen, little one," she heard him say. "In the rustle of the leaves, you can hear the grandfathers' whispers. In the river, you can hear their laughter. In the sky, you can see and hear their anger and their joy. Listen with your heart, and they will always help you as you grow to lead your people.

"A day will come when there will be great change," he told her. "You will live to see that change. Be strong and trust in the Creator to guide you on the path to beauty. It will come, but not without great struggle. Help your brothers and sisters.

"We will meet in the spirit world in great joy."

Then he was gone.

The vision reassured Weetamoo that her grandfather wanted her to fight with Metacomet and other sachems against white people. She believed that her grandfather's message meant her people would emerge victorious.

She would share her vision at council.

She lifted up her pack basket and pulled her tumpline up to her forehead. Then, she began her descent into the valley of the grandfathers.

Squakeag

As she walked down the big hill, Mary saw a pasture that looked as if it had been grazed by English cattle. It was neatly cleared and fenced and had a road leading to it—a proper English cart road, still showing ruts beneath the snow. *Have we at last come to civilization? Could Albany be close by? Will it be tonight that I will lie down on a soft bed under a sturdy wooden roof?*

She had never ventured so far in all her life so had no idea of the distances she traveled or the geography of the places she went through. Few white men had ventured as far. Mary did not know the Pocumtuc people lived nearby but she sensed that she drew ever closer to the Mohawks in the west where she might be traded for weapons. In the same place, beside the Connecticut River, settlers had taken advantage of fertile, alluvial plains that had long been used to grow native crops. With few trees to clear and fewer rocks than in most places, the terrain offered a place to build frontier towns. They approached the northernmost settlement of Northfield, Squakeag to her captors.

Before long, the travelers passed a field of frozen wheat. The women dropped their loads to harvest and thresh it until there was not a grain standing. Mary joined a group in a nearby cornfield and gathered in two ears of maize. Some found ground nuts as well. Mary looked forward to a good meal that evening.

Once they made their camp, they all got to work preparing and cooking what they had gleaned. Mary started a fire and set her pot to boil. When she looked up, an Indian walked by carrying a bloody piece of horse liver. Mary jumped up and stopped him. "Oh, Good Sir, would you not share some of that meat?"

He laughed at her, saying, "What? You would eat this? Could you eat it?"

"If you were to give me some of it, I would surely try."

Still laughing, he cut a piece for her. She thought to offer him some of her corn, but when she reached into her basket, there was only one ear, not two. She left her hand in the basket cradling her precious food. She took the bit of liver with her other hand. "Thank you, Kind Sir. I will remember this kindness."

Mary laid the meat to cook on the coals, then added her one ear of corn to the pot, thinking to mash it with the meat. But before the meat had even seared, Weetamoo pulled it from the coals and cut it into four pieces. Mary snatched back her share and stuffed it all into her mouth, not taking a chance to lose that little bit. Blood colored her fingers and ran down her chin, but she thought she had never tasted anything so splendid. Although she would never have dreamed of eating such a thing nearly raw in the past, her hunger made it as good as any roast she had ever tasted. Weetamoo looked at her with a wrinkled forehead but said nothing. Mary had a good idea that Weetamoo probably had taken her other ear of corn. *Jealous witch,* she thought.

In spite of her unwillingness to share her own food, Mary made her way around the camp where others cooked up the mess of wheat they had gathered and found several who shared that with her. In time, she returned to Weetamoo's campsite with a full stomach.

Mary sat before the fire and thought about her day. She wondered where she had found the strength to carry on. Never in her life had she imagined she could travel so far with so little to sustain or comfort her. *No feather bedclothes or soft pillow. No warm, strong house with lamps or candles burning before a welcoming hearth. No larder with ample supply of meat, vegetables, and seasoning. And surely no milk or sugar or proper tea. What I would not give for a steaming cup of Asian tea. Would my mother ever have dreamed back in England that her little girl would one day climb over mountains and rivers and live among heathens in a wilderness? Nay, I myself would not have believed it.*

190

That she had managed with so little surprised her. She told herself that she endured the ordeal better than most. *Certainly better than Ann Joslin, God rest her soul.* Some of the heathen ways began to seem ordinary to her. She had a good sense of what might provoke them and avoided it as much as she could. And she knew how to seek out what she needed.

Although in captivity, she could not help but see that no one physically restrained her from coming and going as long as she met Weetamoo's needs before her own. And so far, she had only met with kindness from the others. *Yes,* she thought. *I will survive this. God has made me strong and shown me all that I must do to survive.*

As she watched the flames, she felt something stir in her that she could not describe. Not pride in what she had been able to endure and not satisfaction that she had met a great challenge. It was something else. Something deeper. She felt power kindled from a glowing ember, something always in her but that had never before felt the breath of life.

Her sense of value had always depended on someone else. Her importance related not to her own accomplishments but to those of others. She was her father's daughter. A wealthy barrister, he gave her prominence in her community. She had been matched to Joseph, whose good name and honorable calling invoked prestige, although he did not have wealth. As the minister's wife, Mary became the most important woman in Lancaster. Even when she had children, her worth came from being a good mother. Daughter, wife, mother. She had taken pride in performing all those roles well. Yet, she had never had recognition for anything she did on her own. In truth, she had never done any great thing on her own. Alone for the first time in her life, only she took responsibility for her actions whether she ate or drank, slept or wakened, lived or died. It was all up to her and her alone. And she was surviving.

Mary sat looking at the fire. For the first time in a long while, she felt at peace.

Change in Plans

Seconet ran into camp, breathless. "News from Metacomet," he huffed.

Weetamoo stood beside him, waiting for him to catch his breath. "No help from the Mohawks. United Colonies marching to support Massachusetts Bay," he blurted.

Weetamoo dropped to the ground. "Sit, sit. Tell me the rest." The news stunned her, and she needed more detail to take it all in.

"Connecticut agreed to send Mohawks and soldiers to support the fight. They already march to Boston and may already be there. Metacomet says go north. He will meet you at Coasset."

Weetamoo grew ashen as her courage faded from her face. *What is this? Since when do our neighbors the Mohawks rise against us. That demon Winslow must have filled them, too, with lies. The colonists would use our neighbors once again against us, as they had against the Pequots and the Narragansetts.* The news devastated her.

Quannopinn, standing at the other side of the camp, saw her fall and rushed to her side, "Are you alright? Is it the baby?" He hadn't even noticed Seconet until after he helped her to her feet.

"What did you tell her?" he asked the messenger. "Why did you not wait for me? What is it? What news?"

Seconet started to speak, but Weetamoo put up her hand. She said steadily, "Quannopinn, Seconet is my trusted scout. It is proper for him to share his news first with me. And now he will share it with the council. So go and gather them." She seethed at the idea that he treated her as a submissive, weak woman.

Quannopinn looked at her as if to say, "I am not your child to order about." But he said nothing. He waved Seconet away and looked as if he might speak. Instead, he walked away.

What is wrong with me? she wondered. *Why does he anger me so? Clearly, he has my welfare in mind—or at least his unborn son's. How am I to continue as a sachem and a wife? I've never had this issue with any of my other husbands. Why now does Quannopinn cause me such frustration?*

"Awashonks," she called out. Gather the sachems and sagamores. We have news from Metacom."

Her cousin took no time in ushering the leaders to the council fire where they all heard firsthand what Seconet had told her. Metacomet learned from their allies within the Mohawk tribe that the Connecticut governor had agreed to gather one thousand recruits, from their people and Connecticut settlers, to fight against Metacom and Weetamoo. Some Mohawks already marched from Connecticut. The battle between the Massachusetts Bay Colony and the Wampanoags and their allies had spread west and south. Seconet bore worse news. Metacomet had been told that the Mohawks would not take captives in trade and would not offer safe travel to any of the French settlements within Mohawk borders. Now that Winslow had engaged the Connecticut men, Weetamoo's people had nowhere to go except north. Her people must face a very hard decision.

"There is no choice," Monaco said. "We will go north. And we will have to gather support from the Sokoki and the Wabanaki— even the Micmacs if we have to."

Wonalancet spoke softly. "I know not if my father will do this thing. I have told you before he wants only to fight with spirit power, not guns."

"No matter what path we will take in time, we will go north at once. There we will decide with our friends what is best." Weetamoo plainly made her statement. "There is nothing at the moment for us to debate. We go north, and then we decide."

Quannopinn stood and added, "On this we are agreed. Using scouts at our back to hinder the English, we will continue north, and we will make our way to Coasset."

Weetamoo felt a twinge of annoyance as Quannopinn restated the obvious. *Does he really feel as if he always has to be above me? As if my word is not enough? Or is it just that at last we stand in true agreement and he follows my lead? I must consider this. I will discuss my marriage with Metacom and heed his good advice.*

In the meanwhile, Weetamoo had other considerations. Aside from moving the people, she worried about her children. The baby seemed to be developing a cough and could not be dragged out in foul weather for much longer. And Laughing Water's time approached. She had to get them to a place of shelter where she would not have to worry about them and could concentrate on the fight ahead, for she felt certain that a great battle loomed.

Never before had all the Algonquin people fought together in such numbers nor had they ever fought against one another in such a widespread manner. There had always been boundary disputes to settle, grievances to address, and alliances to forge and reinforce, but chaos now reigned. The whole of her people felt under siege, and if they did not fight with the English, they fought against them. *What madness is upon us? What peril have they unleashed?* For the first time she worried that they may not be able to win this war.

By morning, word arrived from the scouts behind them that the English soldiers, helped by Mohawk guides, neared them once again. With no time to think about anything but getting to safety, they packed up and struck out again.

Rest for the Weary

Mary dropped down heavily on her makeshift bed. Over the past three weeks, over and over she had been forced to trudge along with the wild band. The day's journey had been difficult and cold. They had left in a mindless rush. The tribe had attempted two river crossings but found the current too strong. The banks swelled, and the travelers abandoned efforts to cross at usual places. The warriors had built and portaged heavy wooden canoes, and the people had tromped along upstream seeking better crossing sites. The leaders pressed Mary and the others to carry greater burdens. By nightfall, they reached a new encampment. Mary guessed they had traveled at least fifty miles since they took her from her home. She did not know it was nearer to seventy.

When she could rest at last, Mary felt grateful to get her feet out of her sodden shoes and under her soft fur wrap, although she was so exhausted that she thought she could have slept on the bare ground with no cover. Her side throbbed. Even though she had removed her pack basket, her forehead still felt the weight of the tumpline that supported it. Her neck and shoulders burned as if afire. Her fingers were raw and blistered from dragging and tying branches to construct the temporary shelters. No wigwams were made here, just lean-tos and makeshift skin tents. She assumed this meant the tribe would be moving on soon. She was too tired to seek out oak leaves tonight; she could wait until morning to dress her wound.

Stiffly folding herself into her fur bed, she lay next to Rachel, whom she had walked with earlier that day and the day before. The woman knelt on her own fur and brushed her daughter's hair into neat braids. Mary turned away. Closing her eyes tightly, she saw her own hands teasing tangles from Sarah's soft golden curls. She could almost feel the silky fibers slipping through her fingers. She opened her eyes and sucked in a deep sigh. Nothing but darkness and rough branches. She blinked but couldn't recapture the image of Sarah's soft, long hair in her hands. How she longed for another such moment with her daughter.

She wept.

Why did I take such moments for granted? "Lord, what a great Providence it is for me to see how important this small task was, now it has been taken from me. God, thank you for showing me my laziness in praising you for such daily pleasures. You have opened my eyes to my errors, and forevermore I will praise you for such precious deeds. Thank you for making me an instrument of your love and care."

Mary kept her face toward the sheltering boughs, listening to the mother comfort her children in their skin beds. The words were strange, different from Weetamoo's. Still, Mary could tell by the woman's voice that she was telling her children a bedtime story or prayer. The children settled down. Their breathing grew soft and deep. At last, the mother crawled into her own fur bed with a long deep sigh. Mary faded quickly into sleep, too. Only occasional whispers, coughs, and small fires gave hints of the sleepless in the quiet encampment.

The Sachems' Treaty
March 1, 1675

So, how is it with you and Quannopinn?" Awashonks asked as they made their way to a crossing place on the Kwinitekw River. Both she and Weetamoo stepped lightly on the well-worn path.

"It is better," Weetamoo said.

Laughing Water smiled and said, "We could hear that in the night."

Weetamoo looked back at her jeering daughter, thinking to scold her for minding the business of her elders. Yet she saw not a child but a young woman before her, a woman about to become a mother herself. She smiled back and patted her daughter's swollen abdomen.

"And how are you and my grandson today?"

"Well. He is anxious to meet you. Sometimes I think he will burst out."

"Within a fortnight, we shall see him," Awashonks offered.

"Maybe sooner," Weetamoo said, "See how he has turned down to find his path out." She noted the lower position of the baby in her daughter's womb. "May we cross the river before your time."

"Today we will cross. We are very close to a fording place." Awashonks knew the trail. She had visited with the Sokoki people on other occasions, and they had visited with her. Some of her people were kin with them, and they had always been on friendly terms. "It will be good to be in Sokoki land soon."

As she predicted, they arrived at a good crossing place in a short time and easily found more dugout canoes submerged with stones near the river bank. Weetamoo and Awashonks waded into the low, icy water and tossed the stones to Laughing Water and Mary on the shore to empty and buoy one of the canoes. They tipped it to remove most of the water. Other canoes had already launched and reached the other side by the time they boarded. Weetamoo helped Laughing Water aboard and waited for Mary to step in, but the white woman fretted about getting her feet wet.

"Enough!" Weetamoo shouted. Soaked to the hip already, as was Awashonks, Weetamoo did not believe Mary fussed over a little water on her ankle. "Get in."

Mary lifted her skirt to step into the craft, when a sudden commotion began behind them. Shouts alerted them that Mohawk scouts again followed them. Mohawks knew the trails well.

"Go!" Weetamoo shouted as she pointed upriver. Awashonks pulled Mary by the arm, and nearly knocked her down. Mary caught her balance and ran along behind Awashonks with her pack basket banging on her back with each step. Weetamoo helped Laughing Water out of the dugout, and they followed close behind.

They carried on, running most of the time, avoiding the main path. They ran uphill, away from the river, and only slowed their pace briefly when they had to pick their way through a thicket. By mid day, after traveling four or five miles, they reached a safe resting place with a good view of the main trail below. They stopped to rest and eat.

The morning's dash had caused traveling bands to scatter, and all sought out their own companions. Weetamoo's band had lagged to the rear, as Mary could not keep up with the younger members in spite of her lighter load. Waiting to see if any of her own scouts appeared in their midst, Weetamoo searched those coming from behind. Instead, she saw the white woman's son walking toward her.

"Hmmph," she uttered.

Awashonks spoke up. "It will do no harm to let them greet one another. Perhaps it will speed Mary's step for the afternoon journey. We have a long way to our next crossing place."

"Perhaps you are right. Eat with me, Cousin. We dare not tarry long."

"Nux. So, tell me, how did you settle things with your sannup?"

"Oh, you old gossip, why must you always pry into my private matters?"

"No, not a gossip, young squaw. I am your sponsor, remember. It is my duty to enquire into these things."

"If you must know, I told him how I felt when he tries to make himself seem more important than me all the time. I reminded him that I am a respected sachem, a sunk squaw in my own right, and I reminded him that he is only a sagamore, second to Canonchet, and I demanded that he show me more respect. He agreed that he would."

"You didn't!" Proud of her cousin for standing up to him, Awashonks looked at her with wide eyes. She and the others had grown weary of his constant need to grab their attention. He was younger than most of the leaders, and they felt they all deserved more respect.

"I did. And he was angry at first, but I think he understood. He came to me with promises of better behavior in the future."

"Ah ha. And this was not just before he bedded you last night, was it?"

"It was. Wait. Just what is your meaning?"

"Nothing at all. Just be sure it was his heart speaking to you and not his member."

"Awashonks! It is not like that."

"I'm only saying that you should not let up on keeping him in his place. He is young and has a lot to learn from you and from his elders. He is a strong warrior, and he will make a good leader. But he has no need to rush things."

"What you say is true. Do not worry. I will see that he is in no rush."

"Ah ha. You will use your woman power, then, to subdue him. That is good."

They both chuckled over that idea and finished their meal.

The Lord Hath Chastened Me Sore

Too tired to eat and just grateful to have the pack basket off her shoulders at last, Mary leaned against a tree. Her eyelids were closed when Joseph's shadow fell upon them, and she snapped them open, half expecting Weetamoo to be there raising a hand against her or pulling her up to her feet. She blinked at the outline of the young man before her, caught in the shadow of the sun.

"What's this?" she cried out. "Is it truly you, my dear son?" She made an effort to get up, but Joseph fell against her chest, crying like he had as a boy with a skinned knee. She could not help herself crying, too, as she rocked him in her arms. He moaned into her bosom, "Mama, why? Why have they done this to us? I am so weary. So weary."

"Hush, hush." Mary whispered as she kept a watch that no one could hear him in this weakened state. "We cannot see God's plan, but we must be strong. Even when we are apart."

"But Mama, where will we go? Our home is burned. Our town is burned. Our family is gone. William, Joseph, Sarah, Aunt Elizabeth, too. Mama, I keep seeing them . . ."

"Shush, Son. I, too, see them, but we must not let that weaken our spirit." Her words did not disguise her own pain and fear. Her voice shook, and she squeezed her son so tightly that he might lose his breath.

"Son, let us not dwell on the past but let us look to our future. For we will have a new future at the end of this. It is promised in the Good Book. In fact, wait now, let's read some of the good Word of God together." She dug into her pack and pulled out her Bible.

Joseph looked over both shoulders, "Mama, put that down. Where did you get it? Don't let them see."

"It is fine, Son. We are allowed to pray and read His Holy Word if it does not get in the way of our work. Here, now. Take that and see what comfort you will find in it."

Joseph took the book from her, flipped it open to Psalm 118.17-18, and read out quietly, "'I shall not die, but live and declare the works of the Lord: The Lord hath chastened me sore, yet he hath not given me over to death.' Look here, Mother. It is true. We have been unmercifully chastened, but we are not yet dead."

"Nay, Son, and we will not die here in this wild place. We will accept God's mercy, and we will get back to find your father and sister."

Mary saw Weetamoo rise from her resting place and walk toward her. In that moment, Mary tore her precious Bible in half, shocking her son.

"Mama, what are you doing!"

"Here, son. Take half of the Bible with you that you might be refreshed by the word of scripture in the wilderness. Go now, as my dame approaches, and she might not favor us together." She squeezed his hand, and he departed.

Mary pushed her torn Bible back into her pack, got up, and lifted it onto her shoulders. Mary resigned herself to another long frigid journey with little comfort at the end of it, save a hard earthen bed and an exhausted slumber. Without another word, the two women walked to the north.

They walked on until nightfall, at last arriving at the crossing place, but too late to make their way to the other side. Laughing Water told Mary they would cross the river in the morning and meet Metacomet. That night, she had a sweet dream of going home that was unmercifully shattered by a nightmare of her sister Elizabeth, her daughter Sarah, and her neighbor Ann Joslin all begging to die while heathens danced around them showering them with flames.

She lay awake fearing what might happen to her in the morrow.

Eve of Reunion

"Walk with me Weetamoo. We will talk about our future." Quannopinn offered her his hand.

"More walking? Are you not weary?"

"I wish to be alone with you, my Sunk Squaw. So will you walk with me a little way?"

She reached up for his hand, and he bent down and lifted her into his arms. "Here. I will walk for you." He carried her to the edge of their camp, and they sat upon a great, moss-covered boulder.

"What is the future you wish to share with me? Have you had a vision?" she asked.

"No vision. Just a clear idea of what I want for you. For me. For our son."

"So tell me, then. How will it be when this is all a memory?"

"Wife, you will come to dwell with me in our place in Narragansett, and I will take the mantle from Canonchet when he is gone. That is what he and Ninagret and Quaiapen and all the others want too."

Weetamoo opened her mouth to protest.

"Wait," he said. "We will also dwell in Pocasset, especially in summer months, and I will fish, and you will plant, and we will make many children. In winter, we will go to my home place, and I will hunt while you make us wealthy with all the wampum from the quahog shells the children will collect from the seashore. I will be King of the Narragansetts, and you will be Queen of the Pocassets, and our son will be the Massasoit of both when he comes of age and you and I are too tired. It will be a great union. Do you agree?"

"It is a good dream, Quannopinn. I would like that." She stopped herself from raising a question about their more immediate future.

They sat in silence for a while listening to the sounds of the camp, growing quieter as the people lay down to rest. They looked up at the stars on yet another brutally cold day but were warm in each other's arms, wrapped in one of their sleeping furs. Quannopinn's hand could not resist running itself over the small mound of her belly. He traced her navel round and round, then ran a finger lightly along her middle and in between her breasts. They, too, had grown slightly larger than before. He cupped one of them and bent down to press his lips to her nipple. She leaned back and caught him by the waist. They melded into each other as if one and made love, gently, patiently, tenderly as they had never done before.

While cherishing the sweet moment, Weetamoo worried that it might be their last lovemaking. She wanted her bliss to last forever. For a moment, she wished to be simply a woman—not a sachem, not a warrior, not a leader. Simply a bride honored by her sannup in the most precious way. She pretended to be merely that and felt the world fall away as her lover carried her along with his passion.

They reached the height of their ecstasy together and fell apart, both panting and letting the chill air dry their sweaty limbs. Again, caught in their own thoughts, they lay in silence.

Weetamoo was sure Quannopinn thought only of future days when he would be a chieftain. She alone worried about news they would gather in the morning from Metacom. She alone worried about her two children from her other marriages and the one in her belly from this one.

Would Quannopinn's dream be real for them? Or must she make another plan?

Tomorrow, I will talk with you, Metacom, and you and I will know the way.

Arriving at Coasset
Eighth Remove

The wide Connecticut River curved into an oxbow at the native place called Coasset. Too deep to ford, the river here flowed with current slow enough to cross. Several heavy wood canoes on the opposite shore revealed the native path to Mohawk country. At a call from one of the leaders on Mary's side of the river, shrubbery began to move on the opposite bank. Indians noiselessly emerged from the bushes and slipped over the sides, into the canoes. They paddled swiftly and silently, guiding the crafts with steady precision toward the great mass of weary people waiting on the eastern shore.

Mary counted at least a dozen canoes in the water. As each one pushed off, another appeared from the thicket on the western edge of the river and then nosed quietly into the water with the two Indians guiding it toward the east bank. Before the last one slipped into the water, the first one slid onto the silty edge in front of Mary. Those behind nudged her forward. She turned to see a press of Indians leaving her no quarter save the muddy course to waiting canoes. A wall of people covered the slope behind her. They seemed to swarm downhill toward her. Not one face among them was white.

Feeling lost to her own kind, Mary suddenly resisted being swept further into the hostile wilderness. She stood still and let them all pass around her. In their momentum, she thought they might forget her here. She might find her way back from that frontier to some outpost where the colonies had posted militia or soldiers who could bring her home, she thought. Perhaps she could work her way to the edge of the teeming bodies and melt away into the woods. Perhaps she could . . .

"You come now," the Indian in one of the boats called out to her. He looked right into her eyes as if he had seen what she was thinking. She felt a push against her shoulder, then another at her injured hip. She winced and tried to turn aside but was jostled by women pushing past her with angry looks. She stepped sideways and nearly lost her footing. She glanced behind and thought. *Lord, can you not stop this wave of heathens coming down upon me?*

"You come now," the Indian in the canoe repeated, louder. He held up his hand to stop an old woman making her way toward him.

Mary felt a strong hand take her elbow and roughly push her at the man in the canoe. She tried to dig into the bank with her heels, but her feet slid on the slimy skin of mud covering the frozen ground. Another hand clapped on her shoulder, and she heard her mistress Weetamoo's cursing tone in her ear. "You go now," Weetamoo whispered harshly as she shoved Mary down the embankment.

Only the people in front of her kept Mary on her feet as they reached out to push her past them toward the waiting canoe. As soon as she set her foot in the canoe, the pilot used his paddle to force her to the front of the long hollowed tree. Coming to a rest in the bow, she felt the rocking and bobbing as more and more people piled into the craft. It sank lower and lower into the icy water. Mary feared it would capsize. *Oh Lord, am I to drown with this devilish mob or would you have me climb into the frigid water to escape?* She felt the boat lurch suddenly. Too late. Her momentary chance to escape had passed.

The canoe glided in quick rhythms across the broad river. The current drifted slightly, but the canoe steadily thrust forward. The pilot deftly kept a distance between other full canoes crossing and empty ones returning.

Mary looked behind and saw a wave of human flesh pressing down the bank like lemmings. Each canoe filled to capacity and pushed off just as another slid ashore beside it. No pauses. Like rhythmic dancers, the seemingly endless human tide pulsed into waiting canoes that ferried across the dark water.

Looking behind her, Mary toppled as the canoe struck the western shore. Two big Indians fiercely yanked the craft, then hoisted her to her feet and shoved her over the bow onto the rocky beach. Two women leaving the boat stepped around her, but Weetamoo came up behind her and pushed her to her feet again. "You useless English. Move. We go to King Philip. Now."

Mary got up and walked over the rough stones. She followed the others to a path between thick brambles. As she stepped through brush into the clearing beyond, her heart stopped. Before her spread an Indian settlement like none she had ever seen. Wigwams stretched as far as she could see. She saw her captors in every direction joyously greeting one another, clapping each other on their backs. Strong men came to lift the loaded pack baskets from tired women's calloused shoulders. Young men wrapped their arms around young women's waists and lifted them in passionate embraces.

None came to help her. Inky smoke spewed from a forge where Indian smiths hammered iron into gun barrels and poured molten metal into pellets to kill her brethren. Drums sounded, and a haunting chant repeated all around.

She stood stunned, surrounded by more people than she had ever seen in one place at one time. She felt more alone than ever before. She felt as if she had arrived in hell with Satan's red minions rejoicing all around her.

She fell to her knees and wept without release.

Reunion with Metacomet

Weetamoo strode through brush into the home of the Sokoki and their southern neighbors, the Pocumtuc people at Coasset, the place of pines. The great village was filled with Metacomet's allies. A weight lifted from her heart as she was welcomed into the midst of her people, finally reunited in a safe refuge. Although far from her own home, the place was untouched by English hands.

There would be no more running from the English. No more days and nights of shelterless wandering. No more foraging for withered berries and decaying ground nuts. These people belonged in this place.

The joy of happy reunions echoed off every tree. *Finally together,* Weetamoo thought, *we will reclaim the right to live as our parents and grandparents once did.*

She heard warriors shouting happy greetings to their arriving families. The weary travelers collapsed into the arms of their long absent fathers, brothers, and husbands. Knots of people fused in between the masses climbing the river bank and fighters flooding down to the water's edge. The sweet release of tears and passion fell quietly over families clasping each other tightly. Weetamoo saw a boy excitedly tugging at the elbows of his parents who were locked in their first embrace since summer. A father lifted his infant son high for their first look into one another's eyes.

Amid the joyful noise, cries of anguish sounded as people learned who would not be joining the great reunion. Because her people believed it not good to speak of the dead, Weetamoo felt the ache of their choked words. A mother's tears streamed wordlessly as she held only one of her two warrior sons. A father stood tall and silent as his sister put his motherless daughter's hand in his. Women shook heads sadly in response to questions about some of the elders. With empty eyes, parents with no children to embrace clutched one another.

Weetamoo turned and watched the crowd moving slowly away from the river. She saw some warriors still waiting for the last of the mishoons bearing people across the water. The warriors had left so hurriedly with Metacomet during the Strawberry Moon that many never had a chance to say goodbye to their families. Some of them would never have the chance.

Weetamoo bent down and placed an offering of tobacco on the trodden soil.

"Sister, I greet you with honor and respect," a familiar voice called out. Weetamoo rose and looked for Metacomet in the sea of people. He stood taller than most of the others, and Weetamoo had no trouble finding him.

The crowd parted to allow the great leader to pass.

"My brother, Sachem Metacomet, you honor me with your welcome," she responded, walking toward the statuesque leader with calm dignity. She held out her hands to him.

"You have made a great journey. I thank you for bringing my people here safely," Metacomet said as he reached out to embrace her. "How I have missed you," he whispered in her ear.

Folding herself into his arms, Weetamoo laid her head upon his chest and listened to his strong heartbeat. She quietly said, "Brother, it is good to have you so near to my heart again."

"Nux, Weetamoo. I feel the strength of our people becoming one again. All our hearts are joined in this place. Taubut. It is good." They began walking toward the village.

Looking at the great number of wetus stretching into the distance and the throng of people all around her, Weetamoo asked, "Metacomet, how many do you number? There are more than I even dared to dream."

"Nearly one thousand," he said proudly. "You will see leaders from all the four winds around our council fire tonight. Wequogan has pledged the support of the Pocumtucs," he said pointing toward the large beaver-shaped mountain to the southeast. "Our brothers the Nashaways, Quabaugs, Naticks, and Marlboroughs from the east have joined us." He swept his arm south and said, "And Muttaump is here with the Nipmucs." Turning north, he said, "And many of the Penacooks have come, even after Passaconaway's withdrawal into the grandmother's country."

He stopped walking and looked directly into her eyes, "Weetamoo, we are one nation again, as we have not been since the time of our grandfathers."

She enjoyed hearing the excitement in his voice about his success in uniting the Algonquin people. Although the young men like him had been demanding it, the elders did not want to break treaties with the English. Weetamoo wondered how Metacomet finally turned their hearts. *Or was it English lies that turned them for him?*

"My brother, I bring you three hundred more warriors from Narragansett, Pokanoket, and Sakonnet, and we are joined by Matoonas and Monaco who bring more Nipmucs and Nashaways to fight." She placed her hand on his bare arm. It felt lean and firm. She wondered how many raids he had been on since she last saw him in the Pocasset swamp. Life must have been as hard for him as it had been for her. She had traveled the distance between them only once. He must have covered it many times over.

"Three hundred, Weetamoo?" he asked in surprise. "Say this is not all who have survived."

"Of warriors, yes, My Brother," she answered quietly. "We lost many at Canonchet's swamp fort. But we took as many English to their deaths there as we could," she said through bitter teeth.

Weetamoo looked behind her at people streaming ashore from the mishoons and said, "I also bring you many more women and children. We had to leave the injured and elderly behind with Quaiapen at the old stone fort."

"You have done well, Sister. By bringing women and children here, you have given us seven more generations of life, and warriors you bring will add to our strength. The injured and elders could not make the journey, and Quaiapen will know how to keep the people safe."

"Nux. It is so. After the attack on the Great Swamp camp, Canonchet and Awashonks knew their treaty with the English had ended. Without their alliance, Quaiapen, Pomham, and Pessacus were all anxious to join you. It is a shame we could not bring them all, but some had to stay to defend the stone fort. The English treaties have lost favor with them all."

"You speak the truth, Weetamoo. What we told them all along they saw written in blood and fire at Canonchet's fort. It caused a great sadness for our people." They walked quietly toward the nushweety, a large longhouse near the central fire that Weetamoo assumed was Metacomet's. She looked all around. She had never seen so many native people together in one place. Not even at a summer gathering. Pride welled up in her throat.

"It is so good to be with you again, Brother. I have needed to be nearer to our fight. Surely, no English village can stand against these numbers," she said. "It is we who are now like the leaves in the forest. Within the year, we will have our country back."

"I have missed you, too, Weetamoo." He looked down at her and nodded. "Our council will benefit from your confidence. Come, I will show you where you will rest." He turned her toward the village, and they walked into the midst of the rejoicing celebration.

A growl came from Weetamoo's belly as she neared the village cook fires. Offerings already burned in thanks. She smelled charred venison and horse flesh. She saw pots simmering with peas and corn bubbling in savory brown broth. A fresh bearskin stretched beside a wetu told her that her people would not go to sleep hungry again that night.

She thanked the bear, her brother, for his gift of life as she walked past.

"You may stay here while you are with us," Metacomet said, pointing out a well-made wetu. It was freshly covered with ash bark, and white smoke gently puffed out the vent hole in the top. "All you should need has been attended to," he added.

She nodded and smiled.

"There you are, Wife," Quannopinn called out as he came up behind her and caught her about the waist. "In this great gathering, I was afraid I might not find you again," he nuzzled into her ear. Turning to Metacomet, he added, "And greetings to you, Cousin." He grasped Metacomet's arm heartily.

Each slapping the other's back with calloused hands, the two men drew one another into a spirited embrace.

"Welcome, Quannopinn, but we are brothers now that you and Weetamoo are joined. Thank you for bringing my sister and all these people safely here. Are you well?"

"Well, yes, and more fit than you, I see. This life of raiding has thinned you out, Metacomet. You look as though you have stayed too long in the pesuponk. Have you sweated off all your summer fat?"

Laughing, Metacomet replied, "And you? I see your marriage has made you both into mothers. What is this?" he asked, patting Quannopinn's thickened middle.

"Only one of us is a mother, Philip," Weetamoo answered, patting her own middle.

"Is it so?" he asked, surprised at her news as much as at her use of his English name. She seldom called him Philip unless in a teasing mood. "Will a future sachem of our people come within this year?"

"Yes, it is so," Quannopinn boasted as he slid his arm around Weetamoo's shoulder in proud acknowledgment of his impending paternity.

"Come the season of harvest, a papoose will come to follow his brave father and his famous uncle. There will be no doubt in his future. I promise that, Metacomet," Weetamoo vowed.

"So you know me as Metacomet again, now," her brother said. "Then let the mighty Sachem Metacomet ask you both to join me for supper in my wetu. It would please me to talk a while before we go to the council fire."

"Yes. It would please us, as well," Weetamoo agreed without looking to her husband for approval.

"Sachem Weetamoo!" Laughing Water called out excitedly. She was running toward them from the path to the river. "You must come to the river! The English woman will not move!"

By the Waters of Babylon

Mary lay on the riverbank and wept, indifferent to wet mud dirtying her skirts and snow caking her hair to her face. No longer able to hold the ache in her heart, she let her loud sobs echo through the cold ground. Her shoulders heaved up and down with each wrenching cry. "Oh, Lord," she wailed between gasps, "Why have you forsaken me . . .to this wilderness?"

With no concern for the Indians surrounding her, she rose to her knees and lifted her eyes and fists to the sky, screaming, "Why? . . .Why? . . .WHY?" And then more quietly, "wh-h-h-y?" Her voice trailed as her head fell to the ground. With arms outstretched and fists tearing at muddy, dead grass, she sobbed, "I remember Zion on the banks of the rivers of Babylon." Then she was quiet except for her dry, ragged breathing.

The Indians around her murmured, then parted to let Weetamoo, Quannopinn, and Metacomet near. Metacomet stepped within the circle and asked, "Woman, why do you cry?" Mary did not respond.

He knelt down beside her, touched her shoulder, and gently asked, "Why do you cry?"

Without lifting her head, Mary sobbed, "Now, you will kill me." Until then, she had always remained calm in their presence. She feared her outburst would cause them to torture and kill her as they had Ann Joslin before. But she had no desire to be strong any longer. She was truly frightened that she would never go home again.

"Nay," he said. "None will harm you here." He stood and said something to the others she did not understand. As he left, an Indian woman she didn't know knelt beside her and helped her sit up. She offered Mary a wooden spoon of cornmeal. Mary did not resist but took it on her dry tongue and mouthed it while blankly staring at the woman. The woman smiled and held out another spoonful of meal. Mary opened her mouth like a baby bird and let the woman feed her another mouthful. Another woman squatted beside her and held out a wooden bowl of peas. After weeks of wanting, the small bowl seemed as great as a bushel to Mary. She put both hands in the bowl and scooped as many as she could into her mouth. Then she gathered all the stray peas that had fallen on her skirt and on the ground and pushed those into her mouth as well.

Only then did she look up to see the crowd of people standing round. Only one of them met her eyes with anger. Weetamoo stood over her and glared. Mary stared back. Weetamoo turned abruptly and walked toward the village without saying a word.

The woman who gave Mary the meal offered her a drink, then helped her to her feet. "Mary," said the woman, "Metacomet—King Philip—will see you. Come. I will take you to him."

Mary looked at her in disbelief. Was she to meet the ravenous creature in his own lair? Her fear deepened. He must have heard about her wailing and now wanted to make an example of her. Like Goody Joslin. All about her she saw only Indians. She saw no way to escape. She knew she must go to him.

So be it. She would go to him, but not as his sacrificial lamb. She turned and dipped the hem of her apron into the river water and wiped her face with its damp edge. She tucked her hair up under her coif and smoothed her skirts. Then she straightened up and said, "Take me to King Philip."

The squaw led her into the village. Mary saw so many wigwams and so much smoke coming from within them and from their cook fires without that she could scarcely tell where one ended and another began. Smoke made her cough and burned her eyes. Never had she seen such a large Indian village. She quietly followed the squaw along a wide path until they came to a wigwam with mats covering it that seemed more newly made and finely woven than the others in the village. Fur from a silver wolf covered its doorway. In only such small ways did it differ from the hundreds of other wigwams in the town.

The woman scratched on the mat, and a man's voice spoke, "Enter." Mary ducked under the skin and stepped inside. As her eyes adjusted to the dim light, she strained to see. The wigwam seemed like others she had been in, but subtle differences implied Indian wealth. Thicker furs made the sleeping platforms more lush than Weetamoo's. Some implements tucked into framework branches had richer ornamentation. The woven mats had more colorful and intricately designed patterns.

She gasped upon realizing he had been the man she saw at the riverside. She studied his appearance. Her eyes rested on him—the great King Philip. Part of his head had been shaved with a thick knot of remaining hair tied to one side. He wore a red mantle over one shoulder and a great beaded wampum necklace that covered most of his chest. She saw a very large knife in his belt. "Come. Sit here by the fire," he said and beckoned her closer to him. His clearly spoken English startled her. She settled in a spot that kept the fire between the two of them. He waited calmly as she folded her legs and tucked in her skirts. She looked evenly into his dark eyes.

"You are King Philip?" she asked.

"I am," he answered with a nod. "And you are Mistress Mary Rowlandson?"

"I am," she replied.

"Nux. It is good. Will you smoke?" he asked extending a richly carved and polished wooden pipe out to her.

"Nay," she answered, then nervously explained, "I no longer use tobacco. It was too bewitching over me." As he quietly regarded her, she added, "Thank you."

Philip took back the pipe and shrugged. "I am told that you have come a great distance and have traveled without complaint. This is good. I am also told that you make English clothing. Is this so?"

"I can," she answered. "With wool and cloth enough, I can make fair clothing. Shirts, hats, stockings. 'Tis true," she said with pride, although her skill was no better than any other colonial woman's.

"Nux, I wish you to make clothing for my boy, Metom. Will you do it?" Philip asked her.

"Aye, for a good price, I will make your son clothing," she dared to say.

Philip laughed out loud. Few spoke to him so boldly. "I shall pay you a shilling for a shirt. Do you say that is enough?" he asked.

"It is enough." She put forth her hand to signify the bargain had been struck. Philip leaned forward and gripped her hand tightly and pulled her slightly toward him. He looked right into her eyes and said, "Good. Then I will see you again when the shirt is done." He released her hand.

"So you will," she said. A little shaken, and clearly dismissed, she cautiously rose to leave, trying to keep the king in her sight until she backed out of his wigwam.

Straightening up outside, she thought that one of the squaws of the village smiled at her. Another squaw nodded at her respectfully. Taking in the idea that she had been charged by King Philip to make a shirt for his boy, she brushed her apron into place. She stood up tall, marveling that she had bartered with the villain that the English army had sought for more than half a year. Like Daniel in the lion's den, she had come out safely. She patted her Bible in her pocket and vowed to give more honor and praise to the Lord for watching over her and for giving her the courage she had shown while in the lion's lair.

After her meeting with King Philip, Mary walked through the village. She felt a change in the air. Yes, the daylight lasted longer and the air felt a little warmer, but something else seemed different. Though surrounded by the same dome-shaped dwellings and dark-skinned strangers, she felt more at ease. The people here did not look at her with angry faces. A woman pinning back a mat on her bark-covered home looked her way and smiled as Mary walked past. A child ran across her path and did not skirt widely around her. A group of men smoking pipes outside their shelters did not lift their eyes from their game as she passed. Crying out rants of glee or dismay as their fortune changed, they continued tossing painted plum stones into a wooden tray.

As before, she felt insignificant but somehow with a new sense of belonging. Although she did not hold the elevated status she enjoyed as Mistress in her home town, here the mighty sachem recognized her for her valued skills. He had offered her the opportunity to trade with him and others for her needs. *Why have I not recognized the value of my labor until now,* she wondered. As every school girl learned and as all women must, she could knit and sew, but until her interview with the great sachem, she did not appreciate the preciousness of her skill among the savages.

Of course they coveted the fine needlework of the English. They stole clothing, even torn, blood-soaked clothing from the corpses they had killed. Thus far, she had scratched for sustenance from barren ground or scoured scrub brush for withered berries or begged for scraps at doorways to supplement the scant rations given her by her selfish mistress.

Yes, something has changed tonight, she thought. With the food at the riverbank, her first full meal in weeks nestled under her ribs, her mind felt clear. Meeting King Philip and finding him a civil man and congenial host did much to lighten her spirit. *Had he not said I would come to no harm? Had he not treated me as a guest and not as a captive? Did he not recognize the wealth of my family and status of my husband?* That, more than his food and his kindness, comforted her. She would knit him a cap for his son and sew him a fine shirt, too. Mary wondered if that evil wench, her mistress, would have to give way to her torment, now that the king of all of them had requested her service?

Mary marveled at how God had replied to her desperate cry of only hours before. She believed that through her penitence, in His wisdom, it pleased God to warm her heart and show her that she might survive. He opened her eyes to her own value as an article of trade and offered her means to endure through her own wit and skills.

"Oh, Providence," she prayed, "I thank Thee for watching over me even more than the sparrows or the lilies of the field. I am grateful for the discernment of your wisdom in teaching me from want the many gifts that Thou hath set before me."

Pesuponk

Weetamoo ate a small helping of corn mash and peas with her sister Wootonekanuske, Metacomet, and Quannopinn, and left as soon as she could, saying she had to get ready for the feast. She never relished her sister's cooking and liked even less sharing her company. Instead of going to her own wetu, she walked away from the village to a small stream. She was told she would find a pesuponk, a sweat lodge, along the stream. After her long journey and many deprivations, she needed to bring peace to her body, mind, heart, and spirit.

Laughing Water saw her mother leaving and gathered the items Weetamoo asked her to carry to the pesuponk. She followed a path that led to a dip in the land that muffled village noise. There they found the sweat lodge built into the sloped side of the hill. Laughing Water kindled a fire in the pit outside the lodge. Weetamoo lifted the skin flap covering the opening, slipped into the pesuponk, and passed out stones to Laughing Water to heat them in the fire. Laughing Water drew water from the stream as the stones warmed.

Once the charcoals glowed in the fire pit, Laughing Water dipped a gourd into the water. She used the wet gourd to transfer hot coals into the pit inside the pesuponk. She then placed cedar branches over the coals and covered them with hot stones until they masked the glow of embers.

Weetamoo slipped off her skirt and mantle and removed her moccasins and leggings. She removed all her beaded jewelry and crawled naked into the pesuponk where she sat opposite the door and pit of hot coal and stones.

Laughing Water closed the flap and left Weetamoo in total darkness. She felt heat rising from the hot stones. Sizzling cedar filled the small lodge with curling tendrils of aromatic smoke. She breathed in the hot, sweet scent and let her mind relax.

Slowly, her eyes adjusted to the dim light. A soft red glow from hot embers pulsed from beneath the stones and between the branches. She placed a bit of tobacco on the glowing stones and began to chant. She ladled herbed water over the hot stones and sat back on the cold moist earth. Steam surged into her nostrils and cleansed away all thoughts. She breathed in hot, moist vapor and let her mind drift back to Kistannit, the Creator teaching Maushop the sacred way to cleanse his body, mind, heart, and spirit. She imagined Maushop teaching Weetucks to rekindle the ceremony when many had forgotten the way. She wanted their spirits to come to her and help her to find *her* way.

Weetamoo felt coolness of smooth earth beneath her and prayed thankfully to the sacred Mother of the Earth, Metanokit, for the land and all life it supported. As she closed her eyes, she envisioned forests that yielded trees that built her homes, mishoons, furnishings, and tools. Her mind's eye followed their long trunks to their base on the forest floor and pictured living plants that gave her food and shelter and beauty every day. Among the plants, she saw the wolf whose skins kept her warm and dry and the deer whose flesh fed her body and the bird whose bones became tools to make her people's lives easier. She whispered thanks to them.

She dropped another bit of tobacco on the stones and made a greeting to Potanit, Spirit of Fire. Pouring another ladle over the stones, she offered thanks to Paumagussett, Spirit of Great Waters. She let steamy heat rise through her nostrils into the very depths of her mind and body. She gave thanks to Tashin, Spirit of the Winds that brought cleansing vapors into her heart and her spirit. She felt surrounded by the many spirits who watched over her.

The darkened lodge felt warmer, and its walls seemed to expand and lift away as her thoughts drifted up into the starry night. She felt her spirit freeing itself from her mortal body and ascending into the sky. As her spirit rose, she looked back and saw the lodge and stream growing smaller. She floated above the trees.

Feeling at ease in her inner core, she made thanks and greeting to Keesuckquand, the Grandfather Spirit of the Heavens, visible daily as the sun, Nepaushet. At once she could see both day and night. She gave her thanks to Nanepaushet, Grandmother Spirit of the Moon, who guides all purification, fertility, and creativity. Weetamoo felt the presence of the Nucksuog, all the Spirits in the Star Nations above, especially the Spirit of the Pesuponk. She asked for their help in cleansing her body, mind, heart, and spirit. She let her mind feel warmth, steam, and air as she drifted into pure sensation.

Weetamoo heard drumming in the village or joyful shouts and chanting of people nearby, and in an instant, her spirit traveled back to the darkness of the pesuponk. Her attention focused on the glowing stones and sweet, hot, scented air filling the small lodge. She felt the white spirit being of the north, Nanummy-in, causing sweat to arise in her skin. She felt Nanummy-in cleansing her body of any soil and poison, just as the winter snow cleans the landscape with its whiteness. Dousing rocks again with herbed water, she breathed healing mist into her nostrils, throat, and chest and felt it coursing through her veins and pushing through her skin in sweat released from her pores.

She lay back on the ground and turned her thoughts to the yellow healing power of the east, Wampanand. Asking for help to cleanse her mind, she dwelled upon the passages of dawn and spring, the renewal of life. She let her body sink down, down into cold dark earth and felt her body push its way through darkness like small flowers pushing up through hard earth and the last mantle of snow. She opened her eyes and saw the bright green leaves and grass of spring, fresh with early morning dew.

She yearned for such freshness in her own spirit and tried to put aside her bitterness and anger with white men who had so hurt her people and way of life. She wanted to feel the wisdom and clarity of purpose that makes every living plant reach up to the sun, no matter what blocks the way. She wanted to bring that sense of renewal to her people in their difficult time. Pouring another scoop of water over the glowing rocks, she prayed for understanding for herself and her people.

She breathed hot steam deeply and allowed it to fill her thoughts. Thinking of bright morning sun, she imagined the time of her youth, when peace dwelled in her land, and her people enjoyed their freedom. As her sweat ran freely, she felt the golden warmth of the sun pulsing through her body and her mind.

She thought of Sowanand, the Red Spirit of Summer, and Towuttin, the south wind, and asked them to cleanse her heart. She wanted to feel lightness in her heart as she had as a child, but she could not release her bitter thoughts against Petananuit for his betrayal nor her anger toward vile white men and Mary Rowlandson, her daily reminder of their treachery. Although she wanted release from her anger, she could not fully let it go.

Pouring another ladle of water, she asked for help with shedding her anger. She took deep breaths of healing mist. Steam seemed only to raise anger deeper in her chest, and hatred filled her with desire for revenge.

Pain in her heart beat stronger when she remembered Metacomet kneeling at Mary's side earlier that day. *What made him do that? As just another captive, why would he care to comfort her? Better to dash her brains out and rid ourselves of her once and for all than to drag her along, using up our precious resources.* Weetamoo imagined Metacomet, the fierce warrior, not comforting Mary but instead bringing down his war club on her wretched white head. The image made her heart race. More sweat beaded up on her skin.

Even as she imagined Mary's murder, she knew in her heart it would not happen. *Metacomet needed Mary, a valuable hostage. He could trade her to the French, if not the Mohawks, for guns.* Weetamoo tried to let that knowledge calm her anger. *For Metacomet, I will endure this. For the good of my people, I will.*

She raised her voice to the spirit of Towuttin and asked for favorable winds to blow upon her heart and send her the peace she once knew. She sang a song her mother taught her to sing when she felt angry as a young girl. She tried to push her tension out with her breathing in time with the melody. She doused the stones again and pictured her anger sputtering and vaporizing like scented droplets on the heated surfaces. As steam burned and awakened every hair in her nostrils and on her skin, she felt her anger lift and fade away.

She turned to black Checksuwand of the west to the cleansing she craved for her spirit. In the darkness, she closed her eyes and emptied her mind of everyday thoughts. She focused her attention on the creation of Nope and all her ancestors who came from that time to the present. She sensed her special place in the world and in the circle of life. She remembered her people who belonged with the land for many thousands of summers and winters. She drew upon their spiritual strength that would be with her for all her days.

She doused the dying embers once again and sat chanting a rhythmic song as she let the universe become one in her. She sensed the darkness and, within the darkness, many stars. She felt kinship with the stars as she felt kinship with her people and the creatures of the earth. She felt at once great and small and interwoven in the spirit that binds all life to itself and to all natural beings. She became aware of the insignificance and importance of this moment and of every moment. She sat in the steamy lodge and let it all wash over her body, mind, heart, and spirit.

As the glow of embers died down, she grew aware of the sounds coming from the distant camp. Drummers summoned the people. Guns fired to call warriors to bring their battles to life in dance.

She slowly uncrossed her legs, stiff and sweat covered. She pulled back her matted damp hair and crawled to the lodge opening. Peering out, she saw Laughing Water had left but had neatly folded a warm fur for her by the stream.

She stepped slowly into the bright, moonlit evening and felt winds kissing and cooling her moist skin. She plunged herself into the shallow, icy stream and let the shock revive her drained body. As she poured water over her face and hair and rinsed away poisons that had drained from her flesh, her muscles tightened. Brisk air blew against her as she rubbed her body vigorously with sand from the bottom of the stream to soften her skin.

Weetamoo sat in the knee-deep water, ducked her head and face briefly in, and shuddered with cold. Then she stepped out onto the waiting fur at water's edge. Wrapping herself in the fur, she followed the starlit path to the celebrating village.

Thanksgiving

As Weetamoo approached the village, vibrations of drums throbbed against her chest. Chants of her people echoed in the trees around her. Her heart lifted as muffled voices of the spirits mingled in her ear with sounds of her people. She felt the presence of the spirits strongly around her. She quickened her step up the path to the great feast.

Tension in her shoulders from carrying her heavy pack had evaporated. Strain in her neck from the weight of its tumpline had disappeared. She had left all her burdens in the smoke of the pesuponk, the sweat lodge, and felt lightness in her body, mind, heart, and spirit. She rolled her head gently in a circle and breathed in cold night air. As she exhaled, she watched mist evaporate like all worries she had carried the past three months. Her muscles felt as supple as young grass, and her flesh moved with the softness of doeskin under her fur garment. For the first time since she left Pocasset, her mind felt at ease.

As she approached the village, she noticed the rows of wetus had emptied. The people gathered in the great circle at the center of the encampment. It pleased her that no one saw her before she slipped into her favorite white dress and adorned herself with a wampum belt and shell ornaments. She wanted to darken her tattoos and freshen her face paint before joining in the dance and war council to follow. The people and sachems would wait for her.

She ducked into her wetu, then called out in her native tongue, "Where is the lazy squaw who let this fire fade to coals?" Laughing Water appeared in a moment with arms laden with kindling, balanced above her heavy abdomen. Weetamoo's teasing did not amuse her. Weetamoo saw that the girl's time approached as she wobbled around the fire pit and clumsily dropped sticks to the floor. Her daughter held on to supporting branches of the wetu as she knelt by the fire. She pulled dry milkweed kapok from her bag and placed it over the coals. Leaning some of the smallest twigs over the downy fluff, she bent to breathe life back into the fire. Flames flickered and spread with each puff.

Weetamoo turned away, without further comment, and began her dressing ritual. Dropping her fur on the ground, she pulled items from her basket, seeking her most ornate garment. She removed her favorite dress. Its deerskin hide had been made soft and white by stretching and rubbing it with macerated brains. It slid pleasingly over her brown skin and she wrapped it tightly about her slender waist with a wampum belt. She left one shoulder bare and straightened the fringed edges over her full breasts. Her nipples stiffened at the touch of soft deerskin. She arched her back and closed her eyes. Lifting her chin and certain that, even with child, she could still raise the interest of the young men in the village, she took a deep breath. Most importantly, she meant to arouse the interest of her husband, Quannopinn, whom she would lay with that night.

She opened her eyes. The firelight glowed brighter now.

"Come and help me with my paints, Laughing Water. We cannot delay. Metacomet awaits my arrival at the dance." She spoke absently as she dug through another pack and tossed strands of shells and leather amulets onto her sleeping platform. She pulled out a necklace made of purple quahog wampum and slid it over her neck. The color stood out against the white dress and her tawny skin. She fastened other bracelets around her wrists and ankles and slid her feet into clean new moccasins that matched her dress. Though it was cold outside, she chose not to wear her leggings. She wanted her legs bare in firelight at the dance.

It pleased Weetamoo that Laughing Water had taken so many of her prized possessions from the burning swamp camp. She had left baskets of food and furs behind but had made certain she brought items her mother valued as they fled. "Come, daughter," Weetamoo repeated. "I need you to darken my tattoos." She held out a small pointed stick.

The young girl struggled to her feet, waddled over to Weetamoo, and took the blackened stick from her hand. She dipped it into a little clay pot of bear fat and charcoal and traced the faint angular patterns on Weetamoo's upper arms. When she finished, she backed up to the wooden sleeping platform and gripped the wooden slats, cautiously lowering herself to sit on its edge. With knees wide apart, she allowed her swollen middle to hang down so she could bend to trace the designs on Weetamoo's ankles and calves. She breathed short heavy breaths as her baby crowded out all the space beneath her ribs.

"You grow very near your time. See how he has turned his head downward. Soon he will be in your arms." Weetamoo put her hand on Laughing Water's abdomen. It was clear that the baby had dropped lower into the birth canal. She touched her daughter's face, looking at the young woman who no longer could be called a child. Laughing Water turned her attention back to the tattoos.

Weetamoo used an English horsehair brush to smooth her hair so it fell down her back between her shoulder blades. She slipped a sinew along the nape of her neck and caught it around her shining black hair. She wrapped it over and under down its length and flipped it forward to tie off the end. She looked down and saw that her sudden movement had caused the young woman to smudge the design. She gently nudged her belly with her knee and said, "What happened, Daughter? Did your papoose want to add to my tattoo?"

The girl looked up at her with a worn smile. "Nay, Mother. It was your movement that changed my stroke. I will fix it," she said, rubbing it off with a bit of leather.

"If you were not so slow-moving, I would not be tying my own hair," she teased. "You used to do this all for me and paint my face. Now I have to do these things for myself. I hope when you wear this papoose on your back you will regain your speed and skill. If not, I will have to find another squaw to help me, and you will sleep outside with the white woman." Weetamoo looked down and smiled at the young girl, who did not look up.

"Listen," Weetamoo said, tilting her chin. "All the people are chanting. They wait for me to begin, and here I am with a fat, tired squaw whose round little papoose gets in the way of dressing her sachem. You make the great King Philip wait, you know," she said, nudging the girl again.

Weetamoo's motion caused another smudge on her calf, but Laughing Water did not alter it. Weetamoo would not see the back of her calf. She straightened up and reached behind herself to rub the small of her back. "There, Sachem," Laughing Water said. "Go to the dance. I will lie here and rest until you return."

"I give thanks to the Creator that your time is near. I cannot manage very much longer with a swollen, tired squaw and lazy, foolish white woman as my only help." She tucked an eagle feather in her hair and laughed as she softly stroked Laughing Water's belly. She smiled and turned, then ducked out of the wetu. Laughing Water lay back on the platform and winced as a birth spasm rocked her pelvis.

Weetamoo stepped out into the cold night and wrapped her fur around her shoulders. Thin tendrils of sweet smoke rose from the embers of cooking fires near the wetus lining the path. The smoldering fires cast a blanket of smoke that reflected the central fire's orange glow. The people made a great circle around the fire. They swayed from side to side in rhythm with the drums and chanted songs of thanksgiving to the Creator and spirits of the ancestors. Their faces lit up with the excitement of the raids to come.

As Weetamoo approached, a small girl turned and saw her. Her mouth fell open at the sight of Weetamoo stepping toward her all in white. Weetamoo smiled at the thought that even a child could be so struck by her beauty. The little girl tugged on her mother's sleeve. The mother leaned down and then looked in the direction the child pointed. She gasped and took a step back, then reached for her nearest neighbors motioning that they should part way for the Sachem Weetamoo. The crowd parted and allowed Weetamoo to step into the circle of light. There was an audible sigh as they turned to see the Pocasset leader in all her famed beauty.

Weetamoo kept her chin high and her eyes down as she walked toward the leaders. At what she thought was just the right moment, she tucked her chin slightly, lifted her eyes, and stared straight into the heart of Metacomet. He shot an approving look straight into her heart and they held one another's gaze for a moment. Then she lowered her eyes and walked to her husband, Quannopinn. Before him, she looked up—straight into his heart. She let her fur slip slightly from her bare shoulder and saw the effect she wanted in his eyes. *Yes,* she thought, *he will follow Metacomet wherever I say.*

Quannopinn reached over to replace her fur and drew her close to his side as he continued shifting his weight from foot to foot in rhythm with the music. Weetamoo heard thin, high melodies of wooden flutes mixed with voices of the people and beats of the drums. She fell into the pattern of the swaying dance, purposefully bumping slightly against Quannopinn's loincloth with her hip. She felt the growing effect she had on him with each touch and looked over her shoulder into his face. He narrowed his brows and bent down to whisper in her ear, "You can taunt me now, Sachem, but it is I who will master you this night."

"Yes, I know you will, my Sannup," she said with a smile, leaning into him again.

Metacomet signaled the drummers, and they played the rhythm to stop. All the music, chanting, and dancing ended simultaneously. Metacomet stepped into the middle of the circle.

"My people," he said, "it is a great honor to be among so many of our nation tonight. We have come great distances to be together in our bodies, minds, hearts, and spirits in this gathering place. Our ancestors look down and smile on us at the bringing of our families to us from Narragansett country. It is good to look upon so many Wampanoags, the People of the First Light. And all our friends from all over the Algonquin land. We thank our hosts, the Sokoki and the Pocumtucs, for sharing their bounty. Let us all offer thanks for this great gift." He placed a pouch of tobacco in the fire. Sparks danced upward in the night between flickering flames and smoke.

The shaman came forward and said, "We offer thanks to the Great Spirit, Kistannit, our Creator, for bringing our people together in the land of our grandfathers. We offer thanks to our Earth Mother, Metanokit for all the bounty of our earth. We thank her for the three sisters—beans, corn, and squash."

A slow, soft drumbeat sounded. Three women stepped forward carrying baskets. One was filled with corn, one with beans, and the last with squash. One by one, they placed them in the fire. It hissed and sputtered and then licked at the reed baskets until they blazed. A sweet aroma wafted from cornhusks curling in the flames. The squash swelled from the heat and split, sending small bursts of yellow flesh into the fire.

"And we thank our Earth Mother Metanokit for our brothers of the earth who give themselves to us as food." The drumbeats sounded stronger but hushed from rabbit fur wrapped around the drumsticks. Two children came forward. The older boy tossed a killed be-nah-nah—a partridge—into the flame. With its wings spread wide, its feathers gave off bright colors as fire consumed their oils. The younger one held out a fish he had caught earlier in the day but, too afraid of the snapping blaze, held on to it. His brother put one hand on his shoulder and took the little fellow's wrist and swung it back, then toward the flames, shaking the fish loose so that it swung almost to the other side of the fire. People laughed as the little boy turned and grinned, showing all his teeth and shining eyes. He puffed up his chest as he strutted back to his parents.

"We thank Potanit, Spirit of Fire who cooks our food and warms our homes and makes our work easy." A man stepped forward with the carcass of a doe slung over his shoulders. The man cast the doe into the heaving fire. People began to sway and hum slightly with the drumming. the savory smell of seared meat soon replaced the acrid smell of burning fur. Fire sizzled as it ate through the fat on the small deer. Weetamoo's empty stomach let out a growl, but no one heard it over the drumming and soft chanting growing a little louder and faster.

"We thank Paumagussett, Spirit of the Great Waters of life in whom swim our brothers the fish and eel and quahog," the shaman called out. A woman drizzled water from a gourd onto the fire, and it sizzled and hissed and set up scented plumes of steam into the night sky. Drumming and chanting intensified.

"And we thank Tashin, the Spirit of the Wind, who will carry our dreams to Keesuckquand, our Grandfather Spirit of the Heavens," the medicine man continued. He sprinkled something into the flames that made the fire sparkle and glitter with color. The people cried, "Hah!" and the drummers beat more loudly.

"We thank our Grandfather Nepaushet, the sun, for warming and lighting our days and our Grandmother Nanepaushet, the moon, for giving us rising and falling seas and for lighting our nights. We give thanks, too, to all the Nucksuog beings of the star nations beyond who hold the stories of our hearts in the heavens. We give thanks to all the spirits in the four winds, in the land, in the sea, and in our living brothers and sisters. We are one with them and with one another." The drumming and chanting was much louder now.

"Let us join in song," one of the drummers cried out. He began to chant, "Hey-ey yunga Ho-o yunga, Hey-ey yung yung," and the people replied, "Hey-ey yunga Ho-o yunga, Hey-ey yung yung." Gently swaying, people began circling the fire in a steady pattern in time to the chanting.

Wearing a coyote skin over his head, the shaman danced into the middle with a burning sweetgrass bundle in his hand. As he danced around the circle, he used an eagle feather to fan smoke from the sweetgrass smudge stick toward the people. After he had circled the fire four times, he stopped before Metacomet and used his feather to paint sacred smoke all around the Sachem. He brushed smoke into Metacomet's eyes and ears and nose and mouth. Metacomet breathed it in deeply. The old medicine man waved feathery smoke over Metacomet's head and heart and all around his body. He chanted as he danced as Metacomet stood tall and proud in the center.

"The earth is our Mother. We must take care of her," the singer called in a steady rhythm, and people echoed their reply, "The earth is our Mother. We will take care of her. Hey-ey yunga Ho-o yunga, Hey-ey yung yung. Hey-ey yunga Ho-o yunga, Hey-ey yung yung."

"The sky is our Father. We must take care of him," he called and the people echoed, "The sky is our Father, we will take care of him. Hey-ey yunga Ho-o yunga, Hey-ey yung yung. Hey-ey yunga Ho-o yunga, Hey-ey yung yung."

"The trees are our brothers. We must take care of them," he called.

"The trees are our brothers. We will take care of them. Hey-ey yunga Ho-o yunga, Hey-ey yung yung. Hey-ey yunga Ho-o yunga, Hey-ey yung yung."

"The lakes are our sisters. We must take care of them," he called.

"The lakes are our sisters. We will take care of them. Hey-ey yunga Ho-o yunga, Hey-ey yung yung. Hey-ey yunga Ho-o yunga, Hey-ey yung yung."

They repeated variations of the chant many times as they circled the fire. With the smoke from the burning sweetgrass, the shaman smudged each person entering the sacred circle. First Metacomet, followed by warriors, then elders, then women, and last, young people. Weetamoo and Quannopinn joined in the swirling dance. They stepped slowly side to side, turning in small circles as they went. Every person made room for the next to join in and attuned their movements to one another. As they tired, they left the spinning circle and took seats on a ring of tree trunks surrounding the fire. The sacred gifts burned to ashes, and the flames died down. The celebration of thanksgiving went on long into the night.

They danced until they were spent, each triumphantly leaving the circle amid chants and drums and loud cheers of respect. Weetamoo walked from the circle panting and holding her side. Her heart thumped in her chest and throbbed in her neck. She felt its steady pumping in her arms and legs and head. She leaned over a stump and beckoned for a drink. A young squaw brought her a gourdful of cold stream water. She tipped her head back and drained the gourd and signaled for another just as Quannopinn walked over to her. Firelight illuminated his sweaty, dark skin, and his hair clung thickly to his forehead and neck. He tipped his chin to her, and she offered him the gourd.

He drank in great gulps, letting the water fall from the edges of the gourd and down his face and chest. "Well, Wife, I have no need for the pesuponk now. I can just go throw myself in the stream as I am," he laughed.

She laughed with him. "And I, as well."

"Then let us go," he said and reached his hand around to catch her by the waist and lead her away from the ring of firelight toward the darkened path.

A seductive smile of a crescent moon slid out from under its veil of clouds. The night's breath blew over her damp skin, but it did not cool the fire in her heart. "It is my honor to bathe with a sannup and sachem who will lead his people in many brave raids," she said. "As we lie together in the darkness, so we shall fight at one another's side." She slid her hand around his back and slipped her fingers between his loincloth and his skin. *Yes*, she thought, *we will fight together. I will not suffer another man who cowers from a fight.*

He slid his arm under her dress and squeezed her firmly. *Hmm*, she thought. *Such a wise choice for me, Metacomet. I will thank you later, Brother.* She walked easily with her sannup toward the water's edge.

Mary's Renewal

Mary walked through the village on a bitter cold day. The sun shone high in the sky and with no clouds above, its brightness amplified the whiteness of snow and smoke to bathe all in a shimmering light. She squinted as she mused about her time here. Grateful they had stopped for over a fortnight, Mary had finally rested and her wound had nearly healed. She'd had time to mend her worn clothes and to ask for help in making leggings and moccasins like the Indians wore to protect her legs from the cold. And her skill in sewing brought her new rewards.

Philip paid her a shilling for the shirt she made. When she received it, she thought she must offer it to her master, but Quannopinn told her, "No, Mary. That is your own. You must accept it in barter for your work." Philip asked her to make a cap and paid her for that with a dinner of a thick pancake, the sweetest she had tasted since her journey began.

After making the items for Philip, others came forward with requests, and she had no lack of work. A squaw offered to pay her for a shirt, and Mary joyfully accepted a piece of bear for that. For a pair of knitted stockings, another paid her with a quart of peas.

Mary decided she would share her bounty with her dame and master and invited them to join her for a meal. They agreed, and she thought perhaps Weetamoo would stop her venomous attacks on her. *Perhaps we can begin to show more respect for one another, since I have shown myself as useful and have learned to barter. Perhaps my resourcefulness will impress her.*

Mary made as savory a meal as she could with no salt or herbs from her garden. When she finished cooking, she took the meal into the wetu and invited them to eat. Quannopinn flashed his approval of her in a broad smile. Weetamoo scowled at her with a countenance as dark as ever. As they all settled down, Mary prepared a dish for them to share. With chunks of charred bear meat and a generous serving of peas, it made a sumptuous feast compared to the boiled horse hoof broth and scanty ground nuts they barely survived on lately.

Mary passed the dish to Quannopinn as her master. He ate ravenously and well, but Weetamoo did not. Quannopinn speared a morsel on his knife, and Weetamoo tasted that piece but no more. Her sullen look spurned Mary's efforts to ingratiate herself with them.

The haughty wench, Mary thought, conscious of her own hungry belly and calluses she raised in the hasty making of the shirt that bought the meal. *Let the devil take her,* Mary thought as she ate heartily and ignored her guest as she never would have thought permissible in her own home. She noticed that Quannopinn, too, paid little mind to Weetamoo's ill mood.

So a truce between the two women did not happen over the meal. Mary took such great offense, she vowed at that moment never to make such an effort again. Especially with the scarcity of food and the difficulty to obtain it. *So Weetamoo, you proud dame, will just have to find her own,* she thought.

Indeed, Mary encountered theft of her own supply of food and clothing in the camp. A few days before, while looking for her children, she met a white woman named Mary Thurston who gave her a cap. Mary wore it with delight until the squaw who owned Mary Thurston came and took it away. Another time, she had a spoon of meal in her pocket and, when she reached in to find it, she found five hard kernels of corn instead. Though the kernels could refresh her, she found it difficult to understand why the people here had no respect for others' property.

As she thought about it, property seemed the crux of all the trouble their two peoples experienced with one another. Property. The natives thought they could sell land and still use it. They had no problem taking food grown on someone else's private land or even helping themselves to tools or livestock if so inclined.

Wasn't it what filled all the courts of late? Protests on both sides involved boundaries not respected or rights to land challenged. She wondered if something simple in their nature prevented them from understanding the permanence of a deed or the concept of ownership. In any case, she would hold on tightly to what belonged to her, and they could do as they would with theirs. She had made her last effort to share with Weetamoo.

Despite the loss of her supplies and cap and Weetamoo's unkind behavior, Mary kept her heart strong. She would use her skills in handwork to make her burden lighter. And she had further reason to feel hopeful.

Earlier that day, when Mary sought out Mary Thurston to thank her for offering her the cap, Goody Thurston replied, "I only regret that my dame took it from you. But, Mistress Rowlandson, I wanted to tell you that I know where you might find your son Joseph."

Mary took her hand and said, "Goody Thurston, your news warms me more than any cap, and I am indebted to you for your kindness. Pray tell, where will I find him?"

So that same morning, Mary saw her son again. It shocked her to find him lying on muddy, cold ground with his arms outstretched. "Joseph, what are you doing? Surely you cannot sleep like that or you will get a chill. Stand up at once." Her voice sounded harsher and shriller than she expected, and the boy jumped to his feet.

"Forgive me, Mother, but I was in prayer, not asleep."

"In prayer? Son, why ever in such a way as this?" She brushed snow and dirt off his coat.

He leaned over to her and whispered, "So they would not see me and know what I am doing. They like it not for me to pray."

"Oh, I see. Could you not just do it away from them?"

"Nay, mother. They want me always in their sight. That is why I could not come to you."

"Ah, yes. They see you as chattel that they can sell and would not want another to take you away from them." She wondered why they understood chattel but not possessions.

"See, they watch us even now, so we dare not pray together. They fear all who pray. They say it brings 'bad magic,' and so whenever I pray, I must do so silently."

"That poses no consequence, Joseph. For the Lord our God hears our every thought, so you just continue being a good boy and pray you in your mind, and all will be fine with you."

"I must go in now, Mother. I see her beckoning me. I think she goes to a war dance. I heard some of the warriors preparing to go on another raid tonight or tomorrow. So she will make me stay in her lodge so I will not walk off. Goodbye, Mother. Thank you for coming."

He gave her a quick hug around her shoulders.

"Goodbye, my son. I will pray for you," she whispered.

Warriors Unite

A s before any battle, the warriors joined in a dance to prepare for the day ahead. Drummers called all to the sacred circle. The shaman called for blessings from the four winds and blessed the circle and musicians with smudge sticks of sage and sweetgrass. Once all had gathered, he motioned for the drummers to lower their music. Metacomet stepped forward to a haunting tune on a bone flute and the shaman caressed him with sacred smoke. Slowly the people quieted to hear what Metacomet had to say.

"My brothers, it is good to be here with you today. We are the people of this country. It is our right granted by the Great Spirit and by our grandfathers. This land was given to us by the Creator. We have come together to prepare for the great fight for our country. We must protect it from harm."

The crowd murmured in agreement.

"We have seen the English take our land and cut down our trees to build their fair houses. They do not live in peace upon the land. They only take from the earth, never giving back. They do not prize the great gifts for their use but only see the profits they can make from them." As he paused, the people were more vocal in their agreement.

"They have slaughtered our brothers of the forest to sell their furs to their countrymen in England. They cut down our brothers, the trees, to make great ships to carry away the abundance of our country and to carry back more English to further their destruction. My brothers, it is time for us to stop them." At his words, younger warriors let out a war whoop, and older ones nodded to each other in assent.

"The English who first came to this country were but a handful of people—forlorn, poor, and distressed," he went on to say. "My father was then sachem; he relieved their distresses in the most kind and hospitable manner. He gave them land to plant and build upon. They flourished and increased. By various means, they got possessed of a great part of his territory. But he remained their friend until he died.

"After my elder brother became sachem, they seized and confined him and thereby threw him into an illness that caused his death."

He paused and then said quietly so everyone would have to hush to hear him, "Soon after I became sachem, they disarmed all my people. They took our land." Angry voices rose here and there among the tribes. He paused again and began a little more loudly, "But a small part of the dominion of my ancestors remains." Then he shouted, "I am determined not to live until I have no country!" Cries of assent answered him.

Young men jumped to their feet, raising their fists and knives in the air. Old men yelled as if young again and got to their feet as well. Even women and children screamed out their pain and anger at the English. Metacomet shouted over their voices, "Stand together with me and fight, my friends! Iotash, Netopash."

At once people rose to their feet again, and a new dance began, a war dance. Metacomet spun around holding his red mantle with outstretched arms, and as he spun, his long wampum chest plate swung, making a wheel of red and white. It reminded Weetamoo of blood on English skin. Her heart sped up at the sight of it. Metacomet threw his head back and let out a scream from the depths of his heart. She threw her head back and let out a scream to match his.

The young bloods gathered up their hatchets and war clubs and raised them into the night air. Jumping in behind Metacomet, they acted out battles as they danced. Matoonas leapt to his feet, eager to show the young pups what true warriors could do. As he swung his club with both hands in diving arcs, others backed away to give him a wide berth. Quannopinn left Weetamoo's side and ran crouching into the circle, feigning the noise of wounded partridge. He then leapt into the air as, with a loud screech, he reached the center.

Young boys added more wood to the central fire and cook fires, ablaze with speared meat sizzling and herbed sobaheg stewing deliciously. Many women prepared parched meal and ground nuts for the men to take on their raids, for they would be off before dawn to raid Northampton.

Weetamoo reached behind her back to free her knife from her belt and raced into the center of the dance, shrieking as she swung her blade in deep, powerful thrusts. Her heart beat faster than the drums as she reached down and pulled her blade across the throat of an imagined fallen enemy. In a swift motion, she enacted a single swipe over her opponent's head and raised her imaginary trophy scalp high, crying out loudly as she danced in a tight circle. Younger fighters backed away from her intensity, and soon only those seasoned in battle remained to demonstrate to the young techniques that, in earlier fights, had won battles with English or native enemies.

The dance in the firelight went on until the last flame flickered out and warriors and their families made their ways home for the night. In the morning, they would take different paths, families with some warriors to the north and Metacomet and his warriors to the south. As they did each time before a battle, the people had quiet thoughts and shared quiet words as they faced another parting, each hoping for a happy reunion before long.

War Drums

There would be little sleep that night. Drumming had already begun, and wetus emptied as each family gathered around the central fire. Mary wrapped her cloak about her and walked out into the night.

She paused in the deserted, smoky village. Through the haze of campfire smoke, she raised her eyes to the spring sky. The rising moon painted the high heavens, and earth's darkness reflected on the low hanging clouds. Unlike their bright whiteness by day, the clouds appeared black against the silvery sky and moved by slow degrees away to the east. Mary thought, *Yes, this darkness that I dwell in is only a filmy vapor that will pass until I, too, shall move east and be redeemed into the fullness of the bright bosom of God's promised land. With God's help I shall see these travails as mere shadows endeavoring to stand between me and my true purpose.*

While immersed in her thoughts, she hadn't noticed how her feet had begun walking in a steady rhythm, following the beat of the distant drums. She moved closer to the source of the sound. Her stride became steadier and more sure. Treading the beaten path between wigwams, she felt drawn to the drummers and the crowd that formed around them.

Pushing between the elbows of her tall captors, she saw several men and boys ringed around a great drum. Each held a wooden stick with a smooth rounded end, and they struck the drum in short, even strokes. Together they thumped, sometimes more heavily, and created a pattern of sound that echoed in her ears and in her breast. Like those around her, she swayed to the slow and even tempo. She shifted her weight from foot to foot with the soldier-like cadence of a funeral march, with an added beat that imitated the thumping of her own heart.

As people around her began odd soft murmurings, she found herself humming along in nameless words. She joined in with the chanting without thinking about the words, just letting her heart sense the spirit of the moment.

Something crept into her, some unnamed emotion. She felt as though the drumming and her heart became one and the voices thrummed in unison with them. Even as she had at times felt rapturous enlightenment when joined in voice with her congregation at prayer meetings in Lancaster, for the present few moments, she felt a oneness with God—and strangely, with the people in the circle and all living creatures under the sun. The intensity of her emotion so moved her that tears blurred her vision. She could see only the flickering firelight casting its glow upon swaying figures and towering trees surrounding them.

Her ears found comfort in the steady rhythm and soft voices. Her mind's eye transformed those around her into saints in the heavens. She blinked, and she felt herself rising into the sky among them, still humming and swaying softly. She had no idea of passage of time, only of deep energy passing within and without her body. When the drumming suddenly stopped, she felt as if a great stone had been hurled into her chest. Her limbs ached, and her body felt its full weight crushing down on her soul.

She took a deep breath of icy air and closed her eyes.

When she opened them again, she recognized herself as the only saint among sinners. She turned on her heels and ran back to the wigwam as if being chased. She hoped God had not seen her writhing in their midst. *What on earth had come over me?* she wondered as she ducked into the wetu.

Forgive me Lord for my weakness, she prayed, wondering still at how she had fallen under such a spell. She told herself she had been bewitched, yet a part of her yearned to go back. *Nay,* she told herself, *I will not succumb to their evil ways. Lord protect me and watch over me,* she whispered.

Listening from her sleeping platform, she heard drumbeats getting stronger and calls of the people growing louder. The sound of their war whoops foretold that the warriors prepared to fight again. She prayed for whoever would suffer next at their hands. She prayed for herself and her children. And she tried to sleep, knowing that, once again, she would have to pack up and move on in the morning.

Northward Path
Ninth Remove
March 14, 1675

The warriors rode out, and Weetamoo was with them. Her heart soared at the thought of taking part in the attack on Northampton at Nonotuck near the bend in the river to the south. She rode with Quannopinn, Metacomet, and his sister Amie's husband, Tispaquin, the black sachem, and Sancumachu, a Pocumtuc sachem. The raid went well, as they easily broke through the fort palisades and burned nine houses, killing six enemies, including one woman.

While some warriors kept the militia busy in their garrison, others took all their sheep and horses. Though victorious, Metacomet's forces suffered many losses, as they discovered too late that two companies of English soldiers had come to reinforce the militia in the garrison.

The British outnumbered her people today, but Weetamoo knew her people would return to fight the foreigners again with their allies. Weetamoo's heart remained lifted knowing that at last she was fighting to push her enemies back, not simply running for her life.

They took horses to ride, fastened sheep to others, and made away, passing briefly through the camp at Coasset before heading a short distance upriver to a crossing place. The people at Coasset had gone ahead to set up a new camp after receiving word from their runners that they had encountered more colonial soldiers close by.

Their new camp sat on the east side of the Kwinitekw, about five miles above Coasset, in Sokoki land still unexplored by white men. For now, they could rest, since without horses, the soldiers could follow only on foot. The mountains and river sheltered them and provided good lookout points from the camp.

Awashonks greeted the warriors with a great smile when she saw them coming into the new camp. "You are just in time with our dinner. Come, come. We've lit the fires to cook your feast."

"Old Sister, have you never any other thought in your mind than when you will enjoy your next meal?" Quannopinn joked with her.

"How well you know me. And I have never seen you walk away from any of my dinners, have I?"

While the cooks prepared the food, the sachems and sagamores sat together drinking sumac tea. It warmed and refreshed them as they shared their news and made plans.

"You encountered two companies at the garrison, you say?" asked Muttaump, the Nipmuc leader. "They will follow us, then. And we cannot fight so many without severe losses."

"True," Metacomet answered. "So we crossed at Coasset to confuse them. Tispaquin and Sancumachu have laid false trails as well on the other side of the river, and we have the advantage of time."

"We will have to go further north," Monaco said.

"I say no," Quannopinn disagreed "We turn on them and destroy or drive them out. We have the warriors now, and they don't."

Weetamoo thought about what to say. She didn't want to dishonor her husband's opinion but felt she must remind him that their numbers included a large band of women, children, and elderly, some of them sick, tired, and hungry. They would not want to expose that vulnerability by fighting so close by. Awashonks spoke up before Weetamoo said something that might again drive a wedge between her and Quannopinn.

"You forget, My Cousin," she said, addressing Quannopinn's idea, "that we have two urgent needs. One, as you say, to stop the English, but the other, to get our people to safety. Which do you think is more important?"

"The one solves the other, does it not?" he answered.

"Not so," answered Monaco. "This enemy does not have a single head we can sever and turn our back on. In the same moment we stop them here, will they not rise up again in another place?"

"We face another worry, too, as planting season approaches," Weetamoo added, "Where will we plant and with what seed? We are living now on gleanings and spoils, but what of tomorrow?"

Canonchet, the old Narragansett leader, stood up. "I will go. I will go south to my country and get our seed. I failed to bring it, and so I will go. They have taken our past, but I will not let them take our future."

"And I will go, too," Amie said. "We are the planters, and we know where we buried the seed corn from the last harvest. I will lead the Narragansett women in this effort." She spoke with the same assuredness as her brother. No one dared to argue with her.

Amie's husband, Tispaquin, nodded at her. "I, too, will go, and I will bring warriors to protect the farming party. And we will make a little havoc along the way to keep the English busy."

"And you will take Laughing Water with you," Weetamoo stated "Camp life bores her, and the travel will do her good while she awaits her son's birth. She, too, knows where to find the seed corn, and you will need many hands to carry it back." While she attributed her daughter's recent behavior to boredom, she wanted her away from the sickness that spread among them, claiming many children. A full moon's time would elapse before the birth of Weetamoo's grandson, but even if Laughing Water gave birth on the way, it would be better than losing him to disease. Weetamoo felt certain that, under Tispaquin's and Canonchet's protection, she had no reason to have concern for her safety.

"Taubut, we have a good plan," Metacomet said. In the morrow, you will prepare for the journey. The rest of us will rest here before taking the path to the north. With the Mohawks now siding with the Connecticut governor against us, we can expect no help from them. We will need support of our brothers in the north to end this war once and for all."

A Fair Bargain

Mary stood outside the wigwam of sagamore Monaco as she had every morning for several days in the new camp.

"Monaco, I call upon you to pay me the wages we agreed for my toil." She had made him a shirt, as agreed, but he had failed to give her compensation. So each day on her way to fill her water buckets at the river, she stopped outside his wigwam to demand her payment.

For many days, no one seemed to notice her boldness, but once it became regular, people showed interest in the morning ritual. Some women dallied at the water's edge giggling over the fact that the white women would confront the Nashaway leader in such a public display. A small knot of young men stood nearby wagering on whether the sagamore would ignore her again, relent to her demands, or knock her on the head and end her nuisance.

As Mary shifted the weight of her buckets, she called out again, "Sachem Monaco, can you hear me?"

The wolf-fur flap of his wigwam swung open, and the bystanders let out gasps and stepped back.

"Good morning, Sir." Mary stood still and tall.

"Ascowequa'ssin, Mistress." His good eye squinted at her, and he had no kindness in his voice.

"I would like to discuss the terms of our agreement, Sir," she began. "It has been three days since . . ."

"Enough!" Monaco shouted. Glancing briefly at the gathered spectators, he put up his hand to stop her from speaking so freely, then said quietly, "Come inside, and we will talk of this." He ducked back into the darkness. The gathering grew silent.

Mary hesitated a moment and said, "Yes, indeed we will." She set down her water buckets and bent to enter the open doorway.

Closing her eyes to allow them to adjust, she said, "Thank you for seeing me, Sir."

Monaco already sat by the fire looking around for his pipe. He found it tucked between the fine rush mats lining the inside of his walls and their bent wooden framework. He took a pinch of tobacco from a mink skin bag hanging on the wall, pressed it into his pipe, and lit it with a long twig he had touched to the fire.

"Yes, I have the shirt you prepared, and it is quite fine. But not so fine as befits a sagamore, for I see no English buttons or lace as on Metacom's goodly shirts." He held up the plain white linen shirt.

"'Tis true, for King Philip I did use such buttons and lace as I had on my own garments, but here in this wilderness, there are no such items ready for my use."

"So, while you made me a shirt, it is not the shirt I was promised." Monaco slowly blinked his one eye.

"But I made no promise," Mary said, smoothing her apron.

"Did I not ask you for a shirt like Metacom's?" Monaco raised his voice slightly.

"Yea, but you did not ask for embellishment as well," Mary parried with an equally firm voice, though inside, she surprised herself with her boldness. The man before her had captured her from her home. She had seen him knock the life from her poor little nephew William in a trice. Without meaning to, her eyes roamed the walls to see if he could reach his war club.

Monaco moved suddenly as if to lunge for her, and she mustered all her strength not to flinch. They sat for a moment staring at one another in silence. Then Monaco laughed.

"So it is. How clever you are, Mary Rowlandson, to withhold that which I did not expressly request." He settled back. After another moment, he said, "Now let us begin a new arrangement. Since this shirt does not satisfy me and since you have no means to do so, why do we not agree to you making me a second shirt of equal quality for my son who will be born under the summer moon?" He puffed on his pipe.

Mary thought about his suggestion, then said, "Oh, Sir, I would be pleased to make you a second shirt but will need further payment for my effort. For you see, without payment for the first, I cannot obtain the makings for a second."

"So, then, Mistress. What shall we do?" He tapped his pipe in his palm. "Shall I beat you so that you will relent from your daily demands?" He knitted his brows and leaned toward her as he said it.

"Sir, if you hurt or kill me, you will invoke the ire of Weetamoo and Quannopinn whom I serve and who would lose my redemption pay. But if you do not, I can make for you many shirts." Mary took care not to use any smugness in her voice but felt the strength of her position.

Mary saw a brief spark of rage in Monaco's eye. He glanced at his club, still fastened to the framework of his lodge. She flinched but hoped he did not notice. He looked at her, a mere white woman in ragged dirty clothes, sitting before him, rationing the affection of her tormentors against him, a mighty warrior. He laughed out loud. Only her audacity surpassed the lunacy of her argument.

"You are a woman of strong heart and weak mind," he laughed. "But I will make the bargain you request because you amuse me. In seven days, you will bring me another shirt as good or better than the first. For both, I will pay you with this knife." He pulled a long hunting knife from its sheath behind his back and thrust it toward her over the fire. He did not move his hand away from the heat and slowly turned the blade from side to side, shining the reflection of the flames into Mary's eyes. Holding it there, he said in a low tone, "Hear me, Woman. This time you will make no public demands, or you will receive your payment in your heart."

Mary did not speak until he lowered the blade and returned it to its sheath. Then she said, "Thank you, Sir, for this meeting. I will return in a week's time with your second shirt, and we can meet again for our exchange. Good day, Sir," she said and backed uneasily toward the door, keeping her eyes on him the whole time.

"Good day," Monaco said, laughing.

Mary backed out and walked straight back to her own campfire, forgetting her buckets in her haste. Loathe to chance another encounter with Monaco so soon, she waited until she saw him leave the camp before collecting them.

After a week, Mary met again with Monaco and, as agreed, he paid her with his knife, this time in its leather sheath. She hurried back from her meeting to give the knife to her master Quannopinn, thinking no slave should have such a gift. Quannopinn accepted her gift, possibly thinking the same. Or perhaps he thought she might use it against him or more likely his squaw who had not softened her ways with Mary in all the long days of her captivity. Weetamoo sat on the other side of their lodge, her baby at her breast, and glared at Mary.

Quannopinn paid little mind to Weetamoo's foul mood. Instead, he listened with pleasure as Mary spoke of how her negotiations had won out over Monaco. He laughed and told her, "Mistress, you have chanced what most brave warriors would never do. It is remarkable that Monaco allowed you to live. I am honored to have this gift from you."

"Why, thank you, Sir," Mary said. His words pleased her and raised a brief flutter of fear that her provocation of so powerful and dangerous a man as Monaco could have ended badly. Weetamoo got up and left without a word to either of them.

"Mary, I must go," Quannopinn said with a tired sigh. "Thank you for this knife and for your skillful negotiations. I will tell Philip that we must enlist your help in trading for your redemption. Thank you again." He rose and left without waiting for her reply. Outside, she heard him and Weetamoo bickering in the moonlight.

What an odd pair the two made. He so polite and wise, and she so angry and rude. It is a wonder he does not throw her out, Mary thought, sopping up remnants of their tea. By the time she went outside the lodge, Quannopinn and Weetamoo had gone. *Good,* she thought, *I shall have a peaceful sleep tonight without notice of their shameless rutting.* It occurred to her that they had not been coupling as often as they had when she first joined them. Whatever the reason, she felt grateful. She turned her mind to daydreaming that she had sweet cake with butter and cream to take with her tea while she gathered up the pot and bowls to clean them.

No Return for Canochet

Weetamoo woke alone in her bed the next morning. The baby slept quietly on his rocking board. Quannopinn must have found another bed in the village. *Good,* she thought. *He must have time to think about his behavior, treating that white woman as an equal. And her, showing such disrespect for Monaco, with him laughing about it. What was he thinking? She should have been whipped or worse for such offensive behavior. Was he losing his mind?* A scratch on the wetu interrupted the questions in her mind.

"Howoh? Who is it?" she called out.

"It is your sister," answered the younger woman.

"What is it?" Weetamoo wondered why she had come so early, and truly, why she came at all. The two women seldom spoke. Each felt jealous of the other, Weetamoo for her sister's marriage to Metacomet and Nanuskooke for Weetamoo's ongoing relationship with him and for her privileges as a sachem.

"We have word from Narragansett country. The black sachem Tispaquin returns," her sister responded.

Weetamoo got up quickly. She flung open the door flap. "What have you heard? Come in quickly," she said, pulling her by the arm.

"They return with food, but not all. Many of our supplies burned in the English fires on the night we fled Canonchet's village. They bring baskets of corn and many seeds to plant." She pulled a small basket of corn from her pack and handed it to her sister.

"Oh, Nanuskooke, I thank you for this good news. And for this corn." Weetamoo resented that as Metacom's wife, Nanuskooke often learned important news before she did. She looked into her own pack baskets, saying, "I must hurry to bring this word to

Quannopinn. Surely he and the others will want to hear the words of Anawan and Canonchet."

"Weetamoo, there is sad news. Laughing Water had her child, but he did not live."

"What! How did this happen? Where is she? When?"

She is resting in my nushweety. It was only yesterday, but she had a hard birth, and the boy tangled in her cord. I am so sorry, Sister. He took no breath after his birth." She held out her arms, and the sisters hugged as they hadn't done since their childhood.

Weetamoo burst into tears, and they cried in each other's arms. "I must go to her," she said when her sobbing subsided. Wiping her eyes with the back of her hand, she looked in her basket for something to wear.

"Wait, Sister. I have more sad news. We will hear no more from Canonchet. The English captured and killed him," Nanuskooke said, and she began crying again.

Weetamoo gasped as Nanuskooke continued, "They say the English took his arms and legs from him while he was still alive, and then they took his head so he cannot enter the spirit world."

Weetamoo dropped the dress she had tugged out of the basket and staggered toward her younger sister. Her knees buckled, and she fell to the ground. "Canonchet murdered?" she said in disbelief. Her eyes fixed on the wall behind her sister, and her voice lost its emotion.

"They said he died bravely. As a warrior."

"As a warrior." Weetamoo repeated listlessly.

"He did not cry out, they said," Nanuskooke told Weetamoo as she knelt next to her. For the first time in many years, they grieved and consoled one another with one heart.

"Did not cry out?" Weetamoo asked in a blank tone that she might have used to say "Is our meal ready?"

"No, Weetamoo. The English offered to spare his life if he surrendered, but he refused."

"But he refused," echoed Weetamoo, staring with vacant eyes at the wall.

"He died with great honor, Weetamoo," her sister told her with tears running freely down to her chin. She looked up at her and said, "When the English offered him his freedom, he told them that he liked it well that he should die before his heart grew soft or he did any unworthy thing. It pains me to tell you that a Pequot warrior called Cassacinamon carried out his execution by gunfire, and Sachem Oneco of the Mohegans beheaded and quartered him."

"What have they done with his body?" Weetamoo looked up and demanded.

"His head is on a pole in Connecticut. We do not know what they did with the rest of his body." Nanuskooke closed her eyes.

"And my grandson?" asked Weetamoo.

"Laughing Water holds him still. The women will prepare a grave at Ashuelot."

"Stop. You have said enough," Weetamoo said, putting her hand up to ward off any more news from her sister. "We must go home and finish our fight. We must go today."

"But, Weetamoo, what of the captives?" Nanuskooke asked.

"We will leave them to Quannopinn. He will finish that. But I am taking my people home. If we cannot defend our own place, then we will die, but with honor as Canonchet has done. I will run no more." She stood up and brushed the dirt off her knees. Looking up at her sister, she said, "Go. Go pack and tell the others."

No, she thought as she looked at her bow tucked into the frame of her wetu. *I will not stay here and let the English take my children and my brothers in my silence.*

She pulled the bow and her skinful of arrows down from the wall and ran her fingers over the sharpened arrowheads. She rubbed the wetness from her face with the back of her hand and vowed, *I will not sleep again until I have made the English suffer as we have suffered. I will take as they have taken and I will avenge my family and my people.*

She snatched the basket that held her war clothes and snapped free her war shirt fringed with the hair of her surviving people. As she thrust her head through the shirt, she screamed out, "Death to all English. I vow that you will not take my people and my land while I am still here."

Small Comforts
Tenth Remove
March 15, 1676

A pallor fell over the lodge, and Weetamoo's dark mood deepened. It surprised Mary that Weetamoo expressed no joy for Laughing Water's return nor for the corn she brought with her. All day, Weetamoo had gone from raging to crying, and Mary thought it best to stay away. She asked Quannopinn if she might go to her son, and he agreed. But on reaching Joseph's shelter, she learned he had left his former household and had moved to a camp a mile or more away.

Mary tried to find the new camp without success. She stopped many of the Indians she saw on the path, but none could help her. None did her any harm, either, for which she thanked God. She had become easy with passing among them and speaking with them at random. After six weeks in captivity, she had forgotten her terror from the early days with them. After a time, Quannopinn came looking for her and guided her to her son.

Joseph complained that he felt unwell and suffered from a great boil on his side. Little daylight remained since Mary had spent most of the afternoon searching for him. Mary tended to Joseph quickly, placing some moss on his wound, as she had learned of its medicinal effect, and promised to see him again soon. She followed Quannopinn back to Weetamoo's campsite.

A crowd had formed around their door and even around their fire outside, and not one of them made room for Mary to sit. She walked away, feeling a bit faint from her day's wandering and thinking about what she might find to eat.

An old squaw from a nearby shelter beckoned her, and Mary went to her.

"Mary, would you have some bear meat? My husband, Attawan, has had a great hunt, and we have more than we need."

"Oh, Mother, this is most kind of you. I will be glad to take it and will make you something in exchange, if that pleases you." The woman pressed a piece of meat into her hand. Looking back to be sure no one from her own house saw, Mary shoved it into her apron pocket.

Seeing Mary's fear, the woman said, "Will you come in? I have tea and stew on the fire." Mary did not waste a minute in accepting the kindness and followed her inside. The shelter looked like her own, sparse but with many well-made mats and ornamented items hanging from the branches. Mary guessed that Attawan, too, was a leader like Quannopinn.

"I am Sarah, wife of Attawan of Musketaquid, the place of grasses. And this is my husband's sister Rebeckah and my daughter Sarah. Here, sit by the fire. Tis a brutal cold night, is it not."

"Tis. Thank you." Mary wasn't sure what to make of the women but nodded to them in greeting, not knowing if they spoke her language. They nodded back, and Sarah smiled at her. Mary had grown accustomed to the idea that some Indians in the midst of the heathens behaved kindly to her. And she realized that these three women practiced Christianity when they all bowed their heads in prayer before taking their food.

"How come you here?" Mary asked.

Sarah took a deep breath and said, "It is a long and woeful story, Mary. Perhaps for another day. For now, let us eat and be glad of the goodness of God who provided this meat. And isn't it good that we have some corn now for seed?"

Mary thought about that. She hoped she would not be long enough among the Indians as to plant seed with them. She much preferred to eat the corn now and return to her own kind before seed-planting should happen. She looked down and saw no corn in her bowl. Only bear and ground nuts in a thick broth. She had not grown accustomed to setting aside rations or reserving seed corn for planting or harder times ahead. Still the food sat well with her and she stayed after her meal in prayer with her new friends, enjoying the company and the warmth.

"Mary, do come again," Sarah said as Mary got up to go. "If we could, you should know we would buy you from them." She nodded in the direction of Weetamoo's lodge. Mary patted her hand in thanks.

In the morning, Mary rose to travel again with a small band to a new camp less than a mile away. The many women among them continually clustered around the new lodge so that Mary once again found it impossible to find a seat at the fire. In all the commotion, Mary ascertained that they would not miss her, so she followed the path they had taken and returned to Sarah's hearth, asking would she mind if she cooked her piece of bear there. She knew if she had shown it to Weetamoo's crew, they would have taken it straight from her and cut it into pieces so small that it would be as if she had none at all.

Sarah welcomed her and offered her a place at her hearth. They shared the bear meat and more ground nuts, and Mary asked again why Sarah traveled with these heathens. "I will tell you, Mary," Sarah said "My family comes from the Christian Indian town of Wamesit, and we lived there until an incident occurred that stole my heart and my will to stay among the colonists. Captain Mosely came and accused several of our people of starting fire to a haystack in Chelmsford belonging to a Captain Richardson. He took them away, among them our daughter and grandson."

"They did not do it, of course. They had been at home the whole time. Rumours circulated that Philip's men had done it, but that did not stop Moseley. I consider him a very bad man, you should know. Anyway, when his men marched them away, some of the villagers at Chelmsford became enraged and fired into them, killing my young grandson and wounding my daughter, Sarah here."

"Oh, Mary, it was a dreadful day. So you see, we had no choice but to come away as soon as we could. We removed to Penacook with

Wonalancet and petitioned to return, but when Wonalancet came hence, we came away with him."

Mary had heard of the happening some time ago, before her capture, but never dreamed she would later find herself in the company of the accused. "I'm sorry for your loss, Sarah. Do you not worry that you will be treated badly here, though?"

"Nay, Mary. We belong here, with our people. Our kin. We have no fear of them. We only can wait and hope and pray that all the suffering and distrust will end soon. And there will come a time when we can live in peace again. Will we not pray for that together?"

"Yea, we will." Mary prayed for her own version of peace, which had developed to hold a little room for some of the kind Christian Indians like Sarah and Rachel. That version had no room for Weetamoo and her ilk. As Mary took her leave, she promised to return and bring her Bible so they could read scripture together.

Mary stepped out the door and heard a screech calling her a name she could not repeat. A tall Indian man ran at her and pulled her by the arm, shouting at her in words she did not know. He pushed her ahead of him along the trail to the new camp, and when she tarried to catch her breath, he kicked her to make her keep going. She panted, half running, half stumbling all the while trying to stay out of his reach, but the devil took amusement in mistreating her all the way back to Weetamoo's new camp, where he threw her to the ground.

Mary sat quietly, chastised for what reason she did not know. She then saw a deer roasting on a spit and smelled its tantalizing aroma. Her hunger overcame her, and she reached out to tear a piece of meat from its haunch when the same Indian struck her hand. Mary did not know why, but she would have no food that night. She looked around at the faces around the fire and saw only frowns and mean looks.

Why could she have no comfort from these mean folk? To take her from a warm and welcoming hearth to cast her down in the cold with no sustenance at all made no sense to her. She wrapped a fur around herself and sat until sleep overcame her hunger.

Across Ashuelot River
Eleventh Remove
April 1676

After wading across the Ashuelot River, Weetamoo's band of people continued steadily uphill through thick forest and steep slopes. A full day's journey brought them to Wantastegok, where the Wantastekw River joined the Kwinitekw. Weakened by her loss of interest in food since the death of her grandson and Canonchet, Weetamoo traveled with little energy. It became hard to keep going forward when she could find only grief or anger to soothe her pain.

Weetamoo looked at her sleeping children, the baby in his papoose and Laughing Water still clutching her dead son to her breast. She ached for her daughter who for two days would not part with her child. But no more. Today they would bury him in a high place where he would be near his ancestors.

Before waking Laughing Water, Weetamoo went outside to light the fire. It would be a long and sad day, so she let her rest as long as she might. Thinking over the last few day, she sat with her tea. So many had come to greet them and help the little infant on his path to the spirit world. With songs to share and gifts to put in his grave, her people offered comfort in the kindest ways. She felt thankful toward those who kept Mary away during such a sad time. Weetamoo did not want the stink of her in her home, which had been blessed and cleansed by the Powwow along with Laughing Water and herself.

As if hearing Weetamoo's thoughts, Mary appeared out of the darkness.

"Where have you been?" Weetamoo asked without looking at her.

"I slept in another wetu since I found no room in yours last night."

"You will find no room again today. We prepare for a burial. You will prepare food for when I return."

"Who has died?" Mary asked.

Weetamoo sensed no heart in her question and chose not to answer it. "Just see to the food," she responded flatly.

The burial took place in a clearing atop a small mountain. The women shared a quiet, respectful time performing a ceremony full of love for the spirit of the tiny being. So perfect did he look, Weetamoo found it very hard to imagine leaving him behind. Her heart ached for him to open his eyes and be well but she knew that would only happen when he completed his spirit journey. *Goodbye, my little one,* she thought as she laid an offering of tobacco beside him. *Go to your ancestors. Caunbitant, my father, awaits you as does your own brave father. They and all the ancestors will be there to hold your hand and guide you. Do not be afraid. Goodbye.* She wiped her eyes and turned to go. She would not stay to see him covered with earth. She could not.

Laughing Water waited until everyone finished saying goodbye. Placing her gifts beside him and stroking his hair, the mourning mother knelt beside the little bundle He looked so very perfect. Weetamoo's throat tightened, and her chest clenched her heart. Laughing Water leaned down to kiss him but instead covered him with her whole body, suddenly crying out, "No! No! You must not go!"

Her action shocked the gathering, as interrupting someone traveling to the ancestors might bring bad luck upon them or halt their journey. Weetamoo quickly reached her and pushed herself between her daughter and her grandson's body.

"Laughing Water, stop," she whispered. "He has already gone from here. You see only his shell. Our ancestors have come to lead him to his home with them. Shhh. Shhh. He will be well and cared for until we join him. Come now, come. Shhh." She tenderly helped her daughter release her grasp on the little form and helped her to stand.

"Come. We will go make an offering for him now." They spent their afternoon making offerings to all the spirits and ancestors to help and guide him. They sent many blessings to his tiny spirit and said goodbye as the little brave made his way up to the heavens. Then, worn and spent as the sun went down, they made their way back to the camp.

When Weetamoo arrived, Mary was not watching the fire. A kettle of stew hung above, but the fire had burned down so it was only warm, not hot. Weetamoo's temper flared. *Where is she, that little cur?* she thought. She pushed her head into the wetu. There was Mary, wrapped up warmly in her furs with a fire blazing inside. She was reading her Bible and took no notice at all of Weetamoo, who charged across the room at her.

Quannopinn was on the other side of the room, gently rocking her son's cradle board. He motioned to Weetamoo, but there was no stopping her.

"Give me that, you sow!" she shouted. "I will have no more of it in my hearth." She yanked the Bible from Mary's hands and threw it across the room and out the door. Mary jumped up after it and ran out, where she shoved it into her apron pocket away from Weetamoo's grasp. Mary stomped away, looking for another bed for the night. The baby woke with a howl.

Quannopinn managed in time to quiet the baby and Weetamoo. With no one in the mood for food, they all settled down for a rest before the next day's journey. Laughing Water wept into her furs, and Weetamoo curled herself up next to Quannopinn.

In the morning, Weetamoo shoved all she could into Mary's pack to ease Laughing Water's burden. *The white woman had not been doing her share, and it was time for her to do more,* Weetamoo thought. When Mary attempted to put it on, she dropped it back on the bed and said, "No. This is too heavy. You must carry some of it yourself, or we must leave it here."

Weetamoo shouted, "You insolent sow!" She slapped Mary across the face. "You will carry whatever you are told to carry." And she stormed out.

Mary stood stroking her face. She felt a hot welt raised upon her cheek. But she said nothing to Weetamoo. She waited until she knew Weetamoo could not hear her and asked Quannopinn "Where are we bound?"

"We are going north," he said.

"North? Will I be ransomed there?"

"Nux, you will." He walked out without another word.

She followed in silence, too stunned and afraid to show any emotion about the prospect of going home.

Weetamoo Turns Back
Twelfth Remove
End of April 1676

The efficiency of the Indian women dismantling the camps always surprised Mary. Before first light, they had already crept out with pack baskets spilling over with the contents of the shelters. They deftly skinned wigwams as they might a deer, leaving only carcasses of bent branches lashed together with sinew.

As Mary watched, Laughing Water packed away the last of the rolled-up bark to carry to the next night's rest. Cooking fires sizzled angrily as women snuffed them out with the remnants of tea water and the smell of sour smoke wafted all around.

Carrying three skin sacks toward the icy river, Mary walked through the barren village. The screeching sound her moccasins made in the snow told her it had gotten much colder during the night. At river's edge, she leaned down, feeling the nagging ache of her scarred side and stiffness of sleeping in the cold again. She tapped away the clear thin sheet of ice that had formed where another woman had broken through the river's thick crust.

As she held the skins down in brutally cold water, changing hands when either got too sore, she looked across the river and watched blocks of torn floes bobbing in the current. They, unlike her, headed toward the ocean, toward home. The way rocks and ice prevented passage of the floes made her think of the obstacles between her and her return to her complacent Christian life.

"If it please you God, I am ready to be redeemed. I am ready to return to my home as a good wife again. I'll not forget these days of want and hardship and will give You glory for Your wisdom. Like

Moses's people in the desert, had I not had these days of wandering, I would not have come to cherish the Promised Land You gave to us.

"Had I not been made hungry and laid low, I would not treasure the bounty You provided. Had I not been made silent, I would not have known my need to sing Your praise and give You glory, Almighty Father.

"If it is Your will to restore me, I will give witness all my days to Your righteous ways. Forgive me my gluttony and wastefulness. Chastise me for every unkind word I spoke. Heal me from my selfishness and if it pleases You, Lord, let these heathens hasten me home."

"Mary!" Laughing Water called, "We go!"

The young woman turned and walked away following one of several lines of people leaving. Mimicking the chunks of ice in the river, they bobbed along the path.

Mary hefted her water bags and pack basket without any complaint about its weight. Somehow it all felt lighter. Her leather moccasins helping to pad a flat path for her haughty mistress, she fell into line behind the others.

As sun warmed the snow, droplets formed at the end of the sparkling branches. Mary's tread felt buoyant. Every step brought her closer to redemption and restoration to her civilized life. Her tightly packed basket for once rested easily on her back, and the tumpline securing it to her forehead didn't chafe as usual. She hardly felt them. She felt the pull of home.

Behind her, her mistress, Weetamoo, followed slowly. Mary wanted to get behind her and propel her forward but knew her place in the front eased the way. *Why does she walk so slowly?* Mary felt some intangible force holding her back as if she were dreaming. The weight of Weetamoo behind her felt like an anchor pulling against the river's current.

"Why does Weetamoo move so slowly?" she asked the Indian woman beside her.

"I know not," the woman said and continued at her own steady pace.

After only an hour, Weetamoo stopped, and Mary felt obliged to rest. She didn't need to, but Weetamoo commanded it. They drank water from one of the skin bags. Mary smiled at Weetamoo as she offered her some dried berries she had found on the grey branches near the water.

Weetamoo lashed out with the back of her hand, sending the berries sprawling across the trodden path. Mary scrambled to gather them, and as she bent over, Weetamoo kicked her backside. Mary's face scraped against the crystalline snow. The items from her basket flew out over her head. She hurriedly rolled away before Weetamoo could land another kick. She left her basket between them.

"Pick it up," Weetamoo ordered her.

"Yes, Mistress," Mary answered, unwilling to allow the transgression to draw her into another skirmish. Mary took care to stay beyond reach as she put the small fur bags of face powders and jewelry back into her pack.

Weetamoo walked off and began a heated discussion with Master Quannopinn. Mary could not make out the words, but Weetamoo defiantly refused something he said. She stood firmly before the tall sagamore and shook her head in opposition to his strong words. He did not cajole her, and in the end, he uttered some sharp words and walked away.

"Pick it up. We go," Weetamoo hissed, and she began walking in the direction they had just come.

"What?" Mary asked. "Are we not following Quannopinn?"

Weetamoo wheeled and landed another backhanded blow across Mary's face. She stepped back in time, causing Weetamoo to lose her balance and fall towards her. Weetamoo regained her footing and shrieked at Mary, "We go! Now!" and pointed south.

Mary looked around and saw streams of people on both sides of her following Quannopinn north. No one stopped or even looked. They cast their eyes down and parted around the small island of immobile people— Mary, Weetamoo, and her daughter. Laughing Water turned south and waited.

Weetamoo glared at Mary and through clenched teeth said, "Go. Now."

Mary's face felt hot and her chest seemed suddenly bigger. She lifted her shoulders, stood firmly on both feet, and said, "No! We follow Quannopinn."

"We go. Now!" Weetamoo said more loudly, leaning hard toward Mary.

"We must follow Quannopinn and the people," Mary said. "I will not go back." Afraid of what might happen, she turned and started walking north. She felt her heart racing in her chest. Nevertheless, she strode through the snow between two lines of natives who acted as though they didn't see her. She lifted her pack basket to readjust the tumpline on her forehead.

Then she felt a bone splitting kick to her wounded side. White-hot pain dropped her to her knees, and she fell onto her undamaged side. She saw Weetamoo coming at her with the expression of a vicious hound protecting a fresh kill. Unable to catch her breath in time to avoid the blow, she watched helplessly as Weetamoo raised a fallen branch high and crashed it into her skull. More white hot pain shot from the top of Mary's head to the bottom of her spine.

Then it was dark.

* * *

In what felt like a moment, Laughing Water shook Mary and urged her to her feet. Mary slowly realized that more than a few minutes had passed. Tracks in the snow parted around the three women, and left the only trace of the people who had followed Quannopinn. The sun looked higher in the sky and the icy coating on the trees had melted away. Mary's skirts felt wet and cold, and it hurt to move her arm and her head. She struggled with her pack.

"We go," Weetamoo snapped and began walking south. Laughing Water followed. Mary adjusted her pack with her good arm. She stepped into their footsteps and watched the river flowing away beside her.

A Papoose Lullaby
May, 1676

H ow tiresome I find it to carry the burden of that white woman, Weetamoo thought. *How can I endure her any longer? She has selfishness greater than that of the youngest child. She places herself above all.*

Pushing thoughts of Mary away, Weetamoo looked at her own child bundled on Laughing Water's back ahead of her. The papoose faced Weetamoo, who smiled at her son. He just looked at her soundlessly. No smile or notice showed in his face. She worried. *Does he not know me?* There was great sadness in her home after the still birth of Laughing Water's papoose, but since then, Laughing Water had cared for Weetamoo's son as if he were her own. She nursed him with her full breasts and cooed to him with the softness of a mother dove. Weetamoo appreciated her help and knew the care Laughing Water gave turned her thoughts away from her own dead son.

But Weetamoo's baby seemed to grow more listless every day. That night, she would have to take him to her own bed even if Laughing Water protested. Weetamoo wanted to hold him near her heart. She wanted him to know how she loved him. She wanted to lull him to sleep herself. They had come more than five miles to the place below Ashuelot, and Weetamoo longed for a night's rest. They stopped and made camp.

Instead of settling down for bed, Mary and Laughing Water began arguing and having a tug of war over an apron. Laughing Water asked Mary for a small piece of cloth to make a flap for Weetamoo's papoose. But Mary refused even after Weetamoo demanded it. The poor infant, strapped in his papoose carrier, struggled to breathe, and still Mary refused. *The woman has no heart,* Weetamoo thought.

Laughing Water grew angry. "I will tear a piece of cloth from this apron if you will not give it willingly," she said.

Growing more defiant each day, Mary answered, "If you try it, I will tear your coat!"

Weetamoo could not bear the argument any longer. She shouted, "Enough! Laughing Water makes a reasonable request. For a sick child! My sick child!"

Weetamoo raised a stick against Mary. The sachem felt angry enough to have killed her captive and would have, too, if Mary had not stepped to the side when Weetamoo swung at her. The stick lodged in the wall of the wetu.

"Mary, no amount of ransom makes you worth all this trouble!" Weetamoo shrieked as she pulled the stick free, tearing away some of the bark covering and leaving a hole in the side of the wetu.

Laughing Water barked at her, "Look. Now we must sleep with the cold wind."

As Weetamoo turned around with the stick raised overhead, Mary must have seen her death anger growing, for she pulled off the apron and gave it all to Laughing Water before creeping out the door like a cowardly dog.

Weetamoo lowered her arms and lay down on her bed.

"Why must she always think first only of herself?" she muttered.

Laughing Water agreed. "In the end, she does what we ask, but she must always stand against us first. How can this discontentment sit well with her?"

"I will never understand these people. They have no sense at all of being in a community of people. They drove all the good spirit energy away with their selfish pride and greed."

"You speak the truth," Laughing Water agreed. "Look, she has wakened the baby. Let me feed him."

Poor Laughing Water, Weetamoo thought. *She cares for my son like her own, feeding him with the milk of her own breasts, milk meant for her lost child. My first grandson. I feel sad to see such young mothers losing their children.* Laughing Water fed and cooed him until he fell asleep again. She put him back in his mother's bed and returned to her own.

How long can the people endure? The weight of this war and the illness among the people bears down on them. Weetamoo wondered, *When will they be well again and living in their villages near the Great Water with all they need to eat? Can they not turn to home and plant their corn and beans and live in aquene, peace, as before— before the English reign brought terror into their land and into their hearts?* She hoped the party heading north would return with more warriors to save her people.

When all was quiet, Mary crept back in. Weetamoo soon heard a new altercation starting between Laughing Water and the white woman. They argued back and forth over placement of a piece of firewood. Laughing Water had banked the fire for the night and tried to settle into sleep, but Mary—selfish Mary to Weetamoo—kept moving the sticks to release more flame in her direction. Weetamoo could not understand her stupidity. By encouraging the flames, she would speed the burning and wake to cold. With sticks keeping the breath of wind away, embers would keep the hearth warm all night. *Does the foolish woman plan to stay awake all night feeding the fire's hunger?* Weetamoo wondered.

The struggle with the stick of wood continued until Laughing Water could bear no more. She reached for a handful of hot ashes and threw them at Mary, striking her in the face. Weetamoo laughed and thought, *Good for you, Laughing Water.*

Mary sputtered and cursed and at last settled down, weeping. Because of the ashes, she could not see to cause any more trouble that night. *Good,* Weetamoo thought. *Now, at last, we can rest.*

In a strange way, Mary's pitiful weeping brought comfort to Weetamoo. Was her steady moaning soothing like a lullaby? Or did Weetamoo simply take comfort in her dismay? Were English sobs any sadder than Wampanoag ones? Weetamoo did not think so.

Living so closely with Mary, Weetamoo had learned that English sob only for their own people or for themselves. *They weep not for my people,* Weetamoo thought. *They shed no tears when they cut down whole forests of trees to send to their king. They cry not for our brothers the amisqua, now so hunted for their skin that the small ponds are all drying up. The English desire for beaver hats is so great that the little brothers swam into the hills where they have turned into mountains, never damming the streams in our land anymore. For want of a hat, the English might cry, but not for the good gifts the creator Kistannit gave them to keep them warm and well and fed.*

Weetamoo felt certain that Matahou, the mischievous spirit who left the Creator's Aquinas Island so many years ago, must have crossed the water and whispered his jealous words to the English. He put his envy into their hearts so they would one day come here and try to take all that Kistannit gave them back to their king on their boats. At the thought of Matahou, she whispered words to her spirit ancestors to protect her from his charms. She rolled her body away from the two warring women.

She looked at her papoose lying close beside her. He slept with eyes barely closed, and he breathed in short, raspy bursts. She stroked his forehead, and he wrinkled his nose and reached up to wrap his tiny fingers around hers. Like gentle tendrils, they clung to her, soft and cold. She reached down to cover him with another fur. She began to hum a soft lullaby into his small, pink-petaled ear:

Fa la me
Shu ta sin
Heyo heyo ah no
Fa la me
Shu ta sin
Heyo heyo ah no
Ee ah hey, ee ah no
Heyo heyo heyo hey
Heyo heyo heyo no

She looked down at his sweet face and saw in it the promise of the future for her people. As one of the seven generations she would know in her lifetime, he made an important link in the circle of life.

As her son grew into a man, a father, and a grandfather, he would become the living reminder to the English that her people always remained, forever and ever, still here.

Hostages Meet
Thirteenth Remove

The travelers arrived at last at a more permanent place. Mary felt relief when Quannopinn sent word to wait in that place for news of her redemption. The new camp had more wigwams and a larger longhouse than the others and, for the first time, she saw more white faces than she had previously. Mary guessed that they too would find redemption on the main path to Albany.

Only that day, she overheard Weetamoo say that Philip lost two in his delegation when they attempted to travel through Mohawk territory. The event spoiled their desire to redeem her and the others to the French. Their plans for her redemption therefore had to change, and they must await word from Massachusetts Bay Colony about her returning to her own people. So she had to wait.

The warriors returned with another small bounty from a raid on nearby Hadley. They brought with them a captive called Thomas Read, whom Mary recognized as an acquaintance of her husband. She saw them coming in with him and went to the central fire to see if she might have a word with him. Three big Indians had him in their midst while they pushed him this way and that all the while shouting questions at him. They raised knives and hatchets and war clubs over him and bade him to speak. The man stood with his mouth agape, covering his eyes, as they tossed him like a rag doll from one to the other. He broke down crying uncontrollably and fell to his knees.

With her late friend Ann Joslin on her mind, Mary walked into their midst and said, "Stop this. If you please, might I speak with him?"

The warriors laughed and said, "What, Mary? You have questions for him, too?"

"I do, and I have words of comfort for him. Will you leave him to me?"

The tallest one laughed. "It is she who called out Monaco for days."

The other two nodded and joined him in his laughter. One said, "Please, Lady, do have a word," imitating an Englishman's accent. They left him to her but stayed close enough to listen.

"Dear Sir, tell me. Are you not Thomas Read?"

With raised eyebrows, he looked up, not believing what he heard. "I-I, am," he stammered.

"I am Mary White Rowlandson, Reverend Joseph Rowlandson's wife. Do you know my husband?"

"Mistress Rowlandson, I do. Indeed, I do. I saw him not a few days ago in Boston."

"Did you, Sir? Oh, pray, tell me how he was. Did you speak to him?"

"I did, brave lady, so I did."

Mary sensed he was regaining his wits. "So please, Sir, how did you find him?"

"He was in a melancholy state, to be sure, but he looked to be physically fit."

"Oh, Sir, that is as good a news as I have had these long weeks. Tell me, now, why are you crying? Are you in pain?"

"No, but I think they are to kill me. I will die if they are to keep handling me as they do."

"Wait," she said. Then she turned to his captors and said, "Is it your desire to kill this man?"

They looked at one another. Some conversation and head shaking ensued.

"It is not," said the tall one.

"Then he will answer your questions, and you will feed him and give him shelter, will you not?

"We will," said the tall one. Then they all burst out laughing again.

"Pay them no mind," said Mary. "If they wanted you dead, you would be that already, miles back. You are here because you are of value to them. You will become a captive like me. And we are all like to be traded for weapons and supplies for their bloody war. You will not die, at least not here. Do take heart." She squeezed his hand.

He squeezed hers back and stood up. "Mistress Rowlandson, you are wise, and you are brave, and I shall remember you for this. Good Woman, I hope we shall meet again."

"And I." With that, Mary left him and went to find her son so she could share the news from home with him. As she went along, she asked, "Has anyone seen my son?" The people had grown used to her comings and goings and most of the time helped her.

That day, one man she judged a warrior by his face paints answered her, "I know where your son is, Mary Rowlandson. My sachem roasted him, and we had him for our dinner last night. He was so tender and good that I myself ate a piece of him this big." He held up two fingers together.

"You, Sir, are rotten, rotten to the core. You cannot frighten me with your filthy lies." She stomped away. From time to time, she had run into others like him who told her frightening lies, and she knew in her heart of hearts that her own son was fine. It happened that only moments after that confrontation, she found Joseph sitting on a log, bemoaning his plight.

"Mother, is it me who brought such melancholy to my father? Have I done wrong that made God judge us so harshly? Did he take Sarah from us and us from Father because I was unkind to my sisters? Or some other thing I should not have done?"

"Of course not, Joseph. You are a good boy and most of the time a very good brother. You did not cause any of it. The brutes here have done it all with their own free will, and they tell vicious lies because they come from the seed of the one who lied first. Come, come, you are not the cause of this at all."

She pulled him close and then, as she stroked his head, she saw something move in his hair. She pushed his head away from her, seeing him covered in lice. Looking at him, she saw dirt on his face and hands and noticed his unkempt hair and clothing. He did not look at all well. "Joseph, I do not like the look of how these people care for you. Here, let me comb out your hair. You must get yourself to the river to wash out your hair, for it is teeming with lice." As she tried to tidy him up, she said, "I think you should run away from such as these who will not care for you." Never dreaming he would do it, she said it in passing.

In two days' time, Joseph came back to her and told her he had run away but had been caught and beaten for it. So he ran away again and found someone willing to buy him.

"And, Mother, they are very good to me. And they want to meet you, too. Will you come with me to them?"

Mary went and could not believe her son's good fortune. The couple told her how they loved her son and how they would take care of him until his ordeal came to an end. They welcomed her to their hearth any time at all.

Mary could not thank them enough, and she could not stop praising the Lord for bringing her son to such kind people. She had no idea how important it had become for Indian people contemplating the latest offers of amnesty to build up evidence and find colonists who would speak kindly of them on their return from captivity.

On her way to visit Joseph again, she found a young man called John Gilberd lying in the snow with a small papoose. Neither had sufficient clothing against the weather, so she bid the young man to get up.

"Mistress, I cannot, for I am too weak due to the bloody flux. The same is true for this babe. They put us both out here to die."

"Well, not if I have anything to say about it, you will not. Get you up and go collect sticks for a fire. Without that, you will both die."

The poor young man did just as Mary said and picked up the child to hold it nearer the fire. Comforted that he would be warmer, she left the child with Gilberd and went home only to find his mistress telling Weetamoo what she had done.

After the woman left, Weetamoo ordered her not to leave the wetu again. In astonishment, Mary demanded to know why.

"So you will not attempt an escape with your friend Gilberd," Weetamoo said.

"Nay, that is not my intent," Mary laughed in reply, "for will you not ransom me very soon?"

"Silence," Weetamoo shouted. The sachem would not risk an escape and certainly did not want to risk the bloody flux coming in her door. She ordered, "From now on, you will only be permitted to go out to get materials for your work, but other than that, you will stay indoors." Neither woman imagined how soon the order would be withdrawn.

Sometime during the night, Mary woke upon hearing Weetamoo cry out. All in the wetu were disturbed from their sleep and they crowded around the infant suspended in his papoose. Weetamoo covered her mouth but could not prevent a blood curdling wail from escaping. From their anxious voices, huddled heads, and following sobs, Mary discerned that the baby had died. She rolled over, thinking, *Good, there will be more room and food for us all now. And no more bickering over the little creature's needs.* She had no idea that his death would widen the rift between herself and Weetamoo and how soon she would once again be turned out into the cold.

Leaving for Mount Wachusett

Weetamoo and Laughing Water sat quietly in their wetu. In the morning, they would leave for the council of the Powwows at Mount Wachusett. They had already placed their belongings in their packs save what they needed for the night's sleep.

Uneasy stillness filled the room and Weetamoo looked at her empty home. Her eyes froze when they caught sight of a small rattle carved from wood behind the leg of the sleeping platform. She felt a stabbing pain in her heart. She no longer needed it. She looked around her wigwam. No, there were no other reminders of her son left.

Her boy had left her for the spirit world, and in great pain, she had buried him that day with all he needed for his journey. She could not think about that.

The rattle held her attention. She crossed the dirt floor and knelt down to pick up the baby's toy. As she touched it, Weetamoo felt the life of his little spirit still warm in its wooden handle.

Remembering his smiling face when Quannopinn first gave it to him, Weetamoo shook the rattle gently. The dried beans inside clicked against the hollow wood. Her sannup had made it for her little son. As Quannopinn shook it, the boy had smiled and reached to touch it. Quannopinn, too, had smiled at the baby's simple delight. Weetamoo smiled again at the thought of it.

She looked at the carved designs on the neck of the rattle and traced her finger over its shape, an amisqua with its small ears and legs and wide slapping tail. The gift for her son had so pleased her.

Shaking it again, Weetamoo recalled hearing its sound only the day before. She had rattled it for her little boy in her bed. She had wanted to see his smile and his alert eyes follow it as she shook it. But that had not happened. He had just lain struggling for breath between coughing spasms. His little face shone red with a fever she could not cool with snow wrapped in soft, wet doeskin. Later, he stopped struggling and only stared.

The rattle slipped from her limp fingers and fell with a hollow, flat noise. Its image blurred in her eyes as she placed it gently in the fire. She began to hum a soft lullaby. As she hummed, the melody stumbled in the places where she sobbed.

She sent her thoughts to the spirits and asked them to hold her little boy because she could not. She sprinkled a little tobacco into the fire and breathed in its smoke. She lifted her eyes and watched her prayers go up through the smoke hole and into the outside air, where the wind would carry them to the spirits.

Laughing Water knelt beside her and joined in her chanting, adding her own pinch of tobacco to the fire. Weetamoo and her daughter shared the same grief. They rubbed one another's faces with black soot from the hearth.

Weetamoo put her arm around Laughing Water's shoulder and curled it around her as the girl placed her head in her lap. She laid her head atop Laughing Water's, and together they cried out their pain.

Sometime after nightfall, Quannopinn arrived with Awashonks. They found the two women curled together by the burned out fire.

Quannopinn took Weetamoo by the shoulders and led her to the edge of the sleeping platform. He wrapped his thick arms around his wife's frail form. His brave sachem felt small and lifeless to him. "Weetamoo, Little Bird, you must eat," he said.

Awashonks called outside for her sons Mamanewa and Tatuck-amna to bring food and drink. Then she helped Laughing Water sit on her own bed. She stroked the girl's hair and whispered into her ear. She knelt before the fire pit, blew on the embers, and twisted a small, frayed bit of wood until it caught. She added little splinters of wood until they caught and then laid three sticks over them, taking care to leave room for air to circulate. With each of her hard breaths on the embers, the flames roared out and then leapt back. She contin-ued blowing on the fire until all three sticks blazed.

As Mamanewa and Tatuckamna entered, the night whistled bitter wind through the bark layers covering the wetu. It had grown cold inside, but neither Weetamoo nor Laughing Water had noticed. Awashonks took the clay pots from her sons and set the rawhide handles on a stick overhanging the flame. She adjusted their height by wedging the stick in the crook of a forked branch pounded into the ground. In one pot, ground nuts simmered in a broth made from a horse's hoof. In the other steeped a spicy tea broth made with winter berries and nettles.

"Weetamoo," Quannopinn said, "the people will come to see you tonight. You must make ready."

She looked at him blankly for a moment and then nodded. She stood up and went to one of the pack baskets and reached for a mixture of face paints. She pulled out a small clay jar containing black-colored bear grease and charcoal. This she spread over her face. Although she usually used red paint on her face, she instead used the hue of mourning. She combed out her hair and pulled it into one long braid.

The task of preparing for guests distracted her. She methodically went through her ritual of getting ready to appear as the strong sachem and leader of her people.

In a short time, people began to arrive. Some stayed and sat with her a while. Others briefly consoled her, leaving gifts as they departed. Some good friends and family stayed the whole night through.

During all the outpouring of love and support, in came Mary. Dirty and worn, she entered through the door and began to push through people toward the fire. With filthy fingers, she tried to dip into the pot of broth and pull out a bit of meat.

Calling it sluttish behavior, Weetamoo reprimanded her. Mary reached for more.

Furious at her dirty habits and unwilling to allow the mangy creature to soil their spare offering for her mourning guests, Weetamoo ordered Mary out of the wigwam.

"But, Mistress, what shall I eat? And where shall I sleep?" Mary asked.

"I do not care, but it will not be here," Weetamoo answered. "Leave us now."

"I will not!" Mary argued and pulled up her skirts to take a seat near the fire.

Weetamoo's eyes flashed with anger. She would have leapt at Mary, but Mamanewa was on his feet first. "You will leave, as you have been asked," he ordered.

"But this is my home!" Mary cried. Weetamoo heard the word home scrape against Mary's tongue as she uttered it.

Mamanewa reached behind his back and pulled out a sword from its scabbard. He held it above her and said, "Not tonight, woman. Go! Or I shall take your head."

At that, Mary quickly got up and backed out into the cold. Relieved to have Mary gone, Weetamoo felt the mounting tension leave with her. She did not care if the woman lived or died. Yet she knew her people would show her kindness and someone would take in the thoughtless woman. Weetamoo did not have to share her home with Mary on her last night in the place where her son had gone to meet the spirits.

A Dream of Home

While she slept, Mary dreamed of home. Under soft fur covers, she felt the warmth of her own kitchen hearth. She smelled a wondrous good cake baking in her brick oven and heard her daughter Mary humming in time to her wooden spoon rhythmically scraping against a crockery bowl. She heard the merry sounds of her other children playing upstairs in her sturdy garrison home.

Sarah's dancing steps tapped lightly, followed by the clumsy clomping of her brother Joseph. Sarah's spirited giggles made Mary smile. Indeed, she considered herself a woman with many blessings. She heard her husband splashing his face with water from her mother's porcelain basin in the corner of their room. She opened her eyes to bid him good morning, and all her comfort vanished when she saw that the person was not her husband, Joseph, but instead Sarah, the old squaw who had taken pity on her once again and let her in from the cold the night before.

The old woman dropped ground nuts and acorns into a kettle over a fire and stirred them with a wooden spoon as she softly hummed. Something cooked on a stone near the fire and filled the wigwam with a sweet aroma. The happy noises Mary mistook for her own family came from heathen children laughing and playing outside with drums. Her heart fell. For a few sweet moments before she woke, she had found herself at home in her own sweet, soft bed. Awake, though, she despaired. *It cannot be so,* she thought. *I do not want to believe that I am still here.*

My dream was so real. If only I could close my eyes and return home again. Oh, Lord, why do you forsake me to this wilderness among the savages? I cannot bear it ever much longer. Please, dear God, if it please You, find it in Your great Providence to send me home. She turned away and covered her head with the soft fur to try to recover her comfort, but it had fled.

The squaw heard her stirring and said, "Ascowequa'ssin, Mary. You slept long. See? We have already greeted the dawn."

Mary wanted to feign sleep to avoid having to leave the warm bed, but she felt obliged to repay the woman's kindness. To lie there while the Indian worked would be seen as a sign of laziness, and the natives had no tolerance for that.

Mary rolled to her side and greeted the woman. "What cheer, netop? Thank you for your kindness during the night." She sat up and straightened the buttons on her greyed and worn shirtwaist. She would never have gone out in such rags before, but in her captivity, she had no choice. She smoothed her hair and tucked it up under her coif.

"It is nothing. Mary. You are no trouble to us, and we have space here since . . ." Her voice trailed off and she did not complete her thought. But Mary knew what she meant to say. Someone in her family had died. Mary knew that some feverish disease had afflicted many of the young and old. Their Powwows or witches often visited the lodges of the sick, and it pained Mary to see that they believed that foolish antics and keening might make them well again. With herbs and charms and smoke and rattles, they hovered around the ailing person until a crowd gathered to answer their howling chants. But it did no good.

It pleased God to send an epidemic to take them in large numbers. Two papooses in her own lodge had gone in the past fortnight. Mary did not regret it and appreciated having more room in their place. Or at least, she had extra room until last night when it seemed that the whole band of them arrived in a steady stream, she supposed to pay their respects to Weetamoo for her lost papoose. *How vile of them to send her out into the cold night without even a fur for warmth!*

Her shoulders stiffened and her jaw tightened as she remembered wandering in the dark night to find someone who would give her shelter. She felt grateful for the kindness of the old woman and her husband. For the first time since her capture, she had slept in great comfort. For once, she felt warm enough and had eaten well.

Mary saw the woman smiling at her. She could not remember the last time she saw a smile. The squaw beckoned her to eat. Mary edged toward her.

"I thank you for your hospitality. It is good of you to welcome me to your home and share with me your food. I am much obliged to you," Mary said as she accepted the burl bowl held out to her. Steam rose from three acorns and a ground nut in broth, and a sweet scent wafted from the small piece of corn bread. "'Tis a savory meal, indeed. I am much pleased," Mary said and nodded at the smiling woman.

Although the slim fare would do little to calm the knot in her belly, it provided more than she had had in days. With so many people foraging in one place, barely any food remained nearby. Too early for the spring ferns and greens and too late for berries which had long since dried and withered. The remaining corn from Narragansett had been set aside for planting. Their only meat came from an occasional partridge or hare foolhardy enough to venture nearby. Most of their hunters had gone away with Quannopinn or went off in other directions with Philip and the others.

Mary helped the squaw clear away her cooking things and fetched water for her before she took her leave. She asked if she could return, and the woman nodded her assent. Mary pressed her hand in thanks and walked away.

She hoped to find it quiet in Quannopinn's lodge so she could gather her things for the journey. She did not have much of her own, just a little cloth and thread she had bartered for, the bone needle one of the men had made for her, and the furs she used when she slept. But she always had to carry a full pack of Weetamoo's belongings.

Weetamoo with all her trumpery and furnishings, Mary thought. *Such a vain woman, that one. Sees herself as greater than the Queen of Sheba, no doubt. At least this time there would be less to carry.* With the loss of the two papooses, Mary expected her burden to be lightened.

Mary had heard they would travel again for Philip and his leaders to attend a council of Powwows at Mount Wachusett. Mary longed to see Mount Wachusett again, for then she would be within sight of her home in Lancaster. She thought about how her home appeared in her dream and then remembered how it looked when last she saw it, her town in flames. Bodies of her neighbors lay strewn about in puddles of their own blood. Her broken nephew lay across her feet, and her sister's blank eyes stared into hers as she gripped her bloody head and fell before her. Mary smelled gunpowder and smoke mixed with salty death and again heard fierce whooping and mournful cries and moans.

She stopped still, then stepped out into the cold morning and sucked in a great gulp of chill air. She stretched her aching back. Would she have a home to return to? If all was gone, where would she go? And who was left there still? Whatever was to be, she had to get back. After her trial, she knew she could endure whatever awaited her.

With Empty Heart
Fourteenth Remove

Staring up through the smoke hole at the morning sky, Weetamoo lay in the dark wetu. She could not leave the place by the river yet. Although she knew it would not help her papoose if she lingered, she found it impossible to walk away from his burial place. She could not call out his name in her grief for fear of stopping his journey to the spirit world. But a part of her heart cried out for the aching in her empty arms.

Alone in the wetu, she could allow her tears to flow. Not in front of her people, though. With so many falling ill, she had to show strength so they could go on without fear. But how could she go on? Her papoose lost his life while so very young. Too young to know the spirit stories—how would he find his way? She took a deep breath.

She had burned offerings and called on the ancestors to show her son the path. She had folded his small body as he had once curled up inside her and given him to the Earth Mother, Metanokit, and gently cradled his head toward the sacred southwest. So small and so cold. She felt as if she only dreamed that he had lived. *What had choked his tiny breath away and left his little form so empty?* She had placed the ritual herbs beside him and given him the three sisters to sustain him on his journey, but her heart could not let him go.

A grown warrior knows what to do. An old man has wisdom to guide him. *Who will hold my little boy's hand? How will he find his way to the spirit world?* As she thought of it, she began to cry out in deep racking sobs. She turned her face into her fur so that the people outside would not hear her. She poured out her grief into the fur like water from a spilled vessel. Wetness from her tears matted her hair together with the fur so that it clung to her face as she let out an anguished wail. Clutching the sides of her sleeping platform, she gasped out, "Why? Why him? He was too small. He had not lived yet."

Oh, how can I go on without him, she thought. *I am so alone. Quannopinn does not understand. He has no son. It was not good to raise my voice in anger with him for leaving, but my heart is heaviest because he does not understand. Quannopinn's desire to ransom Mary and the others blinds him from seeing my pain.*

She felt angry that Quannopinn placed his goals for power in the war above her and her son. Part of her wondered if her sannup felt secretly glad. He had often spoken of her bearing him a son to lead their people, but he knew that sons follow their mothers. Her dead son, Petananuit's son, would have been the sachem of her people, not Quannopinn's future son. She wondered if inside she, too, felt secretly glad. She had hoped her son by Petananuit would never betray his people as his father had. She had worried about it. *Could my fears have brought my son's illness to him? Did the spirits see my secret fears and punish me for my bad thoughts? Did he die because of me?* she wondered.

No! a voice thundered in her head. *No, Weetamoo, the boy's death is no fault of yours. This just is. If you must blame someone, blame the English.*

Yes, she thought. *With their dirty habits and strange sicknesses. Ever since white people first came, my people suffered. With yellow sores and bloody bowels and fevers no Powwow could still, whole villages had disappeared in the time before my birth. Plimoth was built upon the bones of the ancestors of the Patuxet people. I must not blame myself or Quannopinn or even Petananuit. I know in my heart that the sickness came from the English. If not from their filthy ways, then the disease came from their hatred for my people.*

If only they had let my people live as they always had. Why did the English always need more land and more governors who say our ways must change? Have not my people lived here in peace for many thousand years? Why now must I bury my small boy before he even knew his name? Must I watch as generations before and after mine cough out their lives in painful agony? Who will tell their story as the circle of their lives is broken? Will all become Christian or die? Is their god so powerful that he can silence all the spirits in the hearts of the people of my land?

Through the long night before, her people came. One after another, the people of Weetamoo's tribe came to offer her comfort. They held her, they cried with her, they sat in silence and stared into the fire. At times, they sang. *How many people had come,* she wondered. *Two or three hundred or more?* Before dawn she fell asleep. She awoke alone with an empty heart.

She heard noises outside from the people breaking camp. Today, they would leave for Wachusett to gather and decide their future. All wondered what the Powwows would see and what the council would decide. *Will the young men have their way and continue war until our country becomes free again? Will the Praying Indians soften the hearts of my people enough to weaken them into English submission? Will tired and hungry squaws turn their faces from war and go home to plant corn within new English boundaries? Will my people face capture and enslavement as so many have already? Or will they face their end in our world to find a better place in the spirit world?*

Weetamoo felt small and alone.

Awashonks opened the flap and let in morning chill and early light. A misty cloud hung over the camp, and thicker fog followed the river. The snapping sound of ice foretold the coming thaw.

"Ascowequa'ssin, Weetamoo. Did you sleep, cousin?" she asked.

"Nux," Weetamoo replied flatly. She rubbed her eyes and smudged the back of her hand with face paint. Its blackness reminded her of her dead papoose. The thought struck her with the force of a knife to her heart. She wished she had only dreamed of his death.

"The squaws are almost ready to go. I came to help you pack," Awashonks said. Without waiting for Weetamoo's assent, she began rolling up the sleeping furs.

"Thank you for your help, Cousin. I did not mean to sleep so late," Weetamoo said. She sat on the edge of her sleeping platform and slid her feet into her moccasins. Her leggings hung above the other platform. They seemed too far away to bother with them. Her stomach felt hollow and her throat, sore. Her dry, red eyes burned. As she stood, her head ached. She looked down at her bare legs.

Awashonks noticed her leggings and tossed them to her. Weetamoo caught them clumsily. "Namumpum," Awashonks said, calling Weetamoo by her childhood name, "it will do you no good to get sick. You must dress warmly. Do you want me to help you?" She fussed and tucked Weetamoo's belongings into pack baskets.

Weetamoo didn't answer. As if dreaming, she bent down and fastened her leggings. Everything seemed far away. She watched herself moving but felt nothing. Sounds were muffled. She had the feeling of being inside her body looking out while it functioned on its own. She watched her hands folding a mat that Laughing Water had woven for her. Her finger traced the colored pattern as she slid it into her basket. Her hand lifted her mink tobacco pouch from the forked branch that held up the roof. She wondered why she didn't feel its soft fur. Expecting to see the wetu collapse, she hesitated briefly.

Awashonks stomped out the fire's embers and spread them apart with a wet stick. Weetamoo watched dully as Awashonks sprinkled water onto the hot coals. Hushed hisses and smothered trails of smoke rose from the hearth. With only a few handfuls of water, Awashonks doused out the fire's life. Gone. *Just like my boy,* thought Weetamoo.

Awashonks straightened up and saw Weetamoo staring at the wet, black mud. She took her by the shoulders and said, "Weetamoo, daughter of Caunbitant, you are strong. Your father will watch over your boy now. Your people need you. Come. It is time to go."

Weetamoo nodded and lifted up her pack basket. She looked at the bed where she had last cuddled her son. She pulled her eyes away and swallowed hard to push the hollow feeling down into her belly.

As she left the wetu, Weetamoo turned her thoughts to the new life growing in her belly. It had been four moons since she last bled. She would have another son. He would become strong like his father, Quannopinn. He would grow to be a good man who would lead her people. She thought about her first husband, Wamsutta, and his brother Metacom. *If Wamsutta had not died, Metacom would still claim only a sagamore's power. Would Wamsutta have brought the tribes together as Metacom had? Perhaps one brother must die to make another strong. Perhaps a strong leader needs many spirits to give him power.* The idea gave her an odd comfort.

She looked at the camp and realized Mary had not come to prepare their morning meal. Although she did not feel like eating, Mary's omission angered her.

Fog and snow muffled the sounds of women stacking away pottery and iron pots. They folded and packed some bark coverings while others they set afire. They had continued burning all their shelters as they went, both to leave no shelter behind for enemy use but also to purge any lingering disease that plagued her people. Weetamoo wondered if she or her people would ever come here again.

"Will you walk with me, Cousin?" Awashonks asked.

"What?" Weetamoo asked. She had forgotten about her cousin. Although she heard the question, she tried to absorb its meaning. "Oh, yes," she replied after a brief delay. "We will walk, but first I must find Mary Rowlandson. All this must still be packed," she said, pointing at the bowls and cookware left out all night.

"What a miserable woman she is," Weetamoo continued. "She has no slave here but lives as though she does. Awashonks, it tires me so to deal with her."

"Then sell her," Awashonks answered decisively. She bent to pick up some of the cookware.

"You know I can't," Weetamoo said bitterly. "Don't touch that. I will have Mary see to it."

"Why can't you sell her? She's yours." Awashonks asked.

"Because it would offend Quannopinn," Weetamoo answered, still looking around for Mary.

"What do you mean?" Awashonks asked.

"It was he who bought her from Monaco. He believes she has a high value to her people. Metacomet values her ransom price too greatly, and Quannopinn seeks to win Metacomet's favor."

"He has that already, Weetamoo. That doesn't make any sense," Awashonks said.

"Quannopinn dreams of the time after the war. He seeks to lead more than one small band. Don't you see? We have lost so many leaders, Cousin."

"Now I understand what you are saying. He expects a higher place at the council after the war. But how does Mary matter?" she asked.

Weetamoo grew annoyed. She loved Awashonks but sometimes thought her slow-witted. "Think!" Weetamoo snapped. "Her ransom will be great, but more than that, she will establish the trade price for concessions with the English. She belongs to Quannopinn to trade. Do you see it now?"

She stared at her cousin waiting for her to grasp why Mary's ransom might impact Quannopinn's future. And Weetamoo's.

"Ah, yes I do." Awashonks answered patiently. As she hoped, her provocation snapped Weetamoo into more of her usual state of mind. "Look, Weetamoo. I see your Mary coming out of Attawan's wetu."

Weetamoo's brow and shoulders tightened. "No wonder she is so lazy," Weetamoo observed. "That one treats her like a child." Hands on hips, Weetamoo walked toward Mary.

Mary stretched and yawned. She had not slept as well in months. She arched her back to loosen it and heard Weetamoo shrieking from across the camp.

Attawan's wife said to her, "We would buy you if we could." Then, like an old tortoise, she ducked back into her shell.

Mary saw right away that her short respite had ended. She thanked the old squaw for her kindness and went to help Laughing Water break down the camp.

Who Will Buy This Woman?

Over the past several weeks, Mary had adjusted to a new way of life that she had not imagined possible before. Weetamoo seemed happier as they neared Wachusett and grew less difficult to live with, especially when she spent time with Metacomet. Mary did not know what caused the change but did not question it. She completed her duties in her own household and gratefully still found time for her industry.

On a warm spring day in mid April, Mary and Weetamoo gathered kindling in the nearby forest when they heard a shout from the path.

"Mary," called Laughing Water loudly. Weetamoo saw Mary stop gathering tinder. "Come," she called from the edge of the thicket. "You are needed."

Weetamoo turned toward Laughing Water. "Why?"

Mary picked her way back through the brambles, freeing her skirts from clawing berry bushes as she passed. "Needed for what?" she asked. She stepped over a vernal pool onto a tuffet of crispy brown grass.

"Metacomet summons you," she said. "And you, Mother." Laughing Water offered her hand to help Weetamoo cross a small spring stream. She lowered her voice and said, "The Christian Indians, Tom and Peter, have come with a second letter. They ask to see the woman, and Metacomet wants to speak with you."

"Where are the Christians now?" Weetamoo asked.

"They wait in Metacomet's nushweety."

"Take the woman to my wetu, and I will go to Metacomet. He waits in his nushweety?"

"Yes." Laughing Water walked to Mary and took her by the elbow. "Come, Mary." They walked along the trail closest to Weetamoo's wigwam.

Weetamoo took a different path through the woods. The snow had melted, and days grew warmer. Thickening red buds clamped tightly to the tips of branches. All remained bare and grey or brown, but bird songs and flowing water held the promise of an early Wapicummilcom when buds open. *As soon as the buds are the size of a mouse's ear, the people will need to plant corn,* Weetamoo thought. *It is good that Canonchet had led the people to Narragansett to bring back corn for planting and to eat.* She took a moment to wish him peace in the spirit world for his gift of life to them all. *If the war does not end, we will have to plant here.* She looked at the flat land surrounding this river. *The land is good for planting. The river feeds it well.*

Soon the river would run with salmon in the season of namassack kesos, catching fish. She wanted to believe their time of hunger would end and the people would live their lives as they had before the English and before the war. News of English visitors disturbed her.

As she approached Metacomet's nushweety, she saw saddled horses tied nearby. *Yes, the Christian Indians are here. Only Christians would bind an animal.* It seemed strange that her brothers would keep such ways even when they returned to their old villages. The camp bustled with activity. Instead of a quiet village with people going about their daily chores, all gathered and whispered excitedly in clusters.

Weetamoo passed the band of people and entered Metacomet's nushweety. "Laughing Water says the Christians have come. Do they bring ransom?" she asked.

"Nay, they do not. They bring only this," he spat, shaking a paper at her. "Another letter from the governor. He wants us to release all the captives. Does he think we are fools?" he shouted as he paced and waved the paper in the air.

"For mere money or guns he expects us to release not only this one, but many others? And then once they are free, he will use them and the traitor Christian Indians to find us and take back their ransom," he roared.

"Weetamoo, I am sorely tempted to send him a corpse in answer to his request. How does he dare to make such a demand? And he makes an offer of amnesty if our leaders present themselves to him. Bah! An English amnesty I have seen before. It comes to an Indian with his neck at the end of a rope or his head on a spear." He crumpled the paper and tossed it into the fire.

Weetamoo snatched the paper from the flame. "Is that all, Metacomet?" she asked, flattening the paper against her thigh. "Is there no message from the husband of Mary Rowlandson?" She looked at the English words. She could understand some of the writing but not all.

"James Printer says there is no word on the paper from the husband. But the Christian Indians, Tom and Peter, bring his word and tokens for me and for Mary to show his willingness to trade. They ask to see the woman."

"You have spoken with them?" she asked.

"No, not yet. I await word from our scouts that no English lurk nearby waiting to fall on us while we occupy ourselves with these two."

"Metacomet, you are wise to wait. So they offer amnesty and redemption," she mused. "How can we use this to our advantage? We should think on it."

Gunshots sounded in the distance.

Metacomet looked up. "As I suspected, the English skulk nearby. Once again we will move," he said absently. "To our advantage? Hmmm. Amnesty will never be enough. What we must have is our land and our peace."

"So has the time come for us to sue for peace? Are the English soft enough to give us peace?" Weetamoo asked. She sat on the edge of the wooden sleeping platform and looked down at her stretched out legs.

"It is true that our people tire of war," she agreed. "They feel warm days and see birds returning from the south. They know we must plant corn soon or be hungry another winter. So many are sick and dying, and all have family who have gone on to the spirit world for want or for war." She looked up at him. "But Metacom, is it not the same with the English? Have they not also lost men to war and people to hunger and sickness?"

She stood up and put her hand on his shoulder. "We have driven them away from Baquoag, Squakeag, and Nonotuck. Menameset is no longer surrounded by their filthy villages. We are still many. My heart says we can drive them back. They hide in their wooden garrisons but cannot save their fair houses. If we burn out their villages, they will soon abandon them, and we can take the land back and grow strong again. Do you not agree, Brother?"

Metacomet did not answer right away. He walked across the nushweety and put both hands on the wooden supports holding up the roof. He leaned forward and thought. Weetamoo admired his strength of body and mind. She knew he needed her silence at the moment. She sat down again and waited.

After a few minutes, he turned to her and said, "It is so. The English, too, tire of war and need to plant. Their offer of amnesty is no peace. It is surrender. I will not surrender. My people will not surrender. We will not be slaves in our own country."

"How will you answer those men today, Metacom?"

"This is the time to make our own peace. It is best not to give up one captive after another. Such dealings only make us soft and give way to them tracking and hunting us. Today, I will ask for a ransom for the one woman in two weeks time. During the two weeks, I will call upon all the Powwows to meet us at Wachusett. Our shamans will consult the spirits and give us their wisdom. In two weeks' time, the English will come to Wachusett and we will give them our answer to their amnesty and our terms for all future redemptions." A bitterness in his words made Weetamoo proud to be his kinsman.

"So you will free the woman?" Weetamoo asked.

"It may be so. Many things can come of the council of the Powwows. I will seek the wisdom of the spirits. That means much to our people. One woman cannot change the will of the spirits. My heart tells me the English may want all their captives enough to give us back our land and hold their lusting greed. My head tells me if we do not end the ships full of white men landing here, we will never be free again. My body tells me it is strong and can withstand another season of war if it must, and my mind tells me now is the time to strike. If we demand a peace and show our strength, and the English refuse . . ." He paused and drew a deep breath. "If they refuse, we may not be as strong again."

Weetamoo sat in silence. Then she stood up, also breathing deeply, and said, "It is so. In two weeks we will have the answer from our shamans and our people. But, Metacomet, what will you ask for the ransom of the woman?"

"It matters not. Let her set her own price. She is but the first of many. Today we will greet our visitors and give them the words they wish to hear," he said.

"Yes, Brother." Weetamoo took his hand and said, "Let us give the English what they have asked for." Before her mind, her heart held an image of many dead white men.

Word from Home

Laughing Water and Mary hurried along the trail back toward the village. "What is happening?" Mary asked. She followed as she wondered why Laughing Water led her to Weetamoo's lodge.

"Inside. Quickly," Laughing Water replied.

Mary ducked inside but not before she saw several warriors carrying guns and knives.

"Are we being attacked?" Mary was afraid but also felt a twinge of hope.

"No, Mary." Laughing Water said, then left, calling one of the men over to guard Mary's door. "Do not let her leave," she said in her own tongue.

Mary knew not to ask the man questions. He either wouldn't or couldn't answer her. So she pushed aside a decorative woven mat and poked an opening through the bark crust of the lodge. She peered through the hole and listened. The word English stood out among the other stranger words, and she held her hands to her mouth so she wouldn't cry out. *Had the English finally come for her? Was she to be redeemed at last?*

She heard the name Hoar and remembered the solicitor John Hoar who had served her husband in legal matters. *Could it be him? Has Master Hoar come to ransom me?* She knelt close to the tiny hole she had made in the wall of the wetu and clutched her hands to her breast. She prayed earnestly that Master Hoar had come. She promised to give glory to the Lord for all her days if He let her ransom come to pass.

Excitement grew outside, and voices called out the names Tom and Peter. With her face pressed firmly against the ash bark wall, she could see two men in English attire. Her spirit sank a little when she saw the warm response the newcomers received as she recognized them as Christian Indians, not true Christians.

She heard several gunshots. Then silence.

"Dear God," she whispered in despair. "Be merciful. Let no harm come to good Christian men. But if it is your will to call good English saints to you, let not my husband be in their number."

The door flap lifted, and in stepped an Indian dressed in a mixture of native and English dress with a man's fancy coat and shirt over leather moccasins and leggings. Mary fell back, then recognized him as James Printer, the Christian Indian who had given her the Bible.

Still on her knees, Mary looked up at him. She remembered his kindness and her shoulders relaxed a little at the sight of him. Her voice shook. "Kind Sir, will you not tell me what has happened? Has there been a killing of Christians nearby?"

"No, Mistress. Calm yourself. There has been no killing. Only shots of warning to draw some men away from our camp." He sat down.

"But, pray tell, who are they and why do they come?" she asked, creeping toward him.

"They are two Christian Indians, Tom Dublet and Peter Conway." He pulled back the door flap and looked out. Turning back to her, he said, "Mary, they come to seek your release."

Mary drew in a great breath and rose from her crouched position as she clasped her hands to her breast. "Oh, gracious God in Heaven! Say it is so! I am to be redeemed? On this very day?"

"Nay, nay, Mary. Not on this day, but one day soon. First, they must negotiate a reasonable price and the men who have come must see that you are unharmed."

"Oh, let them see me, and I will tell them that I am unharmed. I am sure my husband will raise whatever sum he must." She drew nearer to James and put her hand on his. "Talk to Philip, won't you? Make him let me go with them now." She reached over with her other hand and caught his sleeve.

"No, Mary. Not now, but very soon. Today they bring a second letter from the governor asking for your release. But they bring no ransom nor trade goods. Today you will not go." He took her two hands between his strong palms and said, "Be of strong heart, and you will not be forsaken. I pray with you that your time of trouble comes near to its end."

He gripped her hands more tightly. "Mary, you must think well on what demand your husband will pay. The governor has refused to pay any ransom, so all must come from your own family and friends. Philip must send a demand back today. So you must think quickly and well on it. Philip will meet with you soon. Be ready with your answer."

He patted her hand and left.

Oh, what will I say? she wondered. *Surely Joseph has given an offer as great as he can spare. A second letter? James said second letter. Was the first turned down? How will I know what value I am as a wife to my husband? What of our children? I cannot ask so much that we cannot together redeem our precious children. What shall I say? What terms will make me more valuable alive than dead to this heathen mob?*

Is twelve pounds too little? Is thirty pounds too much? Think. I must think. What does Philip need? Food. Guns. Tobacco. Oh, what shall I say? Barely audible, she whispered, "Guide me, oh Lord. Thou who maketh my redemption, help me choose the right words."

The deerskin flap opened again, and Laughing Water peered in. "Come."

Trembling, Mary obliged. Light-headed as she rose, she needed a moment to clear her vision. Then she followed Laughing Water into Philip's longhouse. The place smelled of burned sage and sweetgrass. They seemed always to burn those. Mary thought she would never clear the smell of it from her hair and clothing. A mob of heathens already gathered, and she could not see through the thick of them. They made her sit behind them all, but at least she could hear the goings-on.

Philip spoke. "We have brought in the woman, Mary Rowland-son, that you may convey word that she is well. Mistress Rowlandson, is it not so?" he asked loudly.

Mary's voice cracked at first. "It . . .It is so, King Philip." She cleared her throat and answered more strongly, "I am unharmed."

"Mary, tell these men the fair price for your redemption. What worth do you place on your return?" Soft murmurs moved through the crowd. The people seemed surprised that Philip would let the woman set her own ransom.

Mary spoke firmly, "King Philip and other noble gentlemen, I have no doubt that my husband will pay twenty pounds for my safe return." As soon as she said it, she clapped her hands over her mouth and held them there, eyes wide in apprehension. More murmurs rumbled through the crowd.

"It is so," said Philip. "With that price, I shall also take a payment in guns, powder, and seed corn. That is the price for only this one woman. Take the message to the governor. If he would have the release of all captives, we must strike a great bargain. Return to me with his reply. I will be in Wachusett in a fortnight. I have spoken."

Suddenly, Mary heard a rustling and realized that members of Philip's council had stood up all at once. She saw by the altering of shadow and light on the roof and walls of the longhouse that they exited en masse. With no negotiation, the ransom price had been fixed. She prayed that she had not set the price outside her husband's reach.

Freedom at Hand
Fifteenth to Seventeenth Removes

Mary didn't know what had led to Weetamoo's sudden change in heart but thanked God that her feet at last turned her in the direction of home. She understood that they would go to Mount Wachusett and from there, she thought she could find her way home even if she were not redeemed. Mary fully expected her release upon their arrival there. She trusted her suggested ransom of twenty pounds would be reasonable and hoped Joseph could raise that sum and enough more to ransom the children as well.

She began seeking out people who might have seen her children or who could tell her the names of people who held them. She realized the importance of remembering landmarks and place names that might help her find them again. She casually asked for names of places where they stayed. As they ventured back the way they had come, she recognized familiar places.

At Wachusett, she had last seen her daughter Mary and buried Sarah, God rest her soul. She had never seen Mary again in all her travels after leaving that place, but she had prayed for her every night and believed her safe and alive somewhere, perhaps even redeemed already. Perhaps her daughter had remained at Wachusett and Mary would see her soon.

Seeing her son Joseph on other occasions comforted her, although she worried about his dreadful condition. Yet it remained her deepest desire to see both her children again soon.

Spring approached and days grew longer, but edible green shoots did not yet emerge from the cold ground. Mary reckoned the date as early or mid April. Her hunger remained constant and eating scant roots, nuts, and dried berries along the way did little to relieve it. Corn recovered by the party that went to Narragansett had not lasted long at all. She had only received a very small bit of it to eat.

Mary did not understand the way the people had of eating everything they had as soon as they got it. She had hoarded some kernels in her pocket, but someone had stolen them from her. When Quannopinn lived with them, he often brought a partridge or rabbit and sometimes a deer home for them to eat, but since his absence, they had no more meat. The women and old men felt too tired to hunt after each day's trek, and animals stayed clear of the wide trails they followed.

Mary daydreamed of the food she had wasted when she lived at home in Lancaster. She thought with relish about scraps she had thrown out to the dogs. She knew it did no good to waste her time thinking of food, but it did her less good to try not to think of it.

When she didn't think of food, she worried about what might happen when they reached Wachusett. She worried about whether her husband had received the ransom demand and whether he had raised the money. She worried about whether he was still alive. Mr. Read's description of Joseph as looking poorly and melancholy concerned her. It must have shocked Joseph greatly to lose his home, his wife, his children, and his church all in one day. She said a prayer for his encouragement.

She walked with the pack basket resting on her shoulders. It felt much lighter than before. Little food remained, and many of the things she had carried had worn out or been discarded or burned along the way. She had fewer skins to carry, as they buried some with Laughing Water's or Weetamoo's papoose, or so she assumed. They had disappeared around that same time. Some of the woven mats she carried before had torn and she abandoned them as useless. Now that the sap ran in the trees, they found it easy enough to loosen fresh bark when they needed it for roofing. She stepped more lightly, relieved of the excess weight.

✳ ✳ ✳

Retracing their steps, the band traveled for three days. Wading over, they crossed Baquoag again. Mary felt weary, wet, and cold, but her will carried her forward. It brightened her spirit on the last day to see her niece with a group of children. They comforted one another with prayer and promises of redemption. In a matter of days, she arrived within sight of the Wachusett Hills.

Gathering Courage
Eighteenth Remove

Morning sun shone warmly on her face, and she rejoiced in it because she knew the wanderings of her captors had finally turned to the direction of her Lancaster home. They traveled through hilly terrain that wound through thick woods between the mountains. She could not yet see Mount Wachusett, but she knew it was there.

They followed the edge of a stream, and she stopped to quench her thirst. Water raged through its bed from all the melted snow and spring rainfall.

After they passed through a narrow gorge made long before by rushing water, the view opened up to reveal the path ahead. Looming in the distance was Mount Wachusett. Looking up at it, Mary remembered when she had looked down into the same valley and feared for her life. Her time with the Indians had not been easy. She felt sure now that her trial would end soon. She could let herself think of going home. She would climb up out of this valley and she would again become Reverend Joseph Rowlandson's wife. She would go home and forget all about groveling for food and hiding in hovels through long winter nights. She had the thought just before she fainted from lack of food.

She woke up to see a strange woman holding sharp herbs under her nose. She waved the herbs away and sat up. The woman gave her cold water from the stream and offered her a spoonful of cold samp porridge. Mary drank and ate greedily. She nodded thanks to the woman. It still surprised Mary that many of the people had been kind to her even though she did not know them. She wondered if her own people would have done as much for one of them. *Would I?*

"Thank you," Mary said.

"You're welcome," said the woman. She was Indian but wore English clothes.

"You speak English?"

"Yes, I learned at the Christian school at Hassanamesit. I am Weecum."

"I am Mary. It is good to know you, Weecum. Thank you for helping me and thank you for the food. I shall repay you."

"There is no need. We share what we have. All is given us by the Creator to share with one another. Are you well enough to continue? Can I help you up?

"Thank you. I think I am fine." Mary rose a little unsteadily. The poor diet had weakened her but not enough to allow her to ask for help. "Will you walk with me?"

"Yes, and if you wish to sing psalms, I will sing them with you as we walk," Weecum volunteered. "Or perhaps you wish to pray?"

Mary looked around for Weetamoo. "No, Weecum. That would not be wise for me to do when Weetamoo is near. It offends her. But I will meet with you to pray away from her later, if you would like. Perhaps we could sing a little if we were not too loud."

"Yes," Weecum agreed. Quietly singing, they walked toward the mountain.

Mary asked her when they stopped to rest if she was a Praying Indian. Weecum seemed a little offended and told her curtly, "Mary, I am a Christian. As Christian as you are. I believe the same as you and have been raised in a good Christian home."

"I'm sorry, Weecum," Mary apologized. "I meant not to offend you. It's just . . .well . . .I wonder how it is you come to be with this group of enemy Indians."

"Many of these people are my family, Mary. We have been family for many thousands of years. Your people are new here. Some of us have been Christian for fifty years. The Creator loves us all and He understands that Indians can also be Christian. But sadly, your people do not understand that Christians can also be Indians. I had to leave my home to avoid being taken away."

"Away to the island?" Mary asked.

Weecum nodded. Mary understood. Weecum must have been one of the people Captain Gookin had spoken about. Then Mary had feared those people. But she began to see Weecum as a woman like herself, a Christian woman among heathens. She realized for the first time since her capture that she was not afraid. She was strong and would survive. It had been unpleasant and difficult, but she was going to survive. Even Weetamoo could not threaten her any longer. She was going home.

After gaining sight of the Wachusett Hills, they still had to pass a treacherous swamp. Spring runoff had flooded the swamp by the time they arrived in late April. When they had last crossed it in deep winter, the frozen ice made the way easier. This time, they had to keep reversing their course when paths became too mired to pass. Winter's ire left dead branches and fallen trees across their way and rushing spring water washed away any loose earth, thus exposing stones, rubble, and roots.

Weecum and Mary separated as they each picked their own best way through the wetlands. Mud sucked at Mary's shoes, and icy cold water at times poured over her knees, despite the lateness of the season. After three days of grueling travel, Mary felt exhausted.

During the trip, few had much to eat. Some Indians killed their horses for food, but Mary had only broth with spoonfuls of corn mash. She felt so weak that at each camp she visited other households and asked if anyone could share a morsel with her. Most turned her away, sadly or angrily refusing her, even those who still had beans or corn to eat. One man offered her bits of horse guts, which in other times she would have refused. She accepted, and it tasted like a feast. The meal refreshed her. She offered thanks to God, remembering a verse from Job 6:7, "The things that my soul refused to touch are now my sorrowful meat."

The past months, Mary realized, gave her an appreciation for the value of what she had wasted before. Never having lived in want, the satisfaction and enjoyment she received from meager meals and slight comforts surprised her. She had never relied upon the mercy of strangers and appreciated each time one of Indians shared some small portion of their own sparse supplies.

In Lancaster, she had always prided herself as benefactress of others in need. Now she felt a different aspect of God's grace that she might never have known without the hardships. She whispered a prayer from Samuel 14:29, "Mine eyes have been enlightened because I tasted a little of this honey."

Their travel through the Great Swamp and the climb to the mountaintop was arduous. Mary fell many times, often feeling as if she might never get up again, but from a distance Weecum encouraged her and she pushed on. When they arrived at Wachusett, Mary saw Quannopinn again. He greeted her warmly, though his face showed concern at her disheveled appearance and her weakness.

"Mary, you look so thin. You must come to the wetu of my wife, Onux, and let her feed you. Come with me." It startled her to learn that he called another squaw his wife. Is that why he left, she wondered. Had he and Weetamoo divorced? Or did he practice bigamy, keeping other wives in other places? No matter, she willingly followed him. His old wife welcomed her and gave her a soft fur to sit on. Onux gave her meat, beans, and a bit of corn bread. The meal tasted like a banquet. At first Mary's stomach wanted to refuse to hold the food down, but she swallowed hard to keep it there.

When she finished eating, Quannopinn asked, "How long has it been since you bathed, Mary?"

She could not remember. She had stopped thinking about her appearance.

"It is time for you to make yourself presentable for your return to English life," he told her. Quannopinn left to fetch water for her. When he returned, he gave her one of his own clean shirts to wear and woolen stockings she had made. He heated the water, and they left her alone so she could bathe in private.

Outside, she heard him talking to Weetamoo. They argued loudly. Mary heard her name. She gathered that Quannopinn chastised Weetamoo for not protecting his asset. Weetamoo lashed out at him for caring more about his captive than herself, his new wife. They shouted back and forth for minutes. Mary heard a loud slap and then silence.

Mary finished washing, then changed into the clean shirt and stockings before pulling on her old skirts. She felt warm and safe and dry and lay down on the fur rug. She fell asleep curled up next to the fire like a tired old house cat. They let her stay until the next morning.

Laughing Water came for her the next day. "Weetamoo asks you to return to her wetu. She will make you comfortable in her home. Her sister also welcomes you to her wetu to eat with her and Metacom, uh, King Philip, this evening."

Weetamoo's change in attitude astonished Mary. She wondered what could have brought it about. She guessed that something Quannopinn said struck home. She thanked Onux for her hospitality, and the older woman told her to return any time. If she truly had the choice, she would not have considered going back to Weetamoo. Yet, she did not understand how she might fit into the triangle among Quannopinn and his other two wives.

Mary followed Laughing Water through the village. Mary thought about asking if she belonged to Quannopinn or Weetamoo but decided to stay quiet.

Laughing Water seemed as if she wanted to say something, twice looking at her and opening her mouth, then looking away without a word. At last she said, "Mary, I am sorry for being angry with you before. I do not dislike you, though I do not understand you sometimes."

Mary nodded. "Your English is getting better." She didn't want to accept the girl's apology. She could not forgive her, although she harbored no hatred for her. She conceded by saying, "I do not always understand you, either, Laughing Water."

She admitted to herself that she did not understand Weetamoo either. She remained an enigma. Although Mary skillfully helped her to throw up a wigwam or lean-to for a night's rest and packed up readily each morning for travel, she tried to keep away from Weetamoo by day as much as she could. As if the hardship and hard work did not pose enough difficulty, Mary had endured Weetamoo's wrath whenever she returned to sleep. She wondered, *Why does she welcome me back?*

She decided to wait until nightfall to enter Weetamoo's wigwam. She found her mistress sitting and staring into the fire. A stew simmered over the coals.

Weetamoo looked up and snarled at her, "The people complain to me that you have been begging at their hearths again. Is it true?"

Mary shed her cloak and sat to remove her tattered moccasins. Holes wore through their soles from all the walking she had done in past weeks. Not in all her lifetime had she walked as many miles as she had done with those shoes.

She looked at her captor. "Yes, Weetamoo, it is true. I have been 'begging.' What would you have me do instead? Starve?" she snapped. She had never been so insolent before nor even called Weetamoo by her name. As soon as she said it, she inwardly flinched in anticipation of a harsh reprisal. She saw the angry look in her eyes, but Weetamoo did not get up.

"Do it again, and I will knock you on the head. I will have no more of your shaming me among my own people," Weetamoo responded dully.

Emboldened by the lack of a physical response, Mary replied, "Then knock me on the head if you must, for without food, I will surely die." She lay back on her sleeping fur and wondered what made her dare to say such a thing.

Being so close to home, she felt both frightened and excited. She feared believing she could return home, because the Indians still had it in their power to refuse her return or to end her life. Yet at the same time, her thoughts began to shift from those of a helpless captive to those of a wealthy free woman. The closer she came to Wachusett, the more she felt her inner power growing. But going home brought its own worries. What changes would she face? Could she go back home and resume her old life?

Strangely, Weetamoo's anger melted away. Before, she would have flown at Mary and grasped any nearby object to hit her or throw at her. Instead, she calmly looked at her and offered her a bowl of stew.

Mary only looked at her. Weetamoo had never eaten with her, let alone cooked for her. She did not know how to respond. Could Weetamoo be playing some kind of trick? Or worse? Poison? She sat up, careful to stay on the far side of the fire from her mistress.

"Mary," Weetamoo said, "the Powwows have met. We have decided that you will be ransomed. We wait now for the answer from John Hoar."

"That is good," Mary said. She struggled to hide her excitement. Coming from Weetamoo's mouth, the words expressed the greatest gift she could imagine. She had been fearful that Weetamoo would block her return to civilization. "When do you think that might happen?" she asked in as casual a voice as she could manage.

"In two weeks," Weetamoo replied, staring into the fire. "Until then, you must rest and recover your strength, for you will still have to travel when you leave us."

"I appreciate your consideration. Thank you." Mary found it difficult to sit and pretend to have a civil conversation with her tormentor. In all the long weeks, they had not once spoken so candidly. Weetamoo usually ordered her around like a slave and beat her worse than one. Mary began to understand that she might now have the upper hand, but had been chastened too much to consider lauding it over her captor.

"This has not always been easy," Weetamoo said to her. "We have been unable to offer you the comforts of a guest. What we have had, we have shared with you. Soon you will return to your people and your own ways. I will be happy for you," Weetamoo lied without looking up.

Mary had a harder time swallowing Weetamoo's words than she had the first meal Weetamoo had made for her. *Surely she mocks me. More likely she will be happy to be rid of my company.*

"Thank you," Mary responded at last. "Although I came here against my will, I am thankful to you for sharing what you had with me. I have learned many things from your people."

Mary did not know what else to say. Deep inside, she wanted to scream out, "Thank you for nearly starving me and leaving me out in the bitter cold. I'm grateful that you didn't kill me all the times you tried." She would have liked to yell at her, to grab her and bang her head on the ground, but she still feared Weetamoo's power over her.

She resented having such unChristian thoughts. She knew that she would never have her revenge on the woman. Then she heard the words of the good book echoing in her head: "Revenge is mine sayeth the Lord."

Council of the Powwows
Nineteenth Remove

On the day of their arrival in the Wachusett foothills, the Powwows fasted alone on top of the mountain. Away from the others, the Powwows each spent time in solitude on private vision quests for wisdom on whether the Indians should continue to war or surrender to the English. The well-being of their people rested as a heavy mantle over them. Many had had enough of war and wanted to return to their homes. The people had grown weak, and if they did not return to planting, hunting, and fishing soon, they would die from starvation or sickness.

Older sachems like Awashonks and Monaco felt that the English, too, had equally poor provisions, experienced similar weakness and concern, and would be ready to treat for peace. Younger men like Awashonks's and Tispaquin's sons sided with Metacom, Quannopinn, and Tispaquin and believed the time ripe for strong offensive attacks. With the number of warriors they still had and their new understanding of English warfare, they believed they could burn out remaining villages and send whatever remained of the English back across the sea.

The Powwows would put controversy to rest. They all converged after their separate quests and prepared to relate to the people what they had learned. If they endorsed war, they would attack Sudbury, the largest outlying English town. If not, the people would all return to their homes to make their own choices of submission or defiance.

As darkness grew, the Powwows returned, and people gathered to learn their decision. Powwows from each tribe collected in a circle around Metacom's Powwow, who knelt on a deerskin. Each had capes and head coverings made from skins of their own spirit totems and had painted their faces in unique designs. One wore a cape all of feathers with a hawk's head resting on his own. Another had the skin of a panther with its angry face above his brow. Others wore fox, bear, and deer totems, too. The people also wore their finest clothes. Many wore weapons. They styled their hair knotted or braided, and some wore feather crowns.

Powwows began softly chanting and beating on the ground with sticks. The head Powwow in the middle struck the ground with his palms to call the attention of the spirits.

He said in Algonquin, "Hear me my brothers and sisters. Before you we come to tell you our visions."

The crowd murmured approval.

"We have asked the spirits to guide our people and show us our path. We have been divided."

The crowd voiced agreement.

"Do you wish to see our vision?" he called out.

"Yes" and "Nux" resounded the replies.

"Will you consent to follow the wisdom of the Spirits?" he asked.

Again, "Yes" and "Nux," the people shouted out.

"Then we will show you what we have seen."

The Powwow in the middle came forward with a musket in his hand. He shook it at the other Powwows as a sign of his willingness to fight, but they turned from him and pushed him away, eventually forcing him from their circle. They quietly whispered among themselves and then some called the Powwow back, but reluctant, he did not return. The moment portrayed Metacomet's failed early efforts to bring the tribes together. Over time, some called the musket-bearing Indian back to make alliances with him.

The musket-toting one stayed outside the circle until an earnest demand rose up for his return. When the Powwows in the circle pled with him enough to convince him to return, he rejoined them. All the Powwows rejoiced and sang over his return.

They gave him a second musket. The Powwows' action signified an increase in power when they united, as they had done at the war council in Montaup the summer before when they agreed to resist the English demands for their weapons.

The head Powwow asked the people for support, and they agreed with him, some more adamantly than others. The Powwows sang again and banged on the ground with their weapons to remind the Spirits and the people that they had joined in sacred trust.

To remind the people that the warriors originally agreed to wait one year before starting the war with the English, again they sent away the Powwow who represented Metacomet, this time with two muskets. The crowd loudly agreed that the musket-bearing warrior should go from them.

The head Powwow called out, "Before we could return to our homes and prepare for war, the English struck our people." The people's cheers grew stronger.

"They killed our brothers for a murder they did not commit," he shouted." The crowd responded with anger. Tispaquin's Assawomset voices rang loudest.

"They called again for us to turn in our guns," the chief Powwow reminded them, and the people nodded and shouted. Wampanoags nodded and discussed the situation angrily with one another.

"They killed our child Peebe over the taking of an English cow." Pocasset anger rose.

"They took our brothers and sisters away to Deer Island to freeze or to sell them as slaves," he shouted. People grew more incensed, especially Christian Indians most abused by the English in that manner.

"They marched our families to trials and shot them in the streets," he called out, and the Wamesits let out loud war whoops.

Collective anger grew, and people shouted out their frustration. In the midst of it, the Powwows called out to the man outside the circle, urging him to fight with them. He wavered. Drawn to them, he nevertheless held back. The Powwows called to him more fervently, begging him to come and fight with them. Still he held back.

By turns, pledging his tribe's allegiance and urging the waverer to join with them, each Powwow raised his musket high over his head and called out to the man, while others beat the ground with the heels of their own weapons. Their action kept the spirits close to observe their sacred vows. As each one made his promise, the man outside the group came a step closer. He held both muskets out at arm's length and submitted his will to the will of the Powwows. Returning to the circle, he raised the muskets up to the sky and brought them down to earth, firing each as it struck the ground with two loud cracks.

The Powwows and the crowd grew quiet. The Powwow in the center waited. Then he spoke, "We have formed a sacred trust. Our people have united as one. With great hardship we have had many victories. If we keep our trust, we will have more. If we do not . . ." he bent down and gathered up dirt in both hands and threw it in wide spraying arcs, "we are but grains of sand." He waited again. "Are we united kin of one family? Or will we be the sand washed away from the shore?" he asked loudly.

The Powwows stood in silence. Then the sachems of the tribes spoke up.

Quannopinn raised his musket and shouted, "We fight!" The Narragansetts cheered.

"We fight!" yelled Tispaquin and the Assawomsets shouted their approval.

Matoonas called, "We fight!" and his tribe raised their voices in agreement.

Weetamoo stepped forward and held up her bow, shouting, "We fight!" The Pocassets joined their voices with hers.

One after another the sachems and tribes reaffirmed their consent to war, even Awashonks and Monaco. When all had spoken, Metacomet called out, "Now we are one again. We go to Sudbury. We fight!"

At his word, the crowd hooted, stomped, and sprang to life. They raised their own weapons and ran to their horses, some of them riding two on one horse. With no advance coordination, they had renewed their commitment and set off to destroy the town of Sudbury.

Sudbury Fight

Weetamoo rode by Quannopinn's side on the ride to Sudbury. She already knew it would be her last fight. She saw the schism between young and old and knew they consented this time with their bodies but not with their hearts. Too many losses, too many leaders gone.

Quannopinn led all the Narragansetts, but he had not won their hearts as Canonchet had. Her own warriors numbered fewer than one hundred. So many injured or killed. A great number dead from illness. Unwisely trusting the English promise of amnesty, others deserted. She felt as if she rode to the fight with their ghosts beside her. She felt empty.

"Quannopinn," she said, "today I will fight for the last time."

"What?" he asked sharply.

"After today, I am taking my people home to Pocasset," she stated firmly.

"Weetamoo, you cannot do that. We have made a sacred pledge," he reminded her. She knew what he meant. He could not believe she would do what she said.

"That is so, but I cannot stay here any longer. My fight will be in my home country, where I was born and where I will die."

"Weetamoo, have you spoken to Metacom of this? There is no sense in it. To disband now will insure our failure. It is only in numbers that we have strength. You were at the council!" he shouted at her in anger.

"I was. I will fight, Quannopinn, but now in my own land. I wish to bury no more Pocassets in distant country." She sighed. "Of that I am sure."

Quannopinn dug his heels into his horse's side and rode away from her. His stubborn wife had made up her mind. He could not change it. Her decision would weigh heavily on the other sachems. The weak ones would follow her and go to their separate homes. Just when they could win the war, she would pull it apart. He pushed his fury down. He could not lay his hand on her. He had to get to Metacom and warn him of her treachery before it spread. What would they do? How could they stop her, he worried.

Catching up to Metacom, he told him of Weetamoo's plans. To his surprise, Metacom calmly said, "I expected it, Quannopinn. The Powwows can only hold the people together for so long. If they do not believe in war in their hearts, minds, and spirits, they can commit their bodies but will never gain victory. We must follow our own path." He looked at Quannopinn who stared back in astonishment. He had never heard Metacom so resigned to defeat.

"Take heart, Quannopinn," Metacom said. "Today we fight as one. Tomorrow we fight as many. Tomorrow we will become the grain of sand in the English eye and the pebble in his shoe. Today we show them all our strength and tomorrow our persistence. They may build their houses and decree their laws, but our hearts will always be tied to the land. They may separate us, but they will never grind us away. We are the land. We are the spirit." He said all of it looking straight ahead as he rode.

"Come, My Brother. Let us not think of tomorrow. Today we have a fight. See, there is the town. It will be a good day. Come." He kicked the sides of his horse and rode ahead to the front of the warriors.

Quannopinn sat listlessly on his horse and thought about what Metacomet said. Then he urged his horse forward and rode ahead with a loud whoop. With resounding force, all around him echoed his cry. As one, the riders spurred their horses on. Whooping and screaming they fell upon the town.

Weetamoo screeched out a wail from the belly of her soul and raced to the fore.

Sudbury never had a chance. The fury of the tribes at Sudbury raged greater than in any other place. The five hundred warriors rode in like a thunder storm. They struck like lightning any English where they stood before they could raise an alarm. The Indians set fires as they went and corralled every living person into their garrisons. They burned many alive.

Around noon, English reinforcements arrived to help the beleaguered town. The Indians cornered them, too, and chased them up Green Hill, cut off from the town. The ferocious warriors ringed them all in so tightly that nearly all perished.

By nightfall, Sudbury no longer existed. The Indians packed up their spoils and headed back the way they had come. Metacom ordered James Printer to leave a message on the bridge they destroyed. They rode away, leaving Sudbury to languish in the aftermath of the brutal day.

A gentle breeze loosened the note. It fell into the river and floated off toward the sea.

The Deal Is Struck

Upon their return from Sudbury, the Indians' subdued behavior surprised Mary. She had expected the usual boisterous party. But no victory dance followed. No whooping or rejoicing. At first she thought the English had badly beaten them and she took heart. She learned instead that only five warriors died, so secretly had they attacked. When one of them told her the English lost a hundred or more, her heart tore in two.

The tragedy of the Sudbury folk weighed on her heavily, although her comfort relied on spoils the warriors brought back. Her guilt and her need entwined inside her. She strangely hoped for the Indians to meet both success and defeat. When she ate the English food and wore the English clothing they brought back, she thanked God for her good fortune and tried to imagine and pray for the people who died that she might have them. She wanted to believe that they had survived but knew it unlikely.

Packing and moving again the next day came as no surprise to Mary. As usual, the tribes kept moving to avoid being followed. They moved during the night, and the next morning she found herself at another camp even closer to her home.

While gathering fiddleheads, she heard excited voices from the camp. Such a commotion rarely occurred because usually the Indians spent all of their time shushing each other and hiding themselves from the English.

The raised voices alarmed her. Whether the sounds foretold troubled or joyful news for those who held her, either could bring bad luck for her. Planning to hide in the edge of the wood until she could tell if it was safe to come out, she picked up her basket and started back to camp.

As she drew nearer, Laughing Water ran to her. "Mary, you must come," she said, out of breath.

"What is it?" Mary asked. "What's happened?"

Between breaths, Laughing Water said, "The Englishman. He returns. He comes for you, Mary."

Mary dropped her basket spilling the contents. "The Englishman? Which Englishman?" she asked anxiously. "Mr. Hoar?" She feared for herself and for the man. Only the day before the warriors had killed a hundred English men and women. It made little consequence to them to kill another who may have discovered their hiding place, she thought.

"The same man, Mary, as came before. Yes, I think he is Mr. Hoar," she answered. She bent down to help Mary pick up her fiddleheads and return them to basket.

Mary felt so excited, she didn't know what to do. She felt faint as she reached for the spilled ferns. They rolled away from her fingers. She couldn't seem to get them into her basket fast enough. *Will I truly go home on this very day?*

She could not believe an English rider had come to their new camp. It astounded her when Laughing Water told her that Mr. John Hoar rode in the company of the two Indians, Tom and Peter, and that they brought her ransom! She worried for his safety and her own but also felt enormous excitement welling inside her breast. Her emotions ran amok at the news.

Afraid and relieved, she felt a vulnerability she had tried to bury since the beginning of her captivity. So close to her redemption, she felt confused. *Why do I fear the Indians more than ever before? Will they let me go? Or could this be a cruel trick? But if true, might I ride away from here this very day?* Though she had imagined the day and lived it in her dreams many times, it frightened her to believe it.

"What should I do?" she asked Laughing Water. "Do they ask for me?"

"I come to take you to our wetu. You must hide until they call you to council. Come, now. They are near and will be at council soon."

Mary started walking, then turned back for her basket she had left on the ground. In grabbing it so hurriedly, she spilled the contents again.

"Never mind," Laughing Water said. "I will come back for them. Metacomet wants you to come back now."

Laughing Water's sense of urgency diminished as they approached the camp. She looked about as if wary of some unseen thing or person. Attawan's wife had told Mary that, in Pocasset where Laughing Water lived, very few white men lived or visited. She had only a little contact with them, and they frightened her. After Laughing Water survived December's Great Swamp fight where most of her family died, her fear of white people intensified. Mary understood the young girl's worry and had tried to befriend her. Sometimes they had taught one another words in their own languages when Weetamoo could not see or hear them. But not since the papooses died.

Mary had not been told, but guessed that Laughing Water's baby died in childbirth or very shortly after during the trek to Narragansett. Given her condition at the time, that came as no surprise. Mary didn't understand why they allowed it, but she had seen others in late stages of pregnancy carrying heavy loads and climbing over hill and dale at the same time an English woman would have confined herself to bed. They never spoke of the stillbirth. Mary never even saw the baby. She didn't even know if it had been a boy or a girl. She only knew that since then Laughing Water had stopped being friendly to her.

Laughing Water suddenly talked more than she had in weeks. Mary felt glad for that. She wanted to talk to someone.

"Laughing Water, what happens now? Have you seen how redemptions are arranged?" she asked while they walked back to camp. The shouting had quieted down, and it seemed like any other day.

"No," she answered. "They will summon you when they are ready for you."

"What should I do? Should I pack my things?" she asked. Then she realized she didn't have any things. She had come empty handed. Any things she had acquired really belonged to Weetamoo or Quannopinn.

"If you wish to. There would be no harm in it."

They walked the rest of the way in silence. She saw no outward signs of Mr. Hoar or the Christian Indians. They went into the wetu. Mary looked around at the things that had become familiar over the past four months. She had her own sleeping furs and bone needles for sewing and knitting. She kept them in a leather pouch a woman made her in exchange for a pair of stockings. She had a basket with a bit of yarn taken from Northfield. She had some items of English clothes from Medfield, the remnant of a Bible, and a hairbrush from Sudbury that Monaco had given her only the day before.

At first, she did not like the idea of having such items, but as her captivity lengthened, she grew to treasure them as vestiges of a life she hoped to return to soon. She felt both sorrow for and connection with the former owners and tried to imagine how they lived and to forget how they died. She grew to revere the items as relics from martyred Christians.

She touched the hairbrush and noticed the long grey hair that did not match her own. She began to cry as she thought about all that had happened to the colonists while she lived among the heathen Indians. She regretted not having any power to save them from their fate. She felt guilty for surviving. She thought of her children and worried over the prospect of leaving them behind in the wilderness. All those emotions rushed at her, and she wept inconsolably.

Laughing Water looked at her with surprise. "Mary, why do you cry? You are going home. It is time for you to be glad."

Mary nodded but kept weeping. She should be happy, but she couldn't stop the flow of tears.

"Mary, stop. What is wrong?" Laughing Water asked. Mary's sudden outburst of emotion frightened her. If Mary went mad,

Weetamoo might lose the ransom. Laughing Water did not want the blame if that happened. She shook Mary by the shoulders and shouted, "Stop it! Stop it!"

Weetamoo heard the noise and entered the wetu. "What goes on here?" she asked. "Mary, stop!" she ordered.

Mary looked at her through clouded eyes and thought, suddenly, how silly Weetamoo looked. All dressed up in her red stockings and red paint with countless bracelets dangling from her wrists to her elbows. She had feathers in her hair and ears, and for the first time, Mary did not fear her. Instead, she started to laugh.

Everything suddenly seemed so ridiculous. She had been running around the woods with painted up savages while they had been terrorizing her neighbors all around. *Why had everyone been so afraid of each other?* She giggled. *The war now seems so absurd. These people have so little. They don't want English houses or land. They like living in makeshift hovels and traipsing about in the wilderness. The English want towns and commerce. Why couldn't they both have what they wanted?* She kept laughing at what seemed like an argument between spoiled children. Then she remembered the deaths that both sides had endured. She stopped laughing and sat down dazed on the edge of the platform.

Weetamoo spoke to Laughing Water in her own language or some other dialect. Mary wasn't sure exactly what she said but assumed she wanted Laughing Water to keep Mary hidden until Philip made a deal with Mr. Hoar. *It wouldn't do to turn in a half-starved, half-mad captive, now would it,* thought Mary. She took a deep breath.

Weetamoo looked at her strangely, then left.

By noon, they finally called her into the council. They told her to sit still and wait while they brought in Mr. Hoar and the two Indians, Tom and Peter. After Philip and his sagamores finished questioning them, they gave Mary permission to speak.

It surprised her when they mentioned the day as the Sabbath and the month as May. She had long ago lost track of time by English reckoning. Her captivity lasted eleven weeks and five days—almost three months! Had someone told her before it happened that she would survive that long in the wilderness, she would never have believed it. She felt pride in her endurance and survival skills. She thanked God for his mercy in keeping her safe for all that time.

Mary asked about the welfare of her husband. It reassured her to hear that Joseph anxiously awaited her return and enjoyed improved health knowing he would see her soon. Mr. Hoar gave her gifts from her husband, including more tobacco. Mary thought, *Poor Joseph. He doesn't even know I no longer take a pipe. I have so much to tell him when I see him again.*

Mary asked, "King Philip, may I expect to leave today with Mr. Hoar?" She held her breath waiting for his answer.

"No," answered some of his council folk. It shocked her to hear the fat old squaw named Awashonks and one-eyed Monaco barring her way to freedom.

"It is too late in the day to begin the travel home, Mary," Philip commented. "Darkness would fall before you reached a resting place."

Mary found that strange when she had grown accustomed to sleeping out of doors in all manner of places. "Mr. Hoar has offered to prepare a meal to share with the council of sagamores and they have consented to attend his meal," Philip continued. Mary felt that he was stalling, perhaps to see what more he could demand from his visitors.

As evening approached, excitement fell over the camp. All expected a feast, but upon returning to his wigwam, Mr. Hoar discovered someone had rifled his belongings and taken most of his food store planned for the meal. When he reported that to Philip, he remarked that some matchit or bad Indian had to have done it, not any of his own people.

Mary, however, had no doubt that Philip had ordered the ransacking to take place during the council. It mattered not, though, because the victory at Sudbury made food plentiful again. A dinner feast would go on.

They came in great numbers to the big longhouse. More than a hundred could fit inside, and the excess spilled over into the warm spring evening. A formal dance was made in the longhouse with four men and four women imitating English dancers. Quannopinn and Weetamoo both joined in the dance, but not paired together as before. They both wore an abundance of ornaments, more than at previous dances. Weetamoo wore a new English kersey woolen coat covered with bands of wampum with handfuls of necklaces dripping from her neck. She had powdered her hair white, and she wore English jewels in her ears. *Doubtless the new trinkets came from some home in Sudbury,* Mary thought.

Quannopinn wore a Holland shirt with lace and silver buttons, and he had on white stockings topped with garters ringed with coins that jangled as he danced. He, too, covered himself in wampum. Other dancers dressed in similar English fashion with gaudy Indian touches. They acted out a formal dance to rhythms beaten out on an overturned kettle. The musicians played a strange parody of a minuet or strathspey that set Mary's nerves to jingling like Quannopinn's coins. It seemed like a frightening version of a fancy dress party.

Something felt very wrong to see the strange folk in such fine English clothes snatched from Sudbury houses. She looked away and saw Mr. Hoar seated in the corner with James Printer, Tom Conway, and Peter Dublet. She heard them all speaking in English and asked to join them. All four gentlemen rose and offered her a seat. Mary thought it the most remarkable genteel courtesy given her since her captivity. She sat and felt almost like an English mistress once again. She had so many questions she wanted to ask them, but before she could, Quannopinn came and joined them.

"Mr. Hoar," he said. "Before you can relieve us of Mistress Rowlandson's company, there will be a debt to settle with me, as I have provided for her upkeep all these days."

Mr. Hoar, knowing the matter would come up and unwilling to spoil the bargain said, "Tell me, Sir, what the fair price for this upkeep would be."

"Over the payment promised to Metacomet for the welfare of us all, I should like very much to have a pint of your rum liquor. I have not enjoyed any in a very great time, and if you have that in your possession, it would seem a fair exchange." His request surprised Mary as well as his polite manner in presenting the demand. In all the spoils taken from all the places they had raided, she had never known any of the Indians to take liquor.

Mr. Hoar sent Tom and Peter to collect a pint from his quarters, and when they returned, Quannopinn opened it and drank it down like water. Between draughts, he spoke freely. "There is much to celebrate," he said. "This is the eve of my parting with my newest wife, Weetamoo. She leaves me tomorrow to go take up her fight in Pocasset country."

He took another long gulp of his rum. Mary was shocked by his manner and loose tongue. She was not aware that Weetamoo was planning any such thing. She was sure that if she were, she would not take kindly to Quannopinn letting it be known to strangers.

"Yes," Quannopinn carried on. "The war in Nipmuc country has come to an end, friends. We are now to spread ourselves in great numbers over the land." He finished off his jug and leaned back contentedly.

Mr. Hoar looked surprised with his candor and started to ask Quannopinn a question, but Philip, who stood nearby, promptly put an end to the discussions.

"Quannopinn," he said, "I need you to see that the scouts are posted all around the camp."

"By all means, my liege," Quannopinn mocked in English style with a lavish bow.

He left the longhouse for his inspecting rounds.

Philip sat down and asked, "So what shall you pay me, Mary, to release you tomorrow?" He wore finery, too, with wampum all over and his great red cape draped on one shoulder. She noticed his war club at his side and worried momentarily that he might just end her life rather than trouble with her. She reminded herself to be extra cautious in what she said.

She stared at the club. If she ignored it as a tool to administer death, she could admire its craftsmanship. Many squares of white and purplish black wampum danced along the polished wood. She couldn't pull her gaze away from it, and feared looking into Philip's eyes. She noticed little stick men carved into the handle of the weapon. Many of them. She wondered about the pattern of wampum, up and down the length of the handle. It seemed so random, sometimes four white then one black then six or eight white and another black. She wondered what it signified but didn't dare to ask.

In all her time since her capture, she had never felt more threatened, except on the first day. She felt keenly aware that Philip had it in his power to turn her loose or dash her brains out.

"You want me to name a price?" she said and looked up into his dark face.

"Yes, Mary, tell me. What will you give me for your release?" he asked. He looked smugly at her.

His question puzzled Mary. She thought for a moment, then said, "If I had anything of value, I would give it all to you, but alas, I have nothing. Tell me what you would have of me, King Philip?" she asked.

She noticed a sparkle of light in his eye and knew then that he respected her for not cowering from his question. He paused, then made his demand. "I would have twenty shillings of money, two fine wool coats, a half bushel of seed corn, and a pound of tobacco." He leaned back satisfied with his fair request.

"I am greatly honored by your love for me to name such a high price for my redemption," she said, all the while thinking, *I know as much as you already, you crafty fox.* She had no doubt that his men had scouted out Mr. Hoar's stores so he could name all the Englishman had brought with him.

Before they could settle the demand, Quannopinn burst back into the longhouse. Smelling of rum, he loudly praised Mr. Hoar and then, in the next breath, berated him. He asked him first to have a drink with him, then suddenly threatened to kill him.

Weetamoo heard the disturbance and went to him. "Quannopinn, do you have time to talk with me?" she asked.

He became offensively affectionate and pushed himself on her. She told him to stop. He tried to pick her up but was too drunk to manage it. She took advantage of his stumbling and, embarrassed by his behavior toward her in front of so many people, ran outside.

He followed after her, and everyone could hear them quarreling outside. Mary heard him ranting at her, calling her cold and unloving. Weetamoo shouted back that it was he who failed to be the sannup he promised her he would be. They hurled insults back and forth, and everyone inside tried to pretend they couldn't hear them. They heard a slap and her running off with her bracelets clinking as he followed with his money jangling at his knees.

Quannopinn's old squaw, Onux, left the longhouse and soon returned with the jangling Quannopinn to say good night. She took him back to her wetu, and they had no more trouble from him that night.

The whole episode shocked Mary. She had never seen him or any other Indian drunk. She felt upset by all the confusion.

The negotiation came to a halt but not before Mr. Hoar agreed to deliver the goods and money as requested. Mary walked back to her wetu that night expecting release the next day. She could not sleep. So many feelings pulsed through her. To think her ordeal would end on the morrow frightened her, but to think it would not, made her even more afraid. She suddenly felt as if she could not last even one more day as a captive. As she lay on her hard stick bed, she wondered if the next night she might lie in a soft feather bed in a solid wood house. The luxury of it seemed decadent.

To have clean clothing again and all she wanted to eat seemed like fantastic dreams. Yet the dreams would come to pass. She believed it deep in her heart but dared not say the words.

Thinking giddily of all she had missed and would soon have again, she lay awake most of the night. Each time she began to drift off to sleep with those pleasant dreams, her fears about her family and her home startled her awake again. Over and over through the long night she wondered. *What home do I have left? Where are my children? Would Joseph have changed? Am I so changed that he would not want me back? What would she find on her return?*

Different Paths

In the morning, Mary Rowlandson, Mr. Hoar, and the two Christian Indians, Tom Dublet and Peter Conway, packed up to leave. Many came out to offer Mary good wishes on her departure. She felt touched by the kindness of some and suspicious of others who had never been kind before.

One woman gave her a hood and a scarf to ride with, and another shook her hand. One asked her to send back tobacco, and one of the Christian Indians asked her to send a loaf of wheat bread. Mary understood such longing. One man even said he and his squaw would run away with her if she liked, but she turned down his offer.

She looked around the crowd to see if Laughing Water or Weetamoo had come to say goodbye, but they had not. They stood together outside their wetu, and Weetamoo looked at her as if her heart was made of stone. Laughing Water gently lifted her hand. Mary nodded but did not wave back.

Quannopinn came to her looking poorly from his drunken night. He took her hand and said, "Mary Rowlandson, go in peace back to your people. May your God watch over you. Farewell." His English words and thoughtful sentiment moved her.

She quietly said, "Hawu'nshech," his word for goodbye. She turned away before he could see her tears. She began her trip back following the three men.

She cried silently for a long part of the morning, never thinking to wipe her tears away. She took deep breaths and wondered, as she went, *is this really happening or am I only dreaming? Can I truly believe I am finally going home?*

They rode from morning till sundown, when they arrived at the remnant of Lancaster. The town where she had raised her children, prayed with her neighbors, and slept with her husband for many years no longer existed. No houses. No people. Just fallow gardens gone wild with spring weeds beside doorsteps leading nowhere. She saw her strawberry patch starting to put out runners and delicate white blossoms. She thought of Sarah sitting there all covered in berry juice. She swallowed hard and looked away.

Her horse followed the others, and they rode on until they came to an abandoned farmhouse. They made beds of straw to lie on, and Mary fell asleep under the cover of a wooden roof for the first time in more than eleven weeks. She woke several times in the night thinking someone had come in and wondered at her surroundings. She felt relieved when the morning sun came in through the glass pane. She thought it odd that the windows remained intact. She guessed the inhabitants must have abandoned it before the Indians attacked.

She ate little breakfast with the men. Though hungry, she felt too nervous to eat. By noon, they arrived in Concord and Mary felt blessed to be met by her brother and brother-in-law, Henry. It amazed her that her brother had survived the attack, for she last saw him fighting for his life in Lancaster.

"God bless you, Mary, and welcome home," her brother said, reaching up to swing her down from her horse. It shocked him to realize how narrow her waist felt and how easily he could lift her. She had once been a hearty woman. Now she seemed as light as a child.

She fell into his arms and pulled him close. Mary laid her head between the shoulders of the two men and wept out loud in great wrenching sobs.

Others gathered around, and she at last eased up. She took cheer from the sight of so many of her neighbors still alive and well as each one came forward to comfort and greet her.

Everyone had questions for her, and she could hardly think what to answer them, saying in turns, "Yes, I am fine." "No I wasn't tortured." "I lived in wetus with an Indian woman and her family." "Their food tasted despicable."

When Henry asked his one pressing question, she fell dumbstruck, "Where is Elizabeth? Was she with you?"

She didn't say anything at all at first. Poor Henry never knew that one of many charred bodies he helped to bury from Lancaster had been her darling sister, his own dear wife, Elizabeth. When Mary had to tell him the news, she ended her interviews for the day with other well-wishers. His head dropped into his hands and he backed away. Her brother guided him to sit on the step, and he stared out, repeatedly blinking his eyes and swallowing hard. Mary needed to go inside and sit down.

To step through a doorway into a warm English house seemed an unparalleled providence. The china dishes and lace tablecloth seemed as precious as gold. In disbelief, she touched simple things like doors with latches and windows with curtains as if seeing them for the first time. The kind family that housed the travelers on the first night of her freedom had spread their table with every manner of food: fresh garden peas, warm bread, roasted meat, pickled jellies, and bless their hearts, a Banbury cake.

Mary found it difficult to be reserved as an English lady should. She noticed them all looking at her when she hurriedly pushed bits of beef into her mouth with her fingers and chased stray crumbs off the table into her palm and tucked them into her pocket for later. She tasted everything but became too quickly filled to gorge herself as she wanted.

She drank her fill of cool clear water and by the hearth sipped her first cup of English tea. She had so many questions of her own but felt too dazed to voice them. Especially her biggest question. *Where is my husband?* They told her he had developed a nervousness from his family's prolonged absence and her brother didn't consider him well enough to endure the travel and shock of her sudden return. He had come for two prior trips in hope of her restoration and had done poorly with disappointment, so his family thought it best for him to wait in Boston.

Mary slept that night in a room with a real bed with fresh, clean bedclothes. She bathed herself with heated water and brushed her hair before a mirror. She stared at the stranger in the glass, frightened by her own appearance. Her skin appeared brown and leathery where the sun had touched it, and where it hadn't, it hung in white wrinkles around her thin bones.

She would never have recognized herself and feared her husband would face a horrible shock to see her. As much as her body had withered, so had her spirit. She wept at the thought that nothing would ever be the same again.

✳ ✳ ✳

Weetamoo left the same morning as Mary. She took very little with her on her journey home. She hoped to find her village spared with food stores intact and her gardens in need of tending. She had no desire to think any longer of war. She needed to go home.

Laughing Water also prepared to leave. She had decided to marry Wonalancet and Sagamore Muttaump would accompany her to meet with Wonalancet's family in the North Country. The two women stood with their foreheads touching and wished each other safe journeys. *She will be safer there,* Weetamoo hoped.

Quannopinn and Metacom stayed behind. They didn't want the women and children threatened, so would remain until all disbanded to travel different paths on different days.

Weetamoo wanted to go alone with a small group of her own people. Only a third had survived the war and winter hardships. Awashonks would take her small tribe and Matoonas, his. Young warriors would band together and had many planned raids along their way back to their own places. Some had decided to take their chance with English offers of amnesty. Others resigned themselves to fight to the death in their homelands.

Weetamoo went to Metacom to say goodbye.

"Hawu'nshech, Brother. I ask Kistannit to watch over you and protect you on your journey."

333

"Hawu'nshech, Sister. May our Earth Mother Metanokit give you all you need for your journey and welcome you home in great abundance," he said with one hand on her shoulder.

"You have made a good war, Metacom," she said. "It will be good to see you again soon in our home country." She reached up and touched his scarred cheek. He kissed the palm of her hand.

Then she walked away.

She had slept alone again the night before as she had since her papoose died. She and Quannopinn had not reconciled. That saddened her, but she felt too hurt to make the first move. His hot head made the war and his member the two most important things. She would always be third, and her dead son had not mattered to him at all.

As she rode away, she remembered how at first she had merely wanted him as a mate to help the war and to have a pleasant bed partner, but she had grown to love him deeply. It saddened her that she did not have the same place in his heart as he had in hers.

She rode away and did not look back.

After several days of riding through hidden trails, Weetamoo at last reached Pocasset. It looked more beautiful than she remembered it. Sun shone brightly across the blue water of Narragansett Bay, and grassy wetlands surrounding her summer home danced in vibrant green to the breath of warm winds from the south. Before she could do anything else, she had to put her feet in the wet sand on her native beach. The same shells from her childhood washed up with the tide, and the same crabs crawled along the seaweed-covered rocks. Seagulls called to one another and played on the gentle winds. Nothing had changed. *How has so much changed in my heart since I left less than a year before?*

She turned her horse free and walked back to her village. Grasses had grown up around the path, but her feet never would forget their way. She stepped into the circle of burned out wetus, their remnants worn from winter winds. She came to her own and touched its yellowed mat, bleached by days of sunlight. She stepped within the boundaries of the wetu's frame. She would have to start again.

She looked down at the ashes of her bed where she last slept with Metacom, the one she loved but would never marry. She thought of Petananuit, the one she married and never loved. As if he could hear her thoughts, Quannopinn's baby kicked. She rubbed her stomach and sang him a lullaby,

Fa la me

Shu to shim

Heyo Heyo Ah No

Fa la me

Shu to shim

Heyo Heyo Ah No

She sat down on the floor of her empty home and wept.

From Mary's Journal
February 10, 1683

It has been seven years since my coming in from captivity, and I have been urged to put down a relation of my ordeal. I had been much encouraged by my late husband, Joseph, to do this to bear witness to the goodness of the Lord in watching over me and my family in this trial of great hardships. With the help of my dear friend and advisor, Reverend Increase Mather, and my husband's successor at his parish in Wetherfield, Connecticut, Reverend John Woodbridge, I have undertaken this important task.

It was most difficult to relive it all again to recreate my experience for the reader, but I think it rightly gives glory and praise to God who watches over His flock, though it be led astray. His mercy was shown to my family after my redemption when we lived for nearly a year by the kindness of strangers before we made a home in Connecticut. Praise God that He was pleased to restore my two eldest children to me, both on the very same day only weeks after my own coming in. They came in, as many others did in great numbers, for after the Sudbury fight this great war just fell away to pieces. Of those I lived among, there are scant few remaining, though I did see some of the Praying Indians when I lived in Boston.

It happened that very soon after my coming in the Indian folk took up arms in sundry places and did great mischief. But the good Lord saw fit to let the governor commission Captain Benjamin Church to set out after them in their home territories and that he did right smartly with the help of friendly Mohegan Indians from Connecticut.

Within two months of the Sudbury fight, there were captured or surrendered all of the sagamores in that land. The governor decreed *that those who would come in willingly and in submission to English rule would be found faultless and set free again, but that was not what happened to most of those that were near to me. The leaders of this vile insurrection were dealt with most harshly.*

One by one they surrendered, only to be tried and executed, often the self-same day. I can testify that Boston Common was a frightful place to me with the severed heads of so many I had lived with staring down from atop their mounted posts.

At different times I saw the faces of Tispaquin, the black sachem; that one-eyed devil Monaco; Matoonas; my once master Quannopinn; and Muttaump. Many others I knew by sight but not by name. I did not venture to see the head of Philip, where it stands still atop a post in Plimoth Colony. Nor did I see the head of my tormentor, Weetamoo, on its mount in Taunton. I see them all enough every night when I close my eyes and try to sleep. There was once a time when I slept well and lightly, but that is no more. When all else rest in their beds, I am alone with the ghosts of my ordeal.

Those who submitted and were not found guilty of heinous crimes, like Awashonks and Philip's and Tispaquin's wives, found pity and were packed off with their children to be sold as slaves in Barbados. Yes, this is what was done to most that lived with me those long winter and spring days in 1675 and 1676.

Weetamoo they found washed ashore in Taunton, dead, they say after daring to escape the ship taking her to answer for her crimes. Philip was shot dead in the back by an Indian named Alderman. It is said he has Philip's scarred hand that he keeps in a jar and shows in taverns to those who would part with a pence. Philip was quartered where he lay and left out for the scavengers to feed on. His head was nailed to a post at Plimoth where it still is now and is said will remain for twenty years, that none will forget the price of rebellion.

I shall not forget the awful times and horrible sights I endured in captivity. I can take no mean thing for granted now. Every day is a blessing and every small thing a gift from above. My children are of good health, though Mary, who was skittish before, wakes often with terrors and seldom ventures out of doors alone. Joseph has become quite a fine gentleman now and is studying the law at Harvard. He has forgotten his youthful fascination with becoming a soldier. My poor husband, Joseph, did never overcome the shock of all that happened and went home to his rest with our heavenly Father only two years after my redemption, God rest his soul.

Lancaster has been rebuilt, though I will never venture there again. I live well and comfortably in Whethersfield, Connecticut, with my new husband, Captain Samuel Talcott, a great Indian fighter who promises to always strongly defend me from harm. Those dark days have passed, and we hope never to see the likes of them again.

I have finished my relation and they tell me it has sold many copies already in Boston. James Printer, that good Christian Indian who gave me the word of God in my time of need and who so ably helped in negotiating my release, assisted in the printing of my relation. He is suggesting we consider selling it in London, too, and that I might do. It is published under the title, "The Sovereignty and Goodness of God." It gives me pleasure to know that there are many who will benefit from hearing of my trial and redemption, thanks be to God. I have much to be thankful for and will end my days in praising the Almighty Redeemer. May the good and merciful God bless us all.

I can remember the time when I used to sleep quietly without workings in my thoughts, whole nights together, but now it is other ways with me. When all are fast about me, and no eye open, but His who ever waketh, my thoughts are upon things past, upon the awful dispensation of the Lord towards us, upon His wonderful power and might, in carrying of us through so many difficulties, in returning us in safety, and suffering none to hurt us. I remember in the night season, how the other day I was in the midst of thousands of enemies, and nothing but death before me. It is then hard work to persuade myself, that ever I should be satisfied with bread again. But now we are fed with the finest of the wheat, and, as I may say, with honey out of the rock. Instead of the husk, we have the fatted calf. The thoughts of these things in the particulars of them, and of the love and goodness of God towards us, make it true of me, what David said of himself, "I watered my Couch with my tears" (Psalm 6.6). Oh!

the wonderful power of God that mine eyes have seen, affording matter enough for my thoughts to run in, that when others are sleeping mine eyes are weeping.

I have seen the extreme vanity of this world: One hour I have been in health, and wealthy, wanting nothing. But the next hour in sickness and wounds, and death, having nothing but sorrow and affliction.

Before I knew what affliction meant, I was ready sometimes to wish for it. When I lived in prosperity, having the comforts of the world about me, my relations by me, my heart cheerful, and taking little care for anything, and yet seeing many, whom I preferred before myself, under many trials and afflictions, in sickness, weakness, poverty, losses, crosses, and cares of the world, I should be sometimes jealous least I should have my portion in this life, and that Scripture would come to my mind, "For whom the Lord loveth he chasteneth, and scourgeth every Son whom he receiveth" (Hebrews 12.6). But now I see the Lord had His time to scourge and chasten me. The portion of some is to have their afflictions by drops, now one drop and then another; but the dregs of the cup, the wine of astonishment, like a sweeping rain that leaveth no food, did the Lord prepare to be my portion. Affliction I wanted, and affliction I had, full measure (I thought), pressed down and running over. Yet I see, when God calls a person to anything, and through never so many difficulties, yet He is fully able to carry them through and make them see, and say they have been gainers thereby. And I hope I can say in some measure, as David did, "It is good for me that I have been afflicted." The Lord hath showed me the vanity of these outward things. That they are the vanity of vanities, and vexation of spirit, that they are but a shadow, a blast, a bubble, and things of no continuance. That we must rely on God Himself, and our whole dependence must be upon Him. If trouble from smaller matters begin to arise in me, I have something at hand to check myself with, and say, why am I troubled? It was but the other day that if I had had the world, I would have given it for my freedom, or to have been a servant to a Christian. I have learned to look beyond present and smaller troubles, and to be quieted under them. As Moses said, "Stand still and see the salvation of the Lord" (Exodus 14.13).

Weetamoo's Reflection from the Spirit World
Still Here

*I*t *has been three hundred summers since my passing into the spirit world, and I am shocked when I look upon my former homeland. Instead of the wooded forests and grassy marshes of Pocasset, I see sharp rows of fair wooden houses like unto those of the people of Plimoth but greater in size and color and so many more crowded together. Each one stands greater than our largest longhouse and closed up on all sides. I see no cook fires, no women grinding corn, no children playing outside.*

At times, the people open their large doorways and drive out— hidden behind panes of glass—in metal carriages. Countless angular roads cover the earth with little growth between the houses. Families do not farm. They keep their grasses shaved, though no one treads there. Elders do not meet to game and smoke, and men no longer teach boys the skills of hunting and fishing.

As Passaconaway once foretold, white men now number as many as the leaves in the forest, and the rivers are all dammed up by whirring mills. Smoke spews from mighty towers and flying machines. I look in vain for the still and quiet places I remember. But for the shorelines and thread of rivers, little familiar to me is left of my former home. My people, still fearful of reprisal, have long hid their identity and keep silent as they watch in horror as our Mother Earth suffered rape again and again for progress.

In this spirit life, I can look forward or look back with ease, but I find nothing easy for me in the future land. As I once lived, so I wish it would remain.

I remember my wedding day during the Feast of the Green Corn, when we stood under a bower of crimson cherries and listened while the elders told the people who we and our people were. Under the azure sky, our elders advised us in strong marriage ways. We danced 'round the golden fire and sang and feasted, the elders, the young together under sight of our ancestors.

When they looked down upon us, I wonder did they feel as I do now? Did they yearn for things no longer in existence? Do they wish to linger still here to keep the old ways? I wonder.

I look today upon such ceremonies of my own descendants, and I weep. For though our war long since died, with it died ten thousand lifetimes of caring for the land, water, sky, and fire that nurtured my people. I whisper to my children's children to turn back to our ways before the time of change passes by. And I wait, for my time to change the world has passed out of my hands now forevermore.

I choose to look back to the days of my childhood, when my country existed as the Creator made it for us. I will linger in the past and in the few quiet places left to us and wait to hear the voices of my people cry out, "We are still here! Spirit of Weetamoo, Little Bird, Namumpum, come to us and make us strong. Help us find our way back to the path of beauty."

Look for me in the clouds at sunset and in the tender shoots pressing up to them from the rich brown earth. I will splash in the ocean surf and sometimes toss you a leathery mermaid's pouch or giant sea clam. You may smell my scent mixed with the fragrant wild rose or roasting of the first green corn. My voice may call to you in the wind stirring mountain treetops or in the distant thunder. My passion will stir in you in the tongues of flame in your ceremonial fires. My people, listen for me. Call to me.

For I will always be still here.

Maps

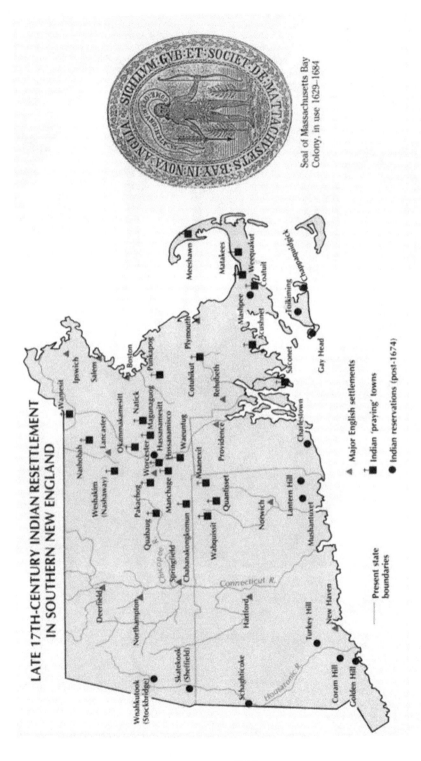

LATE 17TH-CENTURY INDIAN RESETTLEMENT IN SOUTHERN NEW ENGLAND

Wabbaquasset
Ipswich
Salem
Nashobah
Boston
Lancaster
Okommakamesitt
Natick
Ponkapog
Weshakim (Nashaway)
Magunagog
Worcester
Hassanamesitt
Hassanamisco
Pakachog
Manchage
Waeuntug
Cotuhikut
Plymouth
Deerfield
Chabanakongkomun
Quabaug
Chicopee R.
Springfield
Wabaquisset
Maanexit
Quantisset
Rehobeth
Providence
Charlestown
Northampton
Connecticut R.
Hartford
Nameag
Quinnebaug R.
Mushantuxet
Lantern Hill
Schaghticoke
Housatonic R.
Turkey Hill
New Haven
Wnahktukook (Stockbridge)
Skatekook (Sheffield)
Coram Hill
Golden Hill
Weequakut
Coatuit
Mashpee
Saconet
Acushnet
Toikiming
Chappaquidick
Gay Head
Meeshawn
Matakees
Wampeit

▲ Major English settlements
✝ Indian 'praying' towns
◼ Indian reservations (post-1674)

—— Present state boundaries

Seal of Massachusetts Bay Colony, in use 1629–1684

SIGILLVM: GVB: ET: SOCIET: DE: MATTACHVSETS: BAY: IN: NOVA: ANGLIA:

COME: OVER: AND: HELP: VS

From Wilkie R. & J. Tager, Historical Atlas of Massachusetts, University of Massachusetts Press, 1991, page 15

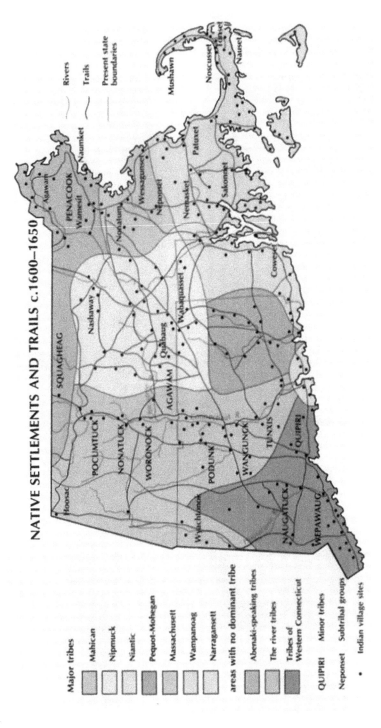

NATIVE SETTLEMENTS AND TRAILS c.1600–1650

Rivers
Trails
Present state boundaries

Agawam
PENACOOK
Wamesit
Naumket
Nashaway
Nashobah
Wessaguscus
Patucket
Patuxet
Nemasket
Sakonnet
Mushawn
Noscusset
Nauset
Tomset

SQUAGHEAG
Wabaquaset
Quabaug
POCUMTUCK
AGAWAM
NONATUCK
WORONOCK
PODUNK
WANGUNGK
TUNXIS
QUIPIRI
Hoosac
Wychumake
NAUGATUCK
WEPAWAUG
Coweset

Major tribes
Mahican
Nipmuck
Niantic
Pequot-Mohegan
Massachusett
Wampanoag
Narragansett
areas with no dominant tribe
Abenaki-speaking tribes
The river tribes
Tribes of Western Connecticut

QUIPIRI   Major tribes
Neponset   Subtribal groups
•   Indian village sites

From Wilkie R. & J. Tager, Historical Atlas of Massachusetts,
University of Massachusetts Press, 1991, page 12

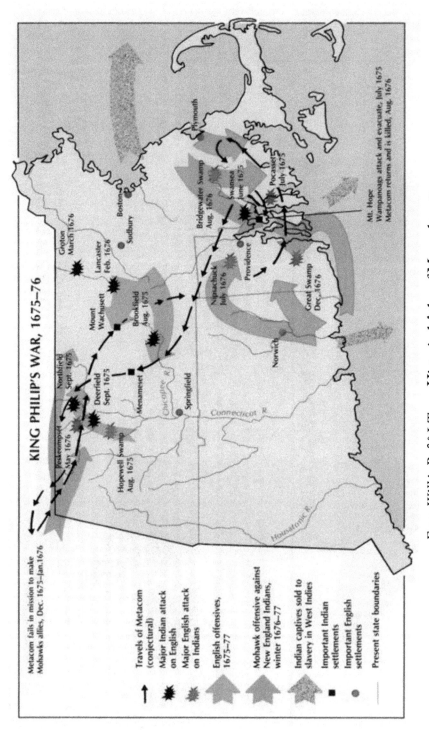

KING PHILIP'S WAR, 1675–76

Metacom fails in mission to make
Mohawks allies, Dec. 1675–Jan.1676

Peskeompsoid
Mar. 1676

Northfield
Sept. 1675

Deerfield
Sept. 1675

Hopewell Swamp
Aug. 1675

Menameset

Chicopee R.

Springfield

Connecticut R.

Housatonic R.

Mount
Wachusett

Brookfield
Aug. 1675

Lancaster
Feb. 1676

Groton
March 1676

Sudbury

Boston

Nipmuck
July 1676

Providence

Great Swamp
Dec. 1676

Norwich

Bridgewater Swamp
Aug. 1676

Swansea
June 1675

Pocasset
July 1675

Plymouth

Mt. Hope
Wampanoags attack and evacuate, July 1675
Metacom returns and is killed, Aug. 1676

Travels of Metacom
(conjectural)

Major Indian attack
on English

Major English attack
on Indians

English offensives,
1675–77

Mohawk offensive against
New England Indians,
winter 1676–77

Indian captives sold to
slavery in West Indies

Important Indian
settlements

Important English
settlements

Present state boundaries

*From Wilkie R. & J. Tager, Historical Atlas of Massachusetts,
University of Massachusetts Press, 1991, page 15*

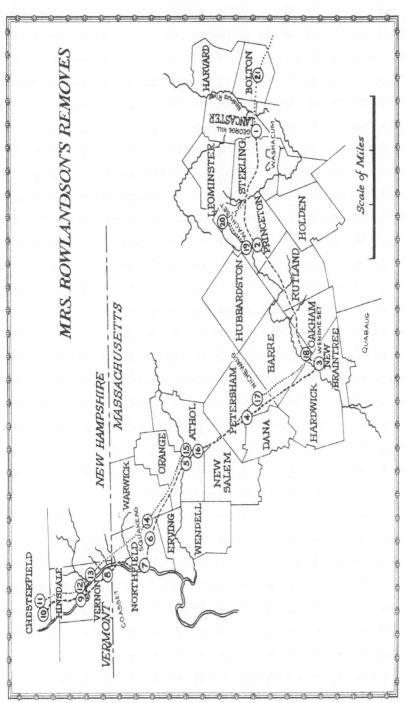

MRS. ROWLANDSON'S REMOVES

NEW HAMPSHIRE

MASSACHUSETTS

Scale of Miles

From Nourse, Henry Stedman, (1884), The Early Records of Lancaster, Massachusetts, 1643-1725
W.J. Coulter, Lancaster, Massachusetts. Courtesy of Lancaster Historical Commission

347

Notes

The reader may find the following information helpful in understanding native words, names, and places.

Clothing

kersey coat-coarse woolen coat from England, often cherished by native people

leggings-leather leg coverings, usually worn affixed to the wearer's belt

pocket-small bag worn under a colonial woman's apron, usually embellished with needlework.

tumpline-A leather strap worn across the forehead to provide support for the weight of a packbasket worn on the back

wampum belt-belt wrought with black and white wampum

belt wrought with black and white wampum, Philip had one nine inches wide with various figures and flowers and pictures of many birds and beasts and another wrought after the former manner which Philip was wont to put upon his head; with two flags on the back part which hung down on his back and another small belt with a Star upon the end of it, which he used to hang on his breast, all edged with red hair which they got in Muhhogs Country. Two horns of glazed powder and a red cloth blank which were royalties which he was wont to adorn himself when he sat in State.

—Church, 1978, 460

Native Seasons or Moons

One of the few surviving records of the Agawam language is recorded in William Pynchon's *Account Book*, c. 1645-1650. On page iii, his son John Pynchon lists the names for the thirteen full moons of the year, including:

1. Squanni kesos-when they set Indian corne (pt of Aprill & pt of May)
2. Moonesquanimock kesos-when women weed their corne (pt of May & pt of June)
3. Towwa kesos-when they hill Indian corne (pt of June & pt of July)
4. Matterlawaw kesos-when squashes are ripe & Indian beans begin to be eatable
5. Micheenee kesos-when Indian corne is eatable
6. Pohquitaqunk kesos-ye middle between harvest & eating Indian corne
7. Pepewarr-because of white frost on ye grass & grain or November
8. Qunni kesos-December
9. Papsapquoho-about ye 6th day of January
10. Lowatannassick-So caled because they account it ye middle of winter
11. Squochee kesos-because ye sun hath strength to thaw
12. Wapicummilcom-because ye ice in ye River is all gone (pt of February & part of March)
13. Namossack kesos-because of catching fish (pt of March and pt of April)

—Day, 1967, 244-247

Eastern Algonquin language had many dialects. Europeans attempted to spell the sounds they heard with varying results, often spelling phonetically and frequently being inconsistent with how they spelled the same word. The following is a compilation of some dates in the native calendar using the modern calendar as a timeline. Many of the references listed here came from Patricia Clark Smith's book, *Weetamoo, Heart of the Pocassets*. Clark Smith notes in an interview for *Scholastic* that she relied heavily upon Roger William's book entitled, *Key into the Language of America*, written in 1643.

early January-Lowatanassick-midwinter

—Clark Smith, 75

late January-Paponakeeswush-winter month

—Clark Smith, 88

February-Squocheekeeswush-when the sun has strength to thaw

—Clark Smith, 112

early March-Wapicummilcum-when ice in the river is gone

—Clark Smith, 128

early April-Namassack Keeswush-time of Catching Fish

—Clark Smith, 105, 140

late March-mid April Namossack Kessos-time of catching fish

April-Snow Crust Moon

May-June-time when Women weed their corn

June-Moon of Leaves

June-July-time when Corn is hilled

July-Strawberry Moon

August-time of First squash and beans and Feast of the Green
Corn

late August-Nepunna Keeswush-Moon when corn is ripe

—Clark Smith, 3

early September-Micheennee Keeswosh-Time of everlasting flies

—Clark Smith, 12

September-time when green corn becomes fit to eat

early October-Taquontikeeswush-Harvest moon

—Clark Smith, 34

October-month of ripening

early November-Pepewarr-White frost moon

—Clark Smith, 51

early December Quinne Keeswush-Long Moon

—Clark Smith, 65

Spirituality and Ceremonies

Feast of the Green Corn-August-first pot of corn harvest offered
in thanks to spirit powers. Fresh fire laid and corn cooked and eaten

only after sacred corn burned to coals. Dancing, singing, through the night up to a week long

—Russell, 1980, 170-171

Pesuponk-sweat lodge ceremony

—Martin, 1999/2001

Thanksgiving-longhouse set up with courtyard, sometimes two hundred feet long where thousands of men and women dance and makes gifts to poor as they can afford. Crowd joins in with rhythmic "hub bub bub."

—Russell, 1980, 173

Spirit Beings

Cowtantowit-god of bounty
Ke-che No-din-Spirit of the Wind
Manitou-[Sha-wain-ne-me-shin]-Great Spirit who created game and all things

—Clark Smith, 53

Maushop-told us when to plant crops and warned us when big storms were coming

—Clark Smith, 24

Squant-the Being who watches over women, wife of Maushop
—Clark Smith, 3, 25

Kistannit-the Creator, showed the way to Maushop to cleanse the body, mind, heart and spirit.
Metanokit-sacred Mother the Earth and all her children-people, animals, trees, grasses, rocks.
Potanit-the spirit of fire
Paumpagusset-the spirit of great waters of life
Tashin-the spirit of the wind
Keesuckquand-Grandfather Spirit of the heavens-seen as
Nepaushet the sun husband and brother to Nanepaushet, the moon
Nanepaushet-Grandmother Spirit of the heavens, seen as the moon, wife and sister of Nepaushet

Munna'mock-Grandmother Moon
—Clark Smith, 84
Nucksuog-unknown beings of the star nations beyond
Nanummy-in-spirit being of the north-color white-for cleansing
and purification. Pray to this spirit for help is sweating away
poisons of the body, and for health, strength and endurance for
selves, families and nation.
Wampanand-healing power of the east, spirit of dawn, renewal,
spring-color yellow-light of Cosmic Intelligence. Pray to this
spirit for help sweating away poisons of the mind.
Sowanand-spirit of summer-color red-behind where the women
sit, rides south wind Towuttin-tends the lodge of the heart. Pray
to this spirit to release the poisons of the heart.
Checksuwand-black being of the west-behind where leader sits.
Pray to this spirit to cleanse spirit.
Thunder controlled by four celestial thundermen
Mon-do-min legend-Wampanoag received gift of corn from
the Great Spirit as a reward to Mon-do-min's kindness to the
starving woman. Corn sprang from the earth over his grave in the
month of June following his death.

—Russell, 1980, 148-149

Animals

amisqua-beaver
—Williams
attuck-deer
—Clark Smith, 181
attuks-herds of deer
—Clark Smith, 42
be-nah-nah-partridge
—Williams
honckock-geese
—Clark Smith, 129

continued on next page

Animals

continued from previous page

nahom-flocks of turkey
—Clark Smith, 42
ohhomons-great horned owl
—Clark Smith, 100

Foods

askutasquash-bright pumpkin
—Clark Smith, 42
mon-do-min-corn
—Russell
nokechick-parched cornmeal
—Williams
openauk-groundnut
—Williams
nuts
—Zabelle
acorns
—Zabelle
hartychokes-Jerusalem artichokes
—Zabelle
Lilly root
—Zabelle
ground beans
—Zabelle
samp-porridge made from ground corn
—Zabelle
sobaheg-stew
—Plimoth
ruffe or ridding-the rough or discarded parts of an animal
—Zabelle

Places

Ashquoash-Quabaug Old Fort-favorite Indian gathering place
four miles southwest of Brookfield, Massachusetts

Assawomset-Lake of the White Stones

Baquoag River-in Athol and Orange, Massachusetts: the Millers
River

Coasset-Algonquin for place of pines, between Northfield, New
Hampshire, and Brattleboro, Vermont

Concord-place of groundnuts

Hassanamesit-"place where there is (much) gravel" or "at the
place of small stones," Grafton, Massachusetts

Kwinitekwa-Algonquin for long tidal river-Connecticut

Montaup-home of Pokanoket Wampanoag people. Modern day
Mount Hope, Rhode Island

Menameset-main camp of warring Nipmucs

Nonotuck-Northampton-Northampton and Hadley,
Massachusetts-in the midst of the river

Patuxet-Little Falls, Massachusetts
   —Clark Smith, 38

Peskeompskut-Exploding Rocks waterfall
in twenty-first-century Turners Falls, Massachusetts
   —Clark Smith, 106

Pocumtuc-Deerfield, Massachusetts, place of swift shallow river

Podunk –place where your foot sinks into the mire
   —Clark Smith, 38

powwow-spiritual leader, healer, medicine man or
a place where powwows hold council or gathering
   —Clark Smith, 187

Quabaug-Brookfield, Massachusetts

Sakonnet-Sogkonate-Little Compton, Rhode Island

Squakeag-Northfield, Massachusetts

Umpane-Plymouth Colony, Massachusetts

Wamesit-near Lowell, Massachusetts

Native Peoples

Abenaki-Dawn People

—Clark Smith, 84

An Algonquin-speaking nation located mainly in northwestern New England and upstate New York. Members of Wabanaki Confederacy

—Clark Smith, 80

Algonquin –largest native language group in North America, extending through Canada, down the Atlantic Seaboard to the Carolinas, and ranging west past the Great Lakes to Montana and southward as far as Oklahoma. In New England, Algonquin includes Wampanoag, Massachusett, Nipmuc, Penacook, Penobscot, Passamaquoddy, Quinnipiac, Mohegan, Pequot, Pocumtuc, Tunxis, Narragansett, and Abenaki people.

Native Words

Ascowequa'ssin-Good Morning (Williams)

Hawu'nshech-Goodbye (Williams)

Howoh-Who is it? (Williams)

hubbub-game played by men: toss five half-painted bones in a basket and bet on how many will land black side up

—Clark Smith, p. 76

iotash-stand to it and fight stoutly

—Williams

mishoon-boat, mishoonash; boats-made by burning out the core of a log, scraping away the burnt wood with stone tools

netop-friend

netopash-my friends

nushweety (nuhsh weh t'oo)-neskwetu-house of two fires-A long house, which is covered with large sheets of bark. A house of this size can be for more than one family, or a large extended family of a person of status.

nux-yes

papoose-baby

sachem-chief

squaw-woman

sunk squaw-squaw sachem; female chief

Taubut-It is well. I am glad.

Wabanaki-Algonquin Confederacy of indigenous people mainly from maritime New England and Canada

Wampanoag-People of the first or morning light

wampum-small beads made from white and purple quahog shells. Used as currency for trade, for decorative purposes, and to symbolize alliances and treaties. Belts, girdles, and necklaces were often designed to represent important events and were used by storytellers as mnemonic devices to aid in the re-telling of spiritual and historical oral traditions. Purple or black wampum was scarcer and more highly prized. *A certain young native leader, 'Prince Philip'...had a coat on and buckskins set thick with these beads of wampum in pleasant wild works and a broad built (belt) of the same. His accoutrements were valued at twenty pounds*

—John Josselyn. 1663

wetu (weh t'oo)-house, wetuash-houses, puttuckakuan-round house: a small round single family home with an outside covering of cattail matting or bark

Wuniish-Go in beauty. May it be beautiful for you.

Yo wuttut'tan-The sun is this high.

Cast of Characters

Native People

Amie-Metacomet's sister, called Amie by the English. Little is known about her other than her marriage to Tispaquin. No birth date known nor death date. She and son, age nine, taken prisoner at Taunton River in 1676 and shipped to Barbados as slaves.

Parents: Massasoit. Ousamequin, Sachem

Children: William Watuspequin, Benjamin Tispaquin

Anawan-Philip's chief captain based in Squannoconk Swamp between Rehoboth and Taunton. He is among those of Philip's people signing several deeds for sale for land in and around Taunton in latter part of the year and earlier mentioned as one of his chiefs or counselors. Annawon led those not captured or killed with Philip at the final battle out of the swamp at Mount Hope. He surrendered to Plymouth under the promise of "good quarter" but was captured on September 11, 1676, and executed at Plymouth at the same time as Tispaquin.

Awashonks-Philip's cousin and squaw sachem of the Sakonnets. She is called Chieftain of the Sakonnets. She agreed in June 1674 to a submission agreeing to give up all her arms. By August 1674, she further put herself in peaceable submission in a letter to Governor Thomas Prence. In spring of 1675, she was a little inclined to join with Philip and convinced by Benjamin Church to put herself under the protection of Plymouth, because Church felt the war would surely prove her ruin if she joined with Philip. After war broke out in July, she joined other tribes seeking refuge in Narragansett. She was married to Tolony.

Children: Mamanewa, Tatuckamna.

Canonchet-Naananto-Great sachem of Narragansetts, son of Miantonomo. Captured by the English at Pawtucket, taken to Stonington and there shot by Oneco, son of Uncas, his lifelong enemy and two sachems of the Pequots of equal rank. It is said "There is no nobler figure in all the annals of the American Indians than Canonchet, son of Miantonimoh, sachem of the Narragansetts."

—New England Historical and Genealogical Register, 44:143
He died in April/May 1676 in Stonington.

Caunbitant-father of Weetamoo-One of nine sachems who came to Plymouth and signed a treaty with the English in 1621. In 1623, he expressed concern to Governor Edward Winslow for coming into Pawtuxet "with the mouth of your pieces presented toward us." Winslow replied that it was a mark of respect and Caunbitant shook his head and answered that he did not like such salutations. Caunbitant is also credited with capturing Squanto threatening "if Squanto were but dead the white men would have lost their tongue." He apparently released Squanto, never carrying out the threat and returned to Mattapoiset. He was considered an enemy of the settlers. His only known child was Weetamoo-Namumpum.

Laughing Water-Weetamoo's daughter, assumed to be young woman mentioned as living with Weetamoo during Mary Rowlandson's captivity. Survived the war and married William Austin, a famous scout and had a son Benoni in 1706 in Biddeford, Maine. She died in 1712.

Massasoit, also called Asuhmequn or Ousemequin, which means Yellow Feather-Wampanoag supreme sachem and Philip's father who entered many treaties with the English settlers. Died in 1661.

Mamanewa-son of Awashonks and Tolony. He and his brother, in disagreement with his mother, refused to acknowledge any authority of Plymouth over them, as did also Awashonks's brother.

Matoonas-sachem of the clan of Nipmucs living at Pakachoog and Nipmuc leader of raid on Mendon. He was a prominent leader in King Philip's war. His son murdered an Englishman and was executed on the gallows on Boston Common. After the execution, his head was cut off and set upon the gallows where it remained for at least five years.

Metacomet-Wampanoag Great sachem King Philip also called Pometacom Massasoit, son of Massasoit, Ousamequin, sachem. In 1656, he and his brother Wamsutta appeared before the court to request English names. He thus became Philip.

Deeded many lots of property to the English settlers and renewed his father's treaties of alliance with Plymouth. In 1671, he was compelled to submit to English laws and customs and to deliver all arms to the English court. Coupled with accusations of complicity in the murder of John Sassamon, Metacomet's former aide, his submitting to English laws led to a build up of hostilities that erupted in war on July 18, 1675. There is disagreement about whether Metacomet masterminded the war or was unable to control growing rage among the warriors. His brother Sankanuhoo was killed in July, 1675, at the onset of the war. Philip united the tribes of New England in a rebellion against British rule. At the time, this was the bloodiest war in history.

In July, 1676, Philip was ambushed in Mount Hope and during escape was killed by an Indian named Alderman. Philip was beheaded, quartered, and left unburied. His hand was given to Alderman as a reward who, it was said by Church, "got many a penny" for showing the hand. His head was put on a spike at Plimoth Plantation where it remained for twenty years.

Monaco, One-Eyed John-leader of Nashaways and Nipmuc leader of Groton attack who eventually betrayed and killed Matoonas; one of the leaders at the Mendon raid

Muttaump-Nipmuc sachem at Quabaug, later Brookfield, Massachusetts; called Mawtamp-alive in 1675 in Quabaug and among the prominent leaders in King Philip's war.

Nanuskooke or Wootonekanuske-Weetamoo's sister married to Metacomet (King Philip). She and her son Metom were captured by the English under Benjamin Church and sold into slavery after the war in Barbados.

Ninigret-sachem of the Niantics, southern Narragansetts and Quaiapen's brother

Oneco-Mohegan son of Uncas. He beheaded and quartered Metacomet after Metacomet was executed.

Peebe-Mount Hope sachem and counselor to King Philip before the war. His residence was in Phebe's Neck in Rhode Island. He was killed in a skirmish with Lieutenant Edward Oakes under the command of Captain Prentice close to Swansea, July 2, 1675.

Pessacus or Mossup-one of the oldest Narragansett sachems, a nephew to Canonicus, and influential counselor of Canonchet, killed in Piscataqua River in 1677, by the Mohawks

Petananuit-Peter Nunnuit, Weetamoo's third husband also known as Petonowowett.

Onux-old squaw wife of Quannopinn.

Pomham or Pumham-one of oldest Narragansett sachems. Killed by a party of English and friendly Indians under Captain Samuel Hunting as he fought for his life in Dedham woods. An unnamed son was captured at the time. He died on July 25, 1676 in Dedham, Massachusetts.

Quannopinn or Quinapin- Weetamoo's fifth husband. A Narragansett chief, son of Cojonoquant, close relative of Canonchet, and second in command at the great fort-fight. He became master of Mary Rowlandson by purchasing her from her capturers. He had two wives other than Weetamoo: Onux, his old squaw, and a young squaw of unknown name. He was captured in the last swamp fight, tried at Newport, and condemned to death with other captives. He was shot on August 25, 1676 in Newport, Rhode Island.

Quaiapen-Narragansetts sunk squaw sachem, Old Queen Magnus. Possibly died when Connecticut forces with their Mohegan and Pequot allies massacred people of the Old Queen Magnus on July 2, 1676. Her son Quequegunent was Weetamoo's second husband. Weetamoo and her husband Quequequanchet are mentioned in court records in October, 1663, as entertaining Naragansett Indians, likely Quaiapen and family.Shortly before March, 1665, Quequegenent and his brother Scuttup died of a "persistent" illness, according to Brooks.

Sancumachu-Pocumtuck sachem. Sancumachu was born about 1640. He was a sachem of the Pocumtuck native American tribe. He and the Pocumtucks or Pocumtucs became an important ally of Metacom King Philip in King Philip's War. Sancumachu was one of the war chiefs who led the successful attacks on Northfield, Massachusetts, and Deerfield, Massachusetts, early in the war. He also was a leader in the Northampton Raid where the Indians were forced to retreat with heavy losses. Sancumachu was killed when Captain William Turner and

150 colonial soldiers and local volunteers made a surprise attack on the Indian camp at Peskeompskut (Falls Fight).

John Sassamon-also known as Sassamon, Woosansaman, Wussausmon. Noted as secretary, interpreter, and a witness for Philip. He is noted as interpreter or witness on "every deed signed by Metacom in 1664-65," and was "eventually ostracized for his betrayal. "Metacom conveyed was a 'bad man' without conscience for his kin," according to Brooks. Said to be murdered by Philip's men for betraying Philip's hostile intents to the English. In January 29, 1674, Tobias or Poggapanossoo, one of Philip's counselors, and his two sons Wampapaquan and Mattashinnamy were indicted, found guilty, and later executed for Sassamon's murder. This trial sparked the onset of King Philip's War.

Sonkanuhoo-brother of King Philip said to have been slain at the fight in a swamp in Pocasset, later Tiverton, Rhode Island, on July 18, 1675.

Squaw Sachem-also known as squaw sachem of Massachusetts, wife of the mighty Nanepashemet. She is among those arriving to see Governor William Bradford on February 5, 1643/4 to "tender themsleves" to the government of Massachusetts, at which time she is noted as the squaw sachem of the Massachusetts. She was married to Nanepashemet.

Children: Montowampate Nanepashemet, Abigail Nanepashemet, Wonohaqueham Nanepashemet, Winnepurkitt Nanepashemet.

She married Webcoit by 1635.

Tatuckamna-Awashonks's son who refused submission to Plymouth along with his brother.

Parents: Tolony and Awashonks

Tispaquin-the "black sachem" at Assawomset Pond and a very famous captain taken in last swamp fight. Beheaded in Boston. Tispaquin was living about 1662 in Titicut, Massachusetts. He survived Philip's death and, under the entreaty of Captain Benjamin Church who promised him and his family safety, he surrendered at Plymouth. Captain Church being absent, he was immediately tried and executed.

He was also known as Tispaquin, Watuspaquin, and Black Sachem.
Called distinguished chieftain or sachem of the Assowampsett or
Assowomset and also the black sachem by the English. Married Amie,
Philip's sister

Children: William Watuspequin and Benjamin Tispaquin.
He died in September, 1676, in Plymouth, Massachusetts.
William Tispaquin or **Mantowapuct**-son of Metacomet's sister
Amie and Tispaquin. Never married. It is thought he lost his life in
King Philip's war, as he was alive until May 14, 1675 and no mention is
made of him after that date.

Tobias or Poggapanossoo-alive in 1673/74 in Plymouth, Massachusetts. Also known as Tobias and one of Philip counselors, he was named
as murderer of John Sassamon. Also implicated were his two sons.

Children: Wampapaquan, Mattashinnamy.
Tolony or Waweyewet-Awashonks's husband and father of her two
sons. He is said to have agreed with her decision of submission, but her
control over her tribe seemed to be fragile.

Children: Mamanewa, Tatuckamna.
Wamsutta-Mooanam Massasoit or Alexander-son of Massasoit.
He was living in 1656 in Pokanoket, Massachusetts. In about the year of
1656, the two sons of Massasoit presented themselves before the court
of Plymouth and requested English names, which accordingly were
bestowed, so Wamsutta or Alexander and Pometacom or Philip.

He was married to Weetamoo or Namumpum by 1656.
He died in July 1662 in Pokanoket, Massachusetts.
Parent: Massasoit or Ousamequin, sachem
Weetamoo or Namumpum or Tatapanum-"as potent a prince as
any round her," she was the daughter of Caunbitant and "heir apparent
and true inheritor" of the territory now included within the limits of the
town of Tiverton Rhode Island, and enjoyed the title of squaw sachem
or queen of the Pocasset. She married Weequequinequa before 1651
in Tiverton. She next married Massasoit or Ousamequin's eldest son,

Wamsutta or Alexander, by 1656. She was married to Quiquequanchett or Quequegunent, son of Quaiapin, sometime after Alexander's death in June 1662 and before October 1663. They took up residence in her own territory, Pocasset. He died shortly before March 1665, according to Brooks. She married Petananuit sometime after and married Quannopinn after July 1675. She died about August 1676 in Taunton, Massachusetts.

Wonalancet-Penacook sachem, son of Passaconaway from what would become New Hampshire.

British People

Benjamin Church-English Captain who befriended Awashonks's tribe and was known for his success with the natives in Rhode Island, Pocasset and Sakonnet

John Eliot-Puritan minister who established segregated Massachusetts convert communities and advocated for peace through change in social structure, rules, clothing, manner, architecture, economic activities, and calendar, although most so-called praying towns were abandoned in 1675

Daniel Gookin-overseer of the Indians

John Leverett-Governor of Massachusetts

Samuel Moseley-English captain dispatched to reinforce the northern frontier

Nathaniel Richardson-fictitious son of William Richardson

William Richardson-fictitious tradesman from Chelmsford commissioned as a lieutenant during King Philip's War.

Joseph Rowlandson-reverend in Lancaster, married Mary White with whom he had four children, Mary, who died at age three, Joseph, Mary, and Sarah, who died in capitivity.

Josiah Winslow-Governor of Plymouth Colony

John Winthrop Jr.-Governor of Connecticut

Christian Indian People

Attawan or Tahattawan, Tahattawants, Attawanee, Ahatawanee-sachem of Musketaquid since Concord and a supporter and propagator of Christianity among his people; also known as John Thomas Attawan. At the death of John Tahattawan before 1670, Pennekennit or Pennahannit became chief. Young Tahattawan died leaving a daughter Sarah, a widow named Sarah, and a young son, a child, the last of the Tahattawans was killed at the age of twelve, November 15, 1675 at Wamesit near Lowell, Massachusetts, a Chelmsford, Massachusetts, party of fourteen white men armed with muskets went to the Indian camp and fired upon them in retaliation for burning of a barn of which the Indians were suspected. Five women and children were wounded, among whom the boys' mother, Sarah, then a widow for the second time, having had as her second husband Oonamog, ruler of the Praying Indians at Marlborough.

Sarah Attawan-a Christian Indian, wife of Attawan, who represents the character in Mary's narrative who offers Mary food and shelter when she is turned out by Weetamoo

Peter Conway-Christian Indian who sided with the English and served as a courier and spy for the British army

Thomas Dublet-Christian Indian who sided with the English and served as a courier and spy for the British army

James Printer or James the Printer-A Nipmuc Christian Indian and print shop apprentice in Cambridge who sought refuge with King Philip during the war to avoid interment on Deer Island

Benjamin Tispaquin-son of Tispaquin and Metacomet's sister Amie. Distinguished warrior who had a piece of his jaw shot off in battle. He married an Indian named Weecum. He died suddenly while sitting in his wigwam, having just before complained of feeling faint. He served the English in Captain James Church's company.

Weecum-fictitious Praying Indian Mary meets along her journey

Bibliography

Beals, Charles Edward Jr. (1916). *Passaconaway in the White Mountains*. Retrieved May 24, 2003, from http://www.sidis.net/PASSChap1.htm

Bennett, Arthur. (1993). *The Valley of Vision*. Carlisle, PA: The Banner of Truth Trust.

Bonfanti, Leo. (1970). *Biographies and Legends of the New England Indians* (Vol. II). Burlington, MA: Pride Publications.

Bonfanti, Leo. (1974). *Biographies and Legends of the New England Indians* (Vol. IV). Salem, MA: Old Saltbox Publishing and Distributing.

Bonfanti, Leo. (1976). *Biographies and Legends of the New England Indians* (Vol. V). Salem, MA: Old Saltbox Publishing and Distributing.

Bonfanti, Leo. (1981). *Biographies and Legends of the New England Indians* (Vol. III). Salem, MA: Old Saltbox Publishing and Distributing.

Bonfanti, Leo. (1993). *Biographies and Legends of the New England Indians, Revised Edition* (Vol. I). Salem, MA: Old Saltbox Publishing and Distributing.

Bradstreet, Anne. (1996). "Some Verses upon the Burning of Our House." In Hugh. Hewitt (Ed.), *Searching for God in America* (p. 184). Dallas, TX: Word Publishing.

Brooks, Lisa. (2018). *Our Beloved Kin: A New History of King Philip's War*. Yale University Press.

Brooks, Lisa. (2018). *Our Beloved Kin: Remapping A New History of King Philip's War*. Retrieved 1 July 2018 at http://ourbeloved-kin.com/awikhigan.

Bruchac, Marge (2005). Historic Deerfield.

Carpenter, Delores Bird. (1994). *Early Encounters - Native Americans and Europeans in New England.* East Lansing, MI: Michigan State University Press.

Chamberlain, Samuel, & Flynt, Henry N. (1965). *Historic Deerfield: Houses and Interiors.* NewYork, NY: Hastings House.

Church, Benjamin. (1975). *Diary of King Philip's War.* Chester, CT: Pequot Press. (Original work published 1716)

Church, Thomas. (1978). Entertaining Passages Relating to King Philip's War. In Richard. Slotkin & James K. Folsom (Eds.), *So Dreadfull a Judgment.* Middletown, CT: Wesleyan University Press.

Clark Smith, Patricia. (2011) *Weetamoo Heart of the Pocassets.* New York: Scholastic, Inc.

Coombs, Linda. (2005, May 6,). Personal interview with Christine Zerillo at Plimoth Plantation, Plymouth, MA.

Cronon, William. (1997). *Changes in the Land - Indians, Colonists, and the Ecology of New England.* New York: Harper Collins Canada Ltd.

Drake, James D. (1999). *King Philip's War, Civil War in New England, 1675-1676.* Amherst: The University of Massachusetts Press.

Easton, John and Royster, Paul (editor). (1675) "A Relation of the Indian War, by Mr.   Easton, of Rhode Island, 1675." Retrieved 8 July 2018 at *Faculty Publications, UNL Libraries.* 33 website. https://digitalcommons.unl.edu/libraryscience/33.

Fiske, John (1903). The Dutch and Quaker Colonies in America. Boston and New York: Houghton, Mifflin and Co. Retrieved 27 October 2018 from *The Internet Archive* website at: https://archive.org/details/dutchandquaker02fiskrich/page/54

Gookin, Daniel. (1972). *An Historical Account of the Doings and Sufferings of the Christian Indians in New England in the years 1675, 1676, 1677* (Richard C. Robey, Ed.). New York: Arno Press. (Original work published 1677)

The History Channel. (Producer). (2005, April 3). *Conquest of America: Episode Three - The Northeast* [Television broadcast]. New York: A&E Television Networks.

Hubbard, William. (1969). *The History of the Indian Wars in New England* (Samuel G. Drake, Ed.). New York: Kraus Reprint Co. (Original work published 1677)

Hubbard, Rev. William. (1966). The Present State of New England. In Charles H. Lincoln (Ed.), *King Philip's War Narratives* (pp. 21-106). Ann Arbor, MI: Ann Arbor University Microfilms, Inc.

(Ed.). (1913). *Narratives of the Indian Wars 1675-1699.*New York: Charles Scribner Sons. Retrieved July 8, 2018 from *The Internet Archive* website at: https://archive.org/details/narrativesofindi00linc.

Leach, Douglas Edward. (1958). *Flintlock and Tomahawk.* New York: The MacMillan Company.

Loewen, James W. (1996). *Lies My Teacher Told Me.* New York: Touchstone.

Mancini, Jason. (2004, February 21,). *Discovering the History of Native and African American Communities in Southern New England.* Native Visions presented at the Mashantucket Pequot Museum Workshop, Mashantucket, CT.

Manitonquat, (Medicine Story). (1991). *Return to Creation.* Spokane, WA: Bear Tribe Publishing.

Martin, Joel W. (2001). *The Land Looks After Us* . New York: Oxford University Press.

Mather, Increase and Royster, Paul (editor). (1676). "A Brief History of the Warr with the Indians in New-England: An Online Electronic Text Edition." Retrieved December 9, 2007 from University of Nebraska-Lincoln, DigitalCommons@University of Nebraska – Lincoln website. http://digitalcommons.unl.edu/libraryscience/31

Mourt, George. (1963). "A Relation or Journal of the Proceedings of the Plantation." In Dwight B. Heath (Ed.), *A Journal of the Pilgrims at Plymouth* (pp. 15-59). New York: Corinth Books, Inc. (Original work published in 1662)

NIAC Publications. (2018) "Nipmuc Place Names - Maine & Massachusetts." Retrieved July 15, 2018, from *Nipmuc Indian Association of Connecticut, Historical Series – Number 3* website. http://www.nativetech.org/Nipmuc/placenames/mainmass.html#Mass

Nickerson, Colin. (2007). Retrieved June 16, 2008 from *Globe Newspaper Company* website at: http://www.boston.com/news/local/articles/2007/10/21/harvard_connecting_to_its_indian_soul/

Nourse, Henry S. (1884). *The Early Records of Lancaster, Massachusetts, 1643-1725.* W. J. Coulter, Lancaster, Massachusetts

Nowell, Samuel. (1978). "Abraham in Arms." In Richard. Slotkin & James K. Folsom (Eds.), *So Dreadfull a Judgment* Middletown, CT: Wesleyan University Press.

Pynchon, John. (c 1650). "Indian Names of the Month." In *William Pynchon's Account Book.* Retrieved July 2, 2019, from Access Genealogy website. https://accessgenealogy.com/native/indian-names-months.htm.

Ramsey, Inez. (Ed.). (2000). *Wampanoag Indian Bibliography.* Retrieved May 24, 2003, from James Madison University, Internet School Library Media Center Web site: http://falcon.jmu.edu/~ramseyil/wampanoag.htm

Rowlandson, Mary. (1998). "A Narrative of the Captivity and Restoration of Mrs. Mary Rowlandson." In Kathryn Zabelle. Derounian-Stodola (Ed.), *Women's Indian Captivity Narratives* New York: Penguin Books.

Russell, Howard S. (1980). *Indian New England Before the Mayflower.* Hanover, NH: University Press of New England.

Schultz, Eric. (Author), & Tougias, Michael. (Author). (2000). *History of King Philip's War* [Documentary Video]. United States: Bride Media International.

Schultz, Eric & Tougias, Michael J. (1999). *King Philip's War.* Woodstock, VT: The Countryman Press.

Shaw, Frank. (2003). *King Philip's War.* Retrieved May 18, 2003, from New England Genealogy Web site: http://www.geocities. com/Heartland/Hills/1094/king.htm

Staples. (1898). Early Mendon & King Philip's War (abridged). Unpublished manuscript. Retrieved May 18, 2003, from http://www.wellswooster.com/tommies/mendon.htm

Sultzman, Lee. (2003). *Wampanoag History.* Retrieved May 18, 2003, from http://www.tolatsga.org/wampa.html

Thatcher, James. (1972). *History of the Town of Plymouth.* Yarmouthport, MA: Parnassus Imprints. (Original work published 1835)

Tompson, Benjamin. (1978). New England's Crisis. In Richard Slotkin & James K. Folsom (Eds.), *So Dreadfull a Judgment* (pp. 207-233). Middletown, CT: Wesleyan University Press.

Tougias, Michael. (2005, March 24,). *Indian Wars of New England.* Lecture and discussion presented at the NH Humanities Council event at Havenwood Heritage Heights, Concord, NH.

Tougias, Michael J. (1996). *Until I Have No Country.* North Attleboro, MA: Covered Bridge Press.

The Trustees of the Reservations. (20019) "Redemption Rock." Retrieved August 20, 2019, from *The Trustees of the Reservations* website at: http://www.thetrustees.org/places-to-visit-central-ma/redemption-rock.html.

Volmar, Mike. "The Dugout Canoe Project - www.fruitlands.org." Retrieved March 9, 2008 from *Scribd, Inc.* website at: https://www.scribd.com/document/248836780/Dugout-Canoe-Article.

Waite, Bill. (2000). *King Philip's War: 1675-1676.* Retrieved April 21, 2001, from http://www.waitegenealogy.org/BillWaite/ kingphilip.htm

Wheeler, Thomas. (1978). "A Thankefull Rembrance of Gods Mercy." In Richard. Slotkin & James K. Folsom (Eds.), *So Dreadfull a Judgment* Middletown, CT: Wesleyan University Press.

Wheeler, Thomas.(1905). *Old South Leaflets. No. 155.* "Captain Thomas Wheeler's Narrative. 1675." Retrieved 27 October 2018 from *The Internet Archive* website at: https://archive.org/ details/captainthomaswhe00whee/page/n3.

Wilkie, R. and J. Tager. (1991). *Historical Atlas of Massachusetts,* University of Massachusetts Press.

Williams, Roger. (1643). *Key into the Language of America.* London: Printed by Gregory Dexter.

Williams, Roger. (1986). *What Cheer, Netop! Selections from A Key into the Language of America.* (Hadassah. Davis, Ed.). Bristol, RI: Haffenreffer Museum of Anthropology. (Original work published 1643)

Winship, Michael P. (1996). *Seers of God, Puritan Providentialism in the Restoration and Early Enlightenment.* Baltimore: The Johns Hopkins University Press.

Winslow, Edward. (1963). "A Journey to Pokanoket." In Dwight B. Heath (Ed.), *A Journal of the Pilgrims at Plymouth* (pp. 60-69). New York: Corinth Books. (Original work published in 1662)

About the Author
Christine Duffy Zerillo

Christine Duffy Zerillo

Christine Duffy Zerillo grew up in Nipmuc Country in Massachusetts. She roamed the woods as she listened to her grandfather tell stories about the area's native people and King Philip's War in 1675. The stories led her to study the people of the time and eventually to write the novel *Still Here.*

Duffy Zerillo worked as a freelance journalist for ten years for *New Hampshire To Do Magazine* and for fourteen years as a college administrator and writing instructor. She retired to Ireland in 2016 to write historical fiction and took classes with writers James Patterson, MJ Hyland, Annemarie Ní Churreáin, and Danielle McLaughlin.

She earned a master of fine arts in creative writing from Goddard College in Vermont in 2006, received a Calderwood Fellowship for Teaching Writing in All Disciplines from the Boston Athenaeum in 2006, and was selected as a winner of National Novel Writing Month in 2017.

Recently returned to America, Duffy Zerillo lives in Connecticut with her husband, Sam, and teaches writing courses for Franklin Pierce University in New Hampshire. She is working on a new novel about her great-grandparents' emigration from Ireland in 1884.

Acknowledgments

It is with grateful thanks that I recognize first my grandfather, Charles F. Duffy, who inspired me with stories of the native people of New England and engaged my interest in the second Puritan war, known as King Philip's War. Secondly, I am eternally grateful to Samuel Zerillo, who supported me as a devoted listener, fabulous chef, printer extraordinaire, and loving husband through every page and chapter as the book evolved. And deepest thanks go to my daughters who encouraged me every step of the way.

Next I owe fond thanks to Richard Panek, who nurtured me through two semesters at Goddard College as I researched history and breathed life into this story, and to Leslie Lee, Rebecca Brown, and Reikko Rizzuto who encouraged me to complete the first draft in the next two semesters.

For their help as I began the revision stage, I am deeply indebted to journalist, novelist, and artist Darlene Olivo and to playwright Lowell Williams who stuck with me through my first year of revisions and inspired me with their talented feedback. Additionally, I owe thanks to the Thursday Night Writers of the Abbey Inn at Tralee, Kerry, Ireland for workshopping my book for two long years and helping me bring it to its final draft state. To Barbara Lovrić thanks for bringing us together and to members Martin O'Brien, Ania Dokurno, Davina O'Neill, Eadbhard McGowan, Gordon Pinckheard, Rachel Pinckheard, and Raffaela Carter, thank you for your input. All of those authors inspired me to be a better writer.

Dave Kobrenski, thank you for your marvelous skill in portraying Weetamoo and Mary in your brilliant cover art, and thanks to Kerri

Helme of Plimoth Plantation for sitting as the model for Weetamoo. Kind thanks to Lancaster Historical Commission and to Richard Wilkie for granting permission to use their maps in *Still Here*. Also thanks to The Trustees of the Reservations for allowing me to use their web content about Redemption Rock. And thank you to Ellen Woodbury, copy editor, for giving it all one last touch-up.

With deepest gratitude, I thank Marcia Gagliardi, my editor and publisher. Thanks to your tender ministrations and gifted expertise, this book became a much better reality than I had ever dreamed.

Colophon

Text, titles, and captions for *Still Here* are set in Adobe Caslon Pro. For her Caslon revival, designer Carol Twombly studied specimen pages printed by William Caslon between 1734 and 1770. Adobe Caslon Pro resides in the Adobe Originals program started in 1989 as an in-house type foundry at Adobe, initiated to create original typefaces.

Still Here dropped capital letters are set in Academy Engraved LET, designed by Letraset's Vince Whitlock and inspired by the Caslon series.